About the author

Steve Berry lives on the coast in Georgia, USA, with his wife and daughter. He is a lawyer who has travelled extensively throughout the Caribbean, Mexico, Europe and Russia. Steve Berry's books have been *New York Times* and international bestsellers, and have been published in forty-two countries and translated into thirty-eight languages.

THE
CHARLEMAGNE
PURSUIT

STEVE BERRY

HODDER

First published in Great Britain in 2009 by Hodder & Stoughton
An Hachette UK company

This paperback edition first published in 2009

1

Published by arrangement with Ballantine Books, an imprint of Random
House Publishing Group, a division of Random House, Inc.

Grateful acknowledgement is made to Beinecke Rare Book and
Manuscript Library, Yale University, for permission to reprint
art on pages 73, 480, 502 and 506.

A CIP catalogue record for this title is available from the British Library

B format ISBN 978 1 444 70976 6
A format ISBN 978 0 340 93348 0

Typeset in Plantin Light by Hewer Text UK Ltd, Edinburgh

Printed and bound by Clays Ltd, St Ives plc

Hodder & Stoughton policy is to use papers that are natural, renewable
and recyclable products and made from wood grown in sustainable
forests. The logging and manufacturing processes are expected to
conform to the environmental regulations of the country of origin.

Hodder & Stoughton Ltd
338 Euston Road
London NW1 3BH

www.hodder.co.uk

For Pam Ahearn and Mark Tavani,
Dream makers

ACKNOWLEDGMENTS

With each book I've recognized all of the wonderful folks at Random House. I make no exception now. So to Gina Centrello, Libby McGuire, Cindy Murray, Kim Hovey, Christine Cabello, Beck Stvan, Carole Lowenstein, and everyone in Promotions and Sales – a heartfelt and sincere thanks. Also, a bow to Laura Jorstad, who has copyedited all of my novels. No writer could ask for a better group of professionals to work with. You're all, without question, the best.

A special thanks to the friendly people in Aachen, who answered my persistent questions with great patience. With long-overdue thanks, I want to mention Ron Chamblin who owns the Chamblin Bookmine in Jacksonville, Florida, where, for years, I've performed the majority of my research. It's an amazing place. Thanks, Ron, for creating it. And a nod to our Aussie Mum, Kate Taperell, who offered her keen insight into how folks talk Down Under.

Finally, this book is dedicated to my agent, Pam Ahearn, and my editor, Mark Tavani. In 1995 Pam signed me as a client, then endured 7 years and 85 rejections before finding us a home. What patience. Then there's Mark. Such a chance he took on a crazy lawyer who wanted to write books.

But we all survived.

I owe Pam and Mark more than any one person could ever repay in a lifetime.

Thank you.

For everything.

Study the past, if you would divine the future.
                                                    – Confucius

*The Ancient Masters were subtle, mysterious, profound,
    responsive.*
The depth of their knowledge is unfathomable.
*Because it is unfathomable, all we can do is describe
    their appearance.*
Watchful, like men crossing a winter stream.
Alert, like men aware of danger.
*Courteous, like visiting guests. Yielding, like ice about to
    melt.*
Simple, like uncarved blocks of wood.
                                          – Lao-tzu (604 BCE)

He that troubleth his own house shall inherit the wind.
                                          – Proverbs 11:29

PROLOGUE

November 1971

The alarm sounded and Forrest Malone came alert.

'Depth?' he called out.

'Six hundred feet.'

'What's beneath us?'

'Another two thousand feet of cold water.'

His gaze raked the active dials, gauges, and thermometers. In the tiny conn the helmsman sat to his right, the planesman squeezed in on the left. Both men kept their hands locked on control sticks. Power flickered on and off.

'Slow to two knots.'

The submarine lurched in the water.

The alarm stopped. The conn went dark.

'Captain, report from reactor room. Circuit breaker has blown on one of the control rods.'

He knew what had happened. The safety mechanisms built into the temperamental thing had automatically dropped the other rods – the reactor had scrammed, shut itself down. Only one possible course of action. 'Switch to batteries.'

Dim emergency lights came on. His engineering officer, Flanders, a neat and deliberate professional on whom he'd come to depend, stepped into the conn. Malone said, 'Talk to me, Tom.'

'I don't know how bad it is or how long it's going to take to fix, but we need to lighten the electrical load.'

They'd lost power before, several times in fact, and he knew batteries could provide temporary power for as long as two days provided they were careful. His crew had trained rigorously for just this kind of situation, but once a reactor scrammed the manual said it had to be restarted within an hour. If more time passed, then the boat had to be taken to the nearest port.

And that was fifteen hundred miles away.

'Shut down everything we don't need,' he said.

'Captain, it's going to be hard holding her steady,' the helmsman noted.

He understood Archimedes' law. An object that weighed the same as an equal volume of water would neither sink nor float. Instead it would remain level at neutral buoyancy. Every sub functioned by that basic rule, kept underwater with engines that drove it forward. Without power, there'd be no engines, no diving planes, no momentum. All problems that could easily be alleviated by surfacing, but above them wasn't open ocean. They were pinned beneath a ceiling of ice.

'Captain, engine room reports a minor leak in the hydraulic plant.'

'Minor leak?' he asked. 'Now?'

'It was noticed earlier, but with the power down they request permission to shut a valve to stop the leak so a hose can be replaced.'

Logical. 'Do it. And I hope that's the end of the bad news.' He turned toward the sonar tech. 'Anything in front of us?'

Submariners all took their cues from others who'd sailed before them, and those who'd first fought frozen seas passed down two lessons. Never hit anything frozen if you don't have to and, if that's not possible, place the bow to the ice, push gently, and pray.

'Clean ahead,' sonar reported.

'Starting to drift,' the helmsman said.

'Compensate. But go easy on the power.'

The sub's nose suddenly pitched down.

'What the hell?' he muttered.

'Stern planes have gone to full dive,' yelled the planesman, who rose to his feet and pulled back on the control stick. 'I can't get them to respond.'

'Blount,' Malone hollered. 'Help him.'

The man fled the sonar station and rushed to assist. The downward angle increased. Malone gripped the plotting table as everything that wasn't attached tumbled forward in a wild avalanche.

'Emergency plane control,' he barked.

The angle increased.

'Beyond forty-five degrees,' the helmsman reported. 'Still on full dive. Not working.'

Malone gripped the table harder and fought to maintain his balance.

'Nine hundred feet and dropping.'

The depth indicator changed so fast the numbers blurred. The boat was rated to three thousand feet, but the bottom was coming up fast and the outside water pressure was rising – too much, too fast, and the hull would implode. But slamming into the seabed in a powered dive wasn't a pleasant prospect, either.

Only one thing left to do.

'All back emergency. Blow all ballast tanks.'

The boat shook as machinery obeyed his command. Propellers reversed and compressed air thundered into tanks, forcing water out. The helmsman held tight. The planesman readied himself for what Malone knew was coming.

Positive buoyancy returned.

The descent slowed.

The bow angled upward, then leveled.

'Control the flow,' he ordered. 'Keep us neutral. I don't want to go up.'

The planesman responded to his command.

'How far to the bottom?'

Blount returned to his station. 'Two hundred feet.'

Malone's gaze shot to the depth indicator. Twenty-four hundred. The hull groaned from the strain, but held. His eyes locked on the OPENINGS indicators. Lights showed all valves and breaches closed. Finally, some good news.

'Set us down.'

The advantage of this sub over all others was its ability to rest on the ocean floor. It was just one of many specialized traits the design possessed – like the aggravating power and control system, of which they'd just experienced a graphic demonstration.

The sub settled on the bottom.

Everyone in the conn stared at one another. No one spoke. No one had to. Malone knew what they were thinking. *That was close.*

'Do we know what happened?' he asked.

'Engine room reports that when that valve was closed for repair, the normal and emergency steering and dive systems failed. That's never happened before.'

'Could they tell me something I don't know?'

'The valve is now reopened.'

He smiled at his engineer's way of saying, *If I knew*

more I'd tell you. 'Okay, tell them to fix it. What about the reactor?'

They'd surely used a crapload of battery power fighting the unscheduled descent.

'Still down,' his executive officer reported.

That hour for restart was fast expiring.

'Captain,' Blount said from the sonar station. 'Contact outside the hull. Solid. Multiple. We seem to be nestled in a boulder field.'

He decided to risk more power. 'Cameras and outside lights on. But this will be a quick look-see.'

The video displays sprang to life in clear water speckled with glistening bits of life. Boulders surrounded the sub, lying at angles across the seabed.

'That's odd,' one of the men said.

He noticed it, too. 'They're not boulders. They're blocks. And large ones. Rectangles and squares. Focus in on one.'

Blount operated the controls and the camera's focus tightened on the face of one of the stones.

'Holy crap,' his exec said.

Markings marred the rock. Not writing, or at least nothing he recognized. A cursive style, rounded and fluid. Individual letters seemed grouped together, like words, but none he could read.

'It's on the other blocks, too,' Blount said, and Malone studied the remaining screens.

They were engulfed by ruin, the pieces of which loomed like spirits.

'Shut down the cameras,' he said. At the moment power, not curiosities, was his main concern. 'Are we okay here, if we sit still?'

'We settled in a clearing,' Blount said. 'We're fine.'

An alarm sounded. He located the source. Electrical panels.

'Captain, they need you forward,' yelled his second in command over the squelch.

He scrambled from the conn and hustled toward the ladder that led up into the sail. His engineer was already standing at its base.

The alarm stopped.

He felt heat and his eyes locked on the decking. He bent down and lightly touched the metal. Hot as hell. Not good. One hundred fifty silver-zinc batteries lay beneath the decking in an aluminum well. He'd learned from bitter experience that their makeup was far more artistic than scientific. They constantly malfunctioned.

An engineer's mate worked four screws that held the decking in place, freeing them one by one. The cover was removed, which revealed a churning storm of boiling smoke. Malone instantly knew the problem. Potassium hydroxide fluid in the batteries had overflowed.

Again.

The deck plate was slammed back into place. But that would buy them only a few minutes. The ventilation system would soon disperse the acrid fumes throughout the boat and, with no way to vent the poisonous air, they'd all be dead.

He raced back to the control room.

He didn't want to die, but their choices were rapidly diminishing. Twenty-six years he'd served on subs – diesels and nukes. Only one in five recruits made it into naval submarine school where physical exams, psychological interviews, and reaction times tested everyone to their limits. His silver dolphins had been pinned on by his first captain, and he'd bestowed the honor to many others since.

So he knew the score.

Ball game over.

Strangely, only one thought filled his mind as he entered the conn and prepared to at least act like they had a chance. His boy. Ten years old. Who would grow up without a father.

I love you, Cotton.

PART ONE

I

Garmisch, Germany
Tuesday, December 11, The Present, 1:40 p.m.

Cotton Malone hated enclosed spaces.

His current unease was amplified by a packed cable car. Most of the passengers were on vacation, dressed in colorful garb, shouldering poles and skis. He sensed a variety of nationalities. Some Italians, a few Swiss, a handful of French, but mainly Germans. He'd been one of the first to climb aboard and, to relieve his discomfort, he'd made his way close to one of the frosty windows. Ten thousand feet above and closing, the Zugspitze stood silhouetted against a steel-blue sky, the imposing gray summit draped in a late-autumn snow.

Not smart, agreeing to this location.

The car continued its giddy ascent, passing one of several steel trestles that rose from the rocky crags.

He was unnerved, and not simply from the crowded surroundings. Ghosts awaited him atop Germany's highest peak. He'd avoided this rendezvous for nearly four decades. People like him, who buried their past so determinedly, should not help it from the grave so easily.

Yet here he was, doing exactly that.

Vibrations slowed as the car entered, then stopped, at the summit station.

Skiers flooded off toward another lift that would take them down to a high-altitude corrie, where a chalet and slopes waited. He didn't ski, never had, never wanted to.

He made his way through the visitor center, identified by a yellow placard as Müncher Haus. A restaurant dominated one half of the building, the rest housed a theater, a snack bar, an observatory, souvenir shops, and a weather station.

He pushed through thick glass doors and stepped out onto a railed terrace. Bracing Alpine air stung his lips. According to Stephanie Nelle his contact should be waiting on the observation deck. One thing was obvious. Ten thousand feet in the high Alps certainly added a heightened measure of privacy to their meeting.

The Zugspitze lay on the border. A succession of snowy crags rose south toward Austria. To the north spanned a soup-bowl valley ringed by rock-ribbed peaks. A gauze of frosty mist shielded the German village of Garmisch and its companion, Partenkirchen. Both were sports meccas, and the region catered not only to skiing but also bobsledding, skating, and curling.

More sports he'd avoided.

The observation deck was deserted save for an elderly couple and a few skiers who'd apparently paused to enjoy the view. He'd come to solve a mystery, one that had preyed on his mind ever since that day when the men in uniforms came to tell his mother that her husband was dead.

'Contact was lost with the submarine forty-eight hours ago. We dispatched search and rescue ships to the North Atlantic, which have combed the last known position. Wreckage was found six hours ago. We waited to tell the families until we were sure there was no chance of survivors.'

His mother had never cried. Not her way. But that didn't mean she wasn't devastated. Years passed before questions formed in his teenage mind. The government offered little explanation beyond official releases. When he'd first joined the navy he'd tried to access the court of inquiry's investigative report on the sub's sinking, but learned it was classified. He'd tried again after becoming a Justice Department agent, possessed of a high security clearance. No luck. When Gary, his fifteen-year-old, visited over the summer, he'd faced new questions. Gary had never known his grandfather, but the boy had wanted to know more about him and, especially, how he died. The press had covered the sinking of the USS *Blazek* in November 1971, so they'd read many of the old accounts on the Internet. Their talk had rekindled his own doubts – enough that he'd finally done something about them.

He plunged balled fists into his parka and wandered the terrace.

Telescopes dotted the railing. At one stood a woman, her dark hair tied in an unflattering bun. She was dressed in a bright outfit, skis and poles propped beside her, studying the valley below.

He casually walked over. One rule he'd learned long ago. Never hurry. It only bred trouble.

'Quite a scene,' he said.

She turned. 'Certainly is.'

Her face was the color of cinnamon which, combined with what he regarded as Egyptian features in her mouth, nose, and eyes signaled some Middle Eastern ancestry.

'I'm Cotton Malone.'

'How did you know I was the one who came to meet you?'

He motioned at the brown envelope lying at the base

of the telescope. 'Apparently this is not a high-pressure mission.' He smiled. 'Just running an errand?'

'Something like that. I was coming to ski. A week off, finally. Always wanted to do it. Stephanie asked if I could bring' – she motioned at the envelope – 'that along.' She went back to her viewing. 'You mind if I finish this? It cost a euro and I want to see what's down there.'

She revolved the telescope, studying the German valley that stretched for miles below.

'You have a name?' he asked.

'Jessica,' she said, her eyes still to the eyepiece.

He reached for the envelope.

Her boot blocked the way. 'Not yet. Stephanie said to make sure you understand that the two of you are even.'

Last year he'd helped out his old boss in France. She'd told him then that she owed him a favor and that he should use it wisely.

And he had.

'Agreed. Debt paid.'

She turned from the telescope. Wind reddened her cheeks. 'I've heard about you at the Magellan Billet. A bit of a legend. One of the original twelve agents.'

'I didn't realize I was so popular.'

'Stephanie said you were modest, too.'

He wasn't in the mood for compliments. The past awaited him. 'Could I have the file?'

Her eyes sparked. 'Sure.'

He retrieved the envelope. The first thought that flashed through his mind was how something so thin might answer so many questions.

'That must be important,' she said.

Another lesson. Ignore what you don't want to answer. 'You been with the Billet long?'

'Couple of years.' She stepped from the telescope mount. 'Don't like it, though. I'm thinking about getting out. I hear you got out early, too.'

As carelessly as she handled herself, quitting seemed like a good career move. During his twelve years he'd taken only three vacations, during which he'd stayed on constant guard. Paranoia was one of many occupational hazards that came with being an agent, and two years of voluntary retirement had yet to cure the malady.

'Enjoy the skiing,' he said to her.

Tomorrow he'd fly back to Copenhagen. Today he was going to make a few stops at the rare-book shops in the area – an occupational hazard of his new profession. Bookseller.

She threw him a glare as she grabbed her skis and poles. 'I plan to.'

They left the terrace and walked back through the nearly deserted visitor center. Jessica headed for the lift that would take her down to the corrie. He headed for the cable car that would drop him ten thousand feet back to ground level.

He stepped into the empty car, holding the envelope. He liked the fact that no one was aboard. But just before the doors closed, a man and woman rushed on, hand in hand. The attendant slammed the doors shut from the outside and the car eased from the station.

He stared out the forward windows.

Enclosed spaces were one thing. Cramped, enclosed spaces were another. He wasn't claustrophobic. More a sense of freedom denied. He'd tolerated it in the past – having found himself underground on more than one occasion – but his discomfort was one reason why, years ago, when he joined the navy, unlike his father, he hadn't opted for submarines.

'Mr. Malone.'

He turned.

The woman stood, holding a gun.

'I'll take that envelope.'

2

Baltimore, Maryland, 9:10 a.m.

Admiral Langford C. Ramsey loved speaking to crowds. He'd first realized that he enjoyed the experience while at the Naval Academy and, over a career that now spanned forty-plus years, he'd constantly sought ways to feed his desire. He was speaking today to the national gathering of Kiwanians – a bit unusual for the head of naval intelligence. His was a clandestine world of fact, rumor, and speculation, an occasional appearance before Congress the extent of his public speaking. But lately, with the blessing of his superiors, he'd made himself more available. No charge, no expenses, no press restrictions. The larger the crowd the better.

And there'd been many takers.

This was his eighth appearance in the last month.

'I came today to tell you about something I'm sure you know little about. It's been a secret for a long time. America's smallest nuclear submarine.' He stared out at the attentive crowd. 'Now, you're saying to yourself, *Is he nuts? The head of naval intelligence is going to tell us about an ultrasecret submarine?*'

He nodded.

'That's exactly what I plan to do.'

'Captain, there's a problem,' the helmsman said.

Ramsey was dozing in and out of a light sleep behind the planesman's chair. The sub's captain, who sat next to him, roused himself and focused on the video monitors.

Every external camera displayed mines.

'Jesus, mother of God,' the captain muttered. 'All stop. Don't move this thing an inch.'

The pilot obeyed the command and punched a sequence of switches. Ramsey may have been only a lieutenant, but he knew explosives became ultrasensitive when immersed in salt water for long periods. They were cruising the Mediterranean Sea's floor, just off the French coast, surrounded by deadly remnants from World War II. A mere touch of the hull to one of the metallic spines and NR-1 would transform from top secret to totally forgotten.

The boat was the navy's most specialized weapon, the idea of Admiral Hyman Rickover, built in secret for a staggering one hundred million dollars. Only 145 feet long and 12 feet wide, with an eleven-man crew, the design was tiny by submarine standards, yet ingenious. Capable of diving to three thousand feet, the craft was powered by a one-of-a-kind nuclear reactor. Three viewing ports allowed external visual inspection. Exterior lighting supported television arrays. A mechanical claw could be used to recover items. A manipulator arm accommodated gripping and cutting tools. Unlike attack-class or missile boats, NR-1 was adorned with a bright orange sail, a flat superstructure deck, an awkward box keel, and numerous protuberances including two retractable Goodyear truck tires, filled with alcohol, that allowed it to drive along the seafloor.

'Downward thrusters online,' the captain said.

Ramsey realized what his captain was doing. Keeping the hull firmly on the bottom. Good thing. There were too many mines on the TV screens to count.

'*Prepare to blow main ballast,*' the captain said. '*I want to rise straight up. No side-to-side.*'

The conn was quiet, which amplified the whine of turbines, whooshes of air, squeals of hydraulic fluid, and bleeps of electronics that, only a short while ago, had acted on him like a sedative.

'*Nice and steady,*' the captain said. '*Hold her still as we rise.*'

The pilot gripped the controls.

The boat had not been equipped with a steering wheel. Instead four sticks had been converted from fighter jets. Typical for NR-1. Though it was state-of-the-art in power and concept, most of its equipment was Stone Age rather than Space Age. Food was prepared in a cheap imitation of an oven used on commercial planes. The manipulator arm was left over from another navy project. The navigation system, adapted from transatlantic airliners, barely worked underwater. Cramped crew quarters, a toilet that rarely did anything but clog, and only TV dinners, bought at a local supermarket before leaving port, to eat.

'*We had no sonar contact on those things?*' the captain asked. '*Before they appeared?*'

'*Zero,*' one of the crew said. '*They just materialized out of the darkness ahead of us.*'

Compressed air rushed into the main ballast tanks and the sub rose. The pilot kept both hands on the controls, ready to use thrusters to adjust their position.

They'd only need to rise a hundred feet or so to be clear.

'As you can see, we made it out of that minefield,' Ramsey told the crowd. 'That was the spring of 1971.' He nodded. 'That's right, a long time ago. I was one of the fortunate to have served on NR-1.'

He saw the look of amazement on faces.

'Not many people know about the sub. It was built in the mid-1960s in total secrecy, hidden even from most admirals at the time. It came with a bewildering array of equipment and could dive three times deeper than any other vessel. It carried no name, no guns, no torpedoes, no official crew. Its missions were classified, and many remain so to this day. What's even more amazing, the boat is still around – now the navy's second oldest serving submersible, on active duty since 1969. Not as secret as it once was. Today it has both military and civilian uses. But when human eyes and ears are needed deep in the ocean, it's NR-1's mission to go. You remember all those stories about how America tapped into transatlantic telephone cables and listened in on the Soviets? That was NR-1. When an F-14 with an advanced Phoenix missile fell into the ocean in 1976, NR-1 recovered it before the Soviets could. After the *Challenger* disaster, it was NR-1 that located the solid rocket booster with the faulty O-ring.'

Nothing grabbed an audience better than a story, and he had plenty from his time on that unique submersible. Far from a technological masterpiece, NR-1 had been plagued with malfunctions and was ultimately kept afloat simply because of its crew's ingenuity. Forget the manual – *innovation* was their motto. Nearly every officer who'd served aboard went on to higher command, himself included. He liked that he could now talk about NR-1, all part of the navy's plan to up recruitment by spouting success. Veterans, like him, could tell the tales, and people, like those now listening from their breakfast tables, would repeat his every word. The press, which he'd been told would be in attendance, would ensure even greater dissemination. *Admiral Langford Ramsey, head of the Office of Naval Intelligence, in a speech before the national Kiwanians, told the audience . . .*

He had a simple view of success.

It beat the hell out of failure.

He should have retired two years ago, but he was the highest-ranking man of color in the US military, and the first confirmed bachelor ever to rise to flag rank. He'd planned for so long, been so careful. He kept his face as steady as his voice, his brow untroubled, and his candid eyes soft and impassive. He'd charted his entire naval career with the precision of an undersea navigator. Nothing would be allowed to interfere, especially when his goal was in sight.

So he gazed out at the crowd and employed a confident voice, telling them more stories.

But one problem weighed on his mind.

A potential bump in the road.

Garmisch.

3

Garmisch

Malone stared at the gun and kept his composure. He'd been a bit tough on Jessica. Apparently his guard had been down, too. He motioned with the envelope. 'You want this? Just some Save the Mountain brochures I promised my Greenpeace chapter I'd post. We get extra credit for field trips.'

The cable car continued to drop.

'Funny man,' she said.

'I considered a career in stand-up comedy. Think it was a mistake?'

Situations like this were precisely why he'd retired. Before taxes, an agent for the Magellan Billet made $72,300 a year. He cleared more than that as a bookseller, with none of the risks.

Or so he thought.

Time to think like he once had.

And play for a fumble.

'Who are you?' he asked.

She was short and squat, her hair some unflattering combination of brown and red. Maybe early thirties. She wore a blue wool coat and gold scarf. The man wore a crimson coat and seemed obedient. She motioned with the gun and told her accomplice, 'Take it.'

Crimson Coat lurched forward and jerked the envelope away.

The woman momentarily glanced at the rocky crags flashing past the moisture-laden windows. Malone used that instant to sweep out his left arm and, with a balled fist, pop the gun's aim away.

She fired.

The report stung his ears and the bullet exploded through one of the windows.

Frigid air rushed in.

He slammed a fist into the man, knocking him back. He cupped the woman's chin in his gloved hand and banged her head into a window. Glass fractured into a spiderweb.

Her eyes closed and he shoved her to the floor.

Crimson Coat sprang to his feet and charged. Together they pounded into the far side of the car, then dropped to the damp floor. Malone rolled in an attempt to free himself from a throat grip. He heard a murmur from the woman and realized that soon he would have two to deal with again, one of them armed. He opened both palms and slapped his hands against the man's ears. Navy training had taught him about ears. One of the most sensitive body parts. The gloves were a problem, but on the third pop the man yelped in pain and released his grip.

Malone propelled his attacker off him with a leg thrust and leaped to his feet. But before he could react, Crimson Coat plunged an arm over Malone's shoulder, his throat again clamped tight, his face forced against one of the panes, freezing condensation chilling his cheek.

'Stay still,' the man ordered.

Malone's right arm was wrenched at an awkward angle. He struggled to free himself but Crimson Coat was strong.

'I said stay still.'

He decided, for the moment, to obey.

'Panya, are you all right?' Crimson Coat was apparently trying to draw the woman's attention.

Malone's face remained pressed to the glass, eyes facing ahead, toward where the car was descending.

'Panya?'

Malone spied one of the steel trestles, maybe fifty yards away, approaching fast. Then he realized that his left hand was jammed against what felt like a handle. They'd apparently ended their struggle against the door.

'Panya, answer me. Are you all right? Find the gun.'

The pressure around his throat was intense, as was the lock on his arm. But Newton was right. For every action there was an opposite and equal reaction.

The spindly arms of the steel trestle were almost upon them. The car would pass close enough to reach out and touch the thing.

So he wrenched the door handle up and slid the panel open, simultaneously swinging himself out into the frozen air.

Crimson Coat, caught off guard, was thrown from the car, his body smacking the trestle's leading edge. Malone gripped the door handle in a stranglehold. His assailant fell away, crushed between the car and the trestle.

A scream quickly faded.

He maneuvered himself back inside. A cloudy plume erupted with each breath. His throat went bone-dry.

The woman struggled to her feet.

He kicked her in the jaw and returned her to the floor.

He staggered forward and stared toward the ground.

Two men in dark overcoats stood where the cable car would stop. Reinforcements? He was still a thousand feet high. Below him spread a dense forest that ambled up the mountain's lower slopes, evergreen branches thick with snow. He noticed a control panel. Three lights flashed green, two red. He stared out the windows and saw another of the towering trestles coming closer. He reached for the switch labeled ANHALTEN and flipped the toggle down.

The cable car lurched, then slowed, but did not fully stop. More Isaac Newton. Friction would eventually end forward momentum.

He grabbed the envelope from beside the woman and stuffed it under his coat. He found the gun and slid it into his pocket. He then stepped to the door and waited for the trestle to draw close. The car was creeping but, even so, the leap would be dicey. He estimated speed and distance, led himself, then plunged toward one of the crossbeams, gloved hands searching for steel.

He thudded into the grid and used his leather coat for cushion.

Snow crunched between his fingers and the beam.

He clamped tight.

The car continued its descent, stopping about a hundred feet farther down the cable. He stole a few breaths, then wiggled himself toward a ladder rising on the support beam. Dry snow fluttered away, like talcum, as he continued a hand-over-hand trek. At the ladder, he planted his rubber soles onto a snowy rung. Below, he saw the two men in dark coats race from the station. Trouble, as he'd suspected.

He descended the ladder and leaped to the ground.

He was five hundred feet up the wooded slope.

He trudged his way through the trees, finding an asphalt road that paralleled the mountain's base. Ahead stood a brown-shingled building hemmed by snow-covered bushes. A work post of some sort. Beyond was more black asphalt, cleared of snow. He trotted to the gate leading to the fenced enclosure. A padlock barred entrance. He heard an engine groaning up the inclined road. He retreated behind a parked tractor and watched as a dark Peugeot rounded a curve and slowed, inspecting the enclosure.

Gun in hand, he readied himself for a fight.

But the car sped away and continued upward.

He spotted another narrow path of black asphalt that led through the trees, down to ground level and the station.

He trotted toward it.

High above, the cable car remained stopped. Inside lay an unconscious woman in a blue coat. A dead man wearing a crimson coat waited somewhere in the snow.

Neither was his concern.

His problem?

Who knew his and Stephanie Nelle's business?

4

Stephanie Nelle glanced at her watch. She'd been working in her office since a little before seven am, reviewing field reports. Of her twelve lawyer-agents, eight were currently on assignment. Two were in Belgium, part of an international team tasked with convicting war criminals. Two others had just arrived in Saudi Arabia on a mission that could become dicey. The remaining four were scattered around Europe and Asia.

One, though, was on vacation.

In Germany.

By design, the Magellan Billet was sparsely staffed. Besides her dozen lawyers, the unit employed five administrative assistants and three aides. She'd insisted that the regiment be small. Fewer eyes and ears meant fewer leaks, and over the fourteen years of the Billet's existence, to her knowledge, never had its security been compromised.

She turned from the computer and pushed back her chair.

Her office was plain and compact. Nothing fancy – that wouldn't fit her style. She was hungry, having skipped breakfast at home when she awoke, two hours ago. Meals seemed to be something she worried about less and less.

Part of living alone – part of hating to cook. She decided to grab a bite in the cafeteria. Institutional cuisine, for sure, but her growling stomach needed something. Maybe she'd treat herself to a midday meal out of the office – broiled seafood or something similar.

She left the secured offices and walked toward the elevators. The building's fifth floor accommodated the Department of Interior, along with a contingent from Health and Human Services. The Magellan Billet had been intentionally tucked away – nondescript letters announcing only JUSTICE DEPARTMENT, LAWYER TASK FORCE – and she liked the anonymity.

The elevator arrived. When the doors opened, a tall, lanky man with thin gray hair and tranquil blue eyes strolled out.

Edwin Davis.

He flashed a quick smile. 'Stephanie. Just the person I came to see.'

Her caution flags raised. One of the president's deputy national security advisers. In Georgia. Unannounced. Nothing about that could be good.

'And it's refreshing not to see you in a jail cell,' Davis said.

She recalled the last time Davis had suddenly appeared.

'Were you going somewhere?' he asked.

'To the cafeteria.'

'Mind if I tag along?'

'Do I have a choice?'

He smiled. 'It's not that bad.'

They descended to the second floor and found a table. She sipped orange juice while Davis downed a bottled water. Her appetite had vanished.

'You want to tell me why, five days ago, you accessed the investigatory file on the sinking of USS *Blazek*?'

She concealed her surprise at his knowledge. 'I wasn't aware that act would involve the White House.'

'That file's classified.'

'I broke no laws.'

'You sent it to Germany. To Cotton Malone. Have you any idea what you've started?'

Her radar went to full alert. 'Your information network is good.'

'Which is how we all survive.'

'Cotton has a high security clearance.'

'Had. He's retired.'

Now she was agitated. 'Wasn't a problem for you when you dragged him into all those problems in central Asia. Surely that was highly classified. Wasn't a problem when the president involved him with the Order of the Golden Fleece.'

Davis' polished face creased with concern. 'You're not aware of what happened less than an hour ago at the Zugspitze, are you?'

She shook her head.

He plunged into a full account, telling her about a man falling from a cable car, another man leaping from the same car, scampering down one of the steel trestles, and a woman found partially unconscious when the car was finally brought to the ground, one of the windows shot through.

'Which one of those men do you think is Cotton?' he asked.

'I hope the one who escaped.'

He nodded. 'They found the body. It wasn't Malone.'

'How do you know all this?'

'I had the area staked out.'

Now she was curious. 'Why?'

Davis finished his bottled water. 'I always found it odd the way Malone quit the Billet so abruptly. Twelve years, then just got out completely.'

'Seven people dying in Mexico City took a toll on him. And it was your boss, the president, who let him go. A favor returned, if I recall.'

Davis seemed in thought. 'The currency of politics. People think money fuels the system.' He shook his head. 'It's favors. One given is one returned.'

She caught an odd tone. 'I was returning a favor to Malone by giving him the file. He wants to know about his father—'

'Not your call.'

Her agitation changed to anger. 'I thought it was.'

She finished her orange juice and tried to dismiss the myriad of disturbing thoughts racing through her brain.

'It's been thirty-eight years,' she declared.

Davis reached into his pocket and laid a flash drive on the table. 'Did you read the file?'

She shook her head. 'Never touched it. I had one of my agents retrieve and deliver a copy.'

He pointed at the drive. 'You need to read it.'

5

USS Blazek Court of Inquiry Findings

On reconvening in December 1971, after still not locating any trace of USS *Blazek*, the court focused its attention on 'what if' as opposed to 'what might have been.' While mindful of the lack of any physical evidence, a conscious effort was made to prevent any preconceived notions to influence the search for the most probable cause of the tragedy. Complicating the task is the highly secretive nature of the submarine, and every effort has been made to preserve the classified nature of both the vessel and its final mission. The Court, after inquiring into all known facts and circumstances connected with the loss of the *Blazek*, submits the following:

Finding the Facts

1. USS *Blazek* is a fictitious designation. The actual submarine involved in this inquiry is NR-1A, commissioned in May 1969. The boat is one of two built as part of a classified program to develop advanced submersible capability. Neither NR-1 nor 1A carries an official name, but in light of the tragedy

and unavoidable public attention, a fictitious designation was assigned. Officially, though, the boat remains NR-1A. For purposes of public discussion, USS *Blazek* will be described as an advanced submersible being tested in the North Atlantic for undersea rescue operations.

2. NR-1A was rated to 3,000 feet. Service records indicate a multitude of mechanical problems during its two years of active service. None of those were deemed engineering failures, only challenges of a radical design, one that pushed the limits of submersible technology. NR-1 has experienced similar operational difficulties, which makes this inquiry all the more pressing since that vessel remains in active service and any defects must be identified and corrected.

3. The miniature nuclear reactor on board was built solely for the two NR-class boats. Though the reactor is revolutionary and problematic, there is no indication of any radiation release at the sight of the sinking, which would indicate that a catastrophic reactor failure was not the cause of the mishap. Of course, such a finding does not preclude the possibility of an electrical failure. Both NR-class boats reported repeated problems with their batteries.

4. Eleven men were aboard NR-1A at the time of its sinking. Officer-in-Charge, CDR Forrest Malone; Executive Officer, LCDR Beck Stvan; Navigation Officer, LCDR Tim Morris; Communications, ET1 Tom Flanders; Reactor Controls, ET1 Gordon

Jackson; Reactor Operations, ET1 George Turner; Ship's Electrician, EM2 Jeff Johnson; Interior Communications, IC2 Michael Fender; Sonar and Food Service, MM1 Mikey Blount; Mechanical Division, IC2 Bill Jenkins; Reactor Laboratory, MM2 Doug Vaught; and Field Specialist, Dietz Oberhauser.

5. Acoustic signals attributed to NR-1A were detected at stations in Argentina and South Africa. Individual acoustic signals and stations are outlined on the following pages entitled 'Table of Factual Data Acoustic Events.' The acoustic event number has been determined by experts to be the result of a high-energy release, rich in low frequencies with no discernible harmonic structure. No expert has been able to state whether the event was an explosion or an implosion.

6. NR-1A was operating beneath the Antarctic ice pack. Its course and final destination were unknown to fleet command, as its mission was highly classified. For purposes of this inquiry, the Court has been advised that the last known coordinates of NR-1A were 73°S, 15°W, approximately 150 miles north of Cape Norvegia. Being in such treacherous and relatively uncharted waters has complicated the discovery of any physical evidence. To date, no trace of the submarine has been located. In addition, the extent of underwater acoustic monitoring in the Antarctic region is minimal.

7. An examination of NR-1, performed to ascertain if any obvious engineering deficiencies could be found in the sister vessel, revealed that the

negative battery plates had been impregnated with mercury to increase their life. Mercury is forbidden for use on submersibles. Why that rule was relaxed on this design is unclear. But if batteries on board NR-1A caught fire, which, according to repair logs, has happened on both NR-1 and 1A, the resulting mercury vapors would have proven fatal. Of course, there's no evidence of any fire or battery failure.

8. USS *Holden*, commanded by LCDR Zachary Alexander, was dispatched on November 23, 1971, to NR-1A's last known position. A specialized reconnaissance team reported finding no trace of NR-1A. Extensive sonar sweeps revealed nothing. No radiation was detected. Granted, a large-scale search and rescue operation may have yielded a different result, but the crew of NR-1A signed an operational order, prior to leaving, acknowledging that in the event of a catastrophe, there would be no search and rescue. Clearance for this extra-ordinary action came directly from Chief of Naval Operations in a classified order, a copy of which the Court has reviewed.

Opinions

The failure to find NR-1A does not lessen the obligation to identify and correct any practice, condition, or deficiency subject to correction that may exist, given that NR-1 continues to sail. After carefully weighing the limited evidence, the Court finds there is no proof of cause or causes for NR-1A's loss. Clearly, whatever happened was catastrophic, but the submarine's isolated location and lack of tracking, communications, and surface support make any conclusions that the Court may make, as to what happened, purely speculative.

Recommendations

As part of continuing efforts to obtain additional information as to the cause for this tragedy, and to prevent another incident from happening with NR-1, a further mechanical examination of NR-1 shall be conducted, as and when practicable, using the latest testing techniques. The purpose of such testing would be to determine possible damage mechanisms, to evaluate secondary effects thereof, to provide currently unavailable data for design improvements, and to possibly determine what may have happened to NR-1A.

Malone sat in his room at the Posthotel. The view out the second-floor windows, past Garmisch, framed the Wetterstein Mountains and the towering Zugspitze, but the sight of that distant peak only brought back what had happened two hours ago.

He'd read the report. Twice.

Naval regulations required that a court of inquiry be convened immediately after any maritime tragedy, staffed with flag officers, and charged with discovering the truth.

But this inquiry had been a lie.

His father had not been on a mission in the North Atlantic. USS *Blazek* didn't even exist. Instead, his father had been aboard a top-secret submarine, in the Antarctic, doing God knows what.

He remembered the aftermath.

Ships had combed the North Atlantic, but no wreckage had been found. News reports indicated that *Blazek,* supposedly a nuclear-powered submersible being tested for deep bottom rescue, had imploded. Malone remembered what the man in uniform – not a vice admiral from the submarine force, whom he later learned would normally break the news to a boat commander's wife, but a captain from the Pentagon – had said to his mother: '*They were in the North Atlantic, twelve hundred feet down.*'

Either he'd lied or the navy had lied to him. No wonder the report remained classified.

American nuclear submarines rarely sank. Only three since 1945. *Thresher,* from faulty piping. *Scorpion,* because of an unexplained explosion. *Blazek,* cause unknown. Or more properly, NR-1A, cause unknown.

Every one of the press accounts he'd reread with Gary over the summer had talked of the North Atlantic. The lack of wreckage was attributed to the water's depth and canyon-like bottom features. He'd always wondered about that. Depth would have ruptured the hull and flooded the sub, so debris would have eventually floated to the surface. The navy also wired the oceans for sound. The court of inquiry noted that acoustical signals had been heard, but the sounds explained little and too few were listening in that part of the world to matter.

Dammit.

He'd served in the navy, joined voluntarily, took an oath, and upheld it.

They hadn't.

Instead, when a submarine sank somewhere in the Antarctic, no flotilla of ships had combed the area, probing the depths with sonar. No reams of testimony, charts, drawings, letters, photographs, or operational directives were accumulated as to cause. Just one lousy ship, three days of inquiry, and four pages of a nothing report.

Bells clanged in the distance.

He wanted to ram his fist through the wall. But what good would that do?

Instead he reached for his cell phone.

6

Captain Sterling Wilkerson, US Navy, stared past the frosty plate-glass window at the Posthotel. He was discreetly positioned across the street, inside a busy McDonald's. People trudged back and forth outside, bundled against the cold and a steady snow.

Garmisch was an entanglement of congested strasses and pedestrian-only quarters. The whole place seemed like one of those toy towns at FAO Schwarz, with painted Alpine cottages nestled deep in cotton batting, sprinkled thickly with plastic flakes. Tourists surely came for the ambience and the nearby snowy slopes. He'd come for Cotton Malone and had watched earlier as the ex-Magellan Billet agent, now a Copenhagen bookseller, killed a man then leaped from a cable car, eventually making his way to ground level and fleeing in his rental car. Wilkerson had followed, and when Malone headed straight for the Posthotel and disappeared inside, he'd assumed a position across the street, enjoying a beer while he waited.

He knew all about Cotton Malone.

Georgia native. Forty-eight years old. Former naval officer. Georgetown law school graduate. Judge Advocate General's Corps. Justice Department agent. Two years ago Malone had been involved in a shoot-out in Mexico City, where he'd received his fourth wound in the line of duty and apparently reached his limit, opting for an early retirement, which the president personally granted. He'd then resigned his naval commission and moved to Copenhagen, opening an old-book shop.

All that, Wilkerson could understand.

Two things puzzled him.

First, the name *Cotton*. The file noted that Malone's legal name was *Harold Earl*. Nowhere was the unusual nickname explained.

And second, how important was Malone's father? Or, more accurately, his father's memory? The man had died thirty-eight years ago.

Did that still matter?

Apparently so, since Malone had killed to protect what Stephanie Nelle had sent.

He sipped his beer.

A breeze swirled past outside and enhanced the dance of snowflakes. A colorful sleigh appeared, drawn by two prancing steeds, its riders tucked beneath plaid blankets, the driver snatching at the bridles.

He understood a man like Cotton Malone.

He was a lot like him.

Thirty-one years he'd served the navy. Few rose to the rank of captain, even fewer beyond to the admiralty. Eleven years he'd been assigned to naval intelligence, the past six overseas, rising to Berlin bureau chief. His service record was replete with successful tours at tough assignments. True, he'd never leaped from a cable car a thousand feet in the air, but he'd faced danger.

He checked his watch. 4:20 p.m.

Life was good.

The divorce to wife number two last year had not been costly. She'd actually left with little fanfare. He then lost twenty pounds and added some auburn to his blond hair, which made him appear a decade short of fifty-three. His eyes were more alive thanks to a French plastic surgeon who'd tightened the folds. Another specialist eliminated the need for glasses, while a nutritionist friend taught him how to maintain greater stamina through a vegetarian diet. His strong nose, taut cheeks, and sharp brow would all be assets when he finally rose to flag rank.

Admiral.

That was the goal.

Twice he'd been passed over. Usually that was all the chances the navy offered. But Langford Ramsey had promised a third.

His cell phone vibrated.

'By now Malone's read that file,' the voice said when he answered.

'Every word, I'm sure.'

'Move him along.'

'Men like this can't be rushed,' he said.

'But they can be directed.'

He had to say, 'It's waited twelve hundred years to be found.'

'So let's not let it wait any longer.'

Stephanie sat at her desk and finished reading the court of inquiry report. 'This whole thing is false?'

Davis nodded. 'That sub was nowhere near the North Atlantic.'

'What was the point?'

'Rickover built two NR boats. They were his babies. He allocated a fortune to them during the height of the Cold War, and no one gave a second thought to spending two hundred million dollars to one-up the Soviets. But he cut corners. Safety was not the primary concern, results were what mattered. Hell, hardly anybody knew the subs existed. But the sinking of NR-1A raised problems on many levels. The sub itself. The mission. Lots of embarrassing questions. So the navy hid behind national security and concocted a cover story.'

'They sent only one ship to look for survivors?'

He nodded. 'I agree with you, Stephanie. Malone is cleared to read that. The question is, should he?'

Her answer was never in doubt. 'Absolutely.' She recalled her own pain at the unresolved questions over her husband's suicide and her son's death. Malone had helped resolve both of those agonies, which was the precise reason why she'd owed him.

Her desk phone buzzed, and one of the staff told her that Cotton Malone was on the line demanding to speak with her.

She and Davis exchanged puzzled glances.

'Don't look at me,' Davis said. 'I didn't give him that file.'

She answered with the handset. Davis pointed to a speaker box. She didn't like it, but she activated the unit so he could hear.

'Stephanie, let me just say that, at the moment, I'm not in the mood for bullshit.'

'And hello to you, too.'

'Did you read that file before you sent it to me?'

'No.' Which was the truth.

'We've been friends a long time. I appreciate you doing this. But I need something else and I don't need any questions asked.'

'I thought we were even,' she tried.

'Put this on my bill.'

She already knew what he wanted.

'A naval ship,' he said, '*Holden*. In November 1971 it was dispatched to the Antarctic. I want to know if its captain is still alive – a man named Zachary Alexander. If so, where is he? If he's not breathing, are any of his officers still around?'

'I don't suppose you're going to tell me why.'

'Have you now read the file?' he asked.

'Why do you ask?'

'I can hear it in your voice. So you know why I want to know.'

'I was told a short while ago about the Zugspitze. That's when I decided to read the file.'

'Did you have people there? On the ground?'

'Not mine.'

'If you read that report, then you know the SOBs lied. They left that sub out there. My father and those other ten men could have been sitting on the bottom waiting for people to save them. People who never came. I want to know why the navy did that.'

He was clearly angry. So was she.

'I want to talk to one or more of those officers from *Holden*,' he said. 'Find them for me.'

'You coming here?'

'As soon as you find them.'

Davis nodded, signaling his assent.

'All right. I'll locate them.'

She was tiring of this charade. Edwin Davis was here for a reason. Malone had obviously been played. She had been, too, for that matter.

'Another thing,' he said, 'since you know about the cable car. The woman who was there – I popped her hard in the head, but I need to find her. Did they take her into custody? Let her go? What?'

Davis mouthed, *You'll get back to him*.

Enough. Malone was her friend. He'd stood by her when she really needed it, so it was time to tell him what was happening – Edwin Davis be damned.

'Never mind,' Malone suddenly said.

'What do you mean?'

'I just found her.'

7

Garmisch

Malone stood at the second-story window and gazed down across the busy street. The woman from the cable car, Panya, calmly walked toward a snowy parking lot that fronted a McDonald's. The restaurant was tucked into a Bavarian-style building, only a discreet sign with the golden arches and a few window decorations announcing its presence.

He released his hold on the lace curtains. What was she doing here? Maybe she'd fled? Or had the police simply let her go?

He grabbed his leather jacket and his gloves and stuffed the gun he'd taken from her into one of the pockets. He left the hotel room and descended to ground level, careful in his movements but casual in his gait.

Outside, the air was like the inside of a chest freezer. His rental car was parked a few feet from the door. Across the street he saw the dark Peugeot the woman had walked toward, preparing to exit the lot, its right blinker flashing.

He hopped into his car and followed.

Wilkerson downed the rest of his beer. He'd seen curtains in the second-floor window part as the woman from the cable car strolled before the restaurant.

Timing truly was everything.

He'd thought Malone could not be steered.

But he'd been wrong.

Stephanie was pissed. 'I'm not going to be party to this,' she told Edwin Davis. 'I'm calling Cotton back. Fire me, I don't give a damn.'

'I'm not here in an official capacity.'

She appraised him with suspicious eyes. 'The president doesn't know?'

He shook his head. 'This one's personal.'

'You need to tell me why.'

She'd only dealt directly with Davis once, and he hadn't been forthcoming, actually placing her life in jeopardy. But in the end she'd learned that this man was no fool. He possessed two doctorates – one in American history, the other in international relations – along with superb organizational skills. Always courteous. Folksy. Similar to President Daniels himself. She'd seen how people tended to underestimate him, herself included. Three secretaries of state had used him to whip their ailing departments into line. Now he worked for the White House, helping the administration through the last three years of its final term.

Yet this career bureaucrat was now openly breaking rules.

'I thought I was the only maverick here,' she said.

'You shouldn't have let that file go to Malone. But once I learned that you had, I decided I needed some help.'

'For what?'

'A debt I owe.'

'And now you're in a position to repay it? With your White House power and credentials.'

'Something like that.'

She sighed. 'What do you want me to do?'

'Malone's right. We need to find out about *Holden* and its officers. If any of them are still around, they need to be located.'

Malone followed the Peugeot. Sawtoothed mountains sliced with streaks of snow stretched skyward on both sides of the highway. He was driving north, out of Garmisch, on an ascending zigzag route. Tall, black-trunked trees formed a stately aisle, the picturesque scene clearly something Baedeker would have reveled in describing. Winter this far north brought darkness quickly – not even five o'clock and daylight had already waned.

He grabbed an area map from the passenger seat and noted that ahead lay the Alpine valley of the Ammergebirge, which stretched for miles from the base of Ettaler Mandl, a respectable peak at over five thousand feet. A small village dotted the map near Ettaler Mandl, and he slowed as both he and the Peugeot ahead entered its outskirts.

He watched as his quarry abruptly wheeled into a parking space before a massive white-fronted building, two-storied, ruled by symmetry, populated with gothic windows. A towering dome rose from its center, flanked by two smaller towers, all topped with blackened copper and flooded with light.

A bronze placard announced ETTAL MONASTERY.

The woman exited the car and disappeared into an arched portal.

He parked and followed.

The air was noticeably colder than in Garmisch, confirming a rise in altitude. He should have brought a thicker coat, but he hated the things. The stereotypical image of a spy in a trench coat was laughable. Way too restrictive. He stuffed gloved hands into his jacket pockets and curled his right fingers around the gun. Snow crunched beneath his feet as he followed a concrete walkway into a cloister the size of a football field, surrounded by more baroque buildings. The woman was hustling up an inclined path toward the doors of a church.

People were both entering and exiting.

He trotted to catch up, dashing through a silence broken only by soles slapping the frozen pavement and the call of a distant cuckoo.

He entered the church through a gothic portal topped by an elaborate tympanum displaying biblical scenes. His eyes were immediately drawn to dome frescoes of what appeared to be heaven. The interior walls were alive with stucco statues, cherubs, and complex patterns, all in brilliant shades of gold, pink, gray, and green, that flickered as if in constant movement. He'd seen rococo churches before, most so overladen that the building became lost, but not here. The decorations seemed subordinate to architecture.

People milled about. Some sat in pews. The woman he was following walked fifty feet to his right, beyond the pulpit, heading for another sculpted tympanum.

She entered and closed a heavy wooden door behind her.

He stopped to consider his options.

No choice.

He moved toward the door and grasped its iron handle. His right fingers stayed tightened around the gun, but he kept the weapon tucked into his pocket.

He twisted the latch and eased open the door.

The room beyond was smaller, with a vaulted ceiling supported by slender white columns. More rococo ornamentation sprang from the walls, but it was not as bold. Perhaps this was a sacristy. A couple of tall cupboards and two tables accounted for the only furnishings. Standing beside one of the tables were two women – the one from the cable car and another.

'Welcome, Herr Malone,' the new woman said. 'I've been waiting.'

8

The house was deserted, the surrounding woods barren of people, yet the wind continued to whisper his name.

Ramsey.

He stopped walking.

It wasn't quite a voice, more a murmur that drifted on the winter wind. He'd entered the house through an open rear doorway and now stood in a spacious parlor dotted with furniture draped in filthy brown cloths. Windows in the farthest wall framed a view of a broad meadow. His legs remained frozen, ears attuned. He told himself that his name had not been spoken.

Langford Ramsey.

Was that indeed a voice, or just his imagination soaking in the spooky surroundings?

He'd driven alone from his Kiwanian appearance into the Maryland countryside. He was out of uniform. His job as head of naval intelligence required a more inconspicuous appearance, which was why he routinely shunned both official dress and a government driver. Outside, nothing in the cold earth suggested that anyone had recently visited, and a barbed-wire fence had long rusted away. The house was a rambling structure of obvious additions, many of the windows shattered, a gaping hole in the roof showing no signs of repair. Nineteenth century, he guessed, the structure surely once an elegant country estate, now fast becoming a ruin.

The wind continued to blow. Weather reports indicated that snow was finally headed east. He glanced at the wood floor, trying to see if the grime had been disturbed, but saw only his footprints.

Something shattered far off in the house. Glass breaking? Metal clanking? Hard to say.

Enough of this nonsense.

He unbuttoned his overcoat and removed a Walther automatic. He crept left. The corridor ahead was cast in deep shadows, and an involuntary chill swept over him. He inched forward to the end of the passageway.

A sound came again. Scraping. From his right. Then another sound. Metal on metal. From the rear of the house.

Apparently, there were two inside.

He crept down the hall and decided a rushing advance might give him an advantage, particularly after whoever it was continued to announce their presence with a steady *tat-tat-tat*.

He sucked a breath, readied the gun, then bolted into the kitchen.

On one of the counters, ten feet away, a dog stared back. It was a large mixed breed, its head topped with rounded ears, the coat a tawny color, lighter underneath, with a white chin and throat.

A snarl seeped from the animal's mouth. Sharp canines came into view, and hind legs tensed.

A bark came from the front of the house.

Two dogs?

The one on the counter leaped down and bolted outside through the kitchen doorway.

He rushed back to the front of the house just as the other animal fled through an open window frame.

He exhaled.

Ramsey.

It seemed as if the breeze had formed itself into vowels and consonants, then spoke. Not clear, or loud. Just there.

Or was it?

He forced his brain to ignore the ridiculous and left the front parlor, following a hallway, passing more rooms dotted with sheathed furniture and wallpaper bubbled from the elements. An old piano stood uncovered. Paintings cast a ghostly nothingness from their cloth coverings. He wondered about the artworks and stopped to examine a few – sepia prints of the Civil War. One depicted Monticello, another Mount Vernon.

At the dining room he hesitated and imagined groups of white men two centuries ago gorging themselves on beefsteaks and warm crumb cake. Perhaps whiskey sodas served in the parlor after. A game of bridge might have been played while a brazier warmed the air with an aroma of eucalyptus. Of course, Ramsey's ancestors had been outside, freezing in the slaves' quarters.

He gazed down a long corridor. A room at the end of the passageway drew him forward. He checked the floor, but only dust covered the planks.

He stopped at the end of the hall, in the doorway.

Another view of the barren meadow loomed through a dingy window. The furniture, like the other rooms, was sheathed, except for a desk. Ebony wood, aged and distressed, its inlaid top coated with blue-gray dust. Deer antlers clung to taupe-colored walls and brown sheets shielded what appeared to be bookcases. Dust mites swirled in the air.

Ramsey.

But not from the wind.

He targeted the source, rushed toward a draped chair, and ripped off the sheet, generating another fog-like cloud. A tape recorder lay on the decaying upholstery, its cassette about halfway spun.

His grip on the gun stiffened.

'I see you found my ghost,' a voice said.

He turned to see a man standing in the doorway. Short, midforties, round face, skin as pale as the coming snow. His thin black hair, brushed straight, gleamed with flecks of silver.

And he was smiling. As always.

'Any need for the theatrics, Charlie?' Ramsey asked, as he replaced his gun.

'Much more fun than just saying hello, and I loved the dogs. They seem to like it here.'

Fifteen years they'd worked together and he didn't even know the man's real name. He knew him only as Charles C. Smith Jr., with an emphasis on the *Junior*. He'd asked once about Smith Sr. and had received a thirty-minute family history, all of which was surely bullshit.

'Who owns this place?' Ramsey asked.

'I do now. Bought it a month ago. Thought a retreat in the country would be a wise investment. Thinking about fixing it up and renting it out. Going to call it Bailey Mill.'

'Don't I pay you enough?'

'A man has to diversify, Admiral. Can't be reliant on just a paycheck to live. Stock market, real estate, that's the way to be ready for old age.'

'It'll take a fortune to repair all this.'

'Which brings me to an informational note. Because of unanticipated fuel cost increases, higher-than-expected travel fares, and an overall increase in overhead and expenses, we will be experiencing a slight rate increase. Though we strive to keep costs down while providing excellent customer service, our stockholders demand that we maintain an acceptable profit margin.'

'You're full of shit, Charlie.'

'And besides, this place cost me a fortune and I need more money.'

On paper Smith was a paid asset who performed specialized surveillance services overseas, where wiretapping laws were loose, particularly in central Asia and the Middle East. So he didn't give a damn what Smith charged. 'Send me a bill. Now listen. It's time to act.'

He was glad that preparatory work had all been done over the past year. Files readied. Plans determined. He'd known an opportunity would eventually arrive – not when or how, just that it would.

And so it had.

'Start with the prime target, as we discussed. Then move south for the other two in order.'

Smith gave him a mock salute. 'Aye, aye, Captain Sparrow. We shall make sail and find the fairest wind.'

He ignored the idiot. 'No contact between us until they're all done. Nice and clean, Charlie. Really clean.'

'Satisfaction is guaranteed or your money back. Customer satisfaction is our greatest concern.'

Some people could write songs, pen novels, paint, sculpt, or draw. Smith killed, and with an unmatched talent. And but for the fact that Charlie Smith was the best murderer he'd ever known, he would have shot the irritating idiot long ago.

Still, he decided to make the gravity of the situation perfectly clear.

So he cocked the Walther and rammed the barrel into Smith's face. Ramsey was a good six inches taller, so he glared down and said, 'Don't screw this up. I listen to your mouth and let you rant, but don't. Screw. This. Up.'

Smith raised his hands in mock surrender. 'Please, Miss Scarlett, don't beat me. Please don't beat me . . .' The voice was high-pitched and colloquial, a crude imitation of Butterfly McQueen.

He didn't appreciate racial humor, so he kept the gun pointed.

Smith started to laugh. 'Oh, Admiral, lighten up.'

He wondered what it took to rattle this man. He replaced the weapon beneath his coat.

'I do have one question,' Smith said. 'It's important. Something I really need to know.'

He waited.

'Boxers or briefs?'

Enough. He turned and left the room.

Smith started laughing again. 'Come on, Admiral. Boxers or briefs? Or are you one of those who are free to the wind. CNN says ten percent of us don't wear any underwear. That's me – free to the wind.'

Ramsey kept marching toward the door.

'May the Force be with you, Admiral,' Smith hollered. 'A Jedi Knight never fails. And not to worry, they'll all be dead before you know it.'

9

Malone's gaze raked the room. Every detail became critical. An open doorway to his right drew his alarm, especially the unexplored darkness beyond.

'It's only us,' his hostess said. Her English was good, laced with a mild German accent.

She motioned, and the woman from the cable car strutted toward him. As she approached he saw her caress the bruise on her face from where he'd kicked her.

'Perhaps I'll get the chance to return the favor one day,' she said to him.

'I think you already have. Apparently, I've been played.'

She smiled with clear satisfaction, then left, the door clanging shut behind her.

He studied the remaining woman. She was tall and shapely with ash-blond hair cut close to the nape of a thin neck. Nothing marred the creamy patina of her rosy skin. Her eyes were the color of creamed coffee, a shade he'd never seen before, and cast an allure that he found hard to ignore. She wore a tan rib-necked sweater, jeans, and a lamb's-wool blazer.

Everything about her screamed privilege and problem. She was gorgeous and knew it.

'Who are you?' he asked, bringing out the gun.

'I assure you, I'm no threat. I went to a lot of trouble to meet you.'

'If you don't mind, the gun makes me feel better.'

She shrugged. 'Suit yourself. To answer your question, I'm Dorothea Lindauer. I live near here. My family is Bavarian, with ties back to the Wittelsbachs. We're *Oberbayer*. Upper Bavarian. Connected to the mountains. We also have deep ties to this monastery. So much that the Benedictines grant us liberties.'

'Like killing a man, then leading the killer to their sacristy?'

The skin between Lindauer's eyebrows creased. 'Among others. But that is, you must say, a grand liberty.'

'How did you know that I'd be on that mountain today?'

'I have friends who keep me informed.'

'I need a better answer.'

'The subject of USS *Blazek* interests me. I, too, have wanted to know what really happened. I assume you have now read the file. Tell me, was it informative?'

'I'm out of here.' He turned for the door.

'You and I have something in common,' she said.

He kept walking.

'Both of our fathers were aboard that submarine.'

Stephanie pushed a button on her phone. She was still in her office with Edwin Davis.

'It's the White House,' her assistant informed through the speaker.

Davis kept silent. She immediately opened the line.

'Seems we're at it again,' the booming voice said through both the handset she held and the speaker from which Davis listened.

President Danny Daniels.

'And what is it I did this time?' she asked.

'Stephanie, it would be easier if we could get to the point.' A new voice. Female. Diane McCoy. Another deputy national security adviser. Edwin Davis' equal, and no friend of Stephanie's.

'What is the point, Diane?'

'Twenty minutes ago you downloaded a file on Captain Zachary Alexander, US Navy, retired. What we want to know is why naval intelligence is already inquiring about *your* interest, and why you apparently, a few days ago, authorized the copying of a classified file on a submarine lost thirty-eight years ago.'

'Seems there's a better question,' she said. 'Why does naval intelligence give a damn? This is ancient history.'

'On that,' Daniels said, 'we agree. I'd like that question answered myself. I've looked at the same personnel file you just obtained, and there's nothing there. Alexander was an adequate officer who served his twenty years, then retired.'

'Mr. President, why are *you* involved in this?'

'Because Diane came into my office and told me we needed to call you.'

Bullshit. No one told Danny Daniels what to do. He was a three-term governor and one-term senator who had managed twice to be elected president of the United States. He wasn't a fool, though some thought him so.

'Forgive me, sir, but from everything I've ever seen, you do exactly what you want to do.'

'A perk of this job. Anyway, since you don't want to answer Diane's question, here's mine. Do you know where Edwin is?'

Davis waved his hand, signaling no.

'Is he lost?'

Daniels chuckled. 'You gave that SOB Brent Green hell and probably saved my hide in the process. Balls. That's what you have, Stephanie. But on this one, we have a problem. Edwin's on a lark. He has some sort of personal thing going here. He grabbed a couple of days leave and took off yesterday. Diane thinks he came to see you.'

'I don't even like him. He almost got me killed in Venice.'

'The security log from downstairs,' McCoy said, 'indicates that he's in your building right now.'

'Stephanie,' Daniels said, 'when I was a boy, a friend of mine told our teacher how he and his father went fishing and caught a sixty-five-pound bass in one hour. The teacher was no idiot and said that was impossible. To teach my buddy a lesson about lying, she told him how a bear came from the woods and attacked her, but was fended off by a tiny hound who beat the bear back with just a bark. 'You believe that?' the teacher asked. 'Sure,' my pal said, 'because that was my dog.'

Stephanie smiled.

'Edwin's my dog, Stephanie. What he does gets run straight to me. And right now, he's in a stink pile. Can you help me out on this one? Why are you interested in Captain Zachary Alexander?'

Enough. She'd gone way too far, thinking she was only helping out first Malone, then Davis. So she told Daniels the truth. 'Because Edwin said I should be.'

Defeat flooded Davis' face.

'Let me speak to him,' Daniels said.

And she handed over the phone.

10

Malone faced Dorothea Lindauer and waited for her to explain.

'My father, Dietz Oberhauser, was aboard *Blazek* when it disappeared.'

He noticed her continual reference to the sub's fake name. She apparently did not know much, or was playing him. One thing she said, though, registered. The court of inquiry's report had named a field specialist. Dietz Oberhauser.

'What was your father doing there?' he asked.

Her striking face softened, but her basilisk eyes continued to draw his attention. She reminded him of Cassiopeia Vitt, another woman who'd commanded his interest.

'My father was there to discover the beginning of civilization.'

'That all? I thought it was something important.'

'I realize, Herr Malone, that humor is a tool that can be used to disarm. But the subject of my father, as I'm sure is the case with you, is not one I joke about.'

He wasn't impressed. 'You need to answer my question. What was he doing there?'

A flush of anger rose in her face, then quickly receded. 'I'm quite serious. He went to find the beginning of civilization. It's a puzzle he spent his life trying to unravel.'

'I don't like being played. I killed a man today because of you.'

'His own fault. He was overzealous. Or perhaps he underestimated you. But how you handled yourself confirmed everything I was told about you.'

'Killing is something you seem to take lightly. I don't.'

'But from what I've been told, it's something you're no stranger to.'

'More of those *friends* informing you?'

'They *are* well informed.' She motioned down at the table. He'd already noticed an ancient tome lying atop the pitted oak. 'You're a book dealer. Take a look at this.'

He stepped close and slipped the gun into his jacket pocket. He decided that if this woman wanted him dead, he would be already.

The book was maybe six by nine inches and two inches thick. His analytical mind ticked off its provenance. Brown calf cover. Blind tool stamping without gold or color. Unadorned backside, which pinpointed its age: Books produced before the Middle Ages were stored flat, not standing, so their bottoms were kept plain.

He carefully opened the cover and spied the frayed pieces of darkened parchment pages. He examined them and noticed odd drawings in the margins and an undecipherable text in a language he did not recognize.

'What is this?'

'Let me answer that by telling you what happened north of here, in Aachen, on a Sunday in May, a thousand years after Christ.'

Otto III watched as the last impediments to his imperial destiny were smashed away. He stood inside the vestibule of the palace chapel, a sacred building erected two hundred years earlier by the man whose grave he was about to enter.

'It is done, Sire,' von Lomello declared.

The count was an irritating man who ensured that the royal palatinate remained properly maintained in the emperor's absence. Which, in Otto's case, seemed most of the time. As emperor he had never cared for the German forests, or for Aachen's hot springs, frigid winters, and total lack of civility. He preferred the warmth and culture of Rome.

Workers carried off the last of the shattered floor stones.

They hadn't known exactly where to excavate. The crypt had been sealed long ago with nothing to indicate the precise spot. The idea had been to hide its occupant from the coming Viking invasions, and the ploy worked. When the Normans sacked the chapel in 881, they found nothing. But von Lomello had mounted an exploratory mission before Otto's arrival and had managed to isolate a promising location.

Luckily, the count had been right.

Otto had no time for mistakes.

After all, it was an apocalyptic year, the first of a new millennium when many believed Christ would come in judgment.

Workers busied themselves. Two bishops watched in silence. The tomb they were about to enter had not been opened since January 29, 814, the day on which the Most Serene Augustus Crowned by God the Great Peaceful Emperor, Governing the Roman Empire, King of the Franks and Lombards Through the Mercy of God, died. By then he was already wise beyond mortals, an inspirer of miracles, the protector of Jerusalem, a clairvoyant, a man of iron, a bishop of bishops. One poet proclaimed that no one would be nearer to the apostolic band than he. In life he'd been called Carolus. Magnus first became attached to his name in reference to his great height, but now *indicated greatness. His French label, though, was the one used most commonly, a merger of* Carolus *and* Magnus *into a name presently uttered with heads bowed and voices low, as if speaking of God.*

Charlemagne.

Workers drew back from the black yaw in the floor and von Lomello inspected their labor. A strange odor crept into the vestibule – sweet, musty, sickly. Otto had sniffed tainted meat, spoiled milk, and human waste. This waft was distinct. Like long ago. Air that had stood guard over things men were not meant to see.

A torch was lit and one of the workmen stretched his arm into the hole. When the man nodded a wooden ladder was brought from outside.

Today was the feast of the Pentecost, and earlier the chapel had been filled with worshipers. Otto was on pilgrimage. He'd just come from the tomb of his old friend Adalbert, bishop of Prague, buried at Gnesen, where, as emperor, he'd raised that city to the dignity of an archbishopric. Now he'd come to gaze at the mortal remains of Charlemagne.

'I'll go first,' Otto said to them.

He was a mere twenty years old, a man of commanding height, the son of a German king and a Greek mother. Crowned Holy Roman Emperor at age three, he'd reigned under the guardianship of his mother for the first eight years and his grandmother for three more. The past six he'd ruled alone. His goal was to reestablish a Renovatio Imperii, *a Christian Roman Empire, with Teutons, Latins, and Slavs all, as in the time of Charlemagne, under the common rule of emperor and pope. What lay below might help elevate that dream into reality.*

He stepped onto the ladder and von Lomello handed him a torch. Eight rungs passed before his eyes until his feet found hard earth. The air was bland and tepid, like that of a cave, the strange odor nearly overpowering, but he told himself that it was nothing more than the scent of power.

The torch revealed a chamber sheathed in marble and mortar, similar in size to the vestibule above. Von Lomello and the two bishops descended the ladder.

Then he saw.

Beneath a canopy, Charlemagne waited upon a marble throne.

The corpse was wrapped in purple and held a scepter in a gloved left hand. The king sat as a living person, one shoulder leaned against the throne, the head raised by a golden chain attached to the diadem. The face was covered by a sheer cloth. Decay was evident, but none of the limbs had fallen away save for the tip of his nose.

Otto dropped to his knees in reverence. The others quickly joined him. He was entranced. He'd never expected such a sight. He'd heard tales but had never paid them much heed. Emperors needed legends.

'It is said that a piece of the cross was laid in the diadem,' von Lomello whispered.

Otto had heard the same. The throne rested atop a slab of carved marble, its three visible sides lively with carved reliefs. Men. Horses. A chariot. A two-headed hell-hound. Women holding baskets of flowers. All Roman. Otto had seen other examples of such magnificence in Italy. He took its presence here, in a Christian tomb, as a sign that what he envisioned for his empire was right.

A shield and sword rested to one side. He knew about the shield. Pope Leo himself had consecrated it the day Charlemagne was crowned emperor two hundred years ago, and upon it was emblazoned the royal seal. Otto had seen the symbol on documents in the imperial library.

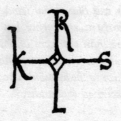

Otto rose to his feet.

One of the reasons he'd come was for the scepter and crown, expecting nothing to greet him but bones.

But things had changed.

He noticed bound sheets resting on the emperor's lap. Carefully, he approached the dais and recognized an illuminated parchment, its writing and artwork faded but still legible. He asked, 'Can any of you read Latin?'

One of the bishops nodded and Otto motioned for him to approach. Two fingers of the corpse's gloved left hand pointed to a passage on the page.

The bishop cocked his head and studied. 'It's the Gospel of Mark.'

'Read it.'

"'For what shall it profit a man, if he shall gain the whole world and lose his own soul?"'

Otto glared at the corpse. The pope had told him the symbols of Carolus Magnus would be ideal tools for reestablishing the splendor of the Holy Roman Empire. Nothing enwrapped power with greater mystique than the past, and he was staring straight at a glorious past. Einhard had described this man as towering, athletic, massive in shoulder, great-chested like a steed, blue-eyed, tawny of hair, ruddy of countenance, abnormally active, incapable of fatigue, having a spirit of energy and mastership that even when in repose, as now, overawed the timid and the quiescent. He finally understood the truth of those words.

The other purpose of his visit flashed through his mind.

He stared around the crypt.

His grandmother, who'd died a few months ago, told him the story that his grandfather, Otto I, told her. Something only emperors knew. Of how Carolus Magnus had ordered certain things be entombed with him. Many knew of the sword, the shield, and the piece of the True Cross. The passage from Mark, though, was a surprise.

Then he saw it. What he'd truly come for. Resting on a marble table.

He stepped close, handed the torch to von Lomello, and stared at a small volume coated in dust. On its cover was imposed a symbol, one his grandmother had described.

Carefully, he lifted the cover. On the pages he saw symbols, strange drawings, and an indecipherable script.

'What is it, Sire?' von Lomello asked. 'What language is that?'

Normally he would not have allowed such an inquiry. Emperors did not accept questions. But the joy of actually finding what his grandmother had told him existed filled him with immeasurable relief. The pope thought crowns and scepters conveyed power, but if his grandmother was to be believed, these strange words and symbols were even more

*powerful. So he answered the count in the same way she'd
answered him.*

'It is the language of heaven.'

Malone listened with a skeptical ear.

'It is said Otto cut off the fingernails, removed a tooth,
had the tip of the nose replaced with gold, then sealed the
tomb.'

'You sound like you don't believe the story,' he told her.

'That time wasn't labeled the Dark Ages without reason.
Who knows?'

On the last page of the book he noticed the same design
that she'd described from the shield in the tomb – a curious
combination of the letters *K, R, L, S*, but with more. He
asked her about it.

'That's the complete signature of Charlemagne,' she said.
'The *A* of *Karl* is found in the center of the cross. A clerk
would add the words left and right. *Signum Caroli gloriosissimi
regis.* The mark of the most glorious King Charles.'

'Is this the book from his grave?'

'It is.'

11

Atlanta, Georgia

Stephanie watched as Edwin Davis squirmed in the chair, clearly uncomfortable.

'Talk to me, Edwin,' Daniels said through the speaker. 'What's going on?'

'It's complicated.'

'I went to college. Served in the military. Was a governor and a US senator. I think I can handle it.'

'I need to do this myself.'

'If it were up to me, Edwin, sure, go for it. But Diane is having a hissy fit. Naval intelligence is asking questions we don't know the answers to. Usually, I'd let the children in the sandbox fight this out among themselves, but now that I've been dragged out into the backyard, I want to know. What's this about?'

In Stephanie's limited experience with the deputy national security adviser, he'd seemed a man who always exhibited a calm, placid exterior. Not now. And Diane McCoy may have reveled in witnessing this man's anxiety, but Stephanie wasn't enjoying the sight.

'Operation Highjump,' Davis said. 'What do you know about it?'

'Okay, you got me,' the president said. 'Round one to you.'

Davis sat silent.

'I'm waiting,' Daniels said.

The year 1946 was one of victory and recovery. World War II had ended and the world would never be the same. Former enemies became friends. Former friends became opponents. America was burdened with a new responsibility, having overnight become a global leader. Soviet aggression dominated political events and the Cold War had begun. Militarily, though, the American navy was being taken apart, piece by piece. At the great bases in Norfolk, San Diego, Pearl Harbor, Yokosuka, and Quonset Point, all was gloom and doom. Destroyers, battleships, and aircraft carriers were slipping into quiet backwaters alongside remote docks. The US Navy was quickly becoming a shadow of what it had been only a year before.

Amid this turmoil, the chief of naval operations signed an astounding set of orders establishing the Antarctic Developments Project, to be carried out during the Antarctic summer from December 1946 to March 1947. Code-named Highjump, the operation called for twelve ships and several thousand men to make their way to the Antarctic rim to train personnel and test materials in frigid zones; consolidate and extend American sovereignty over the largest usable area of the Antarctic continent; determine the feasibility of establishing and maintaining bases in the Antarctic and investigate possible sites; develop techniques for establishing and maintaining air bases on ice, with particular attention to the applicability of such techniques to operations in Greenland, where, it was claimed, physical and climatic conditions resembled those in Antarctica; and amplify existing knowledge of hydrographic, geographic, geological, meteorological, and electromagnetic conditions.

Rear Admirals Richard H. Cruzen and Richard Byrd, the famed explorer known as the admiral of the Antarctic, were

*appointed mission commanders. The expedition would be divided
into three sections. The Central Group included three cargo ships,
a submarine, an icebreaker, the expedition's flagship, and an
aircraft carrier with Byrd aboard. They would establish Little
America IV on the ice shelf at the Bay of Whales. On either
side were the Eastern and Western groups. The Eastern Group,
built around an oiler, a destroyer, and a seaplane tender, would
move toward zero degrees longitude. The Western Group would
be similarly composed and head for the Balleny Islands, then
proceed on a westward course around Antarctica until joining the
Eastern Group. If all went according to plan, the Antarctic would
be encircled. In a few weeks, more would be learned of that great
unknown than had come from a century of previous exploration.*

*Forty-seven hundred men left port in August 1946.
Ultimately, the expedition mapped 5400 miles of coastline,
1400 of which had been entirely unknown. It discovered 22
unknown mountain ranges, 26 islands, 9 bays, 20 glaciers,
and 5 capes, producing 70,000 aerial photographs.*

Machines were tested to the limit.

Four men died.

'The whole thing breathed life back into the navy,' Davis
said. 'It was quite a success.'

'Who gives a rat's ass?' Daniels asked.

'Did you know we went back to Antarctica in 1948?
Operation Windmill. Supposedly those seventy thousand
photographs taken during Highjump were useless because
no one thought to put benchmarks on the ground to
interpret the pictures. They were like sheets of blank white
paper. So they returned to establish the benchmarks.'

'Edwin,' Diane McCoy said, 'what's the point? This is
meaningless.'

'We spend millions of dollars sending ships and men to

Antarctica to take pictures, a place we know is covered in ice, yet we don't establish benchmarks for the pictures while we're there? We don't even anticipate that may be a problem?'

'You saying that Windmill had an alternative purpose?' Daniels asked.

'Both operations did. Part of each expedition was a small force – only six men. Specially trained and briefed. They went inland several times. What they did is why Captain Zachary Alexander's ship was sent to Antarctica in 1971.'

'His personnel file doesn't note anything about that mission,' Daniels said. 'Only that he was assigned command of *Holden* for two years.'

'Alexander sailed to Antarctica to look for a missing submarine.'

More silence from the other end.

'The sub from thirty-eight years ago?' Daniels asked. 'The court of inquiry report Stephanie accessed.'

'Yes, sir. In the late 1960s we built two highly secret subs, NR-1 and 1A. NR-1 is still around, but 1A was lost in Antarctica in 1971. No one was told about its failure – that was covered up. Only *Holden* went looking. Mr. President, NR-1A was captained by Commander Forrest Malone.'

'Cotton's father?'

'And your interest?' Diane asked, with no emotion.

'One of the crew on the sub was a man named William Davis. My older brother. I told myself if I ever was in a position to find out what happened to him, I would.' Davis paused. 'I'm finally in that position.'

'Why is naval intelligence so interested?' Diane asked.

'Isn't it obvious? The sinking was covered up with misinformation. They just let it be lost. Only *Holden* went to look. Imagine what *60 Minutes* would do with that.'

'Okay, Edwin,' Daniels said. 'You connected the dots

pretty good. Round two to you. Carry on. But stay out of trouble and get your ass back here in two days.'

'Thank you, sir. I appreciate the latitude.'

'One piece of advice,' the president said. 'It's true, the early bird gets the worm, but the second mouse gets the cheese.'

The phone clicked.

'I imagine Diane is furious,' Stephanie said. 'She's clearly out of the loop on this one.'

'I don't like ambitious bureaucrats,' Davis muttered.

'Some would say you fit into that category.'

'And they'd be wrong.'

'You seem to be on your own with this one. I'd say Admiral Ramsey at naval intelligence is in damage-control mode, protecting the navy and all that. Talk about an ambitious bureaucrat – he's the definition of one.'

Davis stood. 'You're right about Diane. It won't take her long to get into the loop, and naval intelligence won't be far behind.' He pointed to the hard copies of what they'd downloaded. 'That's why we have to go to Jacksonville, Florida.'

She'd read the file, so she knew that's where Zachary Alexander lived. But she wanted to know, 'Why *we*?'

'Because Scot Harvath told me no.'

She grinned. 'Talk about a Lone Ranger.'

'Stephanie, I need your help. Remember those favors? I'll owe you one.'

She stood. 'That's good enough for me.'

But that was not the reason why she so readily agreed, and her compatriot surely realized it. The court of inquiry report. She'd read it, at his insistence.

No William Davis was listed among the crew of NR-1A.

12

Ettal Monastery

Malone admired the book lying on the table. 'This came from the tomb of Charlemagne? It's twelve hundred years old? If so, it's in remarkable shape.'

'It's a complicated story, Herr Malone. One that spans that full twelve hundred years.'

This woman liked avoiding questions. 'Try me.'

She pointed. 'Do you recognize that script?'

He studied one of the pages, filled with an odd writing and naked women frolicking in bathtubs, connected by intricate plumbing that appeared more anatomical than hydraulic.

He studied more pages and noticed what seemed to be charts with astronomical objects, as if seen through a telescope. Live cells, as they would have appeared from a microscope. Vegetation, all with elaborate root structures. A strange calendar of zodiacal signs, populated by tiny naked people in what looked like rubbish bins. So many illustrations. The unintelligible writing seemed almost an afterthought.

'It's as Otto III noted,' she said. 'The language of heaven.'

'I wasn't aware that heaven required a language.'

She smiled. 'In the time of Charlemagne, the concept of heaven was much different.'

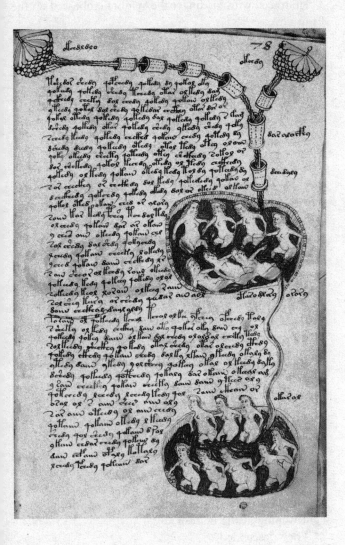

He traced with his finger the symbol embossed on the front cover.

'What is it?' he asked.

'I have no idea.'

He quickly became aware of what was not in the book. No blood, monsters, or mythical beasts. No conflict or destructive tendencies. No symbols of religion, or trappings of secular power. In fact, nothing that pointed to any recognizable way of life – no familiar tools, furniture, or means of transport. Instead the pages conveyed a sense of otherworldliness and timelessness.

'There's something else I'd like to show you,' she said.

He hesitated.

'Come now, you're a man accustomed to situations like this.'

'I sell books.'

She motioned toward the open doorway across the dim room. 'Then bring the book and follow me.'

He wasn't going to be that easy. 'How about you carry the book and I'll carry the gun.' He regripped the weapon.

She nodded. 'If it makes you feel better.'

She lifted the book from the table and he followed her through the doorway. Inside, a stone staircase angled down into more darkness, another doorway filled with ambient light waiting at the bottom.

They descended.

Below was a corridor that stretched fifty feet. Plank doors lined either side and one waited at the opposite end.

'A crypt?' he asked.

She shook her head. 'The monks bury their dead in the cloister above. This is part of the old abbey, from the Middle Ages. Used now for storage. My grandfather spent a great deal of time here during World War II.'

'Hiding out?'

'In a manner of speaking.'

She navigated the corridor, lit by harsh incandescent bulbs. Beyond the closed door, at the far end, spanned a room arranged like a museum with curious stone artifacts and wood carvings. Maybe forty or fifty pieces. Everything was displayed within bright puddles of sodium light. Tables lined the far end, also lit from above. A couple of wooden cabinets painted Bavarian-style abutted the walls.

She pointed at the wood carvings, an assortment of curlicues, crescents, crosses, shamrocks, stars, hearts, diamonds, and crowns. 'Those came off the gables of Dutch farmhouses. Some called it folk art. Grandfather thought they were much more, their significance lost over time, so he collected them.'

'After the Wehrmacht finished?'

He caught her momentary annoyance. 'Grandfather was a scientist, not a Nazi.'

'How many have tried that line before?'

She seemed to ignore his goad. 'What do you know of Aryans?'

'Enough that the notion did not begin with the Nazis.'

'More of your eidetic memory?'

'You're just a wealth of info on me.'

'As I'm sure you'll gather on me, if you decide this is worth your time.'

Granted.

'The concept of the Aryan,' she said, 'a tall, slim, muscular race with golden hair and blue eyes, traces its origins to the eighteenth century. That was when similarities among various ancient languages were noted by, and you should appreciate this, a British lawyer serving on the Supreme Court of India. He studied Sanskrit and saw how that language resembled Greek and Latin. He coined a word, *Arya,* from Sanskrit, meaning "noble", that he used to describe those Indian dialects. More scholars, who began noticing similarities between Sanskrit and other languages, started using *Aryan* to describe this language grouping.'

'You a linguist?'

'Hardly, but Grandfather knew these things.' She pointed at one of the stone slabs. Rock art. A human figure on skis. 'That came from Norway. Maybe four thousand years old. The other examples you see are from Sweden. Carved circles, disks, wheels. To Grandfather, this was the language of the Aryans.'

'That's nonsense.'

'True. But it gets even worse.'

She told him about a brilliant nation of warriors who once lived quietly in a Himalayan valley. Some event, long lost to history, convinced them to abandon their peaceful ways and turn to warmongering. Some swept south and conquered India. Others surged west, finding the cold, rainy forests of northern Europe. Along the way they assimilated their own language with those of native populations, which explained later similarities. These Himalayan invaders possessed no name. A German literary critic finally gave them one in 1808. Aryans. Then another German writer, with no qualifications as a historian or a linguist, linked Aryans with Nordics, concluding them to be one and the same. He wrote a series of books that became German bestsellers in the 1920s.

'Utter nonsense,' she said. 'No basis in fact. So Aryans are, in essence, a mythical people with a fictional history and a borrowed name. But in the 1930s the nationalists seized on that romantic notion. The words *Aryan, Nordic,* and *German* came to be spoken interchangeably. They still are today. The vision of conquering, flaxen-haired Aryans struck a chord with Germans – it appealed to their vanity. So what started out as a harmless linguistic investigation became a deadly racial tool that cost millions of lives and motivated Germans to do things they would have otherwise never done.'

'Ancient history,' he said.

'Let me show you something that isn't.'

She led him through the exhibits to a pedestal that supported four broken pieces of stone. Upon them were deeply carved markings. He bent down and examined the letters.

'They're like the manuscript,' he said. 'Same writing.'

'Exactly the same,' she said.

oﬀ𝖼𝖼𝖼o 𝛿aⲱ) 𝖼𝖼ⲡɑ ɡﬀ𝖼𝖼Ⲍ𝖼𝖼𝖼ᑫ

He stood. 'More Scandinavian runes?'

'Those stones came from Antarctica.'

The book. The stones. The unknown script. His father. Her father. NR-1A. Antarctica. 'What do you want?'

'Grandfather found these stones there and brought them back. My father spent his life trying to decipher them and' – she held up the book – 'these words. Both men were hopeless dreamers. But for me to understand

what they died for – for you to know why your father
died – we need to solve what grandfather called the *Karl
der Große Verfolgung*.'

He silently translated. The Charlemagne pursuit.

'How do you know that any of this is connected with
that sub?'

'Father wasn't there by accident. He was part of what
was happening. In fact, he was the reason it was happening.
I've been trying to obtain the classified report on *Blazek*
for decades, with no success. But you now have it.'

'And you still haven't told me how you knew that.'

'I have sources within the navy. They told me your
former boss, Stephanie Nelle, obtained the report and was
sending it to you.'

'Still doesn't explain how you knew I'd be on that
mountain today.'

'How about we leave that a mystery for the moment.'

'You sent those two to steal it?'

She nodded.

He didn't like her attitude but, dammit, he was intrigued.
He was beneath a Bavarian abbey, surrounded by an array
of ancient stones with strange markings, and staring at a
book, supposedly from Charlemagne, that could not be
read. If what Dorothea Lindauer said was true, there may
well be a connection to his father's death.

But dealing with this woman was nuts.

He didn't need her. 'If you don't mind, I'll pass.' He
turned to leave.

'I agree,' she said, as he headed for the door. 'You and
I could never work together.'

He stopped, turned back, and made clear, 'Don't screw
with me again.'

'*Guten abend*, Herr Malone.'

13

Wilkerson stood under the snowy branches of a beech tree and watched the bookshop. It was located midway into an arcade of picturesque boutiques, just outside the pedestrian-only zone, not far from a boisterous Christmas market where the squeeze of bodies and a hot glow from floodlights infused an element of warmth into the night's wintry blast. The aroma of cinnamon, gingerbread, and sugarcoated almonds drifted on the dry air, along with scents of sizzling schnitzel and bratwurst. High atop a church, strains of Bach rose from a brass ensemble.

Weak lights illuminated the bookshop's front window and signaled that the proprietor was dutifully waiting. Wilkerson's life was about to change. His current naval commanding officer, Langford Ramsey, had promised him that he'd be coming home from Europe with a gold star.

But he wondered about Ramsey.

That was the thing about blacks. Couldn't be trusted. He still recalled when he was nine years old, living in a small town in southern Tennessee, where carpet mills provided a living for men like his father. Where blacks and whites had once lived separately, a shift in law and attitude had started forcing the races together. One summer's night he was curled on a rug, playing. The adjacent kitchen was full of neighbors, and he'd crept to the doorway and listened as people he knew debated their future. It had been hard to understand why they were upset, so the next afternoon, while he and his father were outside in the backyard, he'd asked.

'They destroy a neighborhood, son. Niggers got no business livin' around here.'

He summoned the courage and asked, 'Didn't we bring 'em over from Africa in the first place?'

'So what? That mean we owe 'em? They do it to themselves, son. Down at the mill, not a one of 'em can keep a job. Nothing matters but what white folks give 'em. People like me, and the rest of the folks on this block, work their whole lives and they just come along and destroy it.'

He remembered the night before and what he heard. 'You and the neighbors going to buy the house down the block and tear it down to keep 'em from living here?'

'Seems the smart thing to do.'

'You going to buy every house on the street and tear them down?'

'If that's what it takes.'

His father had been right. *Can't trust none of them.* Especially one who'd risen to become an admiral in the US Navy and the head of the Office of Naval Intelligence.

But what choice did he have? His road to the admiralty passed straight through Langford Ramsey.

He glanced at his watch. A Toyota coupe eased down the street and parked two businesses away from the bookshop. A side window descended and the driver motioned.

He slipped on a pair of leather gloves, then approached

the bookshop's front door. A light rap and the proprietor unlatched the lock. The tinkle of a bell announced his presence as he entered the store.

'*Guten abend,* Martin,' he said to a squat, overweight man with a bushy black mustache.

'Good to see you again,' the man said in German.

The proprietor wore the same bow tie and cloth suspenders he'd worn weeks ago when they'd first met. His shop was an eclectic mixture of old and new, with an emphasis on the occult, and he had a reputation as a discreet broker.

'I trust your workday has gone well?' Wilkerson asked.

'Actually, the day has been slow. Few customers, but with the snow and the Christmas market tonight, people's minds are not on books.' Martin closed the door and twisted the lock.

'Then perhaps I can change your luck. Time to conclude our business.'

For the past three months this German had acted as a conduit, acquiring a variety of rare books and papers from differing sources, all on the same subject and, hopefully, unnoticed by anyone.

He followed the man through a ragged curtain into the back of the shop. During his first visit, he'd learned that the building had once, in the early twentieth century, housed a bank. Left over was a vault, and Wilkerson watched while the German spun the dial, released the tumblers, then eased open a heavy iron door.

Martin entered and yanked the chain on a bare bulb. 'I've been toiling with this most of the day.'

Boxes were stacked in the center. Wilkerson examined the contents of the top one. Copies of *Germanien,* an archaeological and anthropological monthly published by the Nazis in the 1930s. Another box held leather-bound volumes titled *The Research and Educational Society, The Ahnenerbe: Evolution, Essence, Effect.*

'Those were presented to Adolf Hitler by Heinrich Himmler on Hitler's fiftieth birthday,' Martin said. 'Quite a coup to find them. And relatively inexpensive, too.'

The rest of the boxes held more journals, correspondence, treatises, and papers, from before, during, and after the war.

'I was lucky to find sellers who wanted cash. They are becoming harder and harder to locate. Which brings us to my payment.'

Wilkerson retrieved an envelope from inside his coat and handed it to the man. 'Ten thousand euros, as agreed.'

The German thumbed through the bills, clearly pleased.

They left the vault and walked back toward the front of the store.

Martin arrived at the curtain first and suddenly spun around, a gun pointed straight at Wilkerson. 'I'm not an amateur. But whoever you work for must take me for one.'

He tried to wipe the confusion from his face.

'Those men outside. Why are they here?'

'To help me.'

'I did as you asked, bought what you wanted, and left no trail to you.'

'Then you have nothing to worry about. I came solely for the boxes.'

Martin motioned with the envelope. 'Is it the money?'

He shrugged. 'I wouldn't think so.'

'Tell whoever is funding this purchase that they should leave me alone.'

'How do you know I'm not funding it?'

Martin studied him. 'Somebody is using you. Or worse, you're whoring yourself. You're lucky I don't shoot you.'

'Why don't you?'

'No need for me to waste a bullet. You're no threat. But tell your benefactor to leave me be. Now take your boxes and go.'

'I'll need some help.'

Martin shook his head. 'Those two stay in the car. You carry them out yourself. But know this. One trick and I'll shoot you dead.'

14

Ettal Monastery

Dorothea Lindauer stared at the lustrous blue-gray stones supposedly carted here by her grandfather from Antarctica. Through the years she'd rarely visited the abbey. These obsessions had meant little to her. And as she caressed the rough surface, her fingers tracing the strange letters that her grandfather and father had wrestled to understand, she was now sure.

Fools. Both of them.

Especially her grandfather.

Hermann Oberhauser had been born into an aristocratic family of reactionary politicians, passionate in their beliefs, incompetent in doing much about them. He'd latched on to the anti-Polish movement that swept through Germany in the early 1930s, raising money to combat the hated Weimar Republic. As Hitler rose to power, Hermann acquired a publicity firm, sold editorial space to the National Socialists at bargain rates, and aided the rise of the Brown Shirts from terrorists to leaders. He then started a chain of newspapers and headed the German National People's Party, which eventually aligned itself with the Nazis. He also sired three sons. Two never saw the end of the war, one dying in Russia, the other in France. Her father survived only because he was too young to fight.

After the peace, her grandfather became one of the countless disappointed souls who'd made Hitler what he was and survived to endure the shame. He lost his newspapers, but luckily kept his factories, paper mills, and oil refinery, which were needed by the Allies, so his sins, if not forgiven, were conveniently forgotten.

Her grandfather also claimed an irrational pride in his Teutonic heritage. He was enraptured with German nationalism, concluding that Western civilization was on the verge of collapse and its only hope lay in recovering long-lost truths. As she'd told Malone, in the late 1930s he'd spotted strange symbols in the gables of Dutch farmhouses and came to believe that they, along with the rock art from Sweden and Norway, and the stones from Antarctica, were a type of Aryan hieroglyph.

The mother of all scripts.

The language of heaven.

Utter nonsense, but the Nazis loved those romantic ideas. By 1931 ten thousand men were part of the SS, which Himmler eventually transformed into a racial elite of young Aryan males. Its Race and Settlement Office meticulously determined if an applicant was genetically fit for membership. Then, in 1935, Himmler went a step farther and created a brain trust dedicated to reconstructing a golden Aryan past.

The trust's mission was twofold.

Unearth evidence of Germany's ancestors back to the Old Stone Age, and convey those findings to the German people.

A long label lent credibility to its supposed importance. *Deutsches Ahnenerbe – Studiengesellschaft für Geistesurgeschichte*. German Ancestral Heritage – the Society for the Study of the History of Primeval Ideas. Or, more simply, the Ahnenerbe. Something inherited from the forefathers. One hundred thirty-seven scholars and scientists, another eighty-two filmmakers, photographers, artists, sculptors, librarians, technicians, accountants, and secretaries.

Headed by Hermann Oberhauser.

And while her grandfather toiled on fiction, Germans died by the millions. Hitler eventually fired him from the Ahnenerbe and publicly humiliated both him and the entire Oberhauser family. That was when he retreated here, to the abbey, safe behind walls that religion protected, and tried to rehabilitate himself.

But never did.

She remembered the day he died.

'Papa.' She knelt beside the bed and grasped his frail hand.

The old man's eyes opened, but he said nothing. He'd long ago lost all memory of her.

'It's never time to give up,' she said.

'Let me go ashore.' The words came only upon his breath and she had to strain to hear him.

'Papa, what are you saying?'

His eyes glazed over, the oily glare disconcerting. He slowly shook his head.

'You want to die?' she asked.

'I must go ashore. Tell the captain.'

'What do you mean?'

He shook his head again. 'Their world. It is gone. I have to go ashore.'

She started to speak, to reassure him, but his grip relaxed and his chest fluttered. Then his mouth slowly opened and he said, 'Heil . . . Hitler.'

Her spine tingled every time she thought of those final words. Why had he felt compelled, with his dying breath, to proclaim an allegiance to evil?

Unfortunately, she would never know.

The door to the subterranean room opened and the woman from the cable car returned. Dorothea watched as she strolled confidently through the displays. How had things come to this point? Her grandfather had died a Nazi, her father had perished a dreamer.

Now she was about to repeat it all.

'Malone's gone,' the woman said. 'He drove off. I need my money.'

'What happened on the mountain today? Your associate wasn't supposed to be killed.'

'Things blew out of hand.'

'You drew a lot of attention to something that wasn't supposed to be noticed.'

'It worked out. Malone came, and you were able to have that chat you wanted.'

'You may have jeopardized everything.'

'I did what you asked me to do and I want to be paid. And I want Erik's share. He definitely earned it.'

'His death means nothing to you?' she asked.

'He overreacted and it cost him.'

Dorothea had quit smoking ten years ago, but she'd recently started again. Nicotine seemed to calm her constantly frayed nerves. She stepped to one of the painted cabinets, found a pack, and offered one to her guest.

'*Danke,*' the woman said, accepting.

She knew from their first meeting that the woman smoked. She selected a cigarette for herself, found some matches, and lit both.

The woman sucked two deep drags. 'My money, please.'

'Of course.'

She watched as the eyes changed first. A pensive gaze was replaced by rushing fear, pain, then desperation.

Muscles in the woman's face tightened, signaling agony. Fingers and lips released the cigarette and her hands reached for her throat. Her tongue sprang from her mouth and she gagged, sucking for air, and finding none.

Her mouth foamed.

She managed one last breath, coughed, and tried to speak, then her neck relaxed and her body collapsed.

On the waft of her last exhale came a tinge of bitter almond.

Cyanide. Skillfully laced into the tobacco.

Interesting how the dead woman had worked for people she knew nothing about. Never once had she asked a single question. Dorothea had not made the same mistake. She'd thoroughly checked out her allies. The dead woman had been simple – money motivated her – but Dorothea could not risk a loose tongue.

Cotton Malone? He could be a different story.

Since something told her she wasn't done with him.

15

Ramsey returned to the National Maritime Intelligence Center, which housed naval intelligence. He was greeted inside his private office by his chief of staff, an ambitious captain named Hovey.

'What happened in Germany?' Ramsey immediately asked.

'The NR-1A file was passed to Malone on the Zugspitze, as planned, but then all hell broke loose on the cable ride down.'

He listened to Hovey's explanation of what happened, then asked, 'Where's Malone?'

'The GPS on his rental car has him all over the place. At his hotel for a while, then off to a place called Ettal Monastery. It's about nine miles north of Garmisch. Last report had him on the road back toward Garmisch.'

They'd wisely tagged Malone's car, which allowed the luxury of satellite monitoring. He sat at his desk. 'What of Wilkerson?'

'The SOB thinks he's smart as hell,' Hovey said. 'He loosely shadowed Malone, waited in Garmisch awhile, then drove to Füssen and met with some bookstore owner. He had two helpers in a car outside. They carted off boxes.'

'He gets under your skin, doesn't he?'

'He's far more trouble than he's worth. We need to cut him loose.'

He'd sensed a certain distaste before. 'Where'd you two cross paths?'

'NATO headquarters. He almost cost me my captain's bars. Luckily my commanding officer hated the ass-kissing bastard, too.'

He had no time for petty jealousy. 'Do we know what Wilkerson is doing now?'

'Probably deciding who can help him more. Us or them.'

When he'd learned that Stephanie Nelle had acquired the court of inquiry report on NR-1A and its intended destination, he'd immediately sent freelancers to the Zugspitze, intentionally not informing Wilkerson of their presence. His Berlin station chief thought he was the only asset on the ground and had been instructed to keep a loose eye on Malone and report back. 'Did Wilkerson call in?'

Hovey shook his head. 'Not a word.'

His intercom buzzed and he listened as his secretary told him that the White House was on the line. He dismissed Hovey and lifted the phone.

'We have a problem,' Diane McCoy said.

'How do *we* have a problem?'

'Edwin Davis is loose.'

'The president can't rein him in?'

'Not if he doesn't want to.'

'You sense that?'

'I managed to get Daniels to talk to him, but all he did was listen to some rant about Antarctica, then said "have a nice day" and hung up.'

He asked for details and she explained what had happened. Then he asked, 'Our inquiry about Zachary Alexander's file meant nothing to the president?'

'Apparently not.'

'Perhaps we need to increase the pressure.' Which was precisely why he'd dispatched Charlie Smith.

'Davis has hitched his wagon to Stephanie Nelle.'

'She's a lightweight.'

The Magellan Billet liked to think it was a player in international espionage. No way. Twelve friggin' lawyers? Get real. None of them was worth a damn. Cotton Malone? He'd been different. But he was retired, concerned only with his father. Actually, right now he should be pissed off, and nothing clouded judgment better than anger.

'Nelle won't be a factor.'

'Davis went straight to Atlanta. He's not impulsive.'

Granted, but still, 'He doesn't know the game, the rules, or the stakes.'

'You realize he's probably headed for Zachary Alexander?'

'Anything else?'

'Don't screw this up.'

She may have been a national security adviser, but he was no underling to be ordered about. 'I'll try not to.'

'This is my ass, too. Don't forget that. You have a good day, Admiral.'

And she hung up.

This was going to be dicey. How many balloons could he hold underwater at one time? He checked his watch.

At least one of those balloons should pop shortly.

He glanced to his desk at yesterday's *New York Times* and a story in the national section, concerning Admiral David Sylvian, a four-star and vice chairman of the Joint Chiefs of Staff. Thirty-seven years of military service. Fifty-nine years old. Currently hospitalized after a motorcycle accident a week ago thanks to black ice on a Virginia highway. He was expected to recover, but his condition was listed as serious. The White House was quoted as wishing the admiral well. Sylvian was a champion of eliminating waste and had totally rewritten Pentagon budgeting and procurement procedures. A submariner. Well liked. Respected.

An obstacle.

Ramsey had not known when his moment would come, but now that it had, he was ready. Over the past week, everything had dropped into place. Charlie Smith would handle things here.

Time now for Europe.

He reached for the phone and dialed an international number.

The other line was answered after the fourth ring. He asked, 'How's the weather there?'

'Cloudy, cold, and miserable.'

The proper response. He was talking to right person. 'Those Christmas parcels I ordered, I'd like them carefully wrapped and delivered.'

'Overnighted or regular postal?'

'Overnighted. The holidays are fast approaching.'

'We can make that happen within the hour.'

'Wonderful.'

He hung up.

Sterling Wilkerson and Cotton Malone would soon be dead.

PART TWO

16

White Oak, Virginia, 5:15 p.m.

Charlie Smith glanced at the tiny fluorescent hands on his collector's Indiana Jones watch, then stared out the windshield of the parked Hyundai. He'd be glad when spring returned and the time changed. He had some sort of psychological reaction to winter. It had started when he was a teenager, but worsened when he lived in Europe. He'd seen a story about the condition on *Inside Edition*. Long nights, little sun, frigid temperatures.

Depressing as hell.

The hospital's main entrance loomed a hundred feet away. The gray-stuccoed rectangle rose three stories. The file on the passenger seat lay open, ready for reference, but his attention returned to his iPhone and a *Star Trek* episode he'd downloaded. Kirk and a lizardlike alien were battling each other on an uninhabited asteroid. He'd seen every one of the original seventy-nine episodes so many times he usually knew the next line of dialogue. And speaking of babes, Uhura was definitely hot. He watched as the alien lizard cornered Kirk, but glanced away from the screen just as two people pushed through the front doors and walked toward a mocha-colored Ford hybrid.

He compared the license plate with the file.

The vehicle belonged to the daughter and her husband.

Another man emerged from the hospital – midthirties, reddish hair – and headed for a zinc Toyota SUV.

He verified the license plate. The son.

An older woman followed. The wife. Her face matched the black-and-white photo in the file.

What a joy to be prepared.

Kirk ran like hell from the lizard, but Smith knew he wouldn't get far. A showdown was coming.

Same as here.

Room 245 should now be empty.

He knew the hospital was a regional facility, its two operating rooms utilized around the clock, the emergency room accommodating EMS trucks from at least four other counties. Plenty of activity, all of which should allow Smith, dressed as an orderly, to easily move about.

He left the car and strolled through the main entrance.

The lobby reception desk was unoccupied. He knew the employee went off duty at five p.m. and would not return until seven a.m. tomorrow. A few visitors strolled toward the parking lot. Visiting hours ended at five, but the file had reminded him that most people did not clear out until nearly six.

He passed the elevators and followed shiny terrazzo to the far side of the ground floor, stopping in the laundry room. Five minutes later he confidently strode off the second-floor elevator, the rubber soles of his Nurse Mates silent on the shiny tile. The halls to his left and right were quiet, doors to the occupied rooms closed. The nurses' station directly ahead was occupied by two older women, who sat and worked on files.

He carried an armful of neatly folded bedsheets. Downstairs in the laundry room he'd learned that rooms 248 and 250, the closest to 245, could use fresh sheets.

The only difficult decisions he'd faced all day came when choosing what to upload on his iPhone and the actual means of death. Luckily, the hospital's main computer had provided convenient access to the patient's medical records. Though enough internal trauma was present to justify heart or liver failure – his two favorite mechanisms – low blood pressure seemed the doctors' current concern. Medication had already been prescribed to counter the problem, but a note indicated they were waiting for morning before administering the dosage to give the patient time to regain his strength.

Perfect.

He'd already checked Virginia's law on autopsies. Unless death resulted from an act of violence, via suicide, suddenly when in good health, unattended by a physician, or in any suspicious or unusual manner, there'd be no autopsy.

He loved it when rules worked in his favor.

He entered room 248 and tossed the sheets on the bare mattress. He quickly made the bed, tucking tight hospital corners. He then turned his attention across the hall. A gaze in both directions confirmed that all was quiet.

With three steps he entered room 245.

A low-wattage fixture tossed cool white light onto a papered wall. The heart monitor beeped. A respirator hissed. The nurses' station continuously monitored both, so he was careful not to upset either.

The patient lay on the bed – skull, face, arms, and legs heavily bandaged. According to the records, when first brought in by ambulance and rushed into the trauma center, there had been a fractured skull, lacerations, and intestinal damage. Miraculously, though, the spinal cord had not been damaged. Surgery had taken three hours, mainly to repair internal injuries and stitch the lacerations.

The blood loss had been significant, and, for a few hours, the situation teetered on the precarious. But hope eventually turned to promise and the official status was upgraded from serious to stable.

Still, this man had to die.

Why? Smith had no idea. Nor did he care.

He snapped on latex gloves and found the syringe in his pocket. The hospital's computer had also provided the relevant stats so the hypodermic could be preloaded with the proper amount of nitroglycerin.

A couple of squirts and he inserted the bevel-tipped needle into the Y-port receptacle for the intravenous bottle suspended next to the bed. There would be no danger of detection, since the nitro would metabolize within the body as the man died, leaving no traces.

An instant death, though preferable, would set off monitors and bring nurses.

Smith needed time to leave and knew that the death of Admiral David Sylvian would come in about half an hour.

Any discovery of his presence then would be impossible, since he'd be far away, out of uniform, well on the way to his next appointment.

17

Malone reentered the Posthotel. He'd left the monastery and driven straight back to Garmisch, his stomach twisted in knots. He kept visualizing the crew of NR-1A, trapped on the bottom of a frozen ocean, hoping somebody would save them.

But nobody had.

Stephanie had not called back and he was tempted to contact her, but realized that she'd call when there was something to say.

The woman, Dorothea Lindauer, was a problem. Could her father really have been aboard NR-1A? If not, how would she have known the man's name from the report? Though the crew manifest had been part of the official press release issued after the sinking, he recalled no mention of a Dietz Oberhauser. The German's presence aboard the sub was apparently not for public consumption, regardless of the countless other lies that had been told.

What was happening here?

Nothing about this Bavarian sojourn seemed good.

He trudged up the wooden staircase. Some sleep would be welcomed. Tomorrow he'd sort things through. He glanced down the hall. The door to his room hung ajar. Hopes of any respite vanished.

He gripped the gun in his pocket and stepped lightly down the colorful runner that lined the hardwood flooring, trying to minimize squeaks that kept announcing his presence.

The room's geography flashed through his mind.

The door opened into an alcove that led straight ahead into a spacious bath. To the right was the main section that accommodated a queen-sized bed, a desk, a few side tables, a television, and two chairs.

Perhaps the innkeepers had simply failed to close the door? Possible, but after today he wasn't taking any chances. He stopped and, with the gun, nudged the door inward, noticing that the lamps were switched on.

'It's okay, Mr. Malone,' a female voice said.

He peered around the doorway.

A woman, tall and shapely, with shoulder-length ash-blond hair, stood on the other side of the bed. Her unlined face, smooth as a pat of butter, sheathed fine-boned features, sculpted to near perfection.

He'd seen her before.

Dorothea Lindauer?

No.

Not quite.

'I'm Christl Falk,' she said.

Stephanie sat in the window seat, Edwin Davis on the aisle beside her, as the Delta flight from Atlanta began its final approach into Jacksonville International Airport. Below spanned the eastern reaches of the Okefenokee National Wildlife Refuge, the blackwater swamp's vegetation clothed in a wintry brown veneer. She'd left Davis alone with his thoughts during the fifty-minute flight, but enough was enough.

'Edwin, why don't you tell me the truth?'

His head lay on the headrest, eyes closed. 'I know. I didn't have a brother on that sub.'

'Why'd you lie to Daniels?'

He raised up. 'I had to.'

'That's not like you.'

He faced her. 'Really? We hardly know each other.'

'Then why am I here?'

'Because you're honest. Naïve as hell, sometimes. Bullheaded. But always honest. There's something to be said for that.'

She wondered about his cynicism.

'The system is corrupt, Stephanie. Right down to the core. Everywhere you turn, there's poison in government.'

She was baffled by where this was headed.

'What do you know of Langford Ramsey?' he asked.

'I don't like him. He thinks everyone is an idiot and that the intelligence business couldn't survive without him.'

'He's served nine years as head of naval intelligence. That's unheard of. But each time he's come up for rotation, they've allowed him to stay.'

'That a problem?'

'Damn right it is. Ramsey has ambitions.'

'You sound like you know him.'

'More than I ever wanted to.'

'Edwin, stop,' Millicent said.

He was holding the phone, punching the numbers for the local police. She slipped the handset from his grasp and laid it in the cradle.

'Leave it be,' she said.

He stared into her dark eyes. Her gorgeous long brown hair hung tousled. Her face seemed as delicate as ever, but troubled.

In so many ways they were alike. Smart, dedicated, loyal. Only in race were they different – she a beautiful example of African genes, he the quintessential white Anglo-Saxon Protestant. He'd been attracted to her within days of being assigned as Captain Langford Ramsey's State Department liaison, working out of NATO headquarters in Brussels.

He gently caressed the fresh bruise on her thigh. 'He struck you.' He fought the next word. 'Again.'

'It's his way.'

She was a lieutenant, born of a navy family, fourth generation, and Langford Ramsey's aide for the past two years. Ramsey's lover for one of those.

'Is he worth it?' he asked.

She retreated from the phone, clutching her bathrobe tight. She'd called half an hour ago and asked him to come to her apartment. Ramsey had just left. He didn't know why he always came when she called.

'He doesn't mean to do it,' she said. 'His temper gets the best of him. He doesn't like to be refused.'

His gut hurt at the thought of them together, but he listened, knowing she had to relieve herself of false guilt. 'He needs to be reported.'

'It would solve nothing. He's a man on the rise, Edwin. A man with friends. No one would care what I have to say.'

'I care.'

She appraised him with anxious eyes. 'He told me that he would never do it again.'

'He said that last time.'

'It was my fault. I pushed him. I shouldn't have, but I did.'

She sat on the sofa and motioned for him to sit beside her. When he did, she laid her head on his shoulder and, within a few minutes, drifted off to sleep.

'She died six months later,' Davis said in a distant voice.

Stephanie kept silent.

'Her heart stopped. The authorities in Brussels said it was probably genetic.' Davis paused. 'Ramsey had beaten her again, three days before. No marks. Just a few well-placed punches.' He went quiet. 'I asked to be transferred after that.'

'Did Ramsey know how you felt about her?'

Davis shrugged. 'I'm not sure how I felt. But I doubt he'd care. I was thirty-eight years old, working my way up in the State Department. The foreign service is a lot like the military. You take the assignments as they come. But like I said earlier, about the fake brother, I told myself if I ever was in a position to stick it up Ramsey's ass, I would.'

'What does Ramsey have to do with this?'

Davis laid his head back.

The plane swooped in for a landing.

'Everything,' he said.

18

Wilkerson downshifted the Volvo and slowed. The highway was descending, on its way into a broad Alpine valley cut between more towering ranges. Snow appeared from the darkness, swept free from the windshield by the wipers. He was nine miles north of Füssen, in black Bavarian woods, not far from Linderhof, one of mad King Ludwig II's fairy-tale castles.

He came to a stop and turned onto a rocky lane that wound farther into the trees, a dreamy stillness surrounding him. The farmhouse came into view. Typical for the region. Gabled roof, bright colors, walls of stone, mortar, and wood. Green shutters for the ground-floor windows hung shut, just as he'd left them earlier in the day.

He parked and exited the car.

Snow crunched beneath his soles as he walked to the front door. Inside, he switched on a few lamps and stoked the fire he'd left smoldering in the hearth. He then returned to the car and toted the boxes from Füssen inside, storing them in a kitchen closet.

That task was now completed.

He retreated to the front door and stared out into the snowy night.

He would have to report to Ramsey shortly. He'd been

told that within a month he would be reassigned to Washington, inside naval intelligence headquarters, at a high administrative level. His name would be submitted in the next batch of officers hoping for flag rank and Ramsey had promised that, by then, he would be in a position to ensure a successful outcome.

But would that be the case?

He had no choice but to hope. Seemed his whole life lately was dependent on others.

And nothing about that seemed good.

Burning embers settled in the hearth with a hiss. He needed to retrieve a few fresh logs from the pile on the side of the house. A strong fire would be needed later.

He opened the front door.

An explosion rocked the night.

Instinctively, he shielded his face from a sudden flash of intense light and a quick burst of searing heat. He looked up to see the Volvo ablaze, little left but the burning remnant of the undercarriage as flames devoured metal.

He spied movement in the darkness. Two forms. Headed toward him. Carrying weapons.

He slammed the door.

Glass in one of the windows shattered and something thudded onto the plank floor. His gaze locked on the object. A grenade. Soviet configuration. He lunged forward into the next room just as the ordnance exploded. The lodge's walls were apparently well constructed – the partition between the rooms diffused the blast – but he heard wind swirling in what was once a cozy den, the explosion surely annihilating an exterior wall.

He managed to come to his feet and crouched down.

Voices could be heard. Outside. Two men. One on either side of the house.

'Check for a body,' one of them said in German.

He heard pottering through the black rubble, and a flashlight beam pierced the darkness. The assailants were making no effort to mask their presence. He steadied himself against the wall.

'Anything?' one of the men asked.

'*Nein.*'

'Move farther in.'

He braced himself.

A narrow beam of light plunged past the doorway. Then the flashlight itself entered the room, followed by a gun. He waited for the man to step inside, then grabbed for the weapon as he slammed his fist into the man's jaw and wrenched the weapon free.

The man staggered forward, flashlight still in hand. Wilkerson wasted no time. As his assailant regained his balance, he fired once into the man's chest and readied the gun, as a new beam of light probed in his direction.

A black object swished through the air and slammed to the floor.

Another grenade.

He dove over the top of a settee and rolled the sofa onto him just as the bomb exploded and debris rained down. More windows and wall were blown out and the night's bitter cold invaded. The triangle formed by the upended settee had shielded him from the blast, and he thought he'd escaped the worst until he heard a crack and one of the ceiling beams crashed onto the settee.

Luckily, he wasn't pinned.

The man with the flashlight crept closer.

In the attack, Wilkerson had lost the gun, so he searched the darkness. Spotting it, he wiggled free and alligator-crawled forward.

His assailant entered the room, picking his way over the debris.

A bullet ricocheted off the floor just ahead of him.

He scampered behind more rubble as another bullet searched for him. He was running out of options. The gun lay too far away. Cold wind parched his face. The flashlight beam found him.

Damn. He cursed himself, then Langford Ramsey.

A gun blast erupted.

The flashlight beam jiggled, then its rays scattered in all directions.

A body thudded to the floor.

Then silence.

He pushed himself up and spied a darkened form – tall, shapely, feminine – standing in the kitchen doorway, the outline of a shotgun in her arms.

'Are you all right?' Dorothea Lindauer asked.

'Nice shot.'

'I saw you were having trouble.'

He walked over to Lindauer and stared at her through the darkness.

'I assume this resolves all doubts you might have about your Admiral Ramsey and his intentions?' she asked.

He nodded. 'From now on we'll do this your way.'

19

Malone shook his head. Twins? He closed the door. 'I just met your sister. I wondered why she let me go so easily. You two just couldn't speak to me together?'

Christl Falk shook her head. 'We don't speak much.'

Now he was puzzled. 'Yet you're obviously working together.'

'No, we're not.' Her English, unlike her sister's, contained no hint of German.

'Then what are you doing here?'

'She baited you today. Drew you in. I was wondering why. I planned to speak with you when you came down from the summit, but thought better after what happened.'

'You saw?'

She nodded. 'Then I followed you here.'

What the hell had he stumbled into?

'I had nothing to do with what happened,' she made clear.

'Except knowing about it, in advance.'

'I only knew that you'd be there. Nothing else.'

He decided to get to the point. 'You want to know about your father, too?'

'I do.'

He sat on the bed and allowed his gaze to dart to the

far side of the room and the built-in wooden seat beneath the windows, where he'd been talking to Stephanie when he'd spotted the woman from the cable car. The report on *Blazek* still lay where he left it. He wondered if his visitor had peeked.

Christl Falk had made herself comfortable in one of the chairs. She wore a long-sleeved denim shirt and pleated khaki pants, both of which flattered her obvious contours. These two beautiful women, nearly identical in appearance, save for differing hairstyles – hers was shoulder-length, brushed smooth, falling free – seemed quite varied in personality. Where Dorothea Lindauer had conveyed pride and privilege, Christl Falk telegraphed struggle.

'Did Dorothea tell you about Grandfather?'

'I got a synopsis.'

'He did work for the Nazis, heading up the Ahnenerbe.'

'Such a noble endeavor.'

She seemed to catch his sarcasm. 'I agree. It was nothing more than a research institute to manufacture archaeological evidence for political purposes. Himmler believed Germany's ancestors evolved far off, where they'd been some sort of master race. Then that supposed Aryan blood migrated to various parts of the world. So he created the Ahnenerbe – a mix of adventurers, mystics, and scholars – and set out to find those Aryans while eradicating everyone else.'

'Which one was your grandfather?'

She looked puzzled.

'Adventurer, mystic, or scholar?'

'All three, actually.'

'But he apparently was a politician, too. He headed the thing, so he surely knew the Ahnenerbe's true mission.'

'That's where you're wrong. Grandfather only believed in the concept of a mythical Aryan race. Himmler manipulated his obsession into a tool for ethnic cleansing.'

'That rationalization was used at the Nürnberg trials, after the war, with no success.'

'Believe what you want, it's not important to why I'm here.'

'Which I've been waiting – rather patiently, I might add – for you to explain.'

She folded one knee over the other. 'Script and symbol studies were the Ahnenerbe's main interest – looking for ancient Aryan messages. But in late 1935 Grandfather actually found something.' She motioned at her coat, which lay on the bed beside him. 'In the pocket.'

He reached inside and removed a book sheathed in a plastic bag. In size, shape, and condition it looked like the one from earlier, except no symbol was embossed on its cover.

'Do you know about Einhard?' she asked.

'I've read his *Life of Charlemagne*.'

'Einhard was from the eastern part of the Frankish kingdom, the portion that was distinctly German. He was educated at Fulda, which was one of the most impressive centers of learning in the Frankish land. He was accepted into the court of Charlemagne around 791. Charlemagne was unique for his time. Builder, political governor, religious propagandist, reformer, patron of the arts and science. He liked to surround himself with scholarly men, and Einhard became his most trusted adviser. When Charlemagne died in 814, his son Louis the Pious made Einhard his private secretary, too. But sixteen years later, Einhard retired from court when

Louis and his sons started fighting. He died in 840 and was buried at Seligenstadt.'

'You're just a wealth of information.'

'I hold three degrees in medieval history.'

'None of which explains what the hell you're doing here.'

'The Ahnenerbe searched many places for those Aryans. Tombs were opened throughout Germany.' She pointed. 'Inside Einhard's grave, Grandfather found that book you're holding.'

'I thought this came from Charlemagne's tomb?'

She smiled. 'I see Dorothea showed you her volume. *That* one did come from Charlemagne's tomb. This one's different.'

He couldn't resist. He slipped the ancient volume from the bag and carefully opened it. Latin filled the pages, along with examples of the same strange writing and odd art and symbols he'd seen earlier.

'In the 1930s Grandfather found that book, along with Einhard's last will and testament. By Charlemagne's time, men of means were leaving written wills. In Einhard's will, Grandfather discovered a mystery.'

'And how do you know that it's not more fantasy? Your sister didn't speak too kindly of your grandfather.'

'Which is another reason why she and I detest each other.'

'And why are you so fond of him?'

'Because he also found proof.'

Dorothea kissed Wilkerson gently on the lips. She noticed that he was still shaking. They stood in the ruins of the lodge and watched the car burn.

'We're in this together now,' she said.

He surely realized that. And something else. No admiralty for him. She'd told him Ramsey was a snake, but he'd refused to believe her.

Now he knew better.

'A life of luxury and privilege can be a good substitute,' she told him.

'You have a husband.'

'In name only.' She saw he needed reassuring. Most men did. 'You handled yourself well in the house.'

He wiped sweat from his forehead. 'I even managed to kill one of them. Shot him in the chest.'

'Which shows you can handle things, when necessary. I saw them approaching the lodge when I was driving up. I parked in the woods and approached carefully while they made their initial assault. I was hoping you could hold them off until I found one of the shotguns.'

The valley, stretching for kilometers in all directions, belonged to her family. No neighbors anywhere close.

'And those cigarettes you gave me worked,' she said. 'You were right about that woman. Trouble that needed eliminating.'

Compliments were working. He was calming down.

'I'm glad you found that gun,' he said.

Heat from the car fire warmed the freezing air. She still held the shotgun, reloaded and ready, but she doubted there'd be any more visitors tonight.

'We need those boxes I brought,' he said. 'They were in the kitchen closet.'

'I saw them.'

Interesting how danger stimulated desire. This man, a navy captain with good looks, modest brains, and few guts, attracted her. Why were weak men so desirable? Her husband was a nothing who allowed her to do as she pleased. Most of her lovers were similar.

She propped the shotgun against a tree.

And kissed Wilkerson again.

'What kind of proof?' Malone asked.

'You look tired,' Christl said.

'I am, and hungry.'

'Then let's get something to eat.'

He'd had enough of women jerking his chain, and if not for his father's involvement he would have told her, like her sister, to stuff it. But he actually wanted to know more.

'All right. But you're buying.'

They left the hotel and walked in falling snow to a café a few blocks away in one of Garmisch's pedestrian-only zones. Inside, he ordered a slab of roasted pork and fried potatoes. Christl Falk asked for soup and bread.

'Ever heard of the *Deutsche Antarktische Expedition*?' she asked.

The German Antarctic Expedition.

'It left Hamburg in December 1938,' she said. 'The public purpose was to secure a spot in Antarctica for a German whaling station, as part of a plan to increase Germany's fat production. Can you imagine? People actually bought that story.'

'Actually, I can. Whale oil was then the most important raw material for making margarine and soap. Germany was a huge purchaser of Norwegian whale oil. About to go to war and dependent on foreign sources for something that important? Could have been a problem.'

'I see you're informed.'

'I've read about Nazis in Antarctica. The *Schwabenland*,

a freighter capable of catapulting aircraft, went with what – sixty people? Norway had recently claimed a chunk of Antarctica they called Queen Maud Land, but the Nazis charted the same region and renamed it Neuschwabenland. They took a lot of pictures and dropped steel-barbed German flags all over the place from the air. Must have been quite a sight. Little swastikas in the snow.'

'Grandfather was on that 1938 expedition. Though one-fifth of Antarctica was mapped, its real purpose was to see if what Einhard had written in the book I showed you was true.'

He recalled the stones from the abbey. 'And he brought back rocks with the same symbols on them as in the book.'

'You've been to the abbey?'

'At your sister's invitation. But why do I get the feeling you already knew that?' She did not reply, so he asked, 'So what's the verdict? What did your grandfather find?'

'That's the problem. We don't know. After the war the Ahnenerbe's papers were confiscated by the Allies or destroyed. Grandfather had been denounced by Hitler at a party rally in 1939. Hitler didn't agree with some of his views, especially his feminist slants, which asserted that ancient Aryan society may have been ruled by priestesses and female seers.'

'A far cry from the baby machines Hitler believed women to be.'

She nodded. 'So Hermann Oberhauser was silenced, his ideas banned. He was forbidden from publishing or giving lectures. Ten years later his mind began to fail him, and he lived the last years of his life senile.'

'Amazing Hitler didn't simply kill him.'

'Hitler needed our factories, oil refinery, and newspapers. Keeping Grandfather alive was a means to have legitimate control over those. And unfortunately, all he ever wanted to do was please Adolf Hitler, so he willingly made all those available.' She removed the book from her coat pocket and freed it from the plastic bag. 'There are many questions raised by this text. Ones I've been unable to answer. I was hoping you'd help me solve the riddle.'

'The Charlemagne pursuit?'

'I see you and Dorothea did have a long talk. *Ja. Da Karl der Große Verfolgung.*'

She handed him the book. His Latin was okay, so he could roughly decipher the words, but she noticed his struggle.

'May I?' she asked.

He hesitated.

'You might find it interesting. I know I did.'

20

S tephanie studied the older man who opened the door to the modest brick home on the city's south side. He was short and overweight, with a bulbous, fiery-hued nose that reminded her of Rudolph the red-nosed reindeer. According to his service record, Zachary Alexander should be pushing seventy – and he looked it. She listened as Edwin Davis explained who they were and why they'd come.

'What do you think I can tell you?' Alexander asked. 'I've been out of the navy almost thirty years.'

'Twenty-six, actually,' Davis said.

Alexander leveled a pudgy finger at them. 'I don't like wastin' my time.'

She heard a television playing in another room. Some game show. And noticed that the house was immaculate, the inside reeking of antiseptic.

'We only need a few minutes,' Davis said. 'After all, I did come from the White House.'

Stephanie wondered about the lie, but said nothing.

'I didn't even vote for Daniels.'

She smiled. 'A lot of us are in that category, but could we have just a few minutes?'

Alexander finally relented and led them into a den,

where he switched off the television and offered them a seat.

'I served in the navy a long time,' Alexander said. 'But I have to tell you, I don't have fond memories of it.'

She'd read his service record. Alexander had made it to commander but was twice passed over for further promotion. He'd eventually opted out and retired with full benefits.

'They didn't think I was good enough for them.'

'You were good enough to command *Holden*.'

Crinkly eyes narrowed. 'That and a few other ships.'

'We came,' Davis said, 'because of the mission *Holden* completed to Antarctica.'

Alexander said nothing. Stephanie wondered if his silence was calculated or cautionary.

'I actually was excited about those orders,' Alexander finally said. 'I wanted to see the ice. But later, I always thought that trip had somethin' to do with me being passed over.'

Davis leaned forward. 'We need to hear about it.'

'For what?' Alexander spat out. 'The whole thing's classified. May still be. They told me to keep my mouth shut.'

'I'm a deputy national security adviser. She's the head of a government intelligence agency. We can hear what you have to say.'

'Bullshit.'

'Is there any reason you have to be so hostile?' she asked.

'Besides that I hate the navy?' he asked. 'Or besides you two are fishin' and I don't want to be bait.'

Alexander relaxed in his recliner. She imagined that he'd sat there for years thinking about what was running through his mind at this moment. 'I did what I was ordered to do, and I did it well. I always followed orders. But it's been a long time, so what do you want to know?'

She said, 'We know *Holden* was ordered to the Antarctic in November 1971. You went looking for a submarine.'

A puzzled look came to Alexander's face. 'What the hell are you talking about?'

'We've read the court of inquiry report on the sinking of *Blazek,* or NR-1A, whatever you want to call the thing. It specifically mentions you and *Holden* going to search.'

Alexander gazed at them with a mixture of curiosity and enmity. 'My orders were to proceed to the Weddell Sea, take sonar readings, and be alert for anomalies. I had three passengers on board and was told to accommodate their needs, without question. That's what I did.'

'No submarine?' she asked.

He shook his head. 'Nothin' close.'

'What did you find?' Davis asked.

'Not a damn thing. Spent two weeks freezin' my ass off.'

An oxygen bottle rested beside Alexander's chair. Stephanie wondered about its presence, along with an assortment of medical treatises that lined a bookcase across the room. Alexander didn't appear in poor health, and his breathing seemed normal.

'I don't know anythin' about a submarine,' he repeated. 'I recall, at the time, that one sank in the North Atlantic. And it was *Blazek,* that's right. I remember. But my mission had nothing to do with that. We were cruisin' the southern Pacific, rerouted to South America, where we picked up those three passengers. Then we headed due south.'

'What was the ice like?' Davis asked.

'Even though it was nearly summertime, that place is tough sailing. Cold as a freezer, bergs everywhere. But one beautiful spot – that I will say.'

'You learned nothing while you were there?' she asked.

'I'm not the one to ask about that.' His countenance had softened, as if he'd concluded they might not be the enemy. 'Those reports you read didn't mention three passengers?'

Davis shook his head. 'Not a word. Only you.'

'Typical friggin' navy.' His face lost its impassive look. 'My orders were to take those three wherever they wanted to go. They went ashore several times, but when they came back they'd say nothin'.'

'Take any gear with them?'

Alexander nodded. 'Cold-water diving suits and tanks. After the fourth time they went ashore, they said we could leave.'

'None of your men went with them?'

Alexander shook his head. 'No way. Not allowed. Those three lieutenants did it all. Whatever that was.'

Stephanie considered the oddity, but in the military strange things occurred on a daily basis. Still, she needed to ask the million-dollar question. 'Who were they?'

She saw consternation grip the old man. 'You know I've never spoken of this before.' He seemed unable to submerge his depression. 'I wanted to be a captain. I deserved it, but the navy disagreed.'

'It was a long time ago,' Davis said. 'There's not much we can do to repair the past.'

She wondered if Davis meant Alexander's situation or his own.

'This must be important,' the old man said.

'Enough that we came here today.'

'One was a guy named Nick Sayers. Another, Herbert Rowland. Both cocky, like most lieutenants.'

She silently agreed.

'And the third?' Davis asked.

'The cockiest of 'em all. I hated that prick. Trouble is he went on and got his captain's bars. Then gold stars. Ramsey was his name. Langford Ramsey.'

21

The clouds invite me and a mist summons. The course of the stars hasten me and the winds cause me to fly and lift me upward into heaven. I draw to a wall built of crystal and I am surrounded by tongues of ice. I draw to a temple built of stone and the walls are like a tessellated floor made of stone. Its ceiling is like the path of the stars. Heat generates from the walls, fear covers me, and a trembling takes hold. I fall upon my face and see a lofty throne, its appearance is as crystalline as the shining sun. The High Adviser sits and his raiment shines more brightly than the sun and is whiter than any snow. The High Adviser says to me, 'Einhard, thou scribe of righteousness, approach hither and hear my voice.' He speaks to me in my language, which is surprising. 'As He hath created and given to man the power of understanding the word of wisdom, so hath He created me also. Welcome to our land. I am told you are a man of learning. If that be so then you can see the secrets of the winds, how they are divided to blow over the earth, and the secrets of the clouds and dew. We can teach you of the sun and moon, whence they proceed and whither they come again, and their glorious return, and how one is superior to the other, and their stately orbit, and how they do not leave their orbit, and they add nothing to their orbit and they take nothing from it, and they keep faith with each other in accordance with the oath by which they are bound together.'

Malone listened as Christl translated the Latin text, then asked, 'That was written when?'

'Between 814, when Charlemagne died, and 840, when Einhard died.'

'That's impossible. It talks of orbits of the sun and moon and how they're bound to each other. Those astronomical concepts had yet to be developed. Those would have been heresy then.'

'I agree, for men living in western Europe. But for men living elsewhere on this planet, who were not constricted by the church, the situation was different.'

He was still skeptical.

'Let me place this in a historical context,' she said. 'Charlemagne's two elder sons both died before him. His third son, Louis the Pious, inherited the Carolingian empire. Louis' sons fought with their father, and among themselves. Einhard served Louis faithfully, as he'd served Charlemagne, but was so sickened by the infighting that he withdrew from court and spent the rest of his days at an abbey Charlemagne had given him. It was during this time that he wrote his biography of Charlemagne and' – she held up the ancient tome – 'this book.'

'Recounting a great journey?' he asked.

She nodded.

'Who's to say that's real? Sounds like pure fantasy.'

She shook her head. 'His *Life of Charlemagne* is one of the most renowned works of all time. Still in print today.

He was not known for crafting fiction, and he went to a great deal of trouble to conceal these words.'

He still wasn't convinced.

'We know a lot about Charlemagne's deeds,' she said, 'but little about his inner beliefs. Nothing reliable describing those has survived. We do know that he loved ancient histories and epics. Before his time, myths were preserved orally. He was the first to order them written down. We know Einhard supervised that effort. But Louis, after inheriting the throne, destroyed all of those texts for their pagan content. The destruction of those writings would have disgusted Einhard, so he made sure this book survived.'

'By writing it partially in a language no one could understand?'

'Something like that.'

'I've read accounts that say Einhard may not have even written his Charlemagne biography. Nobody knows anything for sure.'

'Mr. Malone—'

'Why don't you call me Cotton? You're making me feel old.'

'Interesting name.'

'I like it.'

She smiled. 'I can explain all of this in much more detail. My grandfather and father spent years researching. There are things I need to show you, things I need to explain. Once you see and hear those, I think you'll agree that our fathers did not die in vain.'

Though her eyes suggested a readiness to take on all his arguments, she was playing her trump card and they both knew it.

'My father was the captain of a submarine,' he said.

'Your father was a passenger on that sub. Granted, I have no idea what either one of them was doing in the Antarctic, but they still died in vain.'

And no one gave a damn, he silently added.

She pushed her soup away. 'Will you help us?'

'Who's *us*?'

'Me. My father. Yours.'

He caught the sound of rebellion, but needed time to hear from Stephanie. 'How about this. Let me sleep on it, and tomorrow you can show me what you want.'

Her eyes softened. 'That's fair. It is getting late.'

They left the café and followed the snowy pavement back toward the Posthotel. Christmas was two weeks away, and Garmisch seemed ready. Holiday time, for him, was a mixed blessing. He'd spent the past two with Henrik Thorvaldsen at Christiangade, and this year would probably be the same. He wondered about Christl Falk and her Christmas traditions. A melancholiness seemed to dominate her, and she made little effort to disguise it. She appeared intelligent and determined – not all that different from her sister – but the two women were unknowns who demanded caution.

They crossed the street. Many of the windows in the gaily frescoed Posthotel were lit to the night. His room, on the second floor, above the restaurant and lobby, had four windows on one side, another three facing the front. He'd left the lamps burning and movement behind one of the windows caught his attention.

He stopped.

Somebody was there. Christl saw it, too.

Curtains were yanked back.

A man's face came into view and his gaze locked onto

Malone's. Then the man glanced right, toward the street, and fled the window, his shadow revealing a rushed exit.

Malone spotted a car with three men inside, parked across the street.

'Come on,' he said.

He knew they needed to leave, and quickly. Thank goodness he still carried the keys to his rental. They rushed to the vehicle and leaped in.

He fired up the engine and whipped from the parking spot. He slammed the transmission into gear and roared from the hotel, tires spinning on the frozen asphalt. He powered his window down, turned onto the boulevard, and spotted a man in his rearview mirror emerging from the hotel.

He gripped the gun from his jacket, slowed as he approached the parked car, and fired a shot into the rear tire, which sent three forms inside ducking for cover.

Then he sped away.

22

Wednesday, December 12, 12:40 a.m.

Malone twisted his way out of Garmisch, using to maximum advantage its maze of unlit narrow streets and his head start on the men who'd been waiting at the Posthotel. He had no way of knowing if they had a second vehicle handy. Satisfied that they were not being pursued, he found the highway leading north that he'd traveled earlier and, following Christl's instructions, realized where they were headed.

'Those things you need to show me are in Ettal Monastery?' he asked.

She nodded. 'No sense waiting until morning.'

He agreed.

'I'm sure when you spoke with Dorothea there, you were told only what she wanted you to know.'

'And you're different?'

She stared at him. 'Totally.'

He wasn't so sure. 'Those men at the hotel. Yours? Or hers?'

'You wouldn't believe me no matter what I said.'

He downshifted as the highway began to descend back toward the abbey. 'A piece of unsolicited advice? You really need to explain yourself. My patience is about gone.'

She hesitated, and he waited.

'Fifty thousand years ago a civilization arose on this planet, one that managed to progress faster than the rest of humankind. Leading the way, if you will. Was it technologically developed? Not really, but it was highly advanced. Mathematics, architecture, chemistry, biology, geology, meteorology, astronomy. That's where it excelled.'

He was listening.

'Our concept of ancient history has been strongly influenced by the Bible. But its texts dealing with antiquity were written from an insular point of view. They distorted ancient cultures and completely neglected some important ones, like the Minoans. This particular culture I'm talking about is not biblical. They were an oceangoing society with worldwide commerce, possessing capable boats and advanced navigational skills. Later cultures like the Polynesians, the Phoenicians, the Vikings, and finally the Europeans would all develop these skills, but Civilization One mastered them first.'

He'd read about those theories. Most scientists now rejected the idea of a linear societal development from the Old Stone Age through the New Stone Age, Bronze Age, and Iron Age. Instead, scholars believed that humans developed independent of one another. Proof of that existed even today, on every continent, where primitive cultures still coexisted with advanced societies. 'So you're saying that, in times past, while Paleolithic peoples occupied Europe, more advanced cultures could have existed elsewhere.' He recalled what Dorothea Lindauer told him. 'Aryans again?'

'Hardly. They're a myth. But that myth may have a basis in reality. Take Crete and Troy. They were long considered fictional, but we now know them to be real.'

'So what happened to this first civilization?'

'Unfortunately, every culture contains the seeds of its own destruction. Progress and decay coexist. History has shown that all societies eventually develop the means of their downfall. Look at Babylon, Greece, Rome, the Mongols, Huns, Turks, and too many monarchical societies to even count. They always do it to themselves. Civilization One was no exception.'

What she said made sense. Man truly did seem to destroy as much as he created.

'Grandfather and Father both were obsessed with this lost civilization. I must confess, I'm drawn to it, too.'

'My bookshop is loaded with New Age materials about Atlantis and a dozen other so-called lost civilizations, not a trace of which has ever been found. It's fantasy.'

'War and conquest have taken their toll on human history. It's a cyclical process. Progress, war, devastation, then reawakening. There's a sociological truism. The more advanced the culture, the more easily it will be destroyed, and the less evidence of it will remain. In more simplistic terms, we find what we look for.'

He slowed the car. 'No, we don't. Most times we stumble onto things.'

She shook her head. 'The greatest human revelations have all started with a simple theory. Look at evolution. It was only after Darwin formulated his concepts that we started noticing things that fortified the theory. Copernicus proposed a radical new way to view the solar system, and when we finally looked we found out he was right. Before the last fifty years no one seriously believed that an advanced civilization could have preceded us. It was regarded as nonsense. So the evidence has simply been neglected.'

'What evidence?'

She removed Einhard's book from her pocket. 'This.'

March 800. Charlemagne rides north from Aachen. He's never before ventured to the Gallic Sea at this time of year, when frigid northern winds pound the shore and fishing is poor. But he insists on this journey. Three soldiers and I accompany him, and the journey takes the better part of a day. Once there, camp is set in the usual location, beyond the dunes, which offers little protection from a strong gale. Three days after arriving sails are seen and we think the boats Danes or part of the Saracenic fleet that threatens the empire north and south. But eventually the king shouts in joy and waits on the beach as the ships raise their oars and smaller boats row ashore carrying the Watchers. Uriel, who rules over Tartarus, leads them. With him are Arakiba, who is over the spirits of men, and Raguel who takes vengeance on the world of luminaries, and Danel, who is set over the best part of mankind and chaos, and Saraqael, who is set over spirits. They wear thick mantles, fur trousers, and fur boots. Their fair hair is neatly trimmed and combed. Charlemagne clasps each in a firm embrace. The king asks many questions and Uriel answers. The king is allowed onto the ships, each fashioned of sturdy timbers and caulked with tar, and he marvels at their sturdiness. We are told they are built away from their land, where trees grow in abundance. They love the sea and understand its ways far better than we do. Danel displays for the king maps of places we do not know exist and we are told how their ships find their way. Danel shows us a piece of sharp iron, resting on a sliver of wood, floating in a shell of water, that points the way over the sea. The king wants to know how that could be and Danel explains that the metal is attracted to one particular direction and he motioned north. No matter how the shell is turned the iron point always finds that direction. They visit for three days and Uriel and the king talk at length. I strike a friendship with Arakiba, who acts as counselor for Uriel, as I do for the king. Arakiba tells me of his land, where fire and ice live together, and I tell him that I would like to see that place.

'The Watchers are what Einhard called the people from Civilization One,' she said. '*Holy Ones* is another term he uses. Both he and Charlemagne thought them from heaven.'

'Who says they were anything other than a culture we already know exists?'

'Do you know of any society that used an alphabet or language like the one you saw in Dorothea's book?'

'That isn't conclusive proof.'

'Was there an oceangoing society in the ninth century? Only the Vikings. But these weren't Vikings.'

'You don't know who they were.'

'No, I don't. But I do know that Charlemagne ordered the book Dorothea showed you buried with him. It was apparently important enough that he wanted it kept from everyone, except emperors. Einhard went to a lot of trouble to hide this book. Suffice it to say that there is more in here that explains why the Nazis really went to Antarctica in 1938, and why our fathers went back in 1971.'

The abbey rose ahead, still illuminated against the limitless night.

'Park over there,' she said, and he wheeled in and stopped.

Still no one following them.

She popped open her door. 'Let me show you what, I'm sure, Dorothea didn't.'

23

Ramsey loved the night. He came alive each day around six pm, his best thoughts and most decisive actions always formulated after dark. Sleep was necessary, though usually no more than four to five hours – just enough to rest his brain, but not enough to waste time. Nighttime also provided privacy, since it was much easier to know if someone was interested in your business at two in the morning as opposed to two in the afternoon. That was why he only met with Diane McCoy at night.

He lived in a modest Georgetown town house that he rented from a longtime friend who liked having a four-star admiral as a tenant. He electronically swept the two floors for monitoring devices at least once a day – and especially before Diane paid a visit.

He'd been fortunate that Daniels had selected her as deputy national security adviser. She was certainly qualified, with degrees in international relations and global economics, and politically connected with both the left and right. She'd come from State as part of the shakeup last year when Larry Daley's career abruptly ended. He'd liked Daley – a negotiable soul – but Diane was better. Smart, ambitious, and determined to stick around longer than the three years left on Daniels' last term.

Thankfully, he could offer her that chance.

And she knew it.

'Things are starting,' he said.

They were comfortable in his den, a fire crackling in the brick hearth. Outside, the temperature had dropped to the midtwenties. No snow yet, but it was on the way.

'Since I know little of what those things are,' McCoy said, 'I can only assume they're good.'

He smiled. 'What about on your end? Can you make the appointment happen?'

'Admiral Sylvian isn't gone yet. He's banged up from that motorcycle accident, but is expected to recover.'

'I know David. He's going to be down for months. He won't want his job unattended during that time. He'll resign.' He paused. 'If he doesn't succumb first.'

McCoy smiled. She was a placid blonde with a capable air and eyes that beamed with confidence. He liked that about her. Modest bearing. Simple. Cool. Yet dangerous as hell. She sat, back straight, in the chair and nursed a whiskey soda.

'I almost believe you can make Sylvian's death happen,' she said.

'What if I can?'

'Then you'd be a man worthy of respect.'

He laughed. 'The game we're about to play has no rules and only one objective. To win. So I want to know about Daniels. Will he cooperate?'

'That's going to depend on you. You know he's no fan, but you're also qualified for the job. Assuming, of course, there's a vacancy to fill.'

He caught her suspicion. The initial plan was simple: Eliminate David Sylvian, secure his spot on the Joint Chiefs of Staff, serve three years, then start phase two.

But he needed to know, 'Will Daniels follow your advice?'

She sipped more of her drink. 'You don't like not being in control, do you?'

'Who does?'

'Daniels is the president. He can do what he pleases. But I think what he does here depends on Edwin Davis.'

He didn't want to hear that. 'How could *he* be a factor? He's a deputy adviser.'

'Like me?'

He caught her resentment. 'You know what I mean, Diane. How could Davis be a problem?'

'That's your flaw, Langford. You tend to underestimate your enemy.'

'How is Davis *my* enemy?'

'I read the report on *Blazek*. Nobody named Davis died in that sub. He lied to Daniels. There was no older brother killed.'

'Did Daniels know that?'

She shook her head. 'He didn't read the inquiry report. He told me to do it.'

'Can't you control Davis?'

'As you so wisely note, we're on the same level. He has as free access to Daniels as I do, per the president's order. It's the White House, Langford. I don't make the rules.'

'What about the national security adviser? Any help there?'

'He's in Europe and not in the loop on this one.'

'You think Daniels is working directly with Davis?'

'How the hell would I know? All I know is Danny Daniels isn't a tenth as stupid as he wants everyone to believe he is.'

He glanced at the mantel clock. Soon the airwaves would be filled with the news of Admiral David Sylvian's untimely death, attributable to injuries sustained in a tragic motorcycle accident. Tomorrow another death in Jacksonville, Florida, might be a local news story. Much was happening, and what McCoy was saying troubled him.

'Involving Cotton Malone in this could also be problematic,' she said.

'How? The man's retired. He just wants to know about his father.'

'That report should not have been given to him.'

He agreed, but it shouldn't matter. Wilkerson and Malone were most likely dead. 'We just used that foolishness to our advantage.'

'I have no idea how that was to *our* advantage.'

'Just know that it was.'

'Langford, am I going to regret this?'

'You're welcome to serve out Daniels' term, then go to work for some think tank writing reports that nobody reads. Ex-White House staffers look great on the letterhead, and I hear they're paid well. Maybe one of the networks would hire you to spout out ten-second sound bites on what other people are doing to change the world. Pays good, too, even if you look like an idiot most of the time.'

'Like I said. Am I going to regret this?'

'Diane, power has to be taken. There's no other way to acquire it. Now, you never answered me. Will Daniels cooperate and appoint me?'

'I read the *Blazek* report,' she said. 'I also did some checking. You were on *Holden* when it went to Antarctica to search for that sub. You and two others. The top brass sent your team under classified orders. In fact, that mission is still classified. I can't even learn about it. I did discover that you went ashore and filed a report on what you found, delivered personally, by you, to the chief of naval operations. What he did with the information, nobody knows.'

'We didn't find anything.'

'You're a liar.'

He gauged her assault. This woman was formidable – a political animal with excellent instincts. She could help and she could hurt. So he shifted. 'You're right. I am lying. But believe me, you don't want to know what really happened.'

'No, I don't. But whatever it is may come back to haunt you.'

He'd thought the same thing for thirty-eight years. 'Not if I can help it.'

She seemed to be restraining a surge of annoyance at his avoidance of her inquiries. 'It's been my experience, Langford, that the past always has a way of returning. Those who don't learn, or can't remember it, are doomed to repeat it. Now you have an ex-agent involved – a damn good one, I might add – who has a personal stake in this mess. And Edwin Davis is on the loose. I have no idea what he's doing—'

He'd heard enough. 'Can you deliver Daniels?'

She paused, taking in his rebuke, then slowly said, 'I'd say that all depends on your friends on Capitol Hill. Daniels needs their help on a great many things. He's doing what every president does at the end. Thinking legacy. He has a legislative agenda so, if the right members of Congress want you on the Joint Chiefs, then he'll give it to them – in return, of course, for votes. The questions are easy. Will there be a vacancy to fill, and can you deliver the right members?'

He'd talked enough. There were things to do before he slept. So he ended the meeting on a note Diane McCoy should not forget. 'The right members will not only endorse my candidacy, they'll insist on it.'

24

Ettal Monastery, 1:05 a.m.

Malone watched as Christl Falk unlocked the door for the abbey church. Clearly, the Oberhauser family had considerable pull with the monks. It was the middle of the night and they were coming and going as they pleased.

The opulent church remained dimly lit. They crossed the darkened marble floor with only their leather heels echoing across the warm interior. His senses were alert. He'd learned that empty European churches, at night, tended to be a problem.

They entered the sacristy and Christl headed straight for the portal that led down into the abbey's bowels. At the bottom of the stairs, the door at the far end of the corridor hung ajar.

He grabbed her arm and shook his head, signaling that they should advance with caution. He gripped the gun from the cable car and kept close to the wall. At the end of the hallway he peered inside the room.

Everything was askew.

'Maybe the monks are pissed?' he said.

The stones and wood carvings lay scattered on the floor, the displays in total disarray. Tables at the far end had been toppled. The two wall cabinets had been rifled through.

Then he saw the body.

The woman from the cable car. No visible wounds or blood, but he caught a familiar scent in the still air.

'Cyanide.'

'She was poisoned?'

'Look at her. She choked on her tongue.'

He saw that Christl didn't want to look at the corpse.

'I can't take that,' she said. 'Dead bodies.'

She was becoming upset, so he asked, 'What did we come to see?'

She seemed to grab hold of her emotions and her gaze raked the debris. 'They're gone. The stones from Antarctica that Grandfather found. They're not here.'

He didn't see them, either. 'Are they important?'

'They have the same writing on them as the books.'

'Tell me what I don't know.'

'This is not right,' she muttered.

'You could say that. The monks are going to be a little upset, regardless of your family's patronage.'

She was clearly flustered.

'Are the stones all we came to see?' he asked.

She shook her head. 'No. You're right. There's more.' She stepped toward one of the gaily decorated cabinets, its doors and drawers open, and glanced inside. 'Oh, my.'

He came up behind her and saw that a hole had been hacked into the rear panel, the splintered opening large enough for a hand to pass through.

'Grandfather and Father kept their papers there.'

'Which somebody seems to have known.'

She inserted her arm. 'Empty.'

Then she rushed for the door.

'Where are you going?' he asked.

'We have to hurry. I only hope we're not too late.'

*   *   *

Ramsey switched off the lights on the ground floor and climbed the stairs to his bedroom. Diane McCoy was gone. He'd considered several times expanding their collaboration. She was attractive in body and brain. But he'd decided that it was a bad idea. How many men of power had been brought down by a piece of ass? Too many to even recall, and he did not intend to join that list.

Clearly, McCoy had been concerned about Edwin Davis. He knew Davis. Their paths had crossed years ago in Brussels with Millicent, a woman he'd enjoyed, many times. She, too, was bright, young, and eager. But also –

'Pregnant,' Millicent said.

He'd heard her the first time. 'What do you want me to do about it?'

'Marrying me would be good.'

'But I don't love you.'

She laughed. 'Yes, you do. You just won't admit it.'

'No, actually, I don't. I enjoy sleeping with you. I enjoy listening to you tell me about what goes on in the office. I enjoy picking your brain. But I don't want to marry you.'

She snuggled close. 'You'd miss me if I were gone.'

He was amazed at how seemingly intelligent women could care so little about their self-respect. He'd struck this woman too many times to count, yet she never fled, almost as if she liked it. Deserved it. Wanted it. A few jabs right now would do them both good, but he decided patience would serve him better, so he held her in a tight embrace and softly said, 'You're right. I would miss you.'

Less than a month later, she was dead.

Within a week, Edwin Davis was gone, too.

Millicent had told him how Davis always came when she called and helped her through his constant rejection.

Why she confessed such things, he could only guess. It was as if his knowing might prevent him from hurting her again. Yet he always did, and she always forgave him. Davis never said a word, but Ramsey many times saw hatred in the younger man's eyes – along with the frustration that came from his utter inability to do anything about it. Davis then was a low-level State Department employee on one of his first foreign assignments, his job to resolve problems not create them – to keep his mouth shut and his ears open. But now Edwin Davis was a deputy national security adviser to the president of the United States. Different time, different rules. *He has free access to Daniels, as I do, per the president's order.* That's what McCoy had said. She was right. Whatever Davis was doing involved him. No proof existed for the conclusion, just a feeling, one he'd learned long ago to never doubt.

So Edwin Davis might have to be eliminated.

Just like Millicent.

Wilkerson trudged through the snow to where Dorothea Lindauer had parked her car. His vehicle was still smoldering. Dorothea seemed unconcerned with the lodge's destruction, even though, as she'd told him weeks ago, the house had been owned by her family since the mid-nineteenth century.

They'd left the bodies among the rubble. *'We'll deal with them later,'* Dorothea had said. Other matters demanded their immediate attention.

He was carrying the last box brought from Füssen and loaded it into the trunk. He was sick of cold and snow. He liked the sun and heat. He would have made a much better Roman than Viking.

He opened the car door and worked his tired limbs in

behind the wheel. Dorothea already sat in the passenger seat.

'Do it,' she said to him.

He glanced at his luminous watch and calculated the time difference. He didn't want to make the call. 'Later.'

'No. He has to know.'

'Why?'

'Men like that have to be kept off balance. He'll make mistakes that way.'

He was torn between confusion and fear. 'I just escaped getting killed. I'm not in the mood for this.'

She touched his arm. 'Sterling, listen to me. This is in motion. There's no stopping. Tell him.'

He could barely make out her face in the darkness, but easily visualized in his mind her intense beauty. She was one of the most striking women he'd ever known. Smart, too. She'd correctly predicted that Langford Ramsey was a snake.

And she'd also just saved his life.

So he found his phone and punched in the number. He provided the operator on the other end his security code and the day's password, then told her what he wanted.

Two minutes later Langford Ramsey came on the line.

'It's mighty late where you are,' the admiral said, his tone amicable.

'You sorry SOB. You're a lying piece of shit.'

A moment of silence, then, 'I assume there's a reason you're speaking to a superior officer this way.'

'I survived.'

'What is it you survived?'

The quizzical tone confused him. But why wouldn't Ramsey lie? 'You sent a team to take me out.'

'I assure you, Captain, if I wanted you dead you would

be. You should be more concerned with who it is that seems to want you dead. Perhaps Frau Lindauer? I sent you to make contact, to get to know her, to find out what I needed to know.'

'And I did exactly what you instructed. I wanted that damn star.'

'And you'll have it, as promised. But have you accomplished anything?'

In the quiet of the car Dorothea had heard Ramsey. She grabbed the phone and said, 'You're a liar, Admiral. It's you who wants him dead. And I'd say he's accomplished a lot.'

'Frau Lindauer, so good to finally speak to you,' he heard Ramsey say through the phone.

'Tell me, Admiral, why do I interest you?'

'You don't. But your family does.'

'You know about my father, don't you?'

'I'm acquainted with the situation.'

'You know why he was on that submarine.'

'The question is, why are you so interested? Your family has been cultivating sources within the navy for years. Did you think I didn't know that? I simply sent you one.'

'We've known there was more,' she said.

'Unfortunately, Frau Lindauer, you'll never know the answer.'

'Don't count on that.'

'Such bravado. I'll be anxious to see if you can make good on that boast.'

'How about you answer one question?'

Ramsey chuckled. 'Okay, one question.'

'Is there anything there to find?'

Wilkerson was baffled by the inquiry. Anything *where* to find?

'You can't imagine,' Ramsey said.

And the line clicked off.

She handed him the phone and he asked her, 'What did you mean? Anything *there* to find.'

She sat back in the seat. Snow coated the car's exterior.

'I was afraid of this,' she muttered. 'Unfortunately, the answers are all in Antarctica.'

'What are you searching for?'

'I need to read what's in the trunk before I can tell you that. I'm still not sure.'

'Dorothea, I'm tossing my whole career, my whole life away for this. You heard Ramsey. He may not have been after me.'

She sat rigid, never moving. 'You'd be dead right now if it weren't for me.' Her head turned his way. 'Your life is locked to mine.'

'And I'll say it again. You have a husband.'

'Werner and I are through. We have been for a long time. It's you and me now.'

She was right and he knew it. Which both bothered and excited him.

'What are you going to do?' he asked.

'A great deal for us both, I hope.'

25

Bavaria

M alone surveyed the castle through the windshield, the ponderous edifice clinging to a sharply rising slope. Mullioned, dormer, and graceful oriel windows shone to the night. Arc lights cast the exterior walls with a mellow medieval beauty. Something Luther once said about another German citadel flashed through his mind. *A mighty fortress is our God, a bulwark never failing.*

He was driving his rental car, Christl Falk in the passenger seat. They'd left Ettal Monastery in a hurry and plunged deep into the frozen Bavarian woods, following a forlorn highway devoid of traffic. Finally, after a forty-minute ride, the castle appeared and he drove them inside, parking in a courtyard. Above, dotting an ink-blue sky, shone a brilliance of sparkling stars.

'This is our home,' Christl said as they exited. 'The Oberhauser estate. Reichshoffen.'

'Hope and empire,' he translated. 'Interesting name.'

'Our family motto. We've occupied this hilltop for over seven hundred years.'

He surveyed the scene of order, meticulous in arrangement, neutral in color, broken only by stains of snow that oozed from the ancient stone.

She turned away and he caught her wrist. Beautiful

women were difficult, and this stranger was indeed beautiful. Even worse, she was playing him and he knew it.

'Why is your name Falk and not Oberhauser?' he asked, trying to throw her off balance.

Her eyes dropped to her arm. He released his grip.

'A marriage that was a mistake.'

'Your sister. Lindauer. Still married?'

'She is, though I can't say it's much of one. Werner likes her money and she likes being married. Gives her an excuse for why her lovers can never be more.'

'You going to tell me why you two don't get along?'

She smiled, which only magnified her allure. 'That depends on whether you agree to help.'

'You know why I'm here.'

'Your father. It's why I'm here, too.'

He doubted that but decided to quit stalling. 'Then let's see what's so important.'

They entered through an arched doorway. His attention was drawn to a huge tapestry that draped the far wall. Another odd drawing, this one stitched in gold upon a deep maroon-and-navy background.

She noticed his interest. 'Our family crest.'

He studied the image. A crown poised over an iconic

drawing of an animal – perhaps a dog or cat, hard to say – gripping what looked like a rodent in its mouth. 'What does it mean?'

'I've never received a good explanation. But one of our ancestors liked it, so he had the tapestry sewn and hung there.'

Outside he heard the unmuffled roar of an engine gunning into the courtyard. He stared out through the open doorway and saw a man emerge from a Mercedes coupe with an automatic weapon.

He recognized the face.

The same one from his room, earlier, at the Posthotel.

What the hell?

The man leveled the gun.

He yanked Christl back as high-velocity rounds whizzed through the doorway and obliterated a table abutting the far wall. Glass shattered from an adjacent floor clock. They rushed forward, Christl leading the way. More bullets strafed the wall behind him.

He gripped the gun from the cable car as they turned a corner and bolted down a short corridor that emptied into a grand hall.

He quickly spied the surroundings and saw a quadrangular-shaped room adorned with colonnades that rose on four sides, long galleries above and beneath. At the far end, illuminated by weak incandescent fixtures, hung the symbol of the former German Empire – a black, red, and gold banner emblazoned with an eagle. The black yaw of a stone fireplace, large enough for several people to stand inside, opened beneath it.

'Split up,' she said. 'You go up.'

Before he could object, she rushed ahead into the darkness.

He spotted a staircase that led up to the second-floor gallery and moved lightly toward the first step. Blackness numbed his eyes. Niches were everywhere, dark voids where, he worried, more ill-disposed retainers could lie in wait.

He crept up the stairs and entered the upper gallery, embracing the darkness, hovering a couple of yards away from the balustrade. A shadow entered the hall below, backlit by light slanting in from the corridor beyond. Eighteen chairs lined a massive dining table. Their gilded backs stood rigid, like soldiers in a line, except for two, which Christl had apparently crawled beneath since she was nowhere to be seen.

A laugh permeated the stillness. 'You're dead, Malone.'

Fascinating. The man knew his name.

'Come and get me,' he called out, knowing the hall would generate an echo and make it impossible to pinpoint his location.

He saw the man probe the darkness, surveying the arches, noticing a tiled stove in one corner, the massive table, and a brass chandelier that loomed over it all.

Malone fired below.

The bullet missed.

Footsteps rushed toward the stairway.

Malone darted ahead, turned the corner, and slowed as he found the opposite gallery. No footsteps could be heard from behind, but the gunman was definitely there.

He stared down at the table. Two chairs remained out of place. Another toppled back and crashed to the floor, sending a thud resounding through the hall.

A gunshot volley, from across the upper gallery, rained down and obliterated the tabletop. Luckily the thick wood handled the assault. Malone fired across the gallery to where the muzzle flashes had appeared. Rounds now came his way, ricocheting off stone behind him.

His eyes searched the darkness, trying to see where the assailant might be. He'd tried to divert attention by calling out, but Christl Falk, whether intentionally or not, had ruined that effort. Behind him, more black niches lined the wall. Ahead was equally bleak. He caught movement on the opposite side – a form, heading his way. He clung to the darkness, crouched and crept forward, turning left to traverse the hall's short side.

What was happening? This man had come for him.

Christl suddenly appeared below in the center of the hall, standing in the weak light.

Malone did not reveal his presence. Instead, he settled into the shadows, hugged one of the arches, and peered around its edge.

'Show yourself,' Christl called out.

No reply.

Malone abandoned his position and moved faster, trying to double back behind the gunman.

'Look, I'm walking away. If you want to stop me, you know what you're going to have to do.'

'Not smart,' a man said.

Malone stopped at another corner. Ahead, halfway down the gallery, the attacker stood, facing away. Malone cast a quick glance downward and saw that Christl was still there.

A cold excitement steadied his nerve.

The shadow before him raised his weapon.

'Where is he?' the man asked her. But she did not reply. 'Malone, show yourself or she's dead.'

Malone crept forward, gun level, and said, 'I'm right here.'

The man's gun stayed angled downward. 'I can still kill Frau Lindauer,' he calmly said.

Malone caught the error but made clear, 'I'll shoot you long before you can pull that trigger.'

The man seemed to consider his dilemma and turned slowly toward Malone. Then his movements accelerated as he tried to swing the assault rifle around, pulling the trigger at the same time. Bullets pinged through the hall. Malone was about to fire when another report banged off the walls.

The man's head wrenched back as he stopped firing.

His body flew away from the railing.

Legs teetered, off balance.

A cry, quick and startled, strangled into silence as the gunman collapsed to the floor.

Malone lowered his weapon.

The top of the man's skull was gone.

He approached the railing.

Below, on one side of Christl Falk stood a tall, thin man with a rifle pointed upward. On the other side was an elderly woman who said to him, 'We appreciate the distraction, Herr Malone.'

'It wasn't necessary to shoot him.'

The old woman motioned and the other man lowered his rifle.

'I thought it was,' she said.

26

Malone descended to ground level. The other man and older woman still stood with Christl Falk.

'This is Ulrich Henn,' Christl said. 'He works for our family.'

'And what does he do?'

'He looks after this castle,' the old woman said. 'He's the head chamberlain.'

'And who are you?' he asked.

Her eyebrows raised in apparent amusement and she threw him a smile with the teeth of a jack-o'-lantern. She was unnaturally gaunt, almost birdlike in appearance, with burnished gray-gold hair. Forked veins lined her spindly arms and liver spots dotted her wrists.

'I am Isabel Oberhauser.'

Though welcome seemed on her lips, the eyes were more uncertain.

'Am I supposed to be impressed?'

'I am the matriarch of this family.'

He pointed at Ulrich Henn. 'You and your employee just killed a man.'

'Who entered my house illegally with a weapon, trying to kill you and my daughter.'

'And you just happened to have a rifle handy, along

with a person who can blow the top of a man's head off from fifty feet away in a dimly lit hall.'

'Ulrich is an excellent shot.'

Henn said nothing. He apparently knew his place.

'I didn't know they were here,' Christl said. 'I was under the impression Mother was away. But when I saw her and Ulrich enter the hall, I motioned for him to stand ready while I drew the gunman's attention.'

'Stupid move.'

'It seemed to work.'

And it also told him something about this woman. Facing down guns took guts. But he couldn't decide if she was smart, brave, or an idiot. 'I don't know too many academicians who'd do what you did.' He faced the older Oberhauser. 'We needed that gunman alive. He knew my name.'

'I noticed that, too.'

'I need answers, not more puzzles, and what you did complicated an already screwed-up situation.'

'Show him,' Isabel said to her daughter. 'Afterward, Herr Malone, you and I can talk privately.'

He followed Christl back to the main foyer, then upstairs into one of the bedchambers where, in a far corner, a colossal tile stove bearing the date 1651 stretched to the ceiling.

'This was my father's and grandfather's room.'

She entered an alcove where a decorative bench jutted below a mullioned window.

'My ancestors, who originally built Reichshoffen in the thirteenth century, were fanatical about being trapped. So every room possessed at least two exits – this one no exception. In fact, it was afforded the utmost in security for the time.'

She applied pressure to one of the mortar joints and a wall section opened, revealing a spiral staircase that wound down in a counterclockwise direction. When she flicked a switch a series of low-voltage lamps illuminated the darkness.

He followed her inside. At the bottom of the staircase she flicked another switch.

He noticed the air. Dry, warm, climate-controlled. The floor was gray slate framed by thin lines of black grout. The coarse stone walls, plastered and also painted gray, bore evidence that they had been hacked from bedrock centuries ago.

The chamber cut a twisting path, one room dissolving into another, forming a backdrop for some unusual objects. There were German flags, Nazi banners, even a replica of an SS altar, fully prepared for the child-naming ceremonies he knew were common in the 1930s. Countless figurines, a toy soldier set laid out on a colorful map of early-twentieth-century Europe, Nazi helmets, swords, daggers, uniforms, caps, windcheater jackets, pistols, rifles, gorgets, bandoliers, rings, jewelry, gauntlets, and photographs.

'This is what my grandfather spent his time, after the war, accumulating.'

'It's like a Nazi museum.'

'Hitler's discrediting profoundly hurt him. He served the bastard well, but never could understand that he meant nothing to the Socialists. For six years, up until the war ended, he tried every way he could to gain back favor. Until he lost his mind utterly in the 1950s, he collected all this.'

'That doesn't explain why the family kept it.'

'My father respected his father. But we rarely come down here.'

She led him to a glass-topped case. Inside, she pointed to a silver ring with SS runes depicted in a way he'd never seen before. Cursive, almost italicized. 'They're in the true Germanic form, as on ancient Norse shields. Fitting, because these rings were only worn by the Ahnenerbe.' She drew his attention to another item in the case. 'The badge with the Odel rune and short-armed swastika was also only for the Ahnenerbe. Grandfather designed them. The stickpin is quite special – a representation of the sacred Irminsul, or Life Tree of the Saxons. It supposedly stood atop the Rocks of the Sun at Detmold and was destroyed by Charlemagne himself, which started the long wars between Saxons and Franks.'

'You speak of these relics almost with reverence.'

'I do?' She sounded perplexed.

'As if they mean something to you.'

She shrugged. 'They're simply reminders of the past. My grandfather started the Ahnenerbe for purely cultural reasons, but it evolved into something altogether different. Its Institute for Military Scientific Research conducted unthinkable experiments on concentration camp prisoners. Vacuum chambers, hypothermia, blood coagulation testing. Horrible things. Its Applied Nature Studies created a Jewish bone collection from men and women whom they murdered, then macerated. Eventually several of the Ahnenerbe were hanged for war crimes. Many more went to prison. It became an abomination.'

He watched her carefully.

'None of which my grandfather participated in,' she said, reading his thoughts. 'All of that happened after he was fired and publicly shamed.' She paused. 'Long after he sentenced himself to this place and the abbey, where he toiled alone.'

Hanging beside the Ahnenerbe banner was a tapestry that depicted the same Life Tree from the stickpin. Writing at the bottom caught his attention. NO PEOPLE LIVE LONGER THAN THE DOCUMENTATION OF THEIR CULTURE.

She saw his interest. 'My grandfather believed that statement.'

'And do you?'

She nodded. 'I do.'

He still did not understand why the Oberhauser family had preserved this collection in a climate-controlled room, with not a speck of dust anywhere. But he could understand one of her stated reasons. He respected his father, too. Though the man had been absent for much of Malone's childhood, he remembered the times they'd spent together throwing a baseball, swimming, or doing chores around the house. He'd remained angry for years after his father died at being denied what his friends, with both parents, took for granted. His mother never let him forget his father but, as he grew older, he came to realize that her memory might have been jaded. Being a navy wife was tough duty – just as being a Magellan Billet wife had eventually proven too much for his ex.

Christl led the way through the exhibits. Each turn revealed more of Hermann Oberhauser's passion. She stopped at another gaily painted wooden cabinet, similar to the one at the abbey. Inside one of its drawers she removed a single page encased within a heavy plastic sheath.

'This is Einhard's original last will and testament, found by Grandfather. A copy was at the abbey.'

He studied what appeared to be vellum, the tight script in Latin, the ink faded to a pale gray.

'On the reverse is a German translation,' she said. 'The final paragraph is the important one.'

In life my oath was given to the most pious Lord
Charles, emperor and augustus, which required me
to withhold all mention of Tartarus. A complete
account of what I know was long ago reverently
placed with Lord Charles on the day he died. If that
sacred tomb ever be opened, those pages shall not
be divided, nor partitioned, but know that Lord
Charles would have them bestowed upon the holy
emperor then holding the crown. To read those truths
would reveal much and, after further considerations
of piety and prudence, especially since witnessing
the utter disregard Lord Louis has shown for his
father's great efforts, I have conditioned the ability
to read those words on knowing two other truths.
The first I do hereby bestow to my son, who is
directed to safeguard it for his son, and his son
thereafter for eternity. Guard it dearly, for it is written
in the language of the church and easily
comprehended, but its message is not complete. The
second, which would bestow a full comprehension
of the wisdom of heaven waiting with Lord Charles,
begins in the new Jerusalem. Revelations there will
be clear once the secret of that wondrous place is
deciphered. Clarify this pursuit by applying the
angel's perfection to the lord's sanctification. But
only those who appreciate the throne of Solomon
and Roman frivolity shall find their way to heaven.
Be warned, neither I, nor the Holy Ones, have
patience with ignorance.

'It's what I told you about,' she said. '*Karl der Große
Verfolgung*. The Charlemagne pursuit. It's what we have
to decipher. It's what Otto III, and every Holy Roman

Emperor after him failed to discover. Solving this puzzle will lead us to what our fathers were searching for in Antarctica.'

He shook his head. 'You said your grandfather went and brought stuff back. Obviously, he solved it. Didn't he leave the answer?'

'He left no records on how or what he learned. As I've said, he went senile and was useless after that.'

'And why has it now become so important?'

She hesitated before answering him. 'Neither Grandfather nor Father cared much for business. The world was what interested them. Unfortunately, Grandfather lived at a time when controversial ideas were banned. So he was forced to labor alone. Father was a hopeless dreamer who did not possess the ability to accomplish anything.'

'He apparently managed to get to Antarctica aboard an American submarine.'

'Which begs a question.'

'Why was the American government interested enough to put him on that sub?'

He knew part of that could be explained by the times. America in the 1950s, '60s, and '70s pursued a number of unconventional investigations. Things like the paranormal, ESP, mind control, UFOs. Every angle was explored in the hope of finding an edge over the Soviets. Had this been another of those wild attempts?

'I was hoping,' she said, 'that you could help explain that.'

But he was still waiting for an answer to his inquiry. So he asked again, 'Why is any of this important now?'

'It could matter a great deal. In fact, it could literally change our world.'

Behind Christl, her mother appeared, the old woman walking slowly toward where they stood, her careful steps making not a sound.

'Leave us,' she ordered her daughter.

Christl left, without a word.

Malone stood, holding Einhard's will.

Isabel straightened. 'You and I have things to discuss.'

27

Charlie Smith waited across the street. One last appointment before his work night ended.

Commander Zachary Alexander, retired USN, had spent the last thirty years doing nothing but complaining. His heart. Spleen. Liver. Bones. Not a body part had escaped scrutiny. Twelve years ago he became convinced he needed an appendectomy until a doctor reminded him that his appendix had been removed ten years before. A pack-a-day smoker in years past, he was sure three years ago that he'd contracted lung cancer, but test after test revealed nothing. Recently, prostate cancer gestated into another of his obsessive afflictions, and he'd spent weeks trying to convince specialists he was afflicted.

Tonight, though, Zachary Alexander's medical worries would all end.

Deciding how best to accomplish that task had been difficult. Since virtually every part of Alexander's body had been thoroughly tested, a medical death would almost certainly be suspicious. Violence was out of the question, as that always attracted attention. But the file on Alexander indicated:

Lives alone. Tired of incessant complaining, wife divorced him years ago. Children rarely visit, gets on their nerves too. Never has a woman over. Considers sex nasty and infectious. Professes to have quit smoking years ago, but most nights, and usually in bed, likes a cigar. A heavy imported brand, specially ordered through a tobacco shop in Jacksonville (address at end). Smokes at least one a day.

That tidbit had been enough to spark Smith's imagination and, coupled with a few other morsels from the file, he'd finally devised the means for Zachary Alexander's death.

Smith had flown from Washington, DC, to Jacksonville on a late-evening shuttle, then followed the directions in the file and parked about a quarter mile beyond Alexander's home. He'd slipped on a denim vest, grabbed a canvas bag from the rental's backseat, and backtracked up the road.

Only a few houses lined the quiet street.

Alexander was noted in the file as a heavy sleeper and chronic snorer, a notation that told Smith a rumble could be heard even outside the house.

He entered the front yard.

A rackety central air compressor roared from one side of the house, warming the interior. The night was chilly, but noticeably less cold than in Virginia.

He carefully made his way to one of the side windows and hesitated long enough to hear Alexander's rhythmic snoring. A fresh pair of latex gloves already encased his hands. He gingerly set down the canvas bag. From inside, he retrieved a small rubber hose with a hollow metal point. Carefully, he examined the window. Just as the file had indicated, silicon insulation sealed both sides from a half-assed repair.

He pierced the seal with the metal tip, then removed a small pressure cylinder from the bag. The gas was a noxious mixture he'd long ago discovered that rendered deep unconsciousness without any residual effects to blood or lungs. He connected the hose to the cylinder's exhaust port, opened the valve, and allowed the chemicals to silently invade the house.

After ten minutes, the snoring subsided.

He closed the valve, yanked the tubing free, and replaced everything in the bag. Though a small hole remained in the silicon, he wasn't concerned. That minuscule piece of incriminating evidence would soon vanish.

He walked toward the rear yard.

Halfway, he dropped the canvas bag, yanked a wooden access door free from the cement block foundation, and wiggled underneath. An assortment of electrical wires spanned the subfloor. The file showed that Alexander, a confirmed hypochondriac, was also a miser. A few years ago he'd paid a neighbor a few dollars to add an outlet for the bedroom, along with providing a direct line from the breaker box to the outside air compressor.

Nothing had been done to code.

He found the junction box the file noted and unscrewed the cover plate. He then loosened the 220-volt line, breaking the connection and silencing the compressor. He hesitated a few anxious seconds, listening, on the off chance Alexander might have escaped the effects of the gas. But nothing disturbed the night.

From another vest pocket he removed a knife and flayed the insulation protecting the electrical wires to and from the junction box. Whoever had performed the work had not encased the wires – their disintegration would be easily attributable to the lack of a protective conduit – so he was careful not to overdue the shearing.

He replaced the knife.

From another vest pocket he slipped out a plastic bag. Inside was a clay-like material and a ceramic connector. He fastened the connector to the screws inside the junction box. Before reestablishing the circuit, he packed the box with the dough, applying globs down the length of the exposed electrical wires. In its present form the material was harmless, but once heated to the requisite temperature for the requisite amount of time, it would vaporize and melt the remaining insulation. The heat necessary to cause that explosion would come from the ceramic connector. A few minutes would be needed for the current to warm the connector to the right temperature, but that was fine.

He needed time to leave.

He retightened the screws.

The compressor sprang to life.

Deliberately, he left the cover off the junction box, stuffing the faceplate into a vest pocket.

He studied his work. Everything appeared in order. As with magicians' flash paper, once the connector and clay ignited, both would become a scorching gas, producing an intense heat. They were ingenious materials, used by colleagues who specialized more in commercial arson than murder, though sometimes, like tonight, the two could be one and the same.

He wormed out from under the house, replaced the door, and retrieved the canvas bag. He checked the ground and made sure nothing remained that might later betray his presence.

He rounded back to the side window.

Using his penlight, he peered through a dingy screen into the bedroom. An ashtray and cigar lay on the table next to Alexander's bed. Perfect. If 'electrical short' was not enough, 'smoking in bed' could certainly be used to close out any arson investigator's file.

He retraced his steps to the road.

The luminous dial of his watch read 1:35 a.m.

He spent a lot of time out at night. A few years ago he'd bought Peterson's guide to the planets and stars and learned about the heavens. It was good to have hobbies. Tonight, he recognized Jupiter shining brightly in the western sky.

Five minutes passed.

A flash spewed from under the house as the connector, then the clay explosive, incinerated. He imagined the scene as the flayed wires joined the conspiracy, electrical current now feeding the fire. The wooden-frame house was well over thirty years old and, like kindling under dried logs, the bottom fire quickly spread. Within minutes the entire structure was engulfed in flames.

Zachary Alexander, though, would never know what happened.

His forced sleep would not be interrupted. He'd be asphyxiated long before flames charred his body.

28

Bavaria

Malone listened to Isabel Oberhauser.

'I married my husband long ago. But, as you can see, both he and his father harbored secrets.'

'Was your husband also a Nazi?'

She shook her head. 'He simply believed that Germany was never the same after the war. I daresay he was right.'

Not answering questions seemed a family trait. She studied him with a calculating gaze and he noticed a tremor that shook her right eye. Her breath came in low wheezes. And only the tick of a clock from somewhere nearby disturbed the intoxicating tranquility.

'Herr Malone, I'm afraid my daughters have not been honest with you.'

'That's the first thing I've heard today that I agree with.'

'Since my husband died, I've been supervising the family wealth. It's an enormous task. Our extensive holdings are wholly owned by the family. Unfortunately, there are no more Oberhausers. My mother-in-law was a hopeless incompetent who, mercifully, died a few years after Hermann. All of the other close relatives either perished in the war or died in the years after. My husband controlled the family when he was alive. He was the last of Hermann's children. Hermann himself lost his mind completely by the mid-1950s. We call it Alzheimer's today, but then it was just senility. Every family wrestles with its succession, and the time has come for my children to take control of this family. Never have Oberhauser assets been divided. Always there have been sons. But my husband and I birthed daughters. Two strong women, each different. To prove themselves, to force them to accept reality, they are on a quest.'

'This is a game?'

The corners of her eyebrows turned down. 'Not at all. It is a search for the truth. My husband, though I loved him dearly, was, like his father, consumed by foolishness. Hitler openly denied Hermann and that rejection, I believe, contributed to his mental downfall. My husband was equally weak. Making decisions proved difficult for him. Sadly, all their lives, my daughters have fought each other. Never were they close. Their father was a source of that friction. Dorothea manipulated his weaknesses, used them. Christl resented them and rebelled. They were both only ten when he died, but their differing relationships with their father seems best how to define them now. Dorothea is practical, grounded, rooted in reality – seeking the complacent man. Christl is the dreamer, a believer – she seeks the strong. They are now engaged in a quest, one neither of them fully comprehends—'

'Thanks to you, I assume.'

She nodded. 'I confess to retaining a certain element of control. But much is at stake here. Literally everything.'

'What's everything?'

'This family owns many manufacturing concerns, an oil refinery, several banks, stocks around the globe. Billions of euros.'

'Two people died today as part of this game.'

'I'm aware of that, but Dorothea wanted the file on *Blazek*. It's part of that reality she craves. Apparently, though, she decided that you were not a route to her success and abandoned the effort. I suspected that would be the case. So I made sure Christl had the opportunity to speak with you.'

'You sent Christl to the Zugspitze?'

She nodded. 'Ulrich was there to watch over her.'

'What if I don't want any part of this?'

Her watery eyes conveyed a look of annoyance. 'Come now, Herr Malone, let's not you and I fool each other. I'm being straightforward. Could I ask the same from you? You want to know, as badly as I do, what happened thirty-eight years ago. My husband and your father died together. The difference between you and I is that I knew he was going to Antarctica. I just didn't realize I would never see him again.'

His mind reeled. This woman possessed a lot of firsthand knowledge.

'He was in search of the Watchers,' she said. 'The Holy Ones.'

'You can't really believe that such people existed.'

'Einhard believed. They're mentioned in the will you hold. Hermann believed. Dietz gave his life for the belief. Actually, they've been called many things by many different cultures. The Aztecs named them Feathered Serpents, supposedly great white men with red beards. The Bible, in the Book of Genesis, calls them Elohim. The Sumerians tagged them as Anunnaki. The Egyptians knew them as Akhu, Osiris, and the Shemsu Hor. Hinduism and Buddhism both describe them. *Ja*, Herr Malone, on this Christl and I agree, they are real. They influenced even Charlemagne himself.'

She was talking nonsense. 'Frau Oberhauser, we're speaking about things that happened thousands of years ago—'

'My husband was utterly convinced the Watchers still exist.'

He realized that the world had been a different place in 1971. No global media, GPS tracking systems, geosynchronous satellites, or Internet. Staying hidden then was actually possible. Not anymore. 'This is ridiculous.'

'So why did the Americans agree to take him there?'

He could see that she possessed the answer to her own question.

'Because they had searched, too. After the war they went to Antarctica in a massive military jaunt called Highjump. My husband spoke of it many times. They went in search of what Hermann found in 1938. Dietz always believed the Americans discovered something during Highjump. Many years passed. Then, about six months before he left for the Antarctic, some of your military came here and met with Dietz. They talked of Highjump and were privy to Hermann's research. Apparently some of his books and papers had been part of what they confiscated after the war.'

He recalled what Christl had just said to him. *It could matter a great deal. In fact, it could literally change the world.* Ordinarily he would consider this whole thing nuts, but the US government had sent one of its most advanced submarines to investigate, then totally covered up its sinking.

'Dietz wisely chose the Americans over the Soviets. They came here also, wanting his help, but he hated communists.'

'Do you have any idea what's in Antarctica?'

She shook her head. 'I've wondered a long time. I knew of Einhard's will, the Holy Ones, the two books Dorothea and Christl have. I've sincerely wanted to know what is there. So my daughters are solving the riddle and, in the process, hopefully learning they may indeed need each other.'

'That may prove impossible. They seem to despise each other.'

Her eyes found the floor. 'No two sisters could hate each other more. But my life will end soon, and I must know that the family will endure.'

'And resolve your own doubts?'

She nodded. 'Precisely. You must understand, Herr Malone, we find what we search for.'

'That's what Christl said.'

'Her father said that many times and, on that, he was right.'

'Why am I involved?'

'Dorothea initially made that decision. She saw you as a means to learn about the submarine. I suspect she rejected you because of your strength. That would truly frighten her. I chose you because Christl can benefit from your strength. But you are also someone who can level things for her.'

As if he cared. But he knew what was coming.

'And by helping us, you may be able solve your own dilemma.'

'I've always worked alone.'

'We know things you don't.'

That, he couldn't deny. 'Have you heard from Dorothea? There's a dead body in the abbey.'

'Christl told me,' she said. 'Ulrich will deal with that, as he will deal with the one here. I'm concerned about who else has involved themselves in this matter, but I believe you're the most qualified person to solve that complication.'

His adrenaline rush from upstairs was rapidly being replaced with fatigue. 'The gunman came here for me and Dorothea. He didn't say anything about Christl.'

'I heard him. Christl has explained to you about Einhard and Charlemagne. That document you're holding clearly contains a challenge – a pursuit. You've seen the book, written in Einhard's hand. And the one from Charlemagne's grave, which only a Holy Roman Emperor was entitled to receive. This is real, Herr Malone. Imagine for a moment if there actually was a first civilization. Think of the ramifications for human history.'

He couldn't decide if the old woman was a manipulator, a parasite, or an exploiter. Probably all three. 'Frau Oberhauser, I could not care less about that. Frankly, I think you're all nuts. I simply want to know where, how, and why my father died.' He paused, hoping he wasn't going to regret what he was about to say. 'If helping you gives me the answer, then that's enough incentive for me.'

'So you have decided?'

'I haven't.'

'Then could I offer you a bed for the night, and you can make your choice tomorrow?'

He felt an ache in his bones and did not want to drive back to the Posthotel – which might not be the safest haven, anyway, considering the number of uninvited visitors over the past few hours. At least Ulrich was here. Strangely, this made him feel better.

'Okay. I won't argue with that suggestion.'

29

Ramsey slipped on his bathrobe. Time for another day. In fact, this could well become the most important day of his life, the first step on a life-defining journey.

He'd dreamed of Millicent and Edwin Davis and NR-1A. A strange combination that wove themselves together in unsettling images. But he was not going to let any fantasy spoil reality. He'd come a long way – and within a few hours he'd claim the next prize. Diane McCoy had been right. It was doubtful he'd be the president's first choice to succeed David Sylvian. He knew of at least two others Daniels would certainly nominate ahead of him – assuming that the decision would be the White House's alone. Thank goodness free choice was a rarity in Washington politics.

He descended to the first floor and entered his study just as his cell phone rang. He carried the thing constantly. The display indicated an overseas exchange. Good. Since speaking to Wilkerson earlier, he'd been waiting to know if the apparent failure had been reversed.

'Those packages for Christmas you ordered,' the voice said. 'We're sorry to say they may not arrive in time.'

He quelled a renewed anger. 'And the reason for the delay?'

'We thought there was inventory in our warehouse, but discovered that none was on hand.'

'Your inventory problems are not my concern. I prepaid weeks ago, expecting prompt delivery.'

'We're aware of that and plan to make sure delivery occurs on time. We just wanted you to be aware of a slight delay.'

'If it requires priority shipping, then incur the cost. It does not matter to me. Just make the deliveries.'

'We're tracking the packages now and should be able to verify delivery shortly.'

'Make sure you do,' he said, and clicked off.

Now he was agitated. What was happening in Germany? Wilkerson still alive? And Malone? Two loose ends he could ill afford. But there was nothing he could do. He had to trust the assets on the ground. They'd performed well before and hopefully would this time.

He switched on the desk lamp.

One of the things that had attracted him to this town house, besides its location, size, and ambience, was a cabinet safe the owner had discreetly installed. Not flawless by any means, but enough protection for files brought home overnight, or the few folders he privately maintained.

He opened the concealed wooden panel and punched in a digital code.

Six files stood upright inside.

He removed the first one on the left.

Charlie Smith was not only an excellent killer, but also gathered information with the zeal of a squirrel locating winter nuts. He seemed to love discovering secrets that people went to great lengths to hide. Smith had spent the past two years collecting facts. Some of it was being used right now, and the rest would be brought into play over the next few days, as needed.

He opened the folder and reacquainted himself with the details.

Amazing how a public persona could be so different from the private person. He wondered how politicos maintained their façades. It had to be difficult. Urges and desires pointed one way – career and image jerked them another.

Senator Aatos Kane was a perfect example.

Fifty-six years old. A fourth-termer from Michigan, married, three children. A career politician since his midtwenties, first at the state level then in the US Senate. Daniels had considered him for vice president when a vacancy came available last year, but Kane had declined, saying that he appreciated the White House's confidence but believed he could serve the president better by staying in the Senate. Michigan had breathed a sigh of relief. Kane was rated by several congressional watchdog groups as one of Congress's most effective purveyors of pork barrel legislation. Twenty-two years on Capitol Hill had taught Aatos Kane all of the right lessons.

And the most important?

All politics were local.

Ramsey smiled. He loved negotiable souls.

Dorothea Lindauer's question still rang in his ears. *Is there anything there to find?* He hadn't thought about that trip to Antarctic in years.

How many times had they gone ashore?

Four?

The ship's captain – Zachary Alexander – had been an inquisitive sort, but, per orders, Ramsey had kept their mission secret. Only the radio receiver his team brought on board had been tuned to NR-1A's emergency transponder. No signal had ever been heard by monitoring stations in the Southern Hemisphere. Which had made the ultimate cover-up easier. No radiation had been detected. It was thought that a signal and radiation might be more discernible closer to the source. In those days ice had a tendency to wreak havoc with sensitive electronics. So they'd listened and monitored the water for two days as *Holden* patrolled the Weddell Sea, a place of howling winds, luminous purple clouds, and ghostly halos around a weak sun.

Nothing.

Then they'd taken the equipment ashore.

'What do you have?' he asked Lt. Herbert Rowland.

The man was excited. 'Signal bearing two hundred and forty degrees.'

He stared out across a dead continent swathed in a mile-thick shroud of ice. Eight degrees below zero and nearly summer. A signal? Here? No way. They were six hundred yards inland from where they'd beached their boat, the terrain as flat and broad as the sea; it was impossible to know if water or earth lay below. Off to the right and ahead, mountains rose like teeth over the glittery white tundra.

'Signal definite at two hundred and forty degrees,' Rowland repeated.

'Sayers,' he called out to the third member of the team.

The remaining lieutenant was fifty yards ahead, checking for fissures. Perception was a constant problem. White snow, white sky, even the air was white with constant breath clouds. This was a place of mummified emptiness, to which the human eye was little better adjusted than pitch darkness.

'It's the damn sub,' Rowland said, his attention still on the receiver.

He could still feel the absolute cold that had enveloped him in that shadowless land where palls of gray-green fog materialized in an instant. They'd been plagued by bad weather, low ceilings, dense clouds, and constant wind. During every Northern Hemisphere winter he'd experienced since, he'd compared its ferocity with the intensity of an ordinary Antarctic day. Four days he'd spent there – four days he'd never forgotten.

You can't imagine, he'd told Dorothea Lindauer in answer to her question.

He stared down into the safe.

Beside the folders lay a journal.

Thirty-eight years ago naval regulations required that commanding officers on all seagoing vessels maintain one.

He slid the book free.

30

Atlanta, 7:22 a.m.

Stephanie roused Edwin Davis from a sound sleep. He came up with a start, at first disoriented until he realized where he lay.

'You snore,' she said.

Even through a closed door and down the hall, she'd heard him during the night.

'So I'm told. I do that when I'm really tired.'

'And who tells you that?'

He swiped the sleep from his eyes. He lay on the bed fully dressed, his cell phone beside him. They'd arrived back in Atlanta a little before midnight on the last flight from Jacksonville. He'd suggested a hotel, but she'd insisted on her guest room.

'I'm not a monk,' he declared.

She knew little of his private life. Unmarried, that much she did know. But had he ever been? Any children? Now, though, was not the time to pry. 'You need a shave.'

He rubbed his chin. 'So good of you to point that out.'

She headed for the door. 'There's towels and some razors – girlie ones, I'm afraid – in the hall bath.'

She'd already showered and dressed, ready for whatever the day might hold.

'Yes, ma'am,' he said, standing. 'You run a tight ship.'

She left him and entered the kitchen, switching on the counter television. Rarely did she eat much breakfast beyond a muffin or some wheat flakes, and she detested coffee. Green tea usually was her choice of a hot beverage. She needed to check with the office. Having a nearly nonexistent staff helped with security but was hell on delegating.

'—it's going to be interesting,' a CNN reporter was saying. 'President Daniels has recently voiced much displeasure with the Joint Chiefs of Staff. In a speech two weeks ago he hinted whether that entire chain of command was even needed.'

The screen shifted to Daniels standing before a blue podium.

'They don't command anything,' he said in his trademark baritone. 'They're advisers. Politicians. Policy repeaters, not makers. Don't get me wrong. I have great respect for these men. It's the institution itself I have problems with. There's no question that the talents of the officers now on the Joint Chiefs could be better utilized in other capacities.'

Back to the reporter, a perky brunette. 'All of which makes you wonder if, or how, he'll fill the vacancy caused by the untimely death of Admiral David Sylvian.'

Davis walked into the kitchen, his gaze locked on the television.

She noticed his interest. 'What is it?'

He stood silent, sullen, preoccupied. Finally, he said, 'Sylvian is the navy's man on the Joint Chiefs.'

She didn't understand. She'd read about the motorcycle accident and Sylvian's injuries. 'It's unfortunate he died, Edwin, but what's the matter?'

He reached into his pocket and found his phone. A few punches of the keys and he said, 'I need to know how Admiral Sylvian died. Exact cause, and fast.'

He ended the call.

'Are you going to explain?' she asked.

'Stephanie, there's more to Langford Ramsey. About six months ago the president received a letter from the widow of a navy lieutenant—'

The phone gave a short clicking sound. Davis studied the screen and answered. He listened a few moments then ended the call.

'That lieutenant worked in the navy's general accounting office. He'd noticed irregularities. Several million dollars channeled to bank after bank, then the money simply disappeared. The accounts were all attached to naval intelligence, director's office.'

'The intelligence business runs on covert money,' she said. 'I have several blind accounts that I use for outside payments, contract help, that kind of thing.'

'That lieutenant died two days before he was scheduled to brief his superiors. His widow knew some of what he'd learned, and distrusted everyone in the military. She wrote the president with a personal plea, and the letter was directed to me.'

'And when you saw Office of Naval Intelligence, your radar went to full alert. So what did you find when you looked into those accounts?'

'They couldn't be found.'

She'd experienced a similar frustration. Banks in various parts of the world were infamous for erasing accounts – provided, of course, enough fees were paid by the account holder. 'So what's got you riled up now?'

'That lieutenant dropped dead in his house, watching

television. His wife went to the grocery store and, when she came home, he was dead.'

'It happens, Edwin.'

'His blood pressure bottomed out. He had a heart murmur for which he'd been treated and, you're right, things like that happen. The autopsy found nothing. With his history and no evidence of foul play, the cause of death seemed easy.'

She waited.

'I was just told that Admiral David Sylvian died from low blood pressure.'

His expression mingled disgust, anger, and frustration.

'Too much of a coincidence for you?' she asked.

He nodded. 'You and I know Ramsey controlled the accounts that that lieutenant found. And now there's a vacancy on the Joint Chiefs of Staff?'

'You're reaching, Edwin.'

'Am I?' Disdain laced his tone. 'My office said they were just about to contact me. Last night, before I dozed off, I ordered two Secret Service agents dispatched to Jacksonville. I wanted them to keep an eye on Zachary Alexander. They arrived an hour ago. His house burned to the ground last night, with him inside.'

She was shocked.

'Indications are an electrical short from wires beneath the house.'

She told herself never to play poker with Edwin Davis. He'd received both bits of news with a nothing face. 'We have to find those other two lieutenants who were in the Antarctic with Ramsey.'

'Nick Sayers is dead,' he said. 'Years ago. Herbert Rowland is still alive. He lives outside Charlotte. I had that checked last night, too.'

Secret Service? White House staff cooperating? 'You're full of crap, Edwin. You're not in this alone. You're on a mission.'

His eyes flickered. 'That all depends. If it works, then I'm okay. If I fail, then I'm going down.'

'You staked your career on this?'

'I owe it to Millicent.'

'Why am I here?'

'Like I told you, Scot Harvath said no. But he told me nobody flies solo better than you.'

That rationalization was not necessarily comforting. But what the hell. The line had already been crossed.

'Let's head to Charlotte.'

31

Malone felt the train slow as they entered the outskirts of Aachen. Even though his worries from last night had receded into better proportion, he wondered what was he doing here. Christl Falk sat beside him, but the ride north from Garmisch had taken about three hours and they'd said little.

His clothes and toiletries from the Posthotel had been waiting for him when he awoke at Reichshoffen. A note had explained that Ulrich Henn had retrieved them during the night. He'd slept on sheets that smelled of clover then showered, shaved, and changed. Of course, he'd only brought a couple of shirts and pants from Denmark, planning to be gone no more than a day, two at the most. Now he wasn't so sure.

Isabel had been waiting for him downstairs, and he'd informed the Oberhauser matriarch that he'd decided to help. What choice did he have? He wanted to know about his father, and he wanted to know who was trying to kill him. Walking away would lead to nothing. And the old woman had made one point clear. *They knew things he didn't.*

'Twelve hundred years ago,' Christl said, 'this was the center of the secular world. The capital of the newly conceived Northern Empire. What two hundred years later we called the Holy Roman Empire.'

He smiled. 'Which was not holy, nor Roman, nor an empire.'

She nodded. 'True. But Charlemagne was quite the progressive. A man of immense energy, he founded universities, generated legal principles that eventually made their way into the common law, organized the government, and started a nationalism that inspired the creation of Europe. I've studied him for years. He seemed to make all the right decisions. He ruled for forty-seven years and lived to be seventy-four at a time when kings barely lasted five years in power and were dead at thirty.'

'And you think all that happened because he had help?'

'He ate in moderation and drank carefully – and this was when gluttony and drunkenness ran rampant. He daily rode, hunted, and swam. One reason he chose Aachen for his capital was the hot springs, which he used religiously.'

'So the Holy Ones taught him about diet, hygiene, and exercise?'

He saw she caught his sarcasm.

'Characteristically, he was a warrior,' she said. 'His entire reign was marked by conquest. But he took a disciplined approach to war. He'd plan a campaign for at least a year, studying the opposition. He also *directed* battles as opposed to participating in them.'

'He was also brutal as hell. At Verden he ordered the beheading of forty-five hundred bound Saxons.'

'That's not certain,' she said. 'No archaeological evidence of that supposed massacre has ever been found. The original source of the story may have mistakenly used the word *decollabat*, beheading, when it should have said *delocabat*, exiling.'

'You know your history. And your Latin.'

'None of this is what I think. Einhard was the chronicler. He's the one who made those observations.'

'Assuming, of course, his writings are authentic.'

The train slowed to a crawl.

He was still thinking about yesterday and what lay below Reichshoffen. 'Does your sister feel the same way about the Nazis, and what they did to your grandfather, as you do?'

'Dorothea could not care less. Family and history are not important to her.'

'What is?'

'Herself.'

'Strange how twins so resent each other.'

'There's no rule that says we're to be bonded together. I learned as a child that Dorothea was a problem.'

He needed to explore those differences. 'Your mother seems to play favorites.'

'I wouldn't assume that.'

'She sent you to me.'

'True. But she aided Dorothea early on.'

The train came to a stop.

'You going to explain that one?'

'She's the one who gave her the book from Charlemagne's grave.'

Dorothea finished her inspections of the boxes Wilkerson had retrieved from Füssen. The book dealer had done well. Many of the Ahnenerbe's records had been seized by the Allies after the war, so she was amazed that so much had been located. But even after reading for the past few hours, the Ahnenerbe remained an enigma. Only in recent years had the organization's existence finally been studied by historians, the few books written on the subject touching mainly on its failures.

These boxes talked of success.

There'd been expeditions to Sweden to retrieve petroglyphs, and to the Middle East, where they'd studied the internal power struggles of the Roman Empire – which, to the Ahnenerbe, had been fought between Nordic and Semitic people. Göring himself funded that journey. In Damascus, Syrians welcomed them as allies to combat a rising Jewish population. In Iran their researchers visited Persian ruins, as well as Babylon, marveling at a possible Aryan connection. In Finland they studied ancient pagan chants. Bavaria yielded cave paintings and evidence of Cro-Magnons, who were, to the Ahnenerbe, surely Aryan. More cave paintings were studied in France where, as one commentator noted, 'Himmler and so many other Nazis dreamed of standing in the dark embrace of the ancestors.'

Asia, though, became a true fascination.

The Ahnenerbe believed early Aryans conquered much of China and Japan and that Buddha himself was an Aryan offspring. A major expedition to Tibet yielded thousands of photographs, head casts, and body measurements, along with exotic animal and plant specimens, all gathered in the hope of proving ancestry. More trips to Bolivia, Ukraine, Iran, Iceland, and the Canary Islands never materialized, though elaborate plans for each journey were detailed.

The records also detailed how, as the war progressed, the Ahnenerbe's role expanded. After Himmler ordered the Aryanization of the conquered Crimea, the Ahnenerbe was charged with replicating German forests and cultivating new crops for the Reich. The Ahnenerbe also supervised the relocation of ethnic Germans to the region, along with the deportation of thousands of Ukrainians.

But as the brain trust grew, more finances were needed.

So a foundation was created to receive donations.

Contributors included Deutsche Bank, BMW, and Daimler-Benz, which were thanked repeatedly in official correspondence. Always innovative, Himmler learned of reflector panels for bicycles that had been patented by a German machinist. He formed a joint company with the inventor and then ensured the passage of a law that required pedals on all bicycles to include the reflectors, which earned tens of thousands of Reichsmarks yearly for the Ahnenerbe.

So much effort had gone into fashioning so much fiction.

But amid the ridiculousness of finding lost Aryans, and the tragedies of participating in organized murder, her grandfather had actually stumbled onto a treasure.

She stared at the old book lying on the table.

Was it indeed from Charlemagne's grave?

Nothing in any of the materials she'd read talked about it, though from what her mother had told her, it had been found in 1935 among the archives of the Weimar Republic, discovered with a message penned by some unknown scribe that attested to its removal from the grave in Aachen on May 19, 1000, by Emperor Otto III. How it managed to survive until the twentieth century remained a mystery. What did it mean? Why was it so important?

Her sister, Christl, believed the answer lay in some mystical appeal.

And Ramsey had failed to alleviate her fears with his cryptic response.

You can't imagine.

But none of that could be the answer.

Or could it?

Malone and Christl exited the train station. Moist, cold air reminded him of a New England winter. Cabs lined the curb. People came and went in steady streams.

'Mother,' Christl said, 'wants *me* to succeed.'

He couldn't decide if she was trying to convince him, or herself. 'Your mother is manipulating you both.'

She faced him. 'Mr. Malone—'

'My name is Cotton.'

She seemed to restrain a surge of annoyance. 'As you reminded me last night. How did you acquire that odd name?'

'A story for later. You were about to berate me, before I knocked you off balance.'

Her face relaxed into a smile. 'You're a problem.'

'From what your mother said, Dorothea thought so, too. But I've decided to take it as a compliment.' He rubbed his gloved hands together and looked around. 'We need to make a stop. Some long underwear would be great. This isn't that dry Bavarian air. How about you? Cold?'

'I grew up in this weather.'

'I didn't. In Georgia, where I was born and raised, it's hot and humid nine months out of the year.' He continued to survey his surroundings with a disinterested appearance, feigning discomfort. 'I also need a change of clothes. I didn't pack for a long trip.'

'There's a shopping district near the chapel.'

'I assume, at some point, you'll explain about your mother and why we're here?'

She motioned for a taxi, which wheeled close.

She opened the door and climbed inside. He followed. She told the driver where they wanted to go.

'*Ja*,' she said. 'I'll explain.'

As they left the station, Malone glanced out the rear window. The same man he'd noticed three hours earlier in the Garmisch station – tall, with a thin, hatchet-shaped face seamed with wrinkles – hailed a cab.

He carried no luggage and seemed intent on only one thing.

Following.

Dorothea had gambled in acquiring the Ahnenerbe records. She'd taken a risk contacting Cotton Malone, but she'd proved to herself that he was of little use. Still, she was not certain that the route to success was more pragmatic. One thing seemed clear. Exposing her family to more ridicule was not an option. Occasionally, a researcher or historian contacted Reichshoffen wanting to inspect her grandfather's papers or talk to the family about the Ahnenerbe. Those requests were always refused, and for good reason.

The past should stay in the past.

She stared at the bed and a sleeping Sterling Wilkerson.

They'd driven north last night and taken a room in Munich. Her mother would know of the hunting lodge's destruction before the day ended. The body in the abbey had also surely been found. Either the monks or Henn would dispose of the problem. More likely, it would be Ulrich.

She realized that if her mother had aided her, by providing the book from Charlemagne's grave, she'd surely given Christl something, too. Her mother had been the one who insisted that she speak to Cotton Malone. That

was why she and Wilkerson had used the woman and led
him to the abbey. Her mother cared little for Wilkerson.
'Another weak soul,' she called him. *'And child, we have no
time for weakness.'* But her mother was nearing eighty and
Dorothea was in the prime of her life. Handsome,
adventurous men, like Wilkerson, were good for many
things.

Like last night.

She stepped to the bed and roused him.

He awoke and smiled.

'It's nearly noon,' she said.

'I was tired.'

'We need to leave.'

He noticed the contents of the boxes scattered across
the floor. 'Where are we going?'

'Hopefully, to get a step ahead of Christl.'

32

Ramsey was energized. He'd checked media websites for Jacksonville, Florida, and was pleased to see a report on a fatal fire at the home of Zachary Alexander, a retired navy commander. Nothing unusual about the blaze, and preliminary reports had targeted the cause as an electrical short due to faulty wiring. Charlie Smith had clearly crafted two masterpieces yesterday. He hoped today would be equally productive.

The morning was mid-Atlantic crisp and sunny. He was strolling the Mall, near the Smithsonian, the sparkling white Capitol looming clear on its hilly perch. He loved a frosty winter's day. With Christmas only thirteen days away and Congress not in session, the business of government had slowed, everything waiting for a new year and the start of another legislative season.

A slow news time, which probably explained the extensive coverage the death of Admiral Sylvian was receiving in the media. Daniels' recent criticisms of the Joint Chiefs had made the untimely death more timely. Ramsey had listened to the president's comments with amusement, knowing that nobody in Congress would be headstrong about changing that command. True, the Joint Chiefs ordered little, but when they spoke people listened.

Which probably explained, more than anything else, the White House's resentment. Particularly Daniels', a lame duck, wobbling toward the climax of his political career.

Ahead, he spotted a short, dapper man dressed in a slim-fitting cashmere overcoat, his pale, cherubic face reddened from the cold. Clean-shaven, he had bristly dark hair that lay close to his scalp. He stomped the pavement in an apparent effort to rid himself of a chill. Ramsey glanced at his watch and estimated the envoy had been waiting for at least fifteen minutes.

He approached.

'Admiral, do you know how friggin' cold it is out here?'

'Twenty-eight degrees.'

'And you couldn't be on time?'

'If I needed to be on time, then I would have been.'

'I'm not in the mood for rank pulling. Not in the mood at all.'

Interesting how being the chief of staff for a US senator bestowed such courage. He wondered if Aatos Kane had told this acolyte to be an ass – or was this improvisation?

'I'm here because the senator said you had something to say.'

'Does he still want to be president?' All of Ramsey's previous contacts with Kane had been shuttled through this emissary.

'He does. And he will be.'

'Spoken with the confidence of a staffer firmly grasping the coattails of his boss.'

'Every shark has its remora.'

He smiled. 'That it does.'

'What do you want, Admiral?'

He resented the younger man's haughtiness. Time to put this man in his place. 'I want you to shut up and listen.'

He noticed the eyes studying him with the calculated gaze of a political pro.

'When Kane was in trouble, he asked for help, and I gave him what he wanted. No questions, it was done.'

He waited a moment before speaking again as three men rushed by.

'I might add,' he said, 'that I violated a multitude of laws, which I'm sure you could not care less about.'

His listener was not a man of age, wisdom, or wealth. But he was ambitious and understood the value of political favors.

'The senator is aware of what you did, Admiral. Though, as you know, we were not aware of the full extent of what you planned.'

'Nor did you reject the benefits afterward.'

'Granted. What is it you want now?'

'I want Kane to tell the president that I'm to be named to the Joint Chiefs of Staff. In Sylvian's vacancy.'

'And you think the president can't tell the senator no?'

'Not without severe consequences.'

The agitated face staring back at him lightened with a fleeting smile. 'It's not going to happen.'

Had he heard right?

'The senator assumed that's what you wanted. Sylvian's corpse probably wasn't even cold when you made that call earlier.' The younger man hesitated. 'Which makes us wonder.'

He spied mistrust in the man's observant eyes.

'After all, as you say, you performed us a *service* once, with no residuals.'

He ignored the implications and asked, 'What do you mean, *not going to happen*?'

'You're too controversial. Too much of a lightning rod.

Too many in the navy either don't like you or don't trust you. Endorsing your appointment would have fallout. And as I mentioned, we're making a White House run, starting early next year.'

He realized that the classic Washington two-step had started. A famous dance that politicians like Aatos Kane were experts at performing. Every pundit agreed. Kane's White House run seemed plausible. In fact, he was his party's leading contender, with little competition. Ramsey knew the senator had been quietly amassing pledges that now totaled in the millions. Kane was a personable, engaging man, comfortable in front of a crowd and a camera. He was neither a true conservative nor a liberal, but a mixture that the press loved to tag *middle of the road*. He'd been married to the same woman for thirty years with not a hint of scandal. He was almost too perfect. Except, of course, for that favor Kane had once needed.

'Fine way to thank your friends,' Ramsey said.

'Who said you were our friend?'

A weariness creased his forehead that he quickly masked. He should have seen it coming. Arrogance. The most common illness afflicting longtime politicians. 'No, you're right. That was presumptuous of me.'

The man's face lost its impassive look. 'Get this straight, Admiral. Senator Kane thanks you for what you did. We would have preferred another way, but he still appreciates it. He repaid you, though, when he blocked the navy from transferring you. Not once, but twice. We sent a full blitz into the backfield on that one. That's what you wanted and that's what we gave you. You don't own Aatos Kane. Not now. Not ever. What you're asking is impossible. In less than sixty days the senator will be an announced

candidate for the White House. You're an admiral who
should retire. Do it. Enjoy a well-earned rest.'

He submerged any defensiveness and simply nodded
in understanding.

'And one more thing. The senator resented your call
this morning demanding that we meet. He sent me to tell
you that this relationship is over. No more visits, no more
calls. Now I have to go.'

'Of course. Don't let me keep you.'

'Look, Admiral, I know you're pissed. I would be, too.
But you're not going on the Joint Chiefs. Retire. Become
a Fox TV analyst and tell the world what a bunch of idiots
we are. Enjoy life.'

He said nothing and simply watched as the prick
paraded off, surely proud of his stellar performance, eager
to report how he'd put the head of naval intelligence in
his place.

He walked to an empty bench and sat.

Cold seeped from its slats through his overcoat.

Senator Aatos Kane had no idea. Neither did his chief
of staff.

But they were both about to find out.

33

Wilkerson had slept well, satisfied both with how he'd handled himself at the lodge and with Dorothea afterward. Having access to money, few responsibilities, and a beautiful woman weren't bad substitutes for not being an admiral.

Provided, of course, that he could stay alive.

In preparation for this assignment, he'd back-checked the Oberhauser family thoroughly. Assets in the billions, and not old money – ancient money that had lasted through centuries of political upheavals. Opportunists? Surely. Their family crest seemed to explain it all. A dog clutching a rat in its mouth, encased inside a crested cauldron. What myriad contradictions. Much like the family itself. But how else could they have survived?

Time, though, had taken a toll.

Dorothea and her sister were all the Oberhausers left. Both beautiful, high-strung creatures. Nearing fifty. Identical in appearance, though each tried hard to distinguish herself. Dorothea had pursued business degrees and actively worked with her mother in the family concerns. She'd married in her early twenties and birthed a son, but he was killed five years ago, a week after his twentieth birthday, in a car accident. All reports indicated that she changed after that. Hardened. Became enslaved to deep anxieties and unpredictable moods. To shoot a man with a shotgun, as she'd done last night, then make love afterward with such an unfettered intensity, proved that dichotomy.

Business had never interested Christl, nor had marriage or children. He'd met her only once, at a social function Dorothea and her husband had attended when he'd first made contact. She was unassuming. An academician, like her father and grandfather, studying oddities, mulling the endless possibilities of legend and myth. Both of her master's theses had been on obscure connections between mythical ancient civilizations – like Atlantis, he'd found after reading both – and developing cultures. Fantasy, all of it. But the male Oberhausers had been fascinated by such ridiculousness, and Christl seemed to have inherited their curiosity. Her childbearing days were over, so he wondered what would happen after Isabel Oberhauser died. Two women who did not like each other – neither one of whom could leave blood heirs – would inherit it all.

A fascinating scenario with endless possibilities.

He was outside, in the cold, not far from their hotel, a magnificent establishment that would satisfy the whims of any king. Dorothea had called from the car last night to speak with the concierge, and a suite had been waiting when they arrived.

The sunny Marienplatz, which he now strolled, was crowded with tourists. A strange hush hung over the square, broken only by the scuff of soles and a murmur of voices. Within sight were department stores, cafés, the central market, a royal palace, and churches. The massive *rathaus* dominated one perimeter, its animated façade streaked with the darkened effects of centuries. He purposefully avoided the museum quarter and headed for one of several bakeries that were enjoying a brisk business. He was hungry and some chocolate pastries would be lovely.

Booths decorated with fragrant pine boughs dotted the square, part of the city's Christmas market, which stretched out of sight down the old town's busy main thoroughfare. He'd heard about the millions who came each year for the festivities but doubted he and Dorothea would have time to attend. She was on a mission. He was, too, which made him think of work. He needed to check with Berlin and maintain a presence for his employees' sake. So he found his cell phone and dialed.

'Captain Wilkerson,' his yeoman said, after answering. 'I was told to direct any call from you directly to Commander Bishop.'

Before he could ask why, the voice of his second in command came on the line. 'Captain, I have to ask where you are.'

His radar went to full alert. Never did Bryan Bishop call him *Captain,* unless other people were listening.

'What's the problem?' he asked.

'Sir, this call is being recorded. You've been relieved of all duties and declared a level-three security risk. Our orders are to locate and detain you.'

He grabbed hold of his emotions. 'Who gave those orders?'

'Office of the Director. Issued by Captain Hovey, signed by Admiral Ramsey.'

He'd actually been the one who recommended Bishop's promotion to commander. He was a compliant officer who followed orders with unquestioned zeal. Great then, bad now.

'Am I being sought?' he asked, and then a realization slammed into him and he clicked off the phone before hearing the answer.

He stared at the unit. They came with a built-in GPS locator for emergency tracking. Damn. That's how they'd found him last night. He hadn't been thinking. Of course, he'd had no idea before the attack that he was a target. After, he'd been rattled and Ramsey – the SOB – had rocked him to sleep, buying time to dispatch another team.

His daddy had been right. Can't trust a one of them.

Suddenly a city of 120 square miles, with millions of inhabitants, transformed from a refuge into a prison. He glanced around at the people, all huddled in thick coats, darting in every direction.

And no longer wanted any pastries.

Ramsey left the National Mall and drove into central Washington, near Dupont Circle. Normally he used Charlie Smith for his special tasks, but that was currently impossible. Luckily he kept a variety of assets – all capable in their own way – on a call list. He had a reputation of paying well and promptly, which helped when he needed things done quickly.

He wasn't the only admiral jockeying for David Sylvian's post. He knew of at least five others who were surely on the phone to congressmen as soon as they'd heard Sylvian had died. Paying the proper respects and burying the man would come in a few days – but Sylvian's successor would be chosen in the next few hours, as slots that high on the military food chain did not stay vacant long.

He should have known Aatos Kane would be a problem. The senator had been around a long time. He knew the lay of the land. But experience came with liabilities. Men like Kane counted on the fact that opponents did not possess either the nerve or the means to exploit those liabilities.

He suffered from neither deficiency.

He grabbed a curbside parking spot just as another car was leaving. At least something had gone right today. He clicked seventy-five cents into the meter and walked through the chill until he found Capitol Maps.

An interesting store.

Nothing but maps from every corner of the globe, including an impressive travel and guidebook collection. He wasn't in the market for cartography today. Instead he needed to speak to the owner.

He entered and spotted her talking to a customer.

She caught a glimpse, but nothing in her countenance revealed any recognition. He assumed the considerable fees he'd paid her through the years for contract services had helped finance the store, but they'd never discussed the matter. One of his rules. Assets were tools, treated the same as a hammer, saw, or screwdriver. Use them. Then put them away. Most of the people he employed understood that rule. Those who didn't were never called again.

The store owner finished with her customer and casually strolled over. 'Looking for a particular map? We have a large assortment.'

He glanced around. 'That you do. Which is good, because I need a lot of help today.'

Wilkerson realized that he was being followed. A man and a woman lurked a hundred feet behind him, most likely alerted by his contact with Berlin. They'd made no move to close, which meant one of two things. They wanted Dorothea and were waiting for him to lead them to her, or he was being herded.

Neither prospect was pleasant.

He elbowed a path through a thick knot of midday Munich shoppers and had no idea how many other adversaries were waiting ahead. A level-three security risk? That meant they would contain with whatever force necessary – including deadly. Worse, they'd had hours to prepare. He knew the Oberhauser operation was important – more personal than professional – and Ramsey had the conscience of an executioner. If threatened, he'd react. At the moment he certainly appeared to be threatened.

He set a sharp pace.

He should call Dorothea and warn her, but he'd resented her intrusion last night during his call with Ramsey. This was his problem and he could handle things. At least she hadn't berated him about being wrong when it came to Ramsey. Instead she'd taken him to a luxurious Munich hotel and pleased them both. Calling her might also require him to explain how they'd been located, and that was a conversation he'd like to avoid.

Fifty yards ahead, the close huddle of the pedestrian-only old town ended at a busy boulevard packed with cars and lined with yellow-fronted buildings that projected a Mediterranean feel.

He glanced back.

The two following closed the gap.

He stared left and right, then across the blare and bustle. A taxi stand lined the boulevard's far curb, drivers propped outside, waiting for fares. Six lanes of chaos lay in between, the noise level as high as his heart rate. Cars began to congeal as traffic signals to his left cycled from green.

A bus approached from his right, in the middle lane. The inside and outside lanes were slowing.

Anxiety gave way to fear. He had no choice. Ramsey wanted him dead. And since he knew what the two pursuers behind him had to offer, he'd take his chances with the boulevard.

He darted out as a driver apparently spotted him and braked.

He timed the next move perfectly and leaped across the middle lane just as the traffic signals changed to red and the bus began its stop for the intersection. He leaped the outside lane, which was luckily car-free for a few moments, and found the grassy median.

The bus ground to a halt and blocked any line of sight from the sidewalk. Honks and screeches, like geese and owls quarreling, signaled opportunity. He'd earned a precious few seconds, so he decided not to waste a single one. He raced across the three lanes ahead of him, empty thanks to the red light, and jumped into the lead taxi, ordering the driver in German, 'Go.'

The man hopped behind the wheel and Wilkerson crouched as the taxi sped away.

He glanced out the window.

The green light appeared and a phalanx of traffic rushed ahead. The man and woman wove their way across the cleared half of the boulevard, now prevented from a complete crossing thanks to the spate of vehicles speeding toward him.

His two pursuers searched all around.

He smiled.

'Where to?' the driver asked in German.

He decided to make another smart play. 'Just a few blocks, then stop.'

When the taxi wheeled to the curb, he tossed the driver ten euros and hopped out. He'd spotted a sign for the U-Bahn and hustled down the stairs, bought a ticket, and rushed to the platform.

The underground train arrived and he stepped into a nearly full car. He sat and activated his cell phone, which came with a special feature. He entered a numeric code and the screen read DELETE ALL DATA? He pressed YES. Like his second wife, who never heard him the first time, the phone asked ARE YOU SURE? He pressed YES again.

The memory was now wiped clean.

He bent over, ostensibly to stretch his socks, and laid the phone beneath the seat.

The train eased into the next station.

He exited. But the phone kept going.

That should keep Ramsey busy.

He made his way up from the station, pleased with his escape. He needed to contact Dorothea, but that had to be done carefully. If he was being watched, so was she.

He stepped out into the sunny afternoon and found his bearings. He was not far from the river, near the Deutsches Museum. Another busy street and crowded sidewalk spread out before him.

A man suddenly stopped beside him.

'*Bitte,* Herr Wilkerson,' he said in German. 'To that car, just down there, at the curb.'

He froze.

The man wore a long wool coat and kept both hands in his pockets.

'I don't want to,' the stranger said, 'but I will shoot you here, if need be.'

His eyes drifted to the man's coat pocket.

A sick feeling invaded his stomach. No way Ramsey's

people had followed him. But he'd been so intent on them, he'd neglect to notice anyone else. 'You're not from Berlin, are you?' he asked.

'*Nein.* I'm something altogether different.'

34

Malone admired one of the last remnants of the Carolingian empire, known then as the Church of Our Lady and now as Charlemagne's chapel. The building seemed to be formed in three distinct sections. A gothic tower, which appeared to stand apart. A round but angular midsection, connected to the tower by a covered bridge, topped with an unusual pleated dome. And a tall, elongated building that seemed all roof and stained-glass windows. The conglomeration had been erected from the latter part of the eighth to the fifteenth centuries, and it was amazing that it had survived, particularly the last hundred years when, Malone knew, Aachen had been mercilessly bombed.

The chapel stood on the low end of a city slope, once connected to the palace proper by a low line of wooden structures that housed a solarium, a military garrison, law courts, and quarters for the king and his family.

Charlemagne's palatinate.

Only a courtyard, the chapel, and the foundations of the palace upon which fourteenth-century builders erected Aachen's town hall remained. The rest had disappeared centuries ago.

They entered the chapel through the west doors, the ancient portal cloistered from the street. Three steps led down into a baroque-style porch, its walls whitewashed and unadorned.

'Those steps are significant,' Christl said. 'Ground levels outside have risen since Charlemagne's time.'

He recalled Dorothea's tale about Otto III. 'Beneath here is where they found Charlemagne's tomb? And the book Dorothea has?'

She nodded. 'Some say Otto III dug through this flooring and found the king sitting upright, his fingers pointing to the Gospel of Mark. *For what shall it profit a man, if he shall gain the whole world and lose his own soul?*'

He caught her cynicism.

'Others say Emperor Barbarossa found the grave site here in 1165, and the body was lying in a marble coffin. That Roman sarcophagus is on display in the treasury next door. Barbarossa supposedly substituted a gilded chest, which is now' – she pointed ahead into the chapel – 'there, in the choir.'

Beyond the altar, he spotted a golden reliquary displayed within an illuminated glass enclosure. They left the porch and stepped into the chapel. A circular passage spanned to the left and right, but he seemed drawn to the center of the inner octagon. Light, like mist, filtered down from windows high in the dome.

'A hexadecagon wrapping an octagon,' he said.

Eight massive pillars folded into each other to form double pillars that held the high dome aloft. Rounded arches rose skyward to the upper galleries where slender columns, marble bridges, and latticework grilles connected everything.

'For three centuries after its completion, this was the tallest building north of the Alps,' Christl told him. 'Stone had been used in the south to construct temples, arenas, palaces, and later churches, but this type of building was unknown among Germanic tribes. This was the first attempt, outside the Mediterranean, to build a stone vault.'

He stared up at the towering gallery.

'Little of what you see is from Charlemagne's time,' she said. 'The structure itself, obviously. The thirty-six marble columns, there, on the second level. Some of them are original – carted from Italy, stolen by Napoleon, but eventually returned. The eight bronze lattices between the arches are also original. Everything else came later. Carolingians whitewashed their churches and painted the insides. Later, Christians added elegance. This remains, though, the only church in Germany built on orders of Charlemagne still standing.'

He had to tilt his back to spy up into the dome. Its golden mosaics depicted twenty-four elders, clad in white, standing before the throne, proffering golden crowns in adoration of the Lamb. From Revelation, if he wasn't mistaken. More mosaics decorated the drum beneath the dome. Mary, John the Baptist, Christ, Archangel Michael, Gabriel, even Charlemagne himself.

Suspended by a wrought-iron chain, whose links thickened as they rose, was a massive, wheel-shaped candelabra replete with intricate goldsmithing.

'Emperor Barbarossa presented that chandelier in the twelfth century,' she said, 'after his coronation. It's symbolic of the heavenly Jerusalem, the city of lights, which will come down from heaven like a victor's crown, as promised to every Christian.'

Revelation again. He thought about another cathedral, St. Mark's in Venice. 'This place has a Byzantine look and feel.'

'It reflects Charlemagne's love of Byzantine richness, as opposed to Roman austerity.'

'Who designed it?'

She shrugged. 'No one knows. A Master Odo is mentioned in some of the texts, but nothing is known about him except that he apparently knew of the architecture from the south. Einhard definitely participated, as did Charlemagne himself.'

The interior didn't impress with its size, instead the illusion was more intimate, the eyes compelled to swing upward, toward heaven.

Admission to the chapel was free, but several paying group tours wandered about, their guides explaining the highlights. Their tail from the train station had wandered inside, too, using one of the crowds for cover. Then, apparently satisfied there was but one entrance, he had drifted back outside.

Malone had guessed right. His rental car had been tagged. How else could the gunman have found them last night? They certainly weren't followed. Today they'd driven the same car from Reichshoffen to Garmisch to catch the train, where he'd first spotted Hatchet Face.

No better way to know if someone was following than to lead him.

Christl pointed up to the second-story gallery. 'That area was reserved exclusively for the monarch. Thirty Holy Roman Emperors were crowned here. Having sat on the throne and followed in the footsteps of Charlemagne, they symbolically gained possession of the empire. No emperor was deemed legitimate until he ascended the throne that sits up there.'

Chairs filled the octagon for worshipers and, as he saw, tourists. He sat off to the side and asked, 'Okay, why are we here?'

'Mathematics and architecture were part of Einhard's love.'

He caught what she'd not voiced. 'Taught to him by the Holy Ones?'

'Look at this place. Quite an accomplishment for the ninth century. A lot of firsts here. That stone vault overhead? It was revolutionary. Whoever designed and built it knew what they were doing.'

'But what does this chapel have to do with Einhard's will?'

'In the will Einhard wrote that a comprehension of the wisdom of heaven begins in the new Jerusalem.'

'This is the new Jerusalem?'

'That's exactly how Charlemagne referred to this chapel.'

He recalled the rest. '*Revelations there will be clear once the secret of that wondrous place is deciphered. Clarify this pursuit by applying the angel's perfection to the lord's sanctification. But only those who appreciate the throne of Solomon and Roman frivolity shall find their way to heaven.*'

'You have a good memory.'

'If you only knew.'

'Riddles are not my strong point, and I've had a hard time with this one.'

'Who says I'm good with them?'

'Mother says you have quite a reputation.'

'It's good to know that I've passed Mama's test. Like I told her and you, she seems to have chosen sides.'

'She's trying to get Dorothea and me to work together. At some point we may have to. But I plan to avoid that as long as possible.'

'In the abbey, when you saw that cabinet had been vandalized, you thought Dorothea was the culprit, didn't you?'

'She knew Father kept his papers there. But I never

told her how the cabinet opened. She was never interested, until lately. She clearly didn't want me to have the documents.'

'But she wanted you to have me?'

'That is puzzling.'

'Maybe she thought I'd be useless?'

'I can't imagine why.'

'Flattery? You'll try anything.'

She smiled.

He wanted to know, 'Why would Dorothea steal the documents at the abbey and leave the originals of at least one of them in the castle?'

'Dorothea rarely ventured beneath Reichshoffen. She knows little of what's down there.'

'So who killed the woman from the cable car?'

Her face hardened. 'Dorothea.'

'Why?'

She shrugged. 'You must know that my sister has little or no conscience.'

'You two are the strangest twins I've ever come across.'

'Though we were born at the same time, that doesn't make us the same. We always maintained a distance from each other that we both enjoy.'

'So what happens when you two inherit it all?'

'I think Mother hopes this quest will end our differences.'

He caught her reservations. 'Not going to happen?'

'We both promised that we'd try.'

'You each have a strange way of trying.'

He stared around at the chapel. A few feet away, within the outer polygon, stood the main altar.

Christl noticed his interest. 'The panel in front is said to have been made from gold that Otto III found in Charlemagne's tomb.'

'I already know what you're going to say. *But nobody knows for sure.*'

Her explanations, so far, had been specific, but that didn't mean they were right. He checked his watch and stood. 'We need to eat something.'

She gave him a puzzled look. 'Shouldn't we deal with this first?'

'If I knew how, I would.'

Before entering the chapel, they'd detoured to the gift shop and learned that the interior stayed open until seven p.m., the last tour starting at six. He'd also noticed an assortment of guidebooks and historical materials, some in English, most in German. Luckily, he was reasonably fluent.

'We need to make a stop, then find a place to eat.'

'The Marktplatz is not far away.'

He motioned toward the main doors. 'Lead the way.'

35

Charlie Smith wore stone-washed jeans, a dark knit shirt, and steel-toed boots, all bought a few hours ago from a Wal-Mart. He imagined himself one of the Duke boys, in Hazzard County, just after climbing out the driver's-side window of the General Lee. Light traffic on the two-lane highway north from Charlotte had allowed a leisurely pace, and now he stood shivering among trees and stared at the house, maybe twelve hundred square feet under one roof.

He knew its history.

Herbert Rowland had bought the property in his thirties, made payments until his forties, then built the cabin in his fifties. Two weeks after retiring from the navy, Rowland and his wife packed a moving van and drove the twenty miles north from Charlotte. They'd spent the past ten years living quietly beside the lake.

On the flight north from Jacksonville, Smith had studied the file. Rowland possessed two genuine medical concerns. The first was a long-standing diabetic condition. Type 1, insulin-dependent. Controllable, provided he maintained daily insulin injections. The second was a love of alcohol, whiskey being Rowland's preference. A bit of a connoisseur, he spent a portion of his monthly navy retirement check on premium blends at a high-priced Charlotte liquor store. He always drank at home, at night, he and his wife together.

His notes from last year suggested a death consistent with diabetes. But devising a method to accomplish that result, while at the same time not raising any suspicion, had taken thought.

The front door opened and Herbert Rowland strolled out into bright sunshine. The older man walked straight to a dirty Ford Tundra and drove away. A second vehicle belonging to Rowland's wife was nowhere to be seen. Smith waited in the thickets ten minutes, then decided to risk it.

He walked to the front door and knocked.

No answer.

Again.

It took less than a minute to pick the lock. He knew there was no alarm system. Rowland liked to tell people he considered it a waste of money.

He carefully opened the door, stepped inside, and found the answering machine. He checked the saved messages. The sixth one, from Rowland's wife, dated and timed a few hours ago, pleased him. She was at her sister's and had called to check on him, ending by noting that she'd be home the day after tomorrow.

His plan immediately changed.

Two days alone was an excellent opportunity.

He passed a rack of hunting rifles. Rowland was an avid woodsman. He checked a couple of the shotguns and rifles. He liked to hunt, too, only his sport walked upright on two legs.

He entered the kitchen and opened the refrigerator. Lining the door shelf, exactly where the file indicated, stood four vials of insulin. With gloved fingers he examined each. All full, plastic seals intact, save for the one currently in use.

He carried the vial to the sink, then removed an empty syringe from his pocket. Puncturing the rubber seal with the needle, he worked the plunger, siphoned out the medicine, then expelled the liquid down the drain. He repeated the process two more times until the vial was empty. From another pocket he found a bottle of saline. He filled the syringe and injected the contents, repeating the process until the vial was once again three-quarters full.

He rinsed the sink and replaced the tampered vial in the refrigerator. Eight hours from now, when Herbert Rowland injected himself, he'd notice little. But alcohol and diabetes didn't mix. Excessive alcohol and untreated diabetes were absolutely fatal. Within a few hours Rowland should be in shock, and by morning he'd be dead.

All Smith would have to do was maintain a vigil.

He heard a motor outside and rushed to the window.

A man and woman emerged from a Chrysler compact.

Dorothea was concerned. Wilkerson had been gone a long time. He'd said he would find a bakery and bring back some sweets, but that had been nearly two hours ago.

The room phone rang and startled her. No one knew she was here except –

She lifted the receiver.

'Dorothea,' Wilkerson said. 'Listen to me. I was followed, but managed to lose them.'

'How did they find us?'

'I have no idea, but I made it back to the hotel and spotted men out front. Don't use your cell phone. It can be monitored. We do that all the time.'

'You sure you lost them?'

'I used the U-Bahn. It's you they're keying on now since they think you'll lead them to me.'

Her mind plotted. 'Wait a few hours, then take the underground to the Hauptbahnhof. Wait near the tourist office. I'll be there at six.'

'How are you going to leave the hotel?' he asked.

'As much business as my family does here, the concierge should be able to handle whatever I ask.'

Stephanie stepped from her car and Edwin Davis emerged from the passenger side. They'd driven from Atlanta to Charlotte, about 240 miles, all interstate highway, the trip a little under three hours. Davis had learned the physical address for Herbert Rowland, LCDR, retired, from navy records and Google had provided directions.

The house sat north of Charlotte, beside Eagles Lake, which, from its size and irregular shape, seemed man-made. The shoreline was steep, forested, and rocky. Few homesites existed. Rowland's wood-sided, hip-roofed house was nestled a quarter mile from the road, among bare hardwoods and green poplars, with a great view.

Stephanie was unsure about all of this and had voiced her concerns during the trip, suggesting that law enforcement should be involved.

But Davis had balked.

'This is still a bad idea,' she said to him.

'Stephanie, if I went to the FBI, or the local sheriff, and told them what I suspected, they'd say I was nuts. And who the hell knows? Maybe I am.'

'Zachary Alexander dying last night isn't a fantasy.'

'But it isn't a provable murder, either.'

They'd heard from the Secret Service in Jacksonville. No evidence of foul play had been detected.

She noticed no cars parked at the house. 'Doesn't seem like anyone's home.'

Davis slammed the car door. 'One way to find out.'

She followed him onto the porch, where he banged on the front door. No answer. He knocked again. After another few moments of silence, Davis tested the knob.

It opened.

'Edwin—' she started, but he'd already entered.

She waited on the porch. 'This is a felony.'

He turned. 'Then stay out there in the cold. I'm not asking you to break the law.'

She knew clear thinking was needed, so she walked inside. 'I have to be out of my mind to be in the middle of this.'

He smiled. 'Malone told me he said the same thing to you last year in France.'

She had no idea. 'Really? What else did Cotton say?'

He did not reply, just headed off to investigate. The décor made her think of Pottery Barn. Ladder-back chairs, sectional sofa, jute rugs across bleached hardwood floors. Everything was neat and orderly. Framed pictures dominated the walls and tables. Rowland was obviously a sportsman. Specimens dotted the walls, mixed with more portraits of what appeared to be children and grand-children. A sectional sofa faced a wooden deck. Across the lake, the far shore was visible. The house seemed to sit in the elbow of a cove.

Davis remained intent on looking around, opening drawers and cabinets.

'What are you doing?' she asked.

He drifted into the kitchen. 'Just trying to get a sense of things.'

She heard him open the refrigerator.

'You learn a lot about someone by studying their refrigerator,' he said.

'Really? What did you learn in mine?'

He'd ventured into hers earlier, before they'd left, to get something to drink.

'That you don't cook. It reminded me of college. Not much there.'

She grinned. 'And what have you learned here?'

He pointed. 'Herbert Rowland is a diabetic.'

She noticed vials with Rowland's name on them marked INSULIN. That wasn't all that hard.'

'And he likes chilled whiskey. Maker's Mark. Good stuff.'

Three bottles stood on the top shelf.

'You a drinker?' she asked.

He closed the refrigerator door. 'I like a shot of sixty-year-old Macallan every once in a while.'

'We need to leave,' she said.

'This is for Rowland's own good. Somebody is going to kill him, in a way he least expects. We need to check the other rooms.'

She still wasn't convinced and walked back into the den. Three doors led off from the great room. Beneath one, she noticed something. Light shifting, shadows, as if someone had just walked past on the other side.

Alarm bells rang in her brain.

She reached beneath her coat and withdrew a Magellan Billet-issue Beretta.

Davis caught sight of the gun. 'You came armed?'

She held up her index finger, signaling for quiet, and pointed to the door.

Company, she mouthed.

* * *

Charlie Smith had been trying to listen. The two intruders had boldly entered the house, forcing him into the bedroom, where he'd shut the door and stood close. When the man had said he planned on checking the remaining rooms, Smith knew he was in trouble. He'd brought no gun. He only toted one when absolutely necessary, and since he'd flown from Virginia to Florida, bringing one along had been impossible. Besides, guns were a poor way to inconspicuously kill somebody. Lots of attention, evidence, and questions.

No one should be here. The file made clear that Herbert Rowland volunteered at the local library every Wednesday until five p.m. He wasn't due back for hours. His wife, of course, was gone. He'd caught snippets of the conversation, which seemed more personal than professional, the woman clearly on edge. But then he'd heard. *You came armed?*

He needed to leave, but there was nowhere to go. Four windows lined the bedroom's exterior walls, but they could provide no ready escape.

A bathroom and two closets opened off the bedroom.

He needed to do something fast.

Stephanie opened the bedroom door. The master suite bed was made, everything tidy, like the rest of the house. A bathroom door hung open, and daylight from the four windows cast a bright glow across the room's Berber carpet. Outside, trees jostled by the breeze shifted and black shapes danced across the floor.

'No ghosts?' Davis said.

She pointed down. 'False alarm.'

Then something caught her eye.

One closet was equipped with pocket doors and appeared to be Mrs. Rowland's, women's clothes hung in a haphazard fashion. A second closet was smaller with a hinged paneled door. She could not see inside, as it sat at a right angle to her, in a short hall that led to the bath. The door hung open, its inner side visible from where she stood. A plastic hanger on the inside knob rocked, ever so slightly, from side to side.

Not much, but enough.

'What is it?' Davis asked.

'You're right,' she said. 'Nothing here. Just nerves from committing a burglary.'

She could see that Davis had not noticed – or if he had, he was keeping the realization close.

'Can we get out of here now?' she asked.

'Sure. I think we've seen enough.'

Wilkerson was terrified.

He'd been forced at gunpoint to make the call to Dorothea, the man from the sidewalk telling him exactly what to say. The barrel of a 9mm automatic had been nestled close to his left temple, and he'd been warned that any variation in the script would result in the trigger being pulled.

But he'd done exactly as instructed.

He'd then been driven across Munich in the rear of a Mercedes coupe, his hands cuffed behind his back, his kidnapper at the wheel. They'd lingered awhile, his captor leaving him alone in the car while he spoke on a cell phone outside.

Several hours had passed.

Dorothea should be at the train station soon, but they were nowhere near its location. In fact, they were driving away from the city center, heading south, out of the city, toward Garmisch and the Alps, sixty miles away.

'How about one thing?' he asked the driver.

The man said nothing.

'Since you're not going to tell me who you work for, how about your name? That a secret, too?'

He'd been taught that to engage your captors was the first step in learning about them. The Mercedes veered right, onto a ramp for the autobahn and sped ahead, merging onto the superhighway.

'My name is Ulrich Henn,' the man finally said.

36

Malone found himself enjoying his meal. He and Christl had walked back to the triangular-shaped Marktplatz and found a restaurant that faced the town's *rathaus*. On the way they'd stopped in the chapel's gift shop and bought half a dozen guidebooks. Their route had led them through a maze of snug, cobbled lanes lined with bourgeois town houses that created a medieval atmosphere, though most were probably only fifty or so years old given that Aachen had been heavily bombed in the 1940s. The afternoon's cold had not deterred shopping. People crowded the trendy shops preparing for Christmas.

Hatchet Face was still following and had entered another café diagonally across from where he and Christl were seated. Malone had asked for and received a table not at, but near, the window, where he could keep an eye outside.

He wondered about their shadow. Only one meant he was dealing with either amateurs or people too cheap to hire enough help. Perhaps Hatchet Face thought himself so good that no one would ever notice? He'd many times met operatives with similar egos.

He'd already skimmed through three of the guidebooks. Just as Christl had said, Charlemagne had considered the chapel his 'new Jerusalem.' Centuries later Barbarossa confirmed that declaration when he donated the copper-gilded chandelier. Earlier Malone had noticed a Latin inscription on the chandelier's bands, and a translation appeared in one of the books. The first line read, 'Here thou appearest in the picture, O Jerusalem, celestial Zion, Tabernacle of peace for us and hope of blessed rest.'

The ninth-century historian Notker was quoted as saying that Charlemagne had the chapel built 'in accordance with a conception of his own,' its length, breadth, and height symbolically related. Work had started sometime around 790 to 800 CE, and the building was consecrated on January 6, 805, by Pope Leo III, in the presence of the emperor.

He reached for another of the books. 'I assume you've studied the history of Charlemagne's time in detail?'

She nursed a glass of wine. 'It's my field. The Carolingian period is one of transition for Western civilization. Before him, Europe was a seething madhouse of conflicting races, incomparable ignorance, and massive political chaos. Charlemagne created the first centralized government north of the Alps.'

'Yet everything he achieved failed after his death. His empire crumbled. His son and grandchildren destroyed it all.'

'But what he believed took root. He thought the first object of government should be the welfare of its people. Peasants were, to him, human beings worth thinking about. He governed not for his glory, but for the common good. He said many times that his mission was not to spread his empire, but to keep one.'

'Yet he conquered new territory.'

'Minimally. Territory here and there for specific purposes. He was a revolutionary in nearly every way.

Rulers of his day gathered men of brawn, archers, warriors, but he summoned scholars and teachers.'

'Still, it all vanished and Europe lingered another four hundred years before real change occurred.'

She nodded. 'That seems the fate of most great rulers. Charlemagne's heirs were not as wise. He was married many times and fathered lots of children. No one knows how many. His firstborn, Pippin, a hunchback, never had the chance to reign.'

Mention of the deformity made him think of Henrik Thorvaldsen's crooked spine. He wondered what his Danish friend was doing. Thorvaldsen would surely either know, or know of, Isabel Oberhauser. Some intel on that personality would be helpful. But if he called, Thorvaldsen would wonder why he was still in Germany. Since he didn't have the answer to that question himself, there was no sense begging it.

'Pippin was later disinherited,' she said, 'when Charlemagne birthed healthy, nondeformed sons by later wives. Pippin became his father's bitter enemy, but died before Charlemagne. Louis, ultimately, was the only son to survive. He was gentle, deeply religious, and learned, but he shrank from battle and lacked consistency. He was forced to abdicate in favor of his three sons, who tore the empire apart by 841. It wasn't until the tenth century that it was reassembled by Otto I.'

'Did he have help, too? The Holy Ones?'

'No one knows. The only direct record of their involvement with European culture are the contacts with Charlemagne, and those come only from the journal I have, the one Einhard left in his grave.'

'And how has all this remained secret?'

'Grandfather told only my father. But because of his

wandering mind, it was hard to know what was real or imagined. Father involved the Americans. Neither Father nor the Americans could read the book from Charlemagne's grave, the one Dorothea has, which is supposed to be the complete account. So the secret has endured.'

As long as she was talking he asked, 'Then how did your grandfather find anything in Antarctica?'

'I don't know. All I know is that he did. You saw the stones.'

'And who has those now?'

'Dorothea, I'm sure. She certainly didn't want me to have them.'

'So she trashed those displays? What your grandfather collected?'

'My sister never cared for Grandfather's beliefs. And she is capable of anything.'

He caught more frost in her tone and decided not to press any further. Instead he glanced at one of the guidebooks and studied a sketch of the chapel, its surrounding courtyards, and adjacent buildings.

The chapel complex seemed to possess an almost phallic shape, circular at one end, an extension jutting forward with a rounded end at the other. It connected to what was once a refectory, now the treasury, by an interior door. Only one set of exterior doors were shown – the main entrance they'd used earlier, called the Wolf's Doors.

'What are you thinking?' she asked.

The question jarred his attention back to her. 'The book you have, from Einhard's grave. Do you have a complete translation of its Latin?'

She nodded. 'Stored on my computer at Reichshoffen. But it's of little use. He talks about the Holy Ones and a few of their visits *with* Charlemagne. The important information is supposedly in the book Dorothea has. What Einhard called a "full comprehension."

'But your grandfather apparently learned that comprehension.'

'It seems so, though we don't know that for sure.'

'So what happens when we finish this pursuit? We don't have the book Dorothea has.'

'That's when Mother expects us to work together. Each of us has a part, compelled to cooperate with the other.'

'But you're both trying like the devil to obtain all the pieces so that you don't need the other.'

How had he managed to get himself involved in such a mess?

'Charlemagne's pursuit is, to me, the only way to learn anything. Dorothea thinks the solution may lie with the Ahnenerbe and whatever it was pursuing. But I don't believe that's the case.'

He was curious. 'You know a lot about what she thinks.'

'My future is at stake. Why wouldn't I know all that I could?'

This stylish woman never hesitated for a noun, searched for the correct tense of a verb, or failed to voice the right phrase. Though beautiful, smart, and intriguing, something about Christl Falk didn't ring quite right. Similar in his mind to when he'd first met Cassiopeia Vitt in France, last year.

Attraction mixed with caution.

But that negative never seemed to deter him.

What was it about strong women with deep contradictions that drew him? Pam, his ex-wife, had been difficult. All of the women he'd known since the divorce had been handfuls, including Cassiopeia. Now this

German heiress who combined beauty, brains, and bravado.

He stared out the window at the neo-gothic town hall, tower roofs at each end, one with a clock that read five thirty.

She noticed his interest in the building. 'There's a story. The chapel stands behind the town hall. Charlemagne had them connected with a courtyard, enclosed by his palace compound. In the fourteenth century, when Aachen built that town hall, they changed the entrance from the north side, facing the courtyard, to the south, facing this way. That reflected a new civic independence. The people had become self-important and, symbolically, turned their

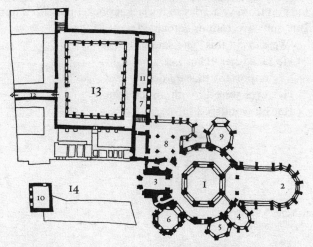

1. Octagon
2. Choir
3. Entrance Hall
4. Matthias Chapel
5. Anna Chapel
6. Hungarian Chapel
7. All Saints' Chapel
8. St. Michael's Chapel
9. Charles and Hubertus Chapel
10. Baptist Chapel
11. All Souls' Chapel
12. Treasury (Small Dragonhole)
13. Cloister
14. Church-yard

backs on the church.' She pointed out the window at the fountain in the Marktplatz. 'That statue atop is Charlemagne. Notice that he faces away from the church. A seventeenth-century reaffirmation.'

He used her invitation to glance outside as an opportunity to examine the restaurant where Hatchet Face had taken refuge – a half-timbered building that reminded him of an English pub.

He listened to the babble of languages mixed with the clanking of plates and cutlery around him. He found himself no longer objecting, either openly or silently, no longer searching out explanations for why he was here. Instead, his mind played with an idea. The cold weight of the gun from yesterday in his jacket pocket reassured him. But only five rounds remained.

'We can do this,' she said.

He faced her. 'Can *we*?'

'It's important that *we* do.'

Her eyes were lit with anticipation.

But he wondered.

37

Charlotte

Charlie Smith waited in the closet. He'd rushed inside, without thinking, relieved to find it deep and cluttered, and positioned himself behind the hanging clothes, leaving the door open in the hope it would deter anyone from looking inside. He'd heard the bedroom door open and the two visitors enter, but it sounded like his ruse had worked. They'd decided to leave and he listened as the front door opened, then closed.

This was the closest he'd ever come to detection. He hadn't expected any interruptions. Who were they? Should Ramsey be informed? No, the admiral had made it clear that there should be no contact until all three jobs were done.

He crept to the window and watched as the car that had been parked out front disappeared down the graveled lane toward the highway – two passengers inside. He prided himself on meticulous preparation. His files were a wealth of useful information. People were generally creatures of habit. Even those who insisted they had no habits practiced predictability. Herbert Rowland was a simple man, enjoying retirement with his wife beside a lake, minding his own business, going about his daily routine. He'd return home later, probably with some take-out food, inject himself, enjoy his dinner, then drink himself to sleep, never realizing that this would be his last day on earth.

He shook his head as the fear left him. An odd way to earn a living, but somebody had to do it.

He needed to do something for the next few hours, so he decided to drive back to town and see a couple of movies. Maybe enjoy a steak for dinner. He loved Ruth's Chris and had already learned there were two in Charlotte.

Later, he'd return.

Stephanie sat silent in the car as Davis drove down a leaf-and-gravel drive back toward the highway. She glanced back and saw that the house was nowhere in sight. Thick woods surrounded them. She'd given Davis the keys and asked him to drive. Luckily he hadn't questioned her, just slid behind the wheel.

'Stop,' she said.

Rock crunched as the tires crept to a halt.

'What's your cell phone number?'

He told her and she punched the digits into hers. She reached for the door handle. 'Drive back to the highway and head off a few miles. Pull over somewhere out of sight and wait till I call you.'

'What are you doing?'

'Playing a hunch.'

Malone walked with Christl across Aachen's Marktplatz. Six p.m. was approaching, and the sun hung low in a sky bruised by storm clouds. The weather had worsened and an icy northern wind sliced into him.

She led them toward the chapel through the old palace courtyard, a rectangular cobbled plaza twice as long as it was wide, lined with bare trees draped with snow. The surrounding buildings blocked the wind, but not the cold. Children ran about, shouting and talking in a joyous confusion. Aachen's Christmas market filled the courtyard. Every German town seemed to have one. He wondered what his son Gary was doing – now out of school for the holidays. He needed to call. He did at least every couple of days.

He watched as children rushed toward a new attraction. A droopy-faced man sporting a purple fur robe and a long tapered cap who reminded him of Father Time.

'St. Nicholas,' Christl said. 'Our Santa Claus.'

'Quite different.'

He used the happy disorder to confirm that Hatchet Face had followed, staying back, casually examining the booths near a towering blue spruce with electric candles and tiny lights balancing on swaying boughs. He caught the scent of boiling vinegar – *glühwein*. A stall selling the spiced port stood a few yards away, gloved patrons cradling steaming brown mugs.

He pointed to another merchant selling what looked like cookies. 'What are they?'

'A local delicacy. *Aachener printen*. Spicy gingerbread.'

'Let's have one.'

She threw him a quizzical look.

'What?' he said. 'I like sweets.'

They walked over and he bought two of the flat, hard cookies.

He tried a bite. 'Not bad.'

He'd thought the gesture would help relax Hatchet Face and he was pleased to see that it had. The man remained casual and confident.

Darkness would be here soon. He'd bought tickets for the chapel's six p.m. tour earlier when they'd stopped to

obtain the guidebooks. He was going to have to improvise.
He'd learned from his reading that the chapel was a
UNESCO world cultural monument. Burglarizing or
damaging it would be a serious offense. But after the
monastery in Portugal and St. Mark's in Venice, what did
it matter?

He seemed to specialize in vandalizing world treasures.

Dorothea entered the Munich train station. The
Hauptbahnhof was conveniently located in the city center,
about two kilometers from the Marienplatz. Trains from
all over Europe arrived and departed by the hour, along
with local connections to the underground lines, trams,
and buses. The station was not a historical masterpiece –
more a modern combination of steel, glass, and concrete.
Clocks throughout the interior noted that it was a little
past six p.m.

What was happening?

Apparently Admiral Langford Ramsey wanted
Wilkerson dead, but she needed Wilkerson.

Actually, she liked him.

She glanced around and spotted the tourist office. A
quick survey of the benches offered no sight of Wilkerson,
but through the crowd she spotted a man.

His tall frame sported a three-button glen-plaid suit
and leather oxfords beneath a wool coat. A dull Burberry
scarf draped his neck. He possessed a handsome face with
child-like features, though age had clearly added some
furrows and valleys. His steel-gray eyes, encircled by wire-
framed glasses, appraised her with a penetrating gaze.

Her husband.

Werner Lindauer.

He stepped close. '*Guten abend,* Dorothea.'

She did not know what to say. Their marriage was entering its twenty-third year, a union that, in the beginning, had been productive. But over the last decade she'd come to resent his perpetual whining and lack of appreciation for anything beyond his own self-interest. His only saving point had been his devotion to Georg, their son. But Georg's death five years ago had chiseled a wide divide between them. Werner had been devastated and so had she, but they'd handled their grief differently. She withdrew into herself. He became angry. Ever since she'd simply led her life and allowed him to lead his, neither answering to the other.

'What are you doing here?' she asked.

'I came for you.'

She was not in the mood for his antics. Occasionally, he'd tried to be a man, more a passing fancy than a fundamental change.

She wanted to know, 'How did you know I'd be here?'

'Captain Sterling Wilkerson told me.'

Her shock evolved into dread.

'Interesting man,' he said. 'A gun to his head and he simply can't stop talking.'

'What have you done?' she asked, not concealing her astonishment.

His gaze zeroed in. 'A great deal, Dorothea. We have a train to catch.'

'I'm not going anywhere with you.'

Werner seemed to restrain a surge of annoyance. Perhaps he hadn't contemplated that reaction. But his lips relaxed into a reassuring smile that actually frightened her. 'Then you shall lose your mother's challenge with your dear sister. Does that not matter?'

She'd had no idea he was aware of what was happening.

She'd told him nothing. Clearly, though, her husband was well informed.

Finally, she asked, 'Where are we going?'

'To see our son.'

Stephanie watched as Edwin Davis drove off. She then switched her phone to silent, buttoned her coat, and plunged into the woods. Old-growth pines and bare hardwoods, many vined with mistletoe, stretched overhead. Winter had only minimally thinned the underbrush. She advanced the hundred yards back toward the house slowly, a heavy layer of pine needles silencing her steps.

She'd seen the hanger moving. No doubt. But was it a mistake by her, or by the person she'd sensed inside?

She repeatedly told her agents to trust their instincts. Nothing worked better than common sense. Cotton Malone had been a master of that. She wondered what he was doing right now. He hadn't called back concerning the information on Zachary Alexander or the rest of *Holden*'s command staff.

Had he found trouble, too?

The house appeared, its form broken by the many trees that stood in between. She crouched behind one of the trunks.

Everyone, no matter how good they may be, eventually screwed up. The trick was being there when it happened. If Davis was to be believed, Zachary Alexander and David Sylvian had been murdered by someone expertly able to mask those deaths. And though he hadn't voiced his reservations, she'd detected them when Davis told her how Millicent had died.

Her heart stopped.

Davis was playing a hunch, too.

The hanger.

It had moved.

And she'd wisely not revealed what she'd seen in the bedroom, deciding to see if Herbert Rowland was, in fact, next.

The door to the house opened and a short, thin man wearing jeans and boots stepped out.

He hesitated, then his darkened form trotted away, disappearing into the woods. Her heart raced. Son of a bitch.

What had he done in there?

She found her phone and dialed Davis's number, which was answered after one ring.

'You were right,' she told him.

'About what?'

'Like you said with Langford Ramsey. Everything. Absolutely everything.'

PART THREE

38

Malone followed the tour group back into the central octagon of Charlemagne's chapel. Inside was fifty degrees warmer than outdoors, and he was grateful to be out of the cold. The tour guide spoke English. About twenty people had bought tickets, Hatchet Face not among them. For some reason their shadow had decided to wait outside. Perhaps the close confines had advised caution. The lack of a crowd may have also played into his decision. The chairs beneath the dome were empty, only the tour group and a dozen or so other visitors loitering about.

A flash strobed the walls as someone snapped a picture. One of the attendants hustled toward the woman with the camera.

'There's a fee,' Christl whispered, 'for taking pictures.'

He watched as the visitor forked over a few euros and the man provided her with a wristband.

'Now she's legal?' he asked.

Christl grinned. 'It takes money to maintain this place.'

He listened as the guide explained about the chapel, most of the information a regurgitation of what he'd read in the guidebooks. He'd wanted to take the tour because only paid groups were allowed in certain parts, upstairs particularly, where the imperial throne was located.

They wandered with the visitors into one of seven side chapels that jutted from the Carolingian core. This one was St. Michael's – recently renovated, the guide explained. Wooden pews faced a marble altar. Several of the group paused to light candles. Malone noticed a door in what he determined to be the west wall and recalled that it should be the other exit he'd discovered while reading the guidebooks. The heavy wooden slab hung closed. He casually wandered through the dim interior while the guide droned on about the history. At the door, he paused and quickly tested the latch. Locked.

'What are you doing?' Christl asked.

'Solving your problem.'

They followed the tour, heading past the main altar toward the gothic choir, another area only open to paying groups. He stopped within the octagon and studied a mosaic inscription that encircled above the lower arches. Black Latin letters on a gold background. Christl carried the plastic shopping bag that held the guidebooks. He quickly found the one he recalled, a thin pamphlet appropriately titled *A Small Guide to Aachen Cathedral*, and noted that the Latin in the printed text matched the mosaic.

CUM LAPIDES VIVI PACIS CONPAGE LIGANTUR INQUE
PARES NUMEROS OMNIA CONVENIUNT CLARET OPUS
DOMINI TOTAM QUI CONSTRUIT AULAM EFFECTUSQUE
PIIS DAT STUDIIS HOMINUM QUORUM PERPETUI
DECORIS STRUCTURA MANEBIT SI PERFECTA AUCTOR
PROTEGAT ATQUE REGAT SIC DEUS HOC TUTUM STABILI
FUNDAMINE TEMPLUM QUOD KAROLUS PRINCEPS
CONDIDIT ESSE VELIT

Christl noticed his interest. 'It's the chapel's consecration. Originally it was painted on the stone. The mosaics are a more recent addition.'

'But the words are the same as in Charlemagne's day?' he asked. 'In the same location?'

She nodded. 'As far as anyone knows.'

He grinned. 'The history of this place is like my marriage. Nobody seems to know anything.'

'And what happened to Frau Malone?'

He caught interest in her tone. 'She decided that Herr Malone was a pain in the ass.'

'She might be right.'

'Believe me, Pam was always right about everything.' But he silently added a qualification that he'd only come to understand years after the divorce. *Almost.* When it came to their son she'd been wrong. But he wasn't about to discuss Gary's parentage with this stranger.

He studied the inscription again. The mosaics, the marble floor, and the marble-sheathed walls were all less than two hundred years old. In Charlemagne's time, which was Einhard's time, the stone surrounding him would have been coarse and painted. To presently do as Einhard instructed – *begin in the new Jerusalem* – could prove daunting since virtually nothing from twelve hundred years ago existed. But Hermann Oberhauser had solved the riddle. How else could he have found anything? So somewhere inside this structure lay the answer.

'We need to catch up,' he said.

They hurried after the tour group and arrived in the choir just as the guide was about to rehang a velvet rope that blocked entrance. Just beyond, the group had congregated around a gilded reliquary, its table-like pedestal elevated four feet off the floor and encased in glass.

'The Shrine of Charlemagne,' Christl whispered. 'From the thirteenth century. Contains the emperor's bones. Ninety-two. Four others are in the treasury, and the rest are gone.'

'They count them?'

'Inside that reliquary is a log that records every time, since 1215, when the lid was opened. Oh, yes, they count.'

She grasped his arm in a light embrace and led him to a spot before the shrine. The tour group had retreated behind the reliquary, the guide explaining how the choir had been consecrated in 1414. Christl pointed to a memorial plaque embedded in the floor. 'Beneath here is where Otto III was buried. Supposedly fifteen other emperors are also buried around us.'

The guide was fielding questions about Charlemagne as the group snapped pictures. Malone studied the choir, a bold gothic design where stone walls seemed to dissolve into expanses of towering glass. He noted how the choir and the Carolingian core joined, the higher parts feeding into the octagon, neither building forfeiting any of its effectiveness.

He studied the upper reaches of the choir, focusing on the second-story gallery that encircled the central octagon. When he'd studied the schematics in the guidebooks he'd thought a vantage point here, in the choir, would offer a clear view of what he needed to see.

And he was right,

Everything on the second level seemed connected.

So far, so good.

The group was led back toward the chapel's main entrance where they climbed what the guide called the emperor's stairway, a circular route that wound into the upper gallery, every stone tread worn down into a drooping curve. The guide held an iron gate open and explained to everyone that only Holy Roman Emperors had been allowed upstairs.

The stairway led to a spacious upper gallery that overlooked the open octagon. The guide drew everyone's attention to a crude hodgepodge of stone fashioned into steps, a bier, a chair, and an altar that jutted from the rear of the raised platform. The strange-looking edifice was encircled by a decorative wrought-iron chain that kept visitors at bay.

'This is Charlemagne's throne,' the guide said. 'It's here on the upper level and elevated like this to be similar to thrones in Byzantine courts. And like those, it sits on the axis of the church, opposite the main altar, facing east.'

Malone listened as the guide described how four slabs of Parian marble had been fitted together with simple brass clamps to form the imperial chair. The six stone risers leading up were cut from an ancient Roman column.

'Six were chosen,' the guide said, 'to correspond with the throne of Solomon, as detailed in the Old Testament. Solomon was the first to have a temple built, the first to establish a reign of peace, and the first to sit on a throne. All similar to what Charlemagne accomplished in northern Europe.'

Part of what Einhard wrote flashed through Malone's mind. *But only those who appreciate the throne of Solomon and Roman frivolity shall find their way to heaven.*

'No one knows for sure when this throne was installed,' the guide was saying. 'Some say it was from Charlemagne's time. Others argue it came later, in the tenth century, with Otto I.'

'It's so plain,' one the tourists said. 'Almost ugly.'

'From the thickness of the four marble pieces used to

form the chair, which, as you can see, vary, it's clear they were floor stones. Definitely Roman. They must have been salvaged from somewhere special. Apparently they were so important that their appearance didn't matter. On this simple marble chair, with a wooden seat, the Holy Roman Emperor would be crowned, then receive homage from his princes.'

She pointed beneath the throne at a small passageway that passed from one side to the other.

'Pilgrims, with backs bent, would creep through under the throne, paying their own homage. For centuries, this place was revered.'

She led the group to the other side.

'Now look here.' The woman pointed. 'See the etchings.'

This was what he'd come for. Pictures had been included in the guidebooks, along with various explanations, but he wanted to see for himself.

Faint lines were visible in the rough marble surface. A square enclosing another square, enclosing still another. Halfway along the sides of the largest, a line jutted inward, bisecting the second form and stopping on the line for the inner square. Not all of the lines had survived, but enough for him to mentally form the completed image.

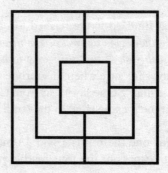

'This is proof,' the guide said, 'that the marble slabs were originally Roman flooring. This is the board used to play Nine Men's Morris, a combination of checkers, chess, and backgammon. It was a simple game that Romans loved. They would etch the squares into a stone and play away. The game was also popular in Charlemagne's time and is still played today.'

'What's it doing on a royal throne?' someone asked.

The guide shook her head. 'No one knows. But it is an interesting aspect, wouldn't you say?'

He motioned for Christl to drift away. The guide droned on about the upper gallery and more cameras flashed. The throne seemed to be a great photo op and, thankfully, everyone sported their official wristbands.

He and Christl rounded one of the upper arches, now out of sight of the tour group.

His eyes searched the semi-darkness.

From the choir below he'd surmised that the throne sat in the west gallery. Somewhere up here, he'd hoped, would be a place to hide.

He led Christl into a dark recess in the outer wall and dissolved into its shadows. He motioned for quiet. They listened as the tour group departed the upper gallery and descended back to ground level.

He checked his watch.

7:00 p.m.

Closing time.

39

Dorothea was in a quandary. Her husband apparently knew all about Sterling Wilkerson, which surprised her. But he also knew of the quest with Christl, and that concerned her – along with the fact that Werner was apparently holding Wilkerson prisoner.

What in the world was happening?

They'd boarded a 6:40 p.m. train out of Munich and headed south to Garmisch. During the eighty-minute trip Werner had said nothing, merely sat and calmly read a Munich newspaper. She'd always found it irritating how he devoured every word, even reading the obituaries and advertisements, commenting here and there on items that struck his interest. She'd wanted to know what he meant by *going to see their son* but decided not to ask. For the first time in twenty-three years this man had shown a backbone, so she chose to keep quiet and see where things led.

They were now driving north on a darkened highway away from Garmisch, Ettal Monastery, and Reichshoffen. A car had been waiting outside the train station with the keys under the front mat. She now realized where they were headed, a location she'd avoided for the past three years.

'I'm not stupid, Dorothea,' Werner finally said. 'You think I am, but I'm not.'

She decided to give him no satisfaction. 'Actually, Werner, I don't think about you at all.'

He ignored her jab and kept driving through the cold. Thankfully, no snow was falling. Traveling this road brought back memories she'd fought hard to erase. From five years ago. When Georg's car careened off an unrailed highway in the Tyrolean Alps. He'd been there skiing and had called just before the accident to tell her that he'd be staying at the same inn he always frequented. They'd chatted for a few minutes – light, brief, and casual, mother and son, the kind of idle chitchat that occurred all the time.

But it was the last time she ever spoke to him.

The next time she saw her only child he was laid in a casket, dressed in a gray suit, ready for burial.

The Oberhauser family plot sat beside an ancient Bavarian church, a few kilometers west of Reichshoffen. After the funeral, the family had endowed a chapel there in Georg's name, and for the first two years she'd gone regularly and lit a candle.

But for the past three years she'd stayed away.

Ahead, she spotted the church, its stained-glass windows faintly lit. Werner parked out front.

'Why do we have to be here?' she asked.

'Believe me, if it wasn't important we wouldn't be.'

He stepped out into the night. She followed him into the church. No one was inside, but the iron gate to Georg's chapel hung open.

'You haven't been in a while,' he said.

'That's my business.'

'I've come quite often.'

That didn't surprise her.

She approached the gate. A marble prie-dieu stood before a small altar. Above, St. George, perched atop a silvery horse, was carved into the stone. She rarely prayed and wondered if she was even a believer. Her father had been a devout atheist, her mother a nonpracticing Catholic. If there was a God, she felt nothing but anger toward him for stripping her of the only person she'd ever loved unconditionally.

'I've had enough of this, Werner. What do you want? This is Georg's grave. He deserves our respect. This is not the place to air our differences.'

'And do you respect *him* by disrespecting me?'

'I don't concern myself with you, Werner. You have your life and I have mine.'

'It's over, Dorothea.'

'I agree. Our marriage has been over a long time.'

'That's not what I meant. No more men. I'm your husband and you are my wife.'

She laughed. 'You have to be joking.'

'Actually, I'm quite serious.'

'And what has suddenly evolved you into a man?'

He retreated to the wall. 'At some point the living must let go of the dead. I've come to that point.'

'You brought me here to tell me that?'

Their relationship had started through their parents. Not an arranged marriage in the formal sense, but nonetheless planned. Thankfully, an attraction blossomed and their early years had been happy. The birth of Georg brought them both great joy. His childhood and teenage years had likewise been wonderful. But his death created irreconcilable differences. There seemed a need to assign blame, and they each directed their frustrations at the other.

'I brought you here because I had to,' he said.

'I haven't come to the point you apparently have.'

'It's a shame,' he said, appearing not to have heard her. 'He would have been a great man.'

She agreed.

'The boy had dreams, ambitions, and we could have fueled his every desire. He would have been the best of us both.' He turned and faced her. 'I wonder what he'd think of us now?'

The question struck her odd. 'What do you mean?'

'Neither of us has treated the other kindly.'

She needed to know, 'Werner, what are you doing?'

'Perhaps he's listening and wants to know your thoughts.'

She resented his pressing. 'My son would have approved of whatever I did.'

'Would he? Would he have approved of what you did yesterday? You killed two people.'

'And how do you know that?'

'Ulrich Henn cleaned up your mess.'

She was confused and concerned, but she was not going to discuss the issue here, in this sacred place. She stepped toward the gate, but he blocked the way and said, 'You cannot flee this time.'

A wave of uneasiness swept through her. She hated him for violating Georg's sanctuary. 'Move.'

'Do you have any idea what you are doing?'

'Go to hell, Werner.'

'You haven't a clue about reality.'

His expression was not one of a man angry or afraid, so she was curious. 'Do you want me to lose to Christl?'

His expression softened. 'I wasn't aware it was a contest. I thought it more a challenge. But that's why I'm here – to help you.'

She needed to know what he knew and how, but could only bring herself to say, 'A dead child does not make a marriage.' Her gaze bore into his. 'I don't need your help. Not anymore.'

'You're wrong.'

'I want to leave,' she said. 'Will you let me pass?'

Her husband remained frozen and, for an instant, she was actually afraid. Werner had always clung to emotions like a drowning man to a life preserver. Good at starting fights, terrible at finishing them. So when he retreated from the doorway she wasn't surprised.

She stepped past.

'There's something you need to see,' he said.

She stopped, turned, and saw something else she'd not seen in this man for a long time. Confidence. Fear again swept through her.

He left the church and walked back to the car. She followed. He found a key and opened the trunk. Inside, a weak light revealed the contorted, dead face of Sterling Wilkerson, a bloody hole in the center of his forehead.

She gasped.

'This is quite serious, Dorothea.'

'Why?' she asked. 'Why did you do that?'

He shrugged. 'You were using him, as he was using you. Here's the point. He's dead. I'm not.'

40

Ramsey was ushered into the living room of Admiral Raymond Dyals Jr., four stars, retired, US Navy. The ninety-four-year-old Missourian had served in World War II, Korea, and Vietnam, then retired in the early 1980s. In 1971, when NR-1A was lost, Dyals had been chief of naval operations, the man who'd signed the classified order not to launch any search and rescue for the missing sub. Ramsey had then been a lieutenant, the one chosen by Dyals for the mission, afterward personally briefing the admiral about *Holden*'s covert Antarctica visit. He'd then been quickly promoted to commander and assigned to Dyals' personal staff. From there, the moves upward had been fast and easy.

He owed this old man everything.

And he knew Dyals still carried clout.

He was the oldest living flag officer. Presidents consulted him, the current one no exception. His judgment was considered sound and meaningful. The press afforded him great courtesy, and senators routinely made pilgrimages to the room into which Ramsey now walked, before a raging fire, a wool blanket spread across the old man's spindly legs, a bushy cat nestled in Dyals' lap. He'd even acquired a label – *Winterhawk* – which Ramsey knew the man relished.

Crinkly eyes flashed as Dyals spotted him entering. 'I always like it when you come by.'

Ramsey stood respectfully before his mentor until he was invited to sit.

'I thought I might hear from you,' Dyals said. 'I heard this morning about Sylvian. He served on my staff once. An okay aide, but too rigid. He seems to have done all right, though. Nothing but glowing reports all day on his life.'

Ramsey decided to come to the point. 'I want his job.'

The admiral's melancholy pupils lit with approval. 'Member, Joint Chiefs of Staff. I never made it that far.'

'You could have.'

The old man shook his head. 'Reagan and I didn't get along. He had his favorites, or at least his aides had their favorites, and I wasn't on that list. Besides, it was time for me to leave.'

'What about you and Daniels? Are you on his favorites list?'

He caught something hard and unbending in Dyals' expression.

'Langford,' Dyals said, 'you know that the president is no friend of ours. He's been hard on the military. Budgets have been slashed, programs curtailed. He doesn't even think we need the Joint Chiefs.'

'He's wrong.'

'Maybe. But he's the president, and he's popular. Like Reagan was, just with a different philosophy.'

'Surely there are military officers he respects. Men you know. Their support of my candidacy could make the difference.'

Dyals lightly stroked the cat. 'Many of them would want the job for themselves.'

He said nothing.

'Don't you find this whole business unsavory?' Dyals asked. 'Begging for favors. Relying on whore politicians for a career. It's one reason I opted out.'

'It's the way of our world. We don't make the rules, we just play by the ones that exist.'

He knew that many flag officers and a good number of those 'whore politicians' could thank Ray Dyals for their jobs. Winterhawk had lots of friends, and knew how to use them.

'I've never forgotten what you did,' Dyals quietly muttered. 'I often think about NR-1A. Those men. Tell me, again, Langford, what was it like?'

A haunting bluish glow seeped through the surface ice, its color gradually deepening with depth, finally evolving into an indigo blackness. Ramsey wore a bulky navy dry suit with tight seals and double layers, nothing exposed except a tiny strip of skin around his lips that had burned when he'd first entered the water but was now numb. Heavy gloves made his hands seem useless. Thankfully, the water dissipated all weight, and floating in the vastness, clear as air, he felt as if he were flying rather than swimming.

The transponder signal Herbert Rowland had detected led them across the snow to a narrow inlet where freezing ocean licked icy shore, a place where seals and birds had congregated for summer. The signal's strength compelled a firsthand inspection. So he'd suited up, Sayers and Rowland helping him don his gear. His orders were clear. Only he went into the water.

He checked his depth. Forty feet.

Impossible to know how far down to the bottom but he was hoping he could at least catch sight of something, enough to confirm the sub's fate. Rowland had told him that the source lay farther inland, toward the mountains that rose from the shoreline.

He kicked through the water.

A wall of black volcanic rock peppered with a dazzling array of orange anemones, sponges, pink staghorns, and yellow-green mollusks rose to his left. But for the fact the water was twenty-eight degrees he could have been on a coral reef. Light dimmed overhead in the frozen ceiling, and what had just appeared as a cloudy sky, in varying shades of blue, steadily went black.

The ice above had apparently been replaced with rock.

He unclipped a light from his belt and switched it on. Little plankton floated around him. He saw no sediment. He shone his light and the beam seemed invisible, as there was nothing to backscatter the photons. They simply hung in the water, revealing themselves only when they struck something.

Like a seal, which shot past, barely flexing a muscle.

More seals appeared.

He heard their trilling call and even felt it in his body, as if he were being sonar-pinged. What an assignment. An opportunity to prove himself to men who could literally make his career. That's why he'd instantly volunteered. He'd also personally chosen Sayers and Rowland, two men he knew could be depended on. Rowland had said the signal source was maybe two hundred yards south. No more. He estimated that he'd swum at least that far. He searched the depths with light that penetrated maybe fifty feet. He was hoping to spot NR-1A's orange conning tower rising from the bottom.

He seemed to be floating in a massive underwater cavern that opened directly into the Antarctic continent, volcanic rock now encircling him.

His gaze searched. Nothing. Just water dissolving into blackness.

Yet the signal was here.

He decided to explore a hundred more yards.

Another seal rocketed past, then one more. Ahead of him, their ballet was entrancing. He watched as they glided with no effort. One of them whirled in a broad somersault, then beat a hasty retreat upward.

He followed with his light.

The animal disappeared.

A second seal flicked its fins and ascended.

It, too, broke through the surface.

How was that possible?

Only rock should be above him.

'Amazing,' Dyals said. 'What an adventure.'

Ramsey agreed. 'My lips felt like I'd been kissing frozen metal when I surfaced.'

The admiral chuckled. 'I would have loved to have done what you did.'

'The adventure's not over, Admiral.'

Dread punctuated his words and the old man now understood that the visit contained a dual purpose.

'Tell me.'

He recounted the Magellan Billet's breach of NR-1A's investigative file. Cotton Malone's involvement. His successful effort to retrieve the file. And White House access into the personnel records of Zachary Alexander, Herbert Rowland, and Nick Sayers. He omitted only what Charlie Smith was handling.

'Someone's looking,' he said.

'It was only a matter of time,' Dyals said in a whisper. 'Secrets seem so hard to keep anymore.'

'I can stop it,' he declared.

The old man's eyes narrowed. 'Then you must.'

'I've taken measures. But you ordered, long ago, that he would be left alone.'

No name was needed. The *he* was known between them.

'So you've come to see if that order still stands?'

He nodded. 'To be complete *he* must also be included.'

'I can't order you any longer.'

'You're the only man I willingly obey. When we disbanded thirty-eight years ago, you gave an order. *Leave him alone.*'

'Is he still alive?' Dyals asked.

He nodded. 'Sixty-eight years old. Lives in Tennessee. Teaches at a college.'

'Still spouting the same nonsense?'

'Nothing has changed.'

'And the other two lieutenants who were there with you?'

He said nothing. He didn't have to.

'You've been busy,' the admiral said.

'I was taught well.'

Dyals continued to stroke the cat. 'We took a chance in '71. True, Malone's crew agreed to the conditions before they left, but we didn't have to hold them to it. We could have looked for them. I've always wondered if I did the right thing.'

'You did.'

'How can you be so sure?'

'The times were different. That sub was our most secret weapon. There's no way we could have revealed its existence, much less that it sank. How long would it have been before the Soviets found the wreckage? And there was the matter of NR-1. It was on missions then, and it's still sailing today. No question – you did the right thing.'

'You believe the president is trying to learn what happened?'

'No. It's a few rungs lower on the ladder, but the man has Daniels' ear.'

'And you think all this might destroy your chances at nomination?'

'Without a doubt.'

No need for him to add the obvious. *And also destroy your reputation.*

'Then I rescind the order. Do as you see fit.'

41

M alone sat on the floor in a tight empty room that opened off the upper gallery. He and Christl had taken refuge inside after avoiding the tour group. He'd watched through a one-inch space beneath the door as lights inside the chapel were dimmed and doors banged shut for the night. That had been over two hours ago and there'd been no sounds since, except the hushed murmur of the Christmas market leaking in through the room's solitary window and a faint whistle of the wind that ravaged the exterior walls.

'It's strange in here,' Christl whispered. 'So quiet.'

'We need time to study this place without interruptions.' He was also hoping that their disappearance would confuse Hatchet Face.

'How long do we wait?' she asked.

'Things need to settle down outside. You never know, there still could be visitors inside before the night is finished.' He decided to take advantage of their solitude. 'I need to know some things.'

In the greenish light from the exterior floodlights he saw her face brighten. 'I was wondering when you'd ask.'

'The Holy Ones. What makes you think they're real?'

She seemed surprised by his inquiry, as if she'd expected

something else. More personal. But she kept her composure and said, 'Have you ever heard of the Piri Reis map?'

He had. It was supposedly created by a Turkish pirate and dated to 1513.

'It was found in 1929,' she said. 'Only a fragment of the original, but it shows South America and West Africa in correct longitudes. Sixteenth-century navigators had no way to confirm longitude – that concept wasn't perfected until the eighteenth century. Gerardus Mercator was one year old when the Piri Reis map was drawn, so it predated his method of projecting the earth on a flat surface, marking everything with latitude and longitude. But the map does just that. It also details the northern coast of Antarctica. That continent wasn't even discovered until 1818. It wasn't until 1949 that the first sonar soundings were made under the ice. Since then, more sophisticated ground radar has done the same thing. There's a near-perfect match between the Piri Reis map and the actual coastline of Antarctica, beneath the ice.

'There's also a notation on the map that indicates the drafter used information from the time of Alexander the Great as source material. Alexander lived in the early part of the fourth century before Christ. By then Antarctica was covered in miles of ice. So those source materials showing the original shoreline would have to be dated somewhere around ten-thousand-plus years before Christ, when there was much less ice, to around fifty thousand years BCE. Also, remember, a map is useless without notations indicating what you're looking at. Imagine a map of Europe with no writing. Wouldn't tell you much. It's generally accepted that writing itself dates from the

Sumerians, around thirty-five hundred years before Christ. That Reis used source maps, which would have to be much older than thirty-five hundred years, means the art of writing is older than we thought.'

'Lots of leaps in logic in that argument.'

'Are you always so skeptical?'

'I've found it's healthy when my ass is on the line.'

'As part of my master's thesis I studied medieval maps and learned of an interesting dichotomy. Land maps of the time were crude – Italy joined to Spain, England misshapen, mountains out of place, rivers inaccurately drawn. But nautical maps were a different story. They were called portolans – it means "port to port." And they were incredibly accurate.'

'And you think that the drafters of those had help.'

'I studied many portolans. The Dulcert Galway of 1339 shows Russia with great accuracy. Another Turkish map from 1559 shows the world from a northern projection, as if hovering over the North Pole. How was that possible? A map of Antarctica published in 1737 showed the continent divided into two islands, which we now know is true. A 1531 map I examined showed Antarctica without ice, with rivers, even mountains that we now know are buried beneath. None of that information was available when those maps were created. But they are remarkably accurate – within *one half-degree* of longitude in error. That's incredible considering the drafters supposedly did not even know the concept.'

'But the Holy Ones knew about longitude?'

'To sail the world's oceans they would have to understand stellar navigation or longitude and latitude. In my research I noticed similarities among the portolans. Too many to be mere coincidence. So if an oceangoing society existed long ago, one that conducted worldwide surveys centuries before the great geological and meteorological catastrophes that swept the world around ten thousand years before Christ, it's logical that information was passed on, which survived and made its way into those maps.'

He was still skeptical but, after their quick tour of the chapel and thinking about Einhard's will, he was beginning to reevaluate things.

He crawled to the door and peered beneath. Still quiet. He propped himself against the door.

'There's something else,' she said.

He was listening.

'The prime meridian. Virtually every country that eventually sailed the seas developed one. There had to be a longitudinal starting point. Finally, in 1884, the major nations of the world met in Washington, DC, and chose a line through Greenwich as zero degree longitude. A world constant, and we've used it ever since. But the portolans tell a different story. Amazingly, they all seemed to use a point thirty-one degrees, eight minutes west as their zero line.'

He did not comprehend the significance of those coordinates, other than they were east of Greenwich, somewhere beyond Greece.

'That line runs straight through the Great Pyramid at Giza,' she said. 'At that same 1884 conference in Washington, an argument was made to run the zero line through that point, but was rejected.'

He didn't see the point.

'The portolans I found all utilized the concept of longitude. Don't get me wrong, those ancient maps did not contain latitude and longitude lines like we know today. They used a simpler method, choosing a center point, then drawing a circle around it and dividing the circle. They would keep doing that outward, generating a crude form of measurement. Each of those portolans I mentioned used the same center. A point in Egypt, near what's now Cairo, where the Giza pyramid stands.'

A pile of coincidences, he had to admit.

'That longitude line through Giza runs south into Antarctica exactly where the Nazis explored in 1938, their Neuschwabenland.' She paused. 'Grandfather and Father both were aware of this. I was first introduced to these concepts from reading their notes.'

'I thought your grandfather was senile.'

'He left some historical notes. Not a lot. Father, too. I only wish they both would have spoken of this pursuit more.'

'This is nuts,' he said.

'How many scientific realities today started out the same way? It's not nuts. It's real. There's something out there, waiting to be found.'

Which his father may have died searching for.

He glanced at his watch. 'We can probably head downstairs. I need to check a few things.'

He came to one knee and pushed himself off the floor. But she stopped him, her hand on his trouser leg. He'd listened to her explanations and concluded that she was not a crackpot.

'I appreciate what you're doing,' she said, keeping her voice hushed.

'I haven't done anything.'

'You're here.'

'As you made clear, what happened to my father is wrapped up in this.'

She leaned close and kissed him, lingering long enough for him to know that she was enjoying it.

'Do you always kiss on the first date?' he asked her.

'Only men I like.'

42

Bavaria

Dorothea stood in shock, Sterling Wilkerson's dead eyes staring up at her.

'You killed him?' she asked her husband.

Werner shook his head. 'Not me. But I was there when it happened.'

He slammed the trunk shut. 'I never knew your father, but I'm told he and I are much alike. We allow our wives to do as they please, provided we're afforded the same luxury.'

Her mind filled with a swarm of confusing thoughts. 'How do you know anything of my father?'

'I told him,' a new voice said.

She whirled.

Her mother stood in the church doorway. Behind her, as always, loomed Ulrich Henn. Now she knew.

'Ulrich killed Sterling,' she said to the night.

Werner brushed by her. 'Indeed. And I daresay he might kill us all, if we don't behave.'

Malone led the way out of their hiding place, back into the octagon's upper gallery. He paused at the bronze railing – Carolingian, he recalled Christl noting, original to the time of Charlemagne – and gazed below. A handful of wall sconces burned as night-lights. Wind continued to wreak havoc against the outer walls, and the Christmas market seemed to be losing enthusiasm. He focused across the open space at the throne on the far side, backdropped by mullioned windows that splashed a luminous glow over the elevated chair. He studied the Latin mosaic that wrapped the octagon below. Einhard's challenge wasn't all that challenging.

Thank goodness for guidebooks and smart women.

He stared at Christl. 'There's a pulpit, right?'

She nodded. 'In the choir. The *ambo*. Quite old. Eleventh century.'

He smiled. 'Always a history lesson.'

She shrugged. 'It's what I know.'

He circled the upper gallery, passed the throne, and headed back down the circular staircase. Interestingly, the iron gate was left open at night. At ground level he traversed the octagon and reentered the choir. A gilded copper pulpit dotted with unique ornamentations perched against the south wall, above an entrance to another of the side chapels. A short staircase led up. He hopped a velvet rope and climbed wooden runners. Luckily what he was looking for was there. A Bible.

He laid the book on the gilded lectern and opened to Revelation. Chapter 21.

Christl stood below and gazed up at him as he read out loud.

'And he carried me away in the spirit to a great and high mountain, and showed me that great city, the holy Jerusalem, descending out of heaven from God, which had a wall great and high, and twelve gates, and at the gates twelve angels, and names written thereon, which are the names of the twelve tribes of the children of Israel. And the wall of the city had twelve

*foundations, and in them the names of the twelve apostles of
the Lamb. And he that talked with me had a golden reed to
measure the city, and the gates thereof, and the wall thereof.
And the city lieth foursquare, and the length is as large as the
breadth, and he measured the city with the reed, twelve
thousand furlongs. The length and the breadth and the height
of it are equal. And he measured the wall thereof, a hundred
and forty and four cubits, according to the measure of a man,
that is, of the angel. And the foundations of the wall of the
city were garnished with twelve precious stones. And the twelve
gates were twelve pearls.*

'Revelation is critical to this place. The chandelier
Emperor Barbarossa donated quotes from it. The mosaic
in the dome is based on it. Charlemagne specifically
called this his "new Jerusalem." And this connection is
no secret – I read about it in all the guidebooks. One
Carolingian foot equaled about one-third of a meter,
which is just a bit more than today's foot. The outer
sixteen-sided polygon is thirty-six Carolingian feet in
length. That translates to one hundred forty-four of
today's feet. The octagon's outer perimeter is the same,
thirty-six Carolingian feet, which is a hundred forty of
today's feet. The height is also precise. Originally eighty-
four of today's feet, without the helmet dome, which
came centuries later. The entire chapel is a factor of
seven and twelve, its breadth and height equal.' He
pointed to the Bible. 'They simply transposed the
dimensions of the celestial city from Revelation, the "new
Jerusalem", into this edifice.'

'That's been studied for centuries,' she said. 'How does
it relate to what we're doing?'

'Remember what Einhard wrote. *Revelations there will
be clear once the secret of that wondrous place is deciphered.*

He used that word cleverly. Not only is Revelation clear.'

He pointed to the Bible.

'But other revelations are clear, too.'

For the first time in years Dorothea felt out of control. She'd seen none of this coming. And now, standing back inside the church, facing her mother and husband, Ulrich Henn obedient and off to the side, she fought to keep her usual composure.

'Don't mourn the loss of that American,' Isabel said. 'He was an opportunist.'

She faced Werner. 'And you're not?'

'I'm your husband.'

'In name only.'

'That's by your choosing,' Isabel said, voice rising, then paused. 'I understand about Georg.' The old woman's gaze drifted toward the side chapel. 'I miss him, too. But he's gone and there's nothing any of us can do about it.'

Dorothea had always despised the way her mother dismissed grief. She never recalled a tear shed when her father disappeared. Nothing seemed to faze her. Yet Dorothea could not shake Wilkerson's lifeless gaze. True, he was an opportunist. But she'd thought their relationship might actually have developed into something more substantial.

'Why did you kill him?' she asked her mother.

'He would have brought immeasurable trouble to this family. And the Americans would have killed him eventually, anyway.'

'You're the one who involved the Americans. You wanted that file on the submarine. You had me arrange that through Wilkerson. You wanted me to get the file, make contact with Malone, and discourage him away. You wanted me

to steal Father's papers and the stones from the monastery.
I did exactly as *you* requested.'

'And did I tell you to kill the woman? No. That was
your lover's idea. Poisoned cigarettes. Ridiculous. And
what of our lodge? Now in ruin. Two men dead inside.
Men whom the Americans dispatched. Which one did you
kill, Dorothea?'

'It had to be done.'

Her mother paced the marble floor. 'Always so practical.
It had to be done. That's right, because of *your* American.
If he'd continued to be involved there would have been
devastating consequences. This did not concern him, so
I ended his participation.' Her mother stepped close, a
few inches away. 'They sent him to spy on us. I simply
encouraged you to play off his weaknesses. But you went
too far. I must say, though, I underestimated their interest
in our family.'

Dorothea pointed at Werner. 'Why did you involve
him?'

'You need assistance. He'll provide it.'

'I need nothing from him.' She paused. 'Or from you,
old woman.'

Her mother's arm swept up and slapped Dorothea's
face. 'You will not address me in such a manner. Not now.
Not ever.'

She did not move, knowing that though she might be
able to overcome her aged mother, Ulrich Henn would
be another matter. She caressed her cheek from the inside
with her tongue.

Her temple pulsed.

'I came here tonight,' Isabel said, 'to make things clear.
Werner is now part of this. I have involved him. This quest
is of my choosing. If you do not want to accept these

rules, then it can end now and your sister will be given control of everything.'

Rapier eyes appraised her. She saw that her mother had not tossed an idle threat.

'You want this, Dorothea. I know you do. You're much more like me. I've watched. You've worked hard in the family businesses, you're good at what you do. You shot that man at the lodge. You have courage, which your sister sometimes lacks. She has vision, which you sometimes ignore. A shame that the best of you both couldn't be merged into one person. Somehow, inside me long ago, everything was scrambled and, sadly, each of you has suffered.'

Dorothea stared at Werner.

She might not love him any longer but, dammit, sometimes she needed him in ways that only those who'd outlived their children could understand. Theirs was a kinship bound by grief. The numbing agony of Georg's death had erected barriers they both had learned to respect. And yet, while her marriage faltered, her life outside of it prospered. Her mother was right. Business was her passion. Ambition is a powerful drug, dulling everything, including caring.

Werner clasped his arms behind him and stood straight, like a warrior. 'Perhaps, before we die, we should enjoy what life we have left.'

'I've never known you to have a death wish. You're quite healthy and could live many years.'

'No, Dorothea. I can *breathe* for many years. Living is an entirely different matter.'

'What is it you want, Werner?'

He lowered his head and stepped close to one of the darkened windows. 'Dorothea, we're at a crossroads. The culmination of your entire life could perhaps occur in the next few days.'

'*Could?* Such confidence.'

The corners of his lips turned down. 'I meant no disrespect. Though we disagree on many matters, I'm not your enemy.'

'Who is, Werner?'

His eyes hardened like iron. 'Actually, you have no need for them. You are your own.'

Malone stepped down from the pulpit. 'Revelation is the final book of the New Testament, where John describes his vision of a new heaven, a new earth, a new reality.' He motioned into the octagon. 'That building symbolized this vision. *They will be His people and He will live among them.* That's what Revelation says. Charlemagne built this and lived here, among his people. Two things, though, were critical. The length, height, and breadth must be the same, and the walls should measure one hundred forty-four cubits. Twelve times twelve.'

'You're quite good at this,' she said.

'Eight was also an important number. The world was created in six days, and God rested on the seventh. The eighth day, when everything was completed, represented Jesus, his resurrection, the start of the glorious crowning work of completion. That's why there's an octagon encircled by a sixteen-sided polygon. Then the designers of this chapel went a step farther.

'*Clarify this pursuit by applying the angel's perfection to the lord's sanctification.* That's what Einhard said. Revelation is about angels and what they did in forming the "new Jerusalem." Twelve gates, twelve angels, twelve tribes of the children of Israel, twelve foundations, twelve apostles, twelve thousand furlongs, twelve precious stones, twelve gates were twelve pearls.' He paused. 'The number twelve, deemed perfection by the angels.'

He left the choir and reentered the octagon.

He pointed to the encircling mosaic band. 'Can you translate it? My Latin is okay, but yours is better.'

A thud echoed off the walls. Like something being forced.

Again.

He identified the direction. From one of the side chapels – St. Michael's. Where the other exit door was located.

He raced inside and rounded the empty pews toward the stout wooden door held shut with an iron latch. He heard a pop from its other side.

'They're forcing the door.'

'Who's *they*?' Christl asked.

He found his gun.

'More trouble.'

43

Dorothea needed to leave, but there was no escape. She was at the mercy of her mother and her husband. Not to mention Ulrich. Henn had worked for the family for over a decade, ostensibly making sure Reichshoffen was maintained, but she'd always suspected that he provided a wider range of services. Now she knew. This man killed.

'Dorothea,' her mother said. 'Your husband wants to make amends. He wants you two to be as you were. Obviously, there are feelings still there or you would have divorced him long ago.'

'I stayed for our son.'

'Your son is dead.'

'His memory isn't.'

'No, it's not. But you're engaged in a battle for *your* heritage. Think. Take what is being offered.'

She wanted to know, 'Why do you care?'

Isabel shook her head. 'Your sister seeks glory, vindication for our family. But that would involve much public scrutiny. You and I have never sought that. It is your duty to prevent that.'

'How did that become my duty?'

Her mother seemed disgusted. 'You are both so like your father. Is none of me inside you? Listen to me, child. The path you're taking is useless. I'm simply trying to help.'

She resented the lack of confidence and the patronizing. 'I learned a good deal from reading those Ahnenerbe periodicals and memos. Grandfather wrote an account of what they saw in Antarctica.'

'Hermann was a dreamer, a man rooted in fantasy.'

'He spoke of areas where the snow gave way to rock. Where liquid lakes existed where none should be. He talked about hollow mountains and ice caves.'

'And what have we to show for all those fantasies? Tell me, Dorothea. Are we any closer to finding anything?'

'We have a dead man in the trunk of the car outside.'

Her mother exhaled a long breath. 'You are hopeless.'

But her patience had worn thin, too. 'You set the rules of this challenge. You wanted to know what happened to Father. You wanted Christl and me to work together. You gave us each part of the puzzle. If you're so damn smart, why are *we* doing all this?'

'Let me tell you something. What your father told me long ago.'

Charlemagne listened in awe as Einhard spoke. They were safe inside the palace chapel, in the room he maintained in the octagon's upper gallery. A summer's night had finally arrived, the exterior windows dark, the chapel equally quiet. Einhard had only yesterday returned from his long journey. The king admired him. A tiny man but, like the bee that makes fine honey or a busy ant, capable of great things. He called him Bezalell, from Exodus, a reference to his great workmanship. No one else would he have sent, and now he listened as Einhard told him of an arduous sea voyage to a place with walls of snow so luminous that sunlight cast their heights in shades of blue and jade green. On one a waterfall formed, the flow of it like silver, and Charlemagne was reminded of the jagged mountains in the south and east. Cold beyond believing, Einhard said, and one of his hands shivered with the memory. The wind blew with such force that not even the chapel surrounding them could have survived. Charlemagne doubted that claim, but did not challenge him. People here live in mud huts, Einhard said, no windows, only a hole in the roof to let smoke escape. Beds are used only by the privileged, clothes are unlined leather. There, it is so different. Houses are all of stone and furnished and heated. Clothes are thick and warm. No social classes, no wealth, no poverty. A land of equals where night comes without end and the water remains still as death, but so beautiful.

'That's what Einhard wrote,' Isabel said. 'Your father told me, as his father told him. It came from the book I gave you, the one from Charlemagne's grave. Hermann learned to read it. Now we must as well. That's why I set this challenge. I want you and your sister to find the answers we need.'

But the book her mother had given her was penned in gibberish, full of fantastical images of unrecognizable things.

'Remember the words of Einhard's will,' Isabel said. '*A full comprehension of the wisdom of heaven waiting with Lord Charles begins in the new Jerusalem.* Your sister is there, right now, in the new Jerusalem, many steps ahead of you.'

She could not believe what she was hearing.

'This is not fiction, Dorothea. The past is not all fiction. The word *heaven* in the time of Charlemagne had a much different meaning than today. The Carolingians called it *ha shemin.* It meant "highlands." We're not talking about religion or God, we're talking about a people who existed far off, in a mountainous land of snow and ice and endless nights. A place Einhard visited. A place where *your* father died. Don't you want to know why?'

She did. Damn her, she did.

'Your husband is here to help,' her mother said. 'I eliminated a potential problem with Herr Wilkerson. Now this quest can continue without interference. I'll make sure the Americans find his body.'

'It wasn't necessary to kill him,' she declared again.

'Wasn't it? Yesterday a man burst into our home and tried to kill Herr Malone. He mistook your sister for you and tried to kill her. Thankfully, Ulrich prevented that from happening. The Americans have little regard for you, Dorothea.'

Her eyes sought and found Henn, who nodded, signaling that what her mother had said was true.

'I knew then that something must be done. Since you are a creature of habit, I found you in Munich where I knew you'd be. Imagine, if I could find you so easily, how long would it have taken the Americans?'

She recalled Wilkerson's panic on the phone.

'I did what needed to be done. Now, child, you do the same.'

But she was at a loss. 'What am I to do? You said I was wasting my time with what I obtained.'

Her mother shook her head. 'I'm sure the knowledge you gained on the Ahnenerbe will be helpful. Are the materials in Munich?'

She nodded.

'I'll have Ulrich retrieve them. Your sister will shortly follow the correct path – it is imperative you join her. She must be tempered. Our family secrets must stay within the family.'

'Where is Christl?' she asked again.

'Attempting what you were trying to do.'

She waited.

'Trusting an American.'

44

Aachen

Malone grabbed Christl and fled St. Michael's Chapel, rushing back into the outer polygon. He turned for the porch and the main entrance.

More pops came from St. Michael's.

He found the main exit doors, which he hoped opened from the inside, and heard a noise. Somebody was forcing the outer latches. Apparently Hatchet Face didn't work alone.

'What's happening?' Christl asked.

'Our friends from last night found us. They've been following all day.'

'And you're just now mentioning it?'

He fled the entranceway and reentered the octagon. His eyes searched the dim interior. 'I figured you didn't want to be bothered with details.'

'Details?'

He heard the door within St. Michael's give way. Behind him, the squeak of ancient hinges confirmed that the main doors had been flung open. He spied the stairway and they raced up the circular risers, all caution abandoned for speed.

He heard voices from below and motioned for quiet.

He needed Christl somewhere safe, so they sure as hell

couldn't be parading around the upper gallery. The imperial throne sat before him. Beneath the crude marble chair was a dark opening where pilgrims once passed, he recalled the guide explaining – a hollow space beneath the bier and six stone steps. Below the altar that jutted from the rear was another opening, this one shielded by a wooden door with iron clasps. He motioned for her to crawl under the throne. She responded with a quizzical look. He wasn't in the mood to argue, so he jerked her toward the iron chain and pointed for her to crawl underneath.

Stay quiet, he mouthed.

Footsteps sounded from the winding staircase. They'd only have a few more seconds. She seemed to realize their predicament and relented, disappearing beneath the throne.

He needed to draw them away. Earlier, when he'd surveyed the upper gallery, he'd noticed a narrow ledge with a profile that ran above the lower arches, marking the dividing line between the floors, wide enough to stand on.

He crept past the throne, rounded the bier, and hopped the waist-high bronze grille. He balanced himself on the cornice, spine rigid against the upper pillars that supported the eight arches of the inner octagon. Thankfully, the pillars were two joined together, a couple of feet wide, which meant he had four feet of marble shielding him.

He heard rubber soles sweep onto the upper gallery's floor.

He began to rethink what he was doing, standing on a ledge ten inches wide, holding a gun with only five rounds, a good twenty-foot drop below. He risked one peek and saw two forms on the far side of the throne.

One of the armed men advanced behind the bier, the other assumed a position on the far side – one probing, the other covering. The smart tactic showed training.

He pressed his head back against the marble and stared out across the octagon. Light from the windows behind the throne cast a glow on the shiny pillars of the far side, and the fuzzy shadow of the imperial chair was clearly visible. He watched as another shadow circled behind the throne, now on the side closest to where he stood.

He needed to draw the attacker closer.

Carefully, his left hand searched his jacket pocket and found a euro coin from the restaurant. He removed it, dropped his hand to one side, then gently tossed the coin in front of the bronze grille, finding the ledge ten feet away, where the next set of pillars rose. The coin tinkled, then dropped to the marble floor below, a ding echoing through the silence. He was hoping that the gunmen would realize he was the source and come forward, looking left, while he struck from the right.

But that didn't take into account what the other armed man would do.

The shadow on his side of the throne grew in size.

He'd have to time the move perfectly. He switched the gun from his right hand to his left.

The shadow approached the grille.

A gun appeared.

Malone pivoted, grabbed the man's coat, and yanked him out over the rail.

The body flew into the octagon.

Malone rolled over the railing as a shot popped and a bullet from the other gunman smacked off the marble. He heard the body slam into the floor twenty feet below, chairs clattering away. He fired one shot across the throne then used the momentum he'd generated to hustle to his feet and find refuge behind the marble pillar, only this time in the gallery as opposed to the ledge.

But his right foot slipped and his knee banged the floor. His spine vibrated with pain. He shook it off and tried to regain his balance, but he'd lost any advantage.

'*Nein,* Herr Malone,' a man said.

He was on all fours, holding the gun.

'Stand,' the man ordered.

He slowly came to his feet.

Hatchet Face had rounded the throne and now stood on the side closest to Malone.

'Drop the weapon,' the man ordered.

He wasn't going to surrender that easily. 'Who do you work for?'

'Drop the weapon.'

He needed to stall but doubted this man was going to allow too many more questions. Behind Hatchet Face, near the floor, something moved. He spotted two soles, toes pointed upward, in the darkness beneath the throne. Christl's legs sprang from her hiding place and slammed into Hatchet Face's knees.

The gunman, caught by surprise, crumpled backward.

Malone used the moment to fire, a bullet thudding into the man's chest. Hatchet Face cried in pain, but seemed to immediately regain his senses, raising his gun. Malone fired again and the man sank to the floor, not moving.

Christl wiggled out from under the bier.

'You're a gutsy lady,' he said.

'You needed help.'

His knee ached. 'Actually, I did.'

He checked for a pulse but found none. Then he walked to the railing and glanced down. The other gunman's body lay contorted among a rubble of chairs, blood oozing onto the marble floor.

Christl came close. For a woman who hadn't wanted to see the corpse in the monastery, she seemed to have no problem with these.

'What now?' she asked.

He pointed below. 'Like I asked you before we were interrupted, I need you to translate that Latin inscription.'

45

Ramsey showed his credentials and drove into Fort Lee. The trip south from Washington had taken a little over two hours. The base was one of sixteen army cantonments built at the outset of World War I, named for Virginia's favorite son, Robert E. Lee. Torn down in the 1920s and converted into a state wildlife sanctuary, the site was reactivated in 1940 and became a bustling center of war activity. Over the past twenty years, thanks to its proximity to Washington, its facilities had been both expanded and modernized.

He wound a path through a maze of training and command facilities that accommodated a variety of army needs, mainly logistics and management support. The navy leased three warehouses in a far corner among a row of military storage units. Access to them was restricted by numeric locks and digital verification. Two of the warehouses were managed by the navy's central command, the third by naval intelligence.

He parked and left the car, drawing his coat closely around his shoulders. He stepped beneath a metal porch and punched in a code, then slid his thumb into the digital scanner.

The door clicked open.

He entered a small anteroom whose overhead lights activated with his presence. He walked to a bank of switches and illuminated the cavernous space beyond, visible through a plate-glass window.

When had he last visited? Six years ago?

No, more like eight or nine.

But his first visit had been thirty-eight years ago. He noticed that things inside weren't much different, besides the modern security. Admiral Dyals had brought him initially. Another blustery winter day. February. About two months after he returned from the Antarctic.

'We're here for a reason,' Dyals said.

He'd wondered about the trip. He'd spent a lot of time at the warehouse the past month, but all that abruptly ended a few days ago when the mission was disbanded. Rowland and Sayers had returned to their units, the warehouse itself had been sealed, and he'd been reassigned to the Pentagon. On the ride south from Washington the admiral had said little. Dyals was like that. Many feared this man – not from temper, which he rarely displayed, nor from verbal abuse, which he avoided as disrespectful. More from an icy stare of eyes that never seemed to blink.

'Did you study the file on Operation Highjump?' Dyals asked. 'The one I provided.'

'In detail.'

'And what did you notice?'

'That where I was in Antarctica corresponded precisely to a location the Highjump team explored.'

Three days ago Dyals had handed him a file marked HIGHLY CLASSIFIED. *The information contained inside was not part of the official record that Admirals Cruzen and Byrd filed after their Antarctic mission. Instead the report was from* a team of army specialists who'd been included among the forty-seven hundred men assigned to Highjump. Byrd himself had commanded them on a special reconnaissance of the northern shoreline. Their reports had only been provided to Byrd, who'd personally briefed the then chief of naval operations. What he'd read amazed him.

'Before Highjump,' Dyals said, 'we were convinced the Germans had constructed Antarctic bases in the 1940s. U-boats had been all over the South Atlantic both during and shortly after the war. The Germans mounted a major exploratory mission there in 1938. Had plans to return. We thought they did and just didn't tell anybody. But it was all crap, Langford. Pure crap. The Nazis didn't go to Antarctica to establish bases.'

He waited.

'They went to find their past.'

Dyals led the way into the warehouse and threaded a path through wooden crates and metal shelving. He stopped and pointed to one row of shelves loaded with rocks covered with a curious mixture of swirls and curlicues.

'Our people in Highjump located some of what the Nazis found in '38. The Germans were following information they'd uncovered that dated back to the time of Charlemagne. One of their own, Hermann Oberhauser, discovered it.'

He recognized the surname, from NR-1A's crew. Dietz Oberhauser, field specialist.

'We approached Dietz Oberhauser about a year ago,' Dyals said. 'Some of our R and D folks were researching German archives captured from the war. The Germans thought that *there might be things to learn in Antarctica. Hermann Oberhauser became convinced that an advanced culture, one that predated our own, lived there. He thought they were long-lost Aryans, and Hitler and Himmler wanted to know if he was right. They also thought that if the civilization was more advanced they might know useful things. In those days, everyone was looking for a break.'*

'Which hadn't changed.

'But Oberhauser fell out of favor. Pissed Hitler off. So he was silenced and shunned. His ideas abandoned.'

Ramsey pointed to the rocks. 'Apparently he was right. There was something to find.'

'You read the file. You were there. Tell me, what do you believe?'

'We didn't find anything like this.'

'Yet the United States spent millions of dollars to send nearly five thousand men to Antarctica. Four men died during that venture. Now eleven more are dead and we've lost a hundred-million-dollar submarine. Come now, Ramsey. Think.'

He didn't want to disappoint this man who'd shown so much confidence in his abilities.

'Imagine a culture,' Dyals said, 'that developed tens of thousands of years before anything we know. Before the Sumerians, the Chinese, the Egyptians. Astronomical observations and measurement, weights, volumes, a realistic concept of the earth, advanced cartography, spherical geometry, navigational skills, mathematics. Let's say they excelled in all these centuries before we ever did. Can you imagine what they may have learned? Dietz Oberhauser told us that his father went to Antarctica in 1938. Saw things, learned things. The Nazis were total fools – pedantic, parochial, arrogant – so they couldn't appreciate what all that meant.'

'But it seems, Admiral, that we too suffered from ignorance.

I read the file. The conclusions from Highjump were that these stones, here in the warehouse, were from some sort of ancient race, perhaps an Aryan race. Everybody seemed concerned about that. It seems we bought into the myth the Nazis formulated about themselves.'

'We did, which was our mistake. But that was a different time. Truman's people thought the whole thing too political to deal with publicly. They didn't want anything around that lent any credence to Hitler or the Germans. So they stamped TOP SECRET on the whole Highjump venture and sealed everything away. But we did ourselves a great disservice.'

Dyals pointed ahead, at a closed steel door. 'Let me show you what you never saw while you were here.'

Ramsey now faced the same door.

A refrigerated compartment.

The one he'd entered thirty-eight years ago for the first and only time. That day Admiral Dyals had issued him an order – one he'd followed ever since – *leave him alone*. That order had now been rescinded but, before he acted, he'd come to make sure they were still here.

He grasped the latch.

46

Aachen

Malone and Christl descended to ground level. The bag that held the guidebooks lay on an unmolested wooden chair. He found one of the booklets and located a translation of the Latin mosaic.

IF THE LIVING STONES SHOULD FIT TOGETHER IN UNITY
IF THE NUMBERS AND DIMENSIONS SHOULD CORRESPOND
THEN THE WORK OF THE LORD WHO ERECTED
THIS GREAT HALL
WILL SHINE BRIGHTLY AND GRANT
SUCCESS TO THE PIOUS ENDEAVORS OF MAN
WHOSE WORKS ALWAYS REMAIN AS AN EVERLASTING
ORNAMENT
IF THE ALMIGHTY ADVISER PROTECTS AND WATCHES OVER IT
SO MAY GOD LET THIS WHOLE TEMPLE EXIST
ON THE FIRM FOUNDATION LAID BY EMPEROR CHARLES

He handed the pamphlet to Christl. 'Is this right?' He'd noticed in the restaurant that a few of the other books contained translations, each one slightly different.

She studied the text, then scanned the mosaic, comparing back and forth. The body lay a few feet away, limbs contorted at odd angles, blood on the floor, and they both seemed to pretend that it wasn't there. He wondered about the gunshots, but doubted with the thickness of the walls and the wind outside that anyone had heard. At least no one had come to investigate so far.

'It's correct,' she said. 'A few minor variations, but nothing that changes the meaning.'

'You told me earlier that the inscription is original, only it's a mosaic instead of paint. The chapel's consecration – which is another word for "sanctification." *Clarify this pursuit by applying the angel's perfection to the lord's sanctification.* The number twelve is the angel's perfection, from Revelation. This octagon was a symbol of that perfection.' He pointed at the mosaic. 'Could be every twelfth letter, but my guess is count every twelfth word.'

A cross signified where the inscription began and ended. He watched as she counted.

'*Claret,*' she said, coming to twelve. Then she found two more words in the twenty-fourth and thirty-sixth positions. *Quorum. Deus.* 'That's all. The last word, *velit,* is number eleven.'

'Interesting, wouldn't you say? Three words, the last stopping at eleven so there'd be no more.'

'*Claret quorum deus.* Brightness of God.'

'Congratulations,' he said. 'You just clarified the pursuit.'

'You already knew, didn't you?'

He shrugged. 'I tried it at the restaurant with one of the translations and found the same three words.'

'You could have mentioned that, along with the fact we were being followed.'

'I could have, but you could have mentioned something, too.'

She tossed him a perplexed look, but he wasn't buying, so he asked, 'Why are you playing me?'

Dorothea stared at her mother. 'You know where Christl is?'

Isabel nodded. 'I watch over both of my daughters.'

She tried to keep her features placid, but a growing anger complicated the task.

'Your sister teamed up with Herr Malone.'

The words stung her. 'You had me send him away. You said he was a problem.'

'He was and still is, but your sister spoke with him after he met with you.'

A feeling of worry passed into foolishness. 'You arranged that?'

Her mother nodded. 'You had Herr Wilkerson. I gave her Malone.'

Her body seemed numb, her mind paralyzed.

'Your sister is in Aachen, at Charlemagne's chapel, doing what needs to be done. Now you must do the same.'

Her mother's face remained impassive. Where her father had been carefree, loving, warm, her mother stayed disciplined, distant, aloof. Nannies had raised both Christl and her, and they'd always craved their mother's attention, competing for what little affection there was to enjoy. Which she'd always thought accounted for much of their animosity – each daughter's desire to be special, complicated by the fact that they were identical.

'Is this just a game for you?' she asked.

'It is far more than that. It is time my daughters grow up.'

'I despise you.'

'Finally – anger. If that will keep you from doing stupid things then by God hate me.'

Dorothea had reached her limit and advanced toward her mother. But Ulrich stepped between them. Her mother held up a hand and stopped him, as she would a trained animal, and Henn stepped back.

'What would you do?' her mother asked. 'Attack me?'

'If I could.'

'And would that obtain what you want?'

The question halted her. Negative emotions ebbed away, leaving only guilt. As always.

A smile crept onto her mother's lips. 'You must listen to me, Dorothea. I have truly come to help.'

Werner watched with a tempered reserve. Dorothea pointed his way. 'You killed Wilkerson and now have given me him. Does Christl get to keep her American?'

'That would not be fair. Though Werner is your husband, he's not a former American agent. I'll deal with it tomorrow.'

'And how do you know where he'll be tomorrow?'

'That's just it, child. I know precisely where he'll be and I'm about to tell you.'

'You have two master's degrees, yet Einhard's will was a problem for you?' Malone asked Christl. 'Get real. You already knew all of this.'

'I won't deny that.'

'I'm an idiot for getting myself in the middle of this disaster. I've killed three people in the past twenty-four hours because of your family.'

She sat in one of the chairs. 'I was able to solve the pursuit to this point. You're right. It was relatively easy. But to someone living in the Dark Ages it was probably insurmountable. So few people then were literate. I have to say, I was curious to see how good you were.'

'Did I pass?'

'Quite well.'

'*But only those who appreciate the throne of Solomon and Roman frivolity shall find their way to heaven.* That's next, so where to?'

'Whether you believe me or not, I don't know the answer. I stopped at this point three days ago and returned to Bavaria—'

'To await me?'

'Mother called me home and told me what Dorothea was planning.'

He needed to make something clear. 'I'm here only because of *my* father. I stayed because somebody is upset that I got a peek at that file, and that reaches straight to Washington.'

'I didn't factor into your decision in any way?'

'One kiss does not make a relationship.'

'And I thought you enjoyed it.'

Time for a reality check. 'Since we both know this much of the pursuit, we can now solve the rest separately.'

He headed toward the exit doors, but stopped at the body. How many people had he killed through the years? Too many. But always for a reason. God and country. Duty and honor.

What about this time?

No answer.

He stared back at Christl Falk, who sat unconcerned. And he left.

47

Stephanie and Edwin Davis huddled in the woods fifty yards from Herbert Rowland's lakeside house. Rowland had arrived home fifteen minutes ago and hurried inside carrying a pizza box. He'd immediately come back out and retrieved three logs from the woodpile. Smoke now puffed from a rough-hacked stone chimney. She wished they had a fire.

They'd spent a couple of hours during the afternoon buying additional winter clothes, thick gloves, and wool caps. They'd also stocked up on snacks and drink, then returned and assumed a position where they could safely watch the house. Davis doubted the killer would return before nightfall, but wanted to be in position just in case.

'He's in for the night,' Davis said, keeping his voice to a whisper.

Though the trees blocked a breeze, the dry air was chilling by the minute. Darkness crept slowly over them in an almost amoebic flow. Their new clothes were all hunter's garb, everything high-tech insulated. She'd never hunted in her life and had felt odd purchasing the stuff at a camping supply store near one of Charlotte's upscale shopping malls.

They nestled at the base of a stout evergreen on a bed

of pine needles. She was munching a Twix bar. Candy was her weakness. One drawer of her desk in Atlanta was filled with temptations.

She was still unsure they were doing the right thing.

'We should call the Secret Service,' she said in a hushed whisper.

'You always so negative?'

'You shouldn't dismiss the idea so quickly.'

'This is my fight.'

'Seems to be mine now, too.'

'Herbert Rowland is in trouble. There's no way he'd believe us if we knocked on the front door and told him. Neither would the Secret Service. We have nothing for proof.'

'Except the guy in the house today.'

'What guy? Who is he? Tell me what we know.'

She couldn't.

'We're going to have to catch him in the act,' he said.

'Because you think he killed Millicent?'

'He did.'

'How about you tell me what's really happening here. Millicent has nothing to do with a dead admiral, Zachary Alexander, or Operation Highjump. This is more than some personal vendetta.'

'Ramsey is the common denominator. You know that.'

'Actually, all I know is I have agents who are trained to do this kind of thing, yet here I am freezing my ass off with a White House staffer who has a chip on his shoulder.'

She finished her candy bar.

'You like those things?' he asked.

'That's not going to work.'

'Because I think they're terrible. Now, Baby Ruth. That's a candy bar.'

She reached into her shopping bag and found one. 'I agree.'

He plucked it from her grasp. 'Don't mind if I do.'

She grinned. Davis was both irritating and intriguing. 'Why have you never married?' she asked.

'How do you know that I haven't?'

'It's obvious.'

He seemed to appreciate her perception. 'Never became an issue.'

She wondered whose fault that had been.

'I work,' he said, as he chewed the candy. 'And I didn't want the pain.'

That she could understand. Her own marriage had been a disaster, ending in a long estrangement, followed by her husband's suicide fifteen years ago. A long time to be alone. But Edwin Davis might be one of the few who understood.

'There's more than pain,' she said. 'Lots of joy there, too.'

'But there's always pain. That's the problem.'

She nestled closer to the tree.

'After Millicent died,' Davis said, 'I was assigned to London. I found a cat one day. Sickly. Pregnant. I took her to the vet who saved her, but not the kittens. After, I took the cat back home. Good animal. Never once would she scratch you. Kind. Loving. I enjoyed having her. Then one day she up and died. It hurt. Real bad. I decided then and there that things I love tend to die. So. No more for me.'

'Sounds fatalistic.'

'More realistic.'

Her cell phone vibrated against her chest. She checked the display – Atlanta calling – and clicked on. After listening a moment, she said, 'Connect him.'

'It's Cotton,' she said to Davis. 'Time he knows what's happening.'

But Davis just kept eating, staring at the house.

'Stephanie,' Malone said in her ear. 'Did you find what I need to know?'

'Things have become complicated.' And, shielding her mouth, she told him some of what had happened. Then she asked, 'The file?'

'Probably gone.'

And she listened as he recounted what had happened in Germany.

'What are you doing now?' Malone asked her.

'You wouldn't believe me if I told you.'

'Considering the dumb-ass things I've done the past two days, I could believe anything.'

She told him.

'I'd say it's not so stupid,' Malone said. 'I'm standing in the freezing cold myself, outside a Carolingian church. Davis is right. That guy will be back.'

'That's what I'm afraid of.'

'Somebody is awfully interested in *Blazek*, or NR-1A, or whatever the damn sub should be called.' Malone's annoyance seemed to have given way to uncertainty. 'If the White House said naval intelligence inquired, that means Ramsey's involved. We're on parallel courses, Stephanie.'

'I got a guy here munching on a Baby Ruth who says the same thing. I hear you two have talked.'

'Anytime somebody saves my ass, I'm grateful.'

She recalled central Asia, too, but needed to know, 'Where's your path leading, Cotton?'

'Good question. I'll get back to you. Careful there.'

'Same to you.'

*   *   *

Malone clicked off the phone. He stood at the far end of the courtyard that accommodated the Christmas market, at the high point of the slope, near Aachen's town hall, facing the chapel a hundred yards off. The snowy building glowed a phosphorescent green. More snow fell in silence, but at least the wind had died.

He checked his watch. Nearly eleven thirty.

All of the booths were shut tight, the swirling currents of voices and bodies silent and still until tomorrow. Only a few people milled about. Christl had not followed him from the chapel and, after speaking with Stephanie, he was even more confused.

Brightness of God.

The term had to be relevant to Einhard's time. Something with a clear meaning. Did the words still possess any significance?

Easy way to find out.

He punched SAFARI on his iPhone, connected to the Internet, and accessed Google. He typed BRIGHTNESS OF GOD EINHARD and pressed SEARCH.

The screen flickered, then displayed the first twenty-five hits.

The top one answered his question.

48

S tephanie heard thrashing. Not loud, but steady enough for her to know somebody was out there. Davis had dozed off. She'd allowed him to sleep. He needed it. He was troubled and she wanted to help, as Malone had helped her, but she continued to question if what they were doing was smart.

She held a gun, her eyes searching the darkness through trees, into the clearing that surrounded Rowland's house. The windows had been quiet for at least two hours. Her ears grabbed the night and she caught another snap. Off to the right. Pine boughs rustled. She pinpointed the location. Maybe fifty yards away.

She laid her hand over Davis' mouth and tapped his shoulder with the gun. He came awake with a start, and she pressed her palm firm across his lips.

'Company,' she whispered.

He nodded in understanding.

She pointed.

Another snap.

Then movement, near Rowland's truck. A dark shadow appeared and merged into the trees, was lost completely for a moment, then there again, heading toward the house.

*   *   *

Charlie Smith approached the front door. Herbert Rowland's cabin had been dark long enough.

He'd spent the afternoon at the movies and enjoyed the steak at Ruth's Chris he'd been craving. All in all, a fairly peaceful day. He'd read newspaper accounts of Admiral David Sylvian's death, pleased that there was no indication of foul play. He'd returned two hours ago and assumed a vigil in the cold woods, waiting.

But everything seemed quiet.

He entered the house through the front door, the lock and dead bolt ridiculously easy to pick, and embraced the central heat inside. He crept first to the refrigerator and checked the insulin vial. The level was definitely lower. He knew each one contained four injections and he estimated another quarter of the saline was gone. With gloved hands, he deposited the vial into a Baggie.

He assessed the chilled whiskey bottles and noticed that one was also noticeably lower. Herbert Rowland had apparently enjoyed his nightly libation. In the kitchen garbage he found a spent syringe and dropped it in the Baggie.

He stepped lightly into the bedroom.

Rowland was nestled under a patchwork quilt, breathing sporadically. He checked the pulse. Slow. The clock on the nightstand read nearly one a.m. Probably seven hours had passed since injection. The file said Rowland medicated himself every night before the six o'clock news, then started drinking. With no insulin in his blood tonight, the alcohol had worked fast, inducing a deep diabetic coma. Death would not be far behind.

He hauled over a chair from one corner. He'd have to stay until Rowland died. But he decided not to be foolish. The two people from earlier still weighed on his mind, so he returned to the den and grabbed two of the hunting guns he'd noticed earlier. One of them was a beauty. A Mossberg high-velocity bolt-action. Seven-shot clip, high caliber, equipped with an impressive telescopic scope. The other was a Remington 12-gauge. One of the commemorative Ducks Unlimited models, if he wasn't mistaken. He'd almost bought one himself. A cabinet beneath the gun rack was filled with shells. He loaded both weapons and returned to his bedside post.

Now he was ready.

Stephanie grabbed Davis by the arm. He was already on his feet ready to advance. 'What are you doing?'

'We have to go.'

'And what is it we're going to do when we get there?'

'Stop him. He's killing that man right now.'

She knew he was right.

'I'll take the front door,' she said. 'The only other way out is through the glass doors on the deck. You cover that. Let's see if we can scare the hell out him and cause a mistake.'

Davis headed off.

She followed, wondering if her ally had ever faced a threat like this before. If not, he was one bold son of a bitch. If so, he was an idiot.

They found the graveled drive and hustled toward the house, making little noise. Davis rounded toward the lake and she watched as he tiptoed up wooden risers to the elevated deck. She saw that the sliding glass doors were curtained on the inside. Davis quietly moved to the opposite side of the deck. Satisfied he was in position, she walked to the front door and decided to take the direct approach.

She banged hard on the door.

Then fled the porch.

Smith bolted up from the chair. Somebody had pounded on the front door. Then he heard thumping, from the deck. More knocking. On the glass doors.

'Come out here, you bastard,' a man screamed.

Herbert Rowland heard nothing. His breath remained labored as his body continued to shut down.

Smith carried both guns and turned for the den.

Stephanie heard Davis scream a challenge.

What in the world?

Smith rushed into the den, laid the rifle on the kitchen counter, and fired two shotgun blasts into the curtains that draped the sliding glass doors. Cold air rushed in as the glass was obliterated. He used the moment of confusion to retreat to the kitchen, crouching behind the bar.

Shots from his right, in the den, sent him hurtling to the floor.

Stephanie fired into the window adjacent to the front door. She followed with another shot. Maybe that would be enough to divert the intruder's attention from the deck, where Davis stood unarmed.

She'd heard two shotgun blasts. She'd planned on simply surprising the killer with the fact that people were outside and wait for him to fumble.

Davis apparently had another idea.

Smith was not accustomed to being cornered. The same two from earlier? Had to be. Police? Hardly. They'd knocked on the door, for God's sake. One of them even called out, inviting a fight. No, these two were something else. But the analysis could wait. Right now he just needed to get his butt out of here.

What would MacGyver do?

He loved that show.

Use your brain.

Stephanie retreated from the porch and darted toward the deck, careful with the windows, using Rowland's truck for cover. She kept her gun aimed at the house, ready to fire. No way to know if it was safe enough to advance, but she needed to find Davis. The grim threat they'd uncovered had quickly escalated.

She trotted past the house, found the stairs that led up to the deck, and arrived just in time to see Edwin Davis hurl what appeared to be a wrought-iron chair into the glass doors.

Smith heard something crash through the remaining glass and rip the curtains from the wall. He leveled the shotgun and fired another blast, then used the moment to grab the sport rifle and flee the kitchen, reentering the bedroom. Whoever was out there would have to hesitate, and he needed to use those few seconds to maximum advantage.

Herbert Rowland still lay in the bed. If he wasn't dead already, he was well on the way. But no evidence of any crime was present. The tampered vial and syringe were safe in his pocket. True, guns had been used, but there was nothing leading to his identity.

He found one of the bedroom windows and lifted the lower pane. Quickly he curled himself out. No one seemed to be on this side of the house. He eased the window shut.

He should deal with whoever was here, but far too many chances had already been taken.

He decided the smart play was the only play.

Rifle in hand, he plunged into the woods.

'Are you completely nuts?' Stephanie screamed at Davis from the ground.

Her compatriot remained on the deck.

'He's gone,' Davis said.

She carefully climbed the stairs, not trusting a word he said.

'I heard a window open, then close.'

'That doesn't mean he's gone, it just means a window opened and closed.'

Davis stepped through the destroyed glass doors.

'Edwin—'

He disappeared into the blackness and she rushed in behind him. He was headed for the bedroom. A light switched on and she came to the door. Davis was taking Herbert Rowland's pulse.

'Barely beating. And he apparently didn't hear a thing. He's in a coma.'

She was still concerned about a man with a shotgun. Davis reached for the phone and she saw him punch three numbers.

911.

49

Ramsey heard the front door chime. He smiled. He'd been sitting patiently, reading a thriller by David Morrell, one of his favorite writers. He closed the book and allowed his late-night visitor to sweat a little. Finally, he stood, walked into the foyer, and opened the door.

Senator Aatos Kane stood outside in the cold.

'You sorry no good—' Kane said.

He shrugged. 'Actually, I thought my response was rather mild considering the rudeness I was shown by your aide.'

Kane stormed inside.

Ramsey did not offer to take the senator's coat. Apparently, the map store operative had already done as instructed, sending a message through Kane's aide, the same insolent prick who'd strong-armed him on the Capitol Mall, that she possessed information concerning the disappearance of an aide who'd worked for Kane three years ago. That woman had been an attractive redhead from Michigan who'd tragically fallen victim to a serial killer who had plagued the DC area. The mass murderer was eventually found, after committing suicide, the whole affair making headlines across the country.

'You sorry bastard,' Kane screamed. 'You said it was over.'

'Let's sit down.'

'I don't want to sit. I want to punch your lights out.'

'Which will change nothing.' He loved twisting the knife. 'I'll still have the upper hand. So you have to ask yourself. Do you want to have a chance to be president? Or would you prefer certain disgrace?'

Kane's anger was accompanied by a clear uneasiness. The view from inside the trap looking out was quite different.

They continued to exchange hard glances, like two lions deciding on who should feast first. Finally, Kane nodded. Ramsey led the senator into the den, where they sat. The room was small, which forced an awkward intimacy. Kane seemed uncomfortable, as he should be.

'I came to you last night, and this morning, to ask for help,' Ramsey said. 'A sincere request made to, what I thought, was a friend.' He paused. 'I was offered nothing in return but arrogance. Your aide was rude and obnoxious. Of course, he was simply doing as you instructed. Hence, my response.'

'You're a deceitful bastard.'

'And you're a cheating husband who managed to conceal his mistake with the convenient death of a serial killer. You even extracted, as I recall, public sympathy for your aide's tragic demise by displaying outrage at her fate. What would your constituents, your family, think if they knew she'd recently aborted a pregnancy – and you were the father?'

'There's no proof of that.'

'Yet you sure were panicked at the time.'

'You know that she could have ruined me, whether I was the father or not. Her allegations would have been all that mattered.'

Ramsey sat ramrod-straight. Admiral Dyals had taught him how to clearly convey who was in charge.

'And your lover knew that,' he said, 'which is why she was able to manipulate you, which is again why you were so appreciative of my help.'

The memory of his past predicament seemed to calm Kane's anger. 'I had no idea what you planned. I would have never agreed to what you actually did.'

'Really? It was the smart play. We killed her, framed another killer, then killed him. As I recall, the press applauded the outcome. The suicide saved a trial and execution and made for some terrific news stories.' He paused. 'And I don't recall a single objection voiced by you at the time.'

He knew that the most dangerous threat any politician faced was an accusation from a supposed lover. So many had been brought down in such a simple manner. It didn't matter if the allegations were unproven or even patently false. All that mattered was they existed.

Kane sat back in the chair. 'I had little choice once I realized what you'd done. What do you want, Ramsey?'

No *Admiral,* nor even the courtesy of a first name. 'I want to ensure that I become the next member of the Joint Chiefs of Staff. I thought I made that clear today.'

'Do you know how many others want that job?'

'Several, I'm sure. But, you see, Aatos, I *created* that vacancy, so it should rightfully be mine.'

Kane stared at him with uncertainty, digesting the admission. 'I should have known.'

'I'm telling you this for three reasons. First, I know

you're not going to tell anyone. Second, you need to understand who you are dealing with. And third, I know you want to be president. The experts say you have a reasonable shot. The party supports you, your poll numbers are excellent, the competition is unimpressive. You have the contacts and the means to raise contributions. I'm told that, privately, you have an assurance of thirty million dollars as seed money from a variety of donors.'

'You've been busy,' Kane said with an air of pained politeness.

'You're reasonably young, in good health, your wife supports you in every way. Your children adore you. All in all, you'd make quite the candidate.'

'Except that I screwed a staffer three years ago, she got pregnant, aborted the baby, and then decided she loved me.'

'Something like that. Unfortunately, for her, she fell victim to a mass murderer, one who, in the throes of insanity, took his own life. Thankfully, he left quite a bit of evidence behind that linked him to all of the crimes, hers included, so a potential disaster for you turned into a plus.'

And Ramsey had wisely hedged his bets by obtaining the abortion records from the South Texas clinic and a copy of the videotaped mandatory counseling session Texas law required before any abortion could be performed. The staffer, though using false identification, had broken down and told the counselor, without naming names, of an affair with her employer. Not a lot of details, but enough to play well on *Inside Edition, Extra,* or *The Maury Show* – and utterly ruin Aatos Kane's chances for the White House.

The operative from the map store had done well,

making clear to Kane's chief of staff that she was that counselor. She wanted to speak with the senator or she planned on calling Fox News, which never seemed to have anything good to say about Kane. Reputations. More fragile than fine crystal.

'You killed Sylvian?' Kane asked.

'What do you think?'

Kane was studying him with an undisguised contempt. But he was so anxious, so willing, so pathetic, that his resistance immediately eroded. 'Okay, I think I can make the appointment happen. Daniels needs me.'

Ramsey's face relaxed into a reassuring smile. 'I knew that to be the case. Now let's discuss the other thing.'

No wit, humor, sympathy invaded his eyes.

'What other thing?'

'I will be your running mate.'

Kane laughed. 'You're insane.'

'Actually, I'm not. The next presidential race is not going to be difficult to predict. Three candidates, maybe four, none in your league. There'll be some primary fights, but you have too many resources, and too much firepower, for anyone to go the distance. Now, you might try to heal the party divide by selecting the strongest loser, or one who does no harm, but neither choice would make sense. The former comes with bitterness and the latter is useless in a fight. You could try to find someone who brings a particular slice of the electorate your way, but that would assume voters favor the top of the ticket because of the bottom, which history shows to be nonsense. More realistically, you could select someone from a state where a running mate could deliver electoral votes. Again, that's nonsense. John Kerry chose John Edwards in 2004 but lost North Carolina. He even lost Edwards' home precinct.'

Kane smirked.

'Your biggest weakness is inexperience in foreign affairs. Senators just don't get many chances there, unless they interject themselves in the process, which you've wisely not done over the years. I can bolster you there. That's my strong point. While you have no military service, I have forty years.'

'And you're black.'

He smiled. 'You noticed? Can't slip anything past you.'

Kane appraised him. 'Vice President Langford Ramsey, one heartbeat away from—'

He held up a halting hand. 'Let's not think about that. I simply want eight years as vice president.'

Kane smiled. 'Both terms?'

'Of course.'

'You've done all this to secure a job?'

'What's wrong with that? Isn't that your goal? You, of all people, can understand what that means. I could never be *elected* president. I'm an admiral, with no political base. But I have a shot at the number two seat. All I have to do is impress one person. You.'

He let his words take hold.

'Surely, Aatos, you see the benefits of this arrangement. I can be a valuable ally. Or, if you choose not to honor our deal, I can become a formidable opponent.'

He watched as Kane assessed the situation. He knew this man well. He was a heartless, amoral hypocrite who'd spent a lifetime in public office assembling a reputation that he now planned to use to vault himself to the presidency.

Nothing seemed to be in the way.

And nothing would be, provided.

'All right, Langford, I'll give you your place in history.'

Finally, a first name. They may be getting somewhere.

'I can also offer something else,' Ramsey said. 'Call it a gesture of good faith to demonstrate that I'm not the devil you think me to be.'

He spied mistrust in Kane's observant eyes.

'I'm told that your chief opponent, especially in the early primaries, will be the governor of South Carolina. You and he don't get along, so the fight could quickly become personal. He's a potential problem, particularly in the South. Let's face it, no one can win the White House without the South. Too many electoral votes to ignore.'

'Tell me something I don't know.'

'I can eliminate his candidacy.'

Kane held up his hands in a halting gesture. 'I don't need anybody else to die.'

'You think me that stupid? No, I have information that would end his chance before it even starts.'

He noticed an amused flicker sweep over Kane's face. His listener was a fast learner, already enjoying the arrangement. No surprise. If nothing else, Kane was adaptable. 'Him out of the way now would make fund-raising much easier.'

'Then call it a gift from a new ally. He'll be gone,' he paused, 'as soon as I'm sworn in on the Joint Chiefs.'

50

Ramsey was thrilled. Everything had played out precisely as he'd predicted. Aatos Kane might or might not be the next president but, if he managed the feat, Ramsey's legacy was assured. If Kane could not be elected, then at least he'd retire from the navy as a member of the Joint Chiefs of Staff.

Definitely a win–win.

He switched off the lights and headed upstairs. A few hours of sleep would be good, as tomorrow would be a critical day. Once Kane made contact with the White House the rumor mill would crank up. He had to be ready to fend off the press, neither denying nor confirming anything. This was a White House appointment and he must appear awed simply by the consideration. By the end of the day, spin doctors would leak news of his possible appointment to test reactions and, barring any great upheaval, by the following day rumor would become fact.

The phone in his robe's pocket rang. Odd at this hour.

He removed the unit and spotted no displayed identification.

Curiosity overtook him. He stopped on the staircase and answered the call.

'Admiral Ramsey, this is Isabel Oberhauser.'

He was rarely surprised, but the pronouncement

genuinely startled him. He caught the aged, gravelly voice, the English tinged with a German accent.

'You're quite resourceful, Frau Oberhauser. For some time now, you've tried to obtain information from the navy, and now you managed a direct call to me.'

'It wasn't all that difficult. Captain Wilkerson gave me the number. With a loaded weapon pointed at his skull, he was most cooperative.'

His trouble had just multiplied.

'He told me a great many things, Admiral. He so wanted to live and he thought that by answering my questions he might have the chance. Alas, it was not to be.'

'He's dead?'

'I saved you the trouble.'

He wasn't about to admit anything. 'What do you want?'

'Actually, I called to offer you something. But before I do, might I ask a question?'

He climbed the stairs and sat on the edge of his bed. 'Go ahead.'

'Why did my husband die?'

He caught a momentary flicker of emotion in her otherwise frigid tone and instantly realized this woman's weakness. He decided truth would be best. 'He volunteered to go on a dangerous mission. One his father had also taken long before. But something happened to the submarine.'

'You speak the obvious and haven't answered the question.'

'We have no idea how the sub sank, only that it did.'

'Did you find it?'

'It never returned to port.'

'Again, not an answer.'

'It's irrelevant whether it was found or not. The crew is still dead.'

'It matters to me, Admiral. I would have preferred to

bury my husband. He deserved to be laid to rest with his ancestors.'

Now he had a question. 'Why did you kill Wilkerson?'

'He was nothing but an opportunist. He wanted to live off this family's fortune. I shall not have that. Also, he was your spy.'

'You seem a dangerous woman.'

'Wilkerson said the same thing. He told me that you wanted him dead. That you lied to him. Used him. He was a weak man, Admiral. But he did tell me what you said to my daughter. How did you put it? *You can't imagine.* That's what you said when she asked if there was anything to find in Antarctica. So answer my question. Why did my husband die?'

This woman thought she possessed the upper hand, calling him in the middle of the night, informing him that his station chief was dead. Bold, he'd give her that. But she was operating at a disadvantage since he knew far more than she did.

'Before your husband was approached about the voyage to Antarctica, both he and his father were thoroughly vetted. What spurred our interest was the Nazis' obsession with their research. Oh, yes, they found things down there in 1938 – you know that. Unfortunately the Nazis were too single-minded to realize what they had found. They silenced your father-in-law. When he finally could speak, after the war, nobody was listening. And your husband failed to learn what his father had. So it all languished – until, of course, we came along.'

'And what did you learn?'

He chuckled. 'Now, what fun would it be to tell you that?'

'As I said, I called to offer you something. You sent a man to kill Cotton Malone and my daughter Dorothea. He invaded my home but underestimated our defenses.

He died. I do not want my daughter harmed, as Dorothea is no threat to you. But Cotton Malone apparently is, since he is now privy to the navy's findings about the sinking of that submarine. Am I wrong?'

'I'm listening.'

'I know precisely where he is and you do not.'

'How can you be so sure?'

'Because a few hours ago, in Aachen, Malone killed two men who had come to kill him. Men you also sent.'

New information, as he'd yet to receive any reports from Germany. 'Your information network is good.'

'*Ja*. Do you want to know where Malone is?'

He was curious. 'What game are you playing?'

'I simply want you out of our family business. You don't want us in your business, so let's separate ourselves.'

He sensed, just as Aatos Kane had with him, that this woman could be an ally, so he decided to offer her something. 'I was there, Frau Oberhauser. In Antarctica. Just after the sub was lost. I dove in the water. I saw things.'

'Things we can't imagine?'

'Things that have never left my mind.'

'Yet you keep them secret.'

'That's my job.'

'I want to know that secret. Before I die, I want to know why my husband never came back.'

'Perhaps I can help you with that.'

'In return for knowing where Cotton Malone is right now?'

'No promises, but I'm your best bet.'

'Which is why I called.'

'So tell me what I want to know,' he said.

'Malone is headed for France, the village of Ossau. He should be there in four hours. More than enough time for you to have men waiting.'

51

Charlotte, 3:15 a.m.

Stephanie stood outside Herbert Rowland's hospital room, Edwin Davis beside her. Rowland had been rushed to the emergency room barely clinging to life, but the doctors had managed to stabilize his condition. She was still furious with Davis.

'I'm calling my people,' she told him.

'I've already contacted the White House.'

He'd disappeared half an hour ago, and she'd wondered what he'd been doing.

'And what does the president say?'

'He's asleep. But the Secret Service is on the way.'

'About time you start thinking.'

'I wanted that son of a bitch.'

'You're lucky he didn't kill you.'

'We're going to get him.'

'How? Thanks to you he's long gone. We could have panicked him, trapped him in the house at least until the cops arrived. But no. You had to throw a chair through the window.'

'Stephanie, I did what I had to do.'

'You're out of control, Edwin. You wanted my help and I gave it to you. If you want to end up dead, fine, do it, but I'm not going to be there to watch.'

'If I didn't know better, I'd think you actually care.'

Charm wasn't going to work. 'Edwin, you were right, there's somebody out there killing people. But this ain't the way, my friend. Not at all. Not even close.'

Davis' cell phone chimed. He checked the display. 'The president.' He clicked on the unit. 'Yes, sir.'

She watched as Davis listened, then he handed the phone to her and said, 'He wants to talk to you.'

She grabbed the phone and said, 'Your aide is nuts.'

'Tell me what happened.'

She gave him a quick recount.

After she finished Daniels said, 'You're right – I need you to take control there. Edwin's too emotional. I know about Millicent. It's one reason I agreed to this whole thing. Ramsey did kill her, no doubt in my mind. I also believe he killed Admiral Sylvian and Commander Alexander. Proving that, of course, is an entirely different matter.'

'We may be at a dead end,' she said.

'We've been there before. Let's find a way to keep going.'

'Why do I always seem to get in the middle of these things?'

Daniels chuckled. 'It's a talent of yours. So that you'll know, I've been informed that two corpses were found in the cathedral at Aachen a few hours ago. The interior had been marred by gunfire. One of the men was shot, the other fell to his death. Both were contract help routinely used by our intelligence agencies. The Germans lodged an official inquiry with us for more information. The tidbit was included in my morning briefing packet. Might there be a connection here?'

She decided not to lie. 'Malone is in Aachen.'

'Why did I know you were going to say that.'

'Something's happening there, and Cotton thinks it relates to what's happening here.'

'He's probably right. I need you to stay on this, Stephanie.'

She stared at Edwin Davis, who stood a few feet away, propped up by the papered wall.

The door to Herbert Rowland's room opened and a man clad in olive scrubs said, 'He's awake and wants to speak with you.'

'I have to go,' she said to Daniels.

'Take care of my boy.'

Malone maneuvered the rental car up the inclined road. Snow framed the rocky countryside on both sides of the asphalt, but the local authorities had done a great job of clearing the highway. He was deep into the Pyrénées, on the French side, near the Spanish border, heading for the village of Ossau.

He'd taken an early-morning train from Aachen to Toulouse then driven southwest into snowy highlands. When he'd Googled BRIGHTNESS OF GOD EINHARD last night he'd immediately learned that the phrase referred to an eighth-century monastery located in the French mountains. The Romans who first came to the area built a vast city, a metropolis of the Pyrénées, which eventually became a center of culture and commerce. But in the fratricidal wars of the Frankish kings, during the sixth century, the city was sacked, burned, and destroyed. Not one inhabitant had been spared. No stone had been left resting upon another. Only a single rock stood amid naked fields, creating, as one chronicler of the time wrote, 'a solitude of silence.' One that lasted until Charlemagne arrived two hundred years later and ordered the construction of a monastery, which included a church, a chapter house, a cloister, and a village nearby. Einhard himself supervised the construction, recruiting the first bishop, Bertrand, who became famous for both his piety and civil administration. Bertrand died in 820 at the foot of the altar and was buried beneath what he'd named the Church of St. Lestelle.

The drive from Toulouse had taken him through a host of picturesque mountain villages. He'd visited the region several times, most recently last summer. Little differed among the countless locations save for names and dates. In Ossau a ragged line of houses straggled up winding streets, each faced with coarse stone and embellished with ornaments, coats of arms, and corbels. Only the peaks of the tiled roofs exposed a confusion of angles, like bricks tossed into the snow. Chimneys exhaled into the cold midday air. About a thousand people lived here and four inns accommodated visitors.

He motored into the center of town and parked. A narrow lane led back to an open square. People in warm clothes, with unreadable eyes, darted in and out of the shops. His watch read 9:40 a.m.

He stared past the rooftops toward a clear morning sky, following the side of an escarpment upward to where a square tower rose from a rocky spur. Scraps of other towers on either side seemed to cling to it.

The ruins of St. Lestelle.

Stephanie stood beside Herbert Rowland's hospital bed, and Davis opposite her. Rowland was groggy but awake.

'You saved my life?' Rowland asked in a voice not much more than a whisper.

'Mr. Rowland,' Davis said. 'We're with the government. We don't have much time. We need to ask you a few things.'

'You saved my life?'

She threw Davis a glance that said, *Let me do this.* 'Mr. Rowland, a man came to kill you tonight. We're not sure how, but he sent you into a diabetic coma. Luckily we were there. Do you feel up to answering questions?'

'Why would he want me dead?'

'You remember the *Holden* and Antarctica?'

She watched as he seemed to search his memory.

'A long time ago,' Rowland said.

She nodded. 'It was. But that's why he came to kill you.'

'Who do you work for?'

'An intelligence agency.' She pointed at Davis. 'He's with the White House. Commander Alexander, who captained *Holden,* was murdered last night. One of the lieutenants who went ashore with you, Nick Sayers, died a few years ago. We thought you might be the next target and we were right.'

'I don't know anything.'

'What did you find in Antarctica?' Davis asked.

Rowland closed his eyes and she wondered if he'd dozed off. A few seconds later he opened them and shook his head. 'I was ordered never to speak of that. Not to anyone. Admiral Dyals himself told me from his own mouth.'

She knew about Raymond Dyals. Former chief of naval operations.

'He ordered NR-1A down there,' Davis said.

That she didn't know.

'You know about the sub?' Rowland asked.

She nodded. 'We've read the report on its sinking, and we talked to Commander Alexander before he died. So tell us what you know.' She decided to make the stakes clear. 'Your life may depend on it.'

'I've got to stop drinking,' Rowland said. 'The doctor told me that it would eventually kill me. I take my insulin—'

'Did you last night?'

He nodded.

She was growing impatient. 'The doctors told us earlier that you had no insulin in your blood. That's why you went into shock – that and the alcohol. But all that's irrelevant now. We need to know what you found in Antarctica.'

52

Malone investigated Ossau's four inns and concluded that L'Arlequin would be the correct choice – all mountain austerity on the outside but elegant on the inside, decorated for Christmas with aromatic pine, a carved nativity scene, and mistletoe over the doors. The proprietor pointed out the guest book – which, he explained, contained the names of all of the famous Pyrenean explorers, along with many nineteenth- and twentieth-century notables. Its restaurant served a wonderful monkfish casserole diced with ham, so he'd enjoyed an early lunch and lingered for over an hour, waiting, finally savoring a log-shaped cake made of chocolate and chestnuts. When his watch read eleven a.m. he decided that he may have chosen wrong.

He learned from the waiter that St. Lestelle closed for the winter, and opened only from May to August to accommodate visitors who flocked to the area to enjoy the summer highlands. Not much there, the man said, mostly ruins. Some restoration work occurred each year, financed by the local historical society and encouraged by the Catholic diocese. Other than that, the site remained quiet.

He decided a visit was in order. Night would come quickly, certainly by five, so he needed to take advantage of what daylight remained.

He left the inn armed, three rounds left in the gun. He estimated that the temperature was in the low twenties. No ice, but lots of dry snow that crunched like cereal beneath his boots. He was glad he'd bought the boots earlier in Aachen, knowing that he was headed into some rough terrain. A new sweater beneath his jacket kept his chest extra warm. Tight leather gloves sheathed his hands.

He was ready.

For what?

He wasn't sure.

Stephanie waited for Herbert Rowland to answer her question about what had happened in 1971.

'I don't owe those bastards a thing,' Rowland muttered. 'I kept my oath. Never said a word. But they still came to kill me.'

'We need to know why,' she said.

Rowland inhaled oxygen. 'It was the damnedest thing. Ramsey came to the base, picked me and Sayers, and said we were going to Antarctica. We were all special ops, used to weird things, but this was the strangest. That's a long way from home.' He savored another breath. 'We flew to Argentina, climbed aboard *Holden*, and stayed to ourselves. We were told to sonar-search for a pinger, but we never heard a thing until we finally went ashore. That's when Ramsey donned his gear and dove into the water. He came back about fifty minutes later.'

'What did you find?' Rowland asked, helping Ramsey from the frozen sea, his grip tight on one shoulder of the dry suit, lifting man and equipment onto the ice.

Nick Sayers tugged on the other shoulder. 'Anything there?'

Ramsey slipped off his faceplate and hood. 'Cold as a Siberian ditch digger's fanny down there. Even with this suit. Hell of a dive, though.'

'You were down nearly an hour. Any depth problems?' Rowland asked.

Ramsey shook his head. 'I stayed above thirty feet the whole time.' He pointed off to the right. 'The ocean juts a long way up there, straight to the mountain.'

Ramsey removed his underwater gloves and Sayer handed him a dry pair. Bare skin could not stay exposed more than a minute in this environment. 'I need to get this suit off and my clothes back on.'

'Anything there?' Sayers asked again.

'Some damn clear water. Place is full of color, like a coral reef.'

Rowland realized they were being ignored, but he also noticed a sealed retrieval bag clipped at Ramsey's waist. The bag had been empty fifty minutes ago.

Now it held something.

'What's in there?' he asked.

'He didn't answer me,' Rowland whispered. 'And he wouldn't let me or Sayers touch the bag.'

'What happened after that?' she asked.

'We left. Ramsey was in charge. We made some more radiation checks, found nothing, then Ramsey ordered *Holden* to head north. He never said a word about what he saw on that dive.'

'I don't get it,' Davis said. 'How are you a threat?'

The older man licked his lips. 'Probably because of what happened on the way back.'

Rowland and Sayers were taking a chance. Ramsey was topside with Commander Alexander, playing cards with some of the other officers. So they'd finally decided to see what their compatriot had found on the dive. Neither of them liked being kept in the dark.

'You sure you know the combination?' Sayers asked.

'The quartermaster told me. Ramsey's been throwing his weight around and this ain't his ship, so he was more than happy to help me out.'

A small safe lay on the deck beside Ramsey's rack. Whatever he'd brought up with him after the dive had rested inside for the past three days while they'd left the Antarctic Circle and found the South Atlantic Ocean.

'Keep an eye on the door,' he told Sayers. He knelt and tried the combination he'd been provided.

Three clicks confirmed that the numbers worked.

He opened the safe and spotted the retrieval bag. He slid it out and felt its rectangular contours, eight by ten or so, maybe an inch thick. He unzipped the top, slid out the contents, and immediately recognized a ship's logbook. On the first page, scrawled in blue ink with a heavy hand, was written MISSION STARTING OCTOBER 17, 1971, ENDING——. The second date would have been added after the sub docked back in port. But he realized that the captain who'd made those entries would never get that chance.

Sayers came close. 'What is it?'

The compartment door swung open.

Ramsey stepped inside. 'I thought you two would try something like this.'

'Stick it up your ass,' Rowland said. 'We're all at the same grade. You're not our superior.'

A smile curled on Ramsey's black lips. 'Actually, I am here. But maybe it's better you went ahead and saw. Now you realize what's at stake.'

'You're damn right,' Sayers said to him. 'We volunteered, just like you, and we want the rewards, just like you.'

'*Believe it or not,*' Ramsey said, '*I was going to tell you before we docked. There are things to be done and I can't do them alone.*'

Stephanie wanted to know, 'Why was it so important?'

Davis seemed to understand. 'It's obvious.'

'Not to me.'

'The logbook,' Rowland said, 'came from NR-1A.'

Malone climbed the rocky path, little more than a thin shelf that zigzagged every hundred feet up the wooded slope. On one side, wrought-iron stations of the cross spanned out in a solemn procession, on the other the vista below steadily grew into a panorama. Sunshine bathed the precipitous valley, and he noticed, in the distance, deep jagged gorges. Bells far away announced midday.

He was headed for one of the cirques, circles of high precipices set into mountainous pockets, accessible only by foot, common in the Pyrénées. Beech trees sustained the slopes, stunted and twisted, their bare snowy branches interlaced in misshapen knots. He kept watch on the uneven path but noticed no footprints, which meant little given the wind and swirling snow.

A final semicircular sweep and the monastery's entrance, perched on the cirque, rose ahead. He paused for a breath and enjoyed another wide-flung view. Snow, refrigerated by cold gusts of wind, swirled in the distance.

Tall masonry walls stretched left and right. If what he'd read was to be believed, those stones had borne witness to Romans, Visigoths, Saracens, Franks, and the crusaders of the Albigensian wars. Many battles had been fought for this vantage point. Silence seemed a physical presence, which gave the place a solemn mood. Its history probably lay buried with the dead, the true record of its glory etched neither in stone nor in parchment.

Brightness of God.

More fiction? Or fact?

He walked the remaining fifty feet, approached an iron gate, and spotted a padlocked chain.

Great.

No way to scale the walls.

He reached out and gripped the gate. Cold seeped though his gloves. What now? Scour the perimeter and see if there was an opening? Seemed like the only course. He was tired, and he knew this stage of exhaustion well – the mind easily became lost in a maze of possibilities, every solution meeting a dead end.

He shook the gate in frustration.

The iron chain slithered to the ground.

53

Charlotte

Stephanie digested exactly what Herbert Rowland had said and asked, 'You're saying NR-1A was intact?'

Rowland appeared to be tiring, but this had to be done.

'I'm saying Ramsey brought the logbook back from the dive.'

Davis threw her a look. 'I told you the SOB was deep in this.'

'Was it Ramsey who tried to kill me?' Rowland asked.

She wasn't going to answer, but saw Davis was not of the same mind.

'He deserves to know,' Davis said.

'This is already out of hand. Do you want more?'

Davis faced Rowland. 'We think he's behind it.'

'We don't *know* that,' she was quick to add. 'But it's a distinct possibility.'

'He was always a bastard,' Rowland said. 'After we got back, he's the one who sucked up all the benefits. Not me or Sayers. Sure, we got a few promotions, but we never got what Ramsey managed.' Rowland paused, clearly fatigued. 'Admiral. All the way to the top.'

'Maybe we should do this later,' she said.

'No way,' Rowland said. 'Nobody comes after me and gets away with it. If I wasn't in this bed, I'd kill him myself.'

She wondered about the bravado.

'I took my last drink tonight,' he said. 'No more. I mean it.'

Anger seemed an effective drug. Rowland's eyes were ablaze.

'Tell us everything,' she said.

'How much do you know about Operation Highjump?'

'Just the official line,' Davis said.

'Which is total garbage.'

Admiral Byrd brought six R4-D aircraft with him to Antarctica. Each was equipped with sophisticated cameras and trailing magnetometers. They launched from a carrier deck using rocket propulsion bottles to assist in takeoff. The aircraft spent over 200 hours in the air and flew 23,000 miles across the continent. On one of the final mapping flights, Byrd's plane returned from its mission three hours late. The official account was that he'd lost an engine and had to limp home. But Byrd's private logs, returned and reviewed by the then chief of naval operations, revealed a different explanation.

Byrd had been flying over what the Germans named Neuschwabenland. He was inland, headed west over a featureless white horizon, when he spotted a bare area dotted with three lakes separated by masses of barren reddish brown rocks. The lakes themselves were colored in shades of red, blue, and green. He noted their position and the following day dispatched to the area a special team, who discovered that the lake water was warm and filled with algae, which provided the pigmentation. The water was also brackish, which indicated a connection to the ocean.

The discovery excited Byrd. He was privy to information from the 1938 German expedition, which had reported similar observations. He'd doubted the claims, having visited the continent and knowing its inhospitable nature, but the special field team explored the area for the next few days.

'I wasn't aware Byrd kept a private log,' Davis said.

'I saw it,' Rowland said. 'The entire Highjump operation was classified, but we worked on a lot of things when we returned and I got a look. It's only during the last twenty years that anything about Highjump has been revealed – most of it false, by the way.'

She asked, 'What is it that you, Sayers, and Ramsey did when you returned?'

'We relocated all the stuff brought home by Byrd in 1947.'

'It still existed?'

Rowland nodded. 'Every bit. Crates of it. The government doesn't throw anything away.'

'What was inside them?'

'I have no idea. We simply moved them, never opened anything. And by the way, I'm concerned about my wife. She's at her sister's.'

'Give me the address,' Davis said, 'and I'll have the Secret Service make contact. But it's you Ramsey's after. And you still haven't told us why Ramsey considers you a threat.'

Rowland lay still, both his arms connected to intravenous bags. 'I can't believe I almost died.'

'The guy we surprised broke into your house yesterday while you were out during the day,' Davis said. 'I'm guessing he screwed with your insulin.'

'My head is pounding.'

She wanted to press harder but knew that this old man would talk only when ready. 'We'll make sure you're protected from here on. We just need to know why it's necessary.'

Rowland's face was a kaleidoscope of twisting emotions. He was struggling with something. His breath came ragged, his watery eyes fixed in a disdainful stare. 'The damn thing was dry as a bone. Not a water smear on any page.'

She registered what he'd said. 'The logbook?'

He nodded. 'Ramsey brought it up from the ocean in the bag. That meant it never got wet before he found it.'

'Mother of God,' Davis muttered.

She now realized. 'NR-1A was intact?'

'Only Ramsey knows that.'

'That's why he wants them all dead,' Davis said. 'When you let that file go to Malone, he panicked. He can't have that get out. Can you imagine what that would do to the navy?'

But she wasn't so sure. There had to be more to the story.

Davis stared at Rowland. 'Who else knows?'

'Me. Sayers, but he's dead. Admiral Dyals. He knew. He commanded the whole thing and gave us the order of silence.'

Winterhawk. That's what the press called Dyals, referring to both his age and his political leanings. He'd long been compared to another aging, arrogant naval officer who also eventually had to be chased off. Hyman Rickover.

'Ramsey became Dyals' favorite,' Rowland said. 'Got assigned to the admiral's personal staff. Ramsey worshiped the man.'

'Enough to protect his reputation, even now?' she asked.

'Hard to say. But Ramsey's a strange bird. Doesn't think like the rest of us. I was glad to be rid of him after we got back.'

'So Dyals is the only one left?' Davis asked.

Rowland shook his head. 'One more knew.'

Had she heard right?

'There's always an expert. He was a hotshot researcher the navy hired. Strange guy. We called him the Wizard of Oz. You know, the guy behind the curtain who nobody ever saw? Dyals himself recruited him, and he reported only to Ramsey and the admiral. He's the one who opened those crates, all by himself.'

'We need a name,' Davis said.

'Douglas Scofield, PhD. He liked to always remind us of that. *Dr. Scofield,* he called himself. None of us was impressed. His head was so far up Dyals' ass he never saw daylight.'

'What happened to him?' she asked.

'Hell if I know.'

They needed to leave, but first there was one more thing. 'What about those crates from Antarctica?'

'We took everything to a warehouse at Fort Lee. In Virginia. And left it with Scofield. After that, I have no idea.'

54

M alone stared down at the iron chain lying in the snow. Think. Be careful. A whole bunch isn't right here. Especially not the clean snip in the chain. Somebody had come prepared with bolt cutters.

He removed the gun from beneath his jacket and pushed open the gate.

Frozen hinges screamed out.

He entered the ruin over crumbling masonry and approached the diminishing arches of a Roman doorway. He descended several crumbling rock steps into an inky interior. What little light existed filtered in with the wind through bare window frames. The thickness of the walls, the slant of the openings, the iron gate at the entrance all indicated the rudimentary times in which they were created. He stared around at what was once important – half place of worship, half citadel, a fortified locale on the outskirts of an empire.

Each exhale vaporized before his eyes.

His gaze continued to rake the ground, but he saw no evidence of others.

He advanced into a maze of columns that supported an intact roof. The sense of vastness disappeared upward into shadowy vaults. He wandered among the columns as he might among tall trees in a petrified forest. He wasn't sure what he was looking for or what he expected, and he resisted the urge to be taken in by the spooky surroundings.

From what he'd read on the Internet, Bertrand, the first bishop, made quite a name for himself. Legend attributed many wonders to his miraculous powers. Nearby Spanish chieftains routinely left a trail of fire and blood across the Pyrénées, and the local population was terrified of them. But before Bertrand they surrendered their prisoners and retreated, never to return.

And there was the miracle.

A woman had brought her baby and complained that the father would not support them. When the man denied any complicity, Bertrand ordered that a vessel of cold water be placed before them and he dropped a rock inside. He told the man to take the stone from the water and, if he was lying, God would give a sign. The man lifted the stone but his hands came away scalded, as if boiled. The father promptly admitted his paternity and made proper amends. For his piety Bertrand eventually acquired a label – *the Brightness of God*. He supposedly shunned the description but allowed it to be applied to the monastery, apparently remembered by Einhard, decades later, as he drew up his last will and testament.

Malone left the columns and passed into the cloister, an irregular-roofed trapezoid lined with arches, columns, and capitals. Roof timbers, which appeared recent, seemed to have been the focus of recent restorations. Two rooms led off the right side of the cloister, both empty, one with no roof, the other with collapsed walls. Surely once refectories for the monks and guests, but only the elements and animals now possessed them.

He turned a corner and advanced down the short side of the gallery, passing several more collapsed spaces, each dusted with snow from either empty window frames or open roofs, brown nettles and weeds infecting their recesses. Above one door a faded carved image of the Virgin Mary stared down. He glanced beyond the doorway into a spacious room. Probably the chapter house where the monks had lived. He stared back out into the cloister garden at a crumbling basin with faint leaf and head decorations. Snow engulfed its base.

Something moved across the cloister.

In the opposite gallery. Fast and faint, but there.

He crouched and crept to the corner.

The long side of the cloister stretched fifty feet before him, ending at a double archway with no doors. The church. He assumed that whatever was to be found would be there, but this was a long shot. Still, somebody had cut the chain outside.

He studied the inner wall to his right.

Three doorways opened between him and the cloister's end. Arches to his left, which framed the windy garden, were all severe, bearing scarcely any ornamentation. Time and the elements had taken their toll. He noticed one lonely cherub that had survived, bearing an armorial shield. He heard something, from his left, in the long gallery.

Footsteps.

Coming his way.

Ramsey left his car and hustled through the cold, entering naval intelligence's main administrative building. He was not required to pass through any security checkpoint. Instead a lieutenant from his staff waited at the door. On the walk to his office, he received his usual morning briefing.

Hovey was waiting in his office. 'Wilkerson's body has been found.'

'Tell me.'

'In Munich, near Olympic Park. Shot in the head.'

'You should be pleased.'

'Good riddance.'

But Ramsey wasn't as thrilled. The conversation with Isabel Oberhauser still weighed on his mind.

'Do you want me to authorize payment to the contract help who handled the job?'

'Not yet.' He'd already called overseas. 'I have them doing something else, in France, at the moment.'

Charlie Smith sat inside Shoney's and finished his bowl of grits. He loved them, especially with salt and three pats of butter. He hadn't slept much. Last night was a problem. Those two had come for him.

He'd fled the house and parked a few miles down the highway. He'd spotted an ambulance rushing to the scene and followed it to a hospital on the outskirts of Charlotte. He'd wanted to go inside, but decided against the move. Instead he'd returned to his hotel and tried to sleep.

He would have to call Ramsey shortly. The only acceptable report was that all three targets had been eliminated. Any hint of a problem and Smith would find himself a target. He taunted Ramsey, took advantage of their long-standing relationship, exploited his successes, all because he knew Ramsey needed him.

But that would change in an instant if he failed.

He checked his watch.

6:15 a.m.

He had to risk it.

He'd noticed a phone outside, so he paid his bill and made the call. When the hospital's menu was recited in his ear, he selected the option for patient information. Since he did not know the room number, he waited until an operator came on the line.

'I need to find out about Herbert Rowland. He's my uncle and was brought in last night.'

He was told to hold a moment, then the woman came back. 'We're sorry to say that Mr. Rowland died shortly after arriving.'

He feigned shock. 'That's horrible.'

The woman offered her condolences. He thanked her, hung up, and exhaled a sigh of relief.

That was close.

He grabbed his composure, found his cell phone, and dialed a familiar number. When Ramsey answered he cheerfully said, 'Three for three. Batting a thousand, as usual.'

'I'm so glad you take pride in your work.'

'We aim to please.'

'Then please me once more. The fourth one. You have the okay. Do it.'

Malone listened. Somebody was both behind and ahead of him. He kept low and darted into one of the rooms that opened off the gallery, this one, he saw, with walls and a ceiling. He pressed his spine taut against the inner wall, adjacent to the doorway. Darkness exaggerated the room's shadowy corners. He was twenty feet from the church entrance.

More footsteps.

From back down the gallery, away from the church.

He gripped the gun and waited.

Whoever was there kept approaching. Had they seen him slip inside? Apparently not, as they made no effort to mask their steps through the brittle snow. He readied himself and cocked his head, using peripheral vision to watch the doorway. The footsteps were now on the opposite side of the wall against which he was pressed.

A form appeared, walking toward the church.

He pivoted and grabbed for a shoulder, swinging the gun around and whirling whoever it was into the outer wall, the gun jammed into ribs.

Shock stared back.

A man.

55

Charlotte, 6:27 a.m.

Stephanie made a call to Magellan Billet headquarters and requested some information on Dr. Douglas Scofield. She and Davis were alone. Half an hour ago two Secret Service agents had arrived and brought with them a secure laptop, which Davis commandeered. The agents were ordered to take custody of Herbert Rowland, who was being moved into a new room under another name. Davis had spoken with the hospital administrator and obtained her cooperation in announcing that Rowland had died. Surely somebody was going to check. Sure enough, the patient information operator had already reported a call twenty minutes ago – from a male who identified himself as a nephew – inquiring into Rowland's condition.

'That should make him happy,' Davis said. 'I doubt our killer will risk a trip inside. To make sure, there'll be an obituary in the paper. I've told the agents to explain it all to the Rowlands and get their cooperation.'

'A bit rough on friends and family,' she said.

'It'll be rougher if the guy realizes his mistake and comes back to finish what he started.'

The laptop signaled an incoming e-mail. Stephanie clicked open the message from her office:

Douglas Scofield is a professor of anthropology at East Tennessee State University. He was associated with the navy from 1968 to 1972 on a contract basis, his activities classified. Access is possible but will leave a trail, so it wasn't done as you indicated silence on these inquiries. His published works are numerous. Besides the usual anthropological journals, he writes for New Age and occult magazines. A quick Internet check revealed subject matters that include Atlantis, UFOs, ancient astronauts, and paranormal events. He's the author of *Maps of Ancient Explorers* (1986), a popular account of how cartography may have been influenced by lost cultures. He is currently attending a conference in Asheville, North Carolina, titled Ancient Mysteries Revealed. Being held at the Inn on Biltmore Estate. About 150 registered. He's one of the organizers and a featured speaker. Seems an annual event, as this is billed as the fourteenth conference.

'He's the only one left,' Davis said. He'd been reading over her shoulder. 'Asheville's not far from here.'

She knew what he was thinking. 'You're not serious.'

'I'm going. You can come if you want. He needs to be approached.'

'Then send the Secret Service.'

'Stephanie, the last thing we need is a show of force. Let's just go and see where it leads.'

'Our friend from last night may be there, too.'

'We can only hope.'

Another ding singled an answer to her second inquiry, so she opened the reply and read:

The navy leases warehouse space at Fort Lee, Virginia. They have since World War II. Presently, they control three buildings. Only one is high security and contains a refrigerated compartment installed in 1972. Access is restricted by numeric code and fingerprint verification through Office of Naval Intelligence. I managed to view its visitor log stored on the navy's database. Interestingly, it's not classified. Only one non–Fort Lee personnel entered during the last 180 days. Admiral Langford Ramsey, yesterday.

'Still want to argue with me?' Davis asked. 'You know I'm right.'

'All the more reason for us to get help.'

Davis shook his head. 'The president won't let us.'

'Wrong. *You* won't let us.'

Davis' face conveyed challenge and submission. 'I have to do this. Maybe you have to do it now, too. Remember, Malone's father was on that boat.'

'Which Cotton should know.'

'Let's get him some answers first.'

'Edwin, you could have been killed last night.'

'But I wasn't.'

'Revenge is the quickest way to get yourself killed. Why don't you let me handle this? I have agents.'

They remained alone in a small conference room the hospital administrator had provided.

'That's not going to happen,' he said.

She could see arguing was pointless. Forrest Malone had been on that sub – and Davis was right, that was enough incentive for her.

She shut down the laptop and stood.

'I'd say we have about a three-hour ride to Asheville.'

'Who are you?' Malone asked the man.

'You scared me to death.'

'Answer my question.'

'Werner Lindauer.'

He made the connection. 'Dorothea's husband?'

The man nodded. 'My passport's in my pocket.'

No time for that. He withdrew the gun and yanked his captive back into the side room, out of the gallery. 'What are you doing here?'

'Dorothea walked here three hours ago. I came to see about her.'

'How did she find this place?'

'You apparently don't know Dorothea that well. She doesn't explain herself. Christl is here, too.'

That, he had expected. He'd waited in the hotel, believing she either knew of this place or would locate it the same way he'd managed.

'She came up here before Dorothea.'

He turned his attention back into the cloister. Time to see what was inside the church. He motioned with the gun. 'You first. To the right and into that doorway at the end.'

'Is that wise?'

'Nothing about this is smart.'

He followed Werner into the gallery, then through the double archway at its end, and immediately sought cover behind a thick column. A wide nave, made to seem narrow by more columns that extended its length, stretched before him. The columns turned in a semicircle behind the altar, following the curve of the apse. Bare walls on either side were high, the aisles broad. No decoration or ornamentation anywhere, the church more ruin than building. The wind's haunting music sounded through bare window frames partitioned by stone crosses. He spotted the altar, a pillar of pitted granite, but what sat before it drew his attention.

Two people. Gagged.

One on either side, on the floor, their arms tied behind them around a column.

Dorothea and Christl.

56

Ramsey marched back toward his office. He was waiting for a report from France and had made clear to the men overseas that he wanted to hear only that Cotton Malone was dead. After that he'd turn his attention to Isabel Oberhauser, but he had not, as yet, decided how best to handle that problem. He'd thought about her during the entire briefing he'd just attended, recalling something he'd once heard. *I've been right and I've been paranoid and it's better being paranoid.*

He agreed.

Luckily he knew a lot about the old woman.

She married Dietz Oberhauser in the late 1950s. He was the son of a wealthy, aristocratic Bavarian family, she the daughter of a local mayor. Her father had been associated with the Nazis during the war, used by the Americans in the years after. She assumed full control of the Oberhauser fortune in 1972, after Dietz disappeared. Eventually, she had him declared legally dead. This activated his will, which left everything to her, in trust, for the benefit of their daughters. Before Ramsey had dispatched Wilkerson to make contact, he'd studied that will. Interestingly, the decision as to when financial control passed to the daughters had been left entirely to

Isabel. Thirty-eight years had elapsed and still she remained in charge. Wilkerson had reported that great animosity existed between the sisters, which might explain a few things, but until today the Oberhauser family discord had meant little to him.

He knew that Isabel had long been interested in *Blazek* and made no secret of her desire to learn what had happened. She'd retained lawyers who'd tried to access information through official channels, and when that failed, she attempted covertly to learn what she could through bribery. His counterintelligence people had detected the attempts and reported them. That's when he assumed personal responsibility and assigned Wilkerson.

Now his man was dead. How?

He knew Isabel employed an East German named Ulrich Henn. The background report noted that Henn's maternal grandfather had commanded one of Hitler's reception camps and supervised the tossing of 28,000 Ukrainians down a ravine. At his war crimes trial he denied nothing and proudly stated, *I was there*. Which made it easy for the Allies to hang him.

Henn was raised by a stepfather who assimilated his new family into communist society. Henn served in the East German military, former Stasi, his current benefactor not all that dissimilar from his communist bosses, both making decisions in the calculating manner of an accountant, then executing them with the unquestioning remorse of a despot.

Isabel was indeed a formidable woman.

She possessed money, power, and nerve. But her weakness was her husband. She wanted to know why he died. Her obsession had been of no real concern until

Stephanie Nelle accessed the file on NR-1A and sent it across the Atlantic to Cotton Malone.

Now it was a problem.

One that he hoped was being solved, right now, in France.

Malone watched as Christl spotted him and struggled against her restraints. Tape sealed her mouth. She shook her head.

Two men showed themselves from the behind the columns. The one on the left was tall, lanky, and dark-haired, the other stout and fair-headed. He wondered how many more were lurking.

'We came for you,' Dark said to him, 'and found these two already here.'

Malone stayed behind a column, gun ready. They didn't know he was limited to three rounds.

'And why am I so interesting?'

'Beats the hell out of me. I'm just glad you are.'

Fair brought a gun barrel close to Dorothea Lindauer's skull.

'We'll start with her,' Dark said.

He was thinking, assessing, noting that there'd been no mention of Werner. He faced Lindauer and whispered, 'Ever shot a man?'

'No.'

'Can you?'

He hesitated. 'If I had to. For Dorothea.'

'Can you shoot?'

'I've hunted all my life.'

He decided to add to his growing résumé of stupid things and handed Werner the automatic.

'What do you want me to do?' Werner asked.

'Shoot one of them.'

'Which one?'

'I don't care. Just shoot, before they shoot me.'

Werner's head bobbed in understanding.

Malone sucked a few deep breaths, steeled himself, and stepped away from the column, his hands exposed. 'Okay, here I am.'

Neither of the assailants moved. Apparently, he'd caught them by surprise. Which had been the whole idea. Fair withdrew his gun from Dorothea Lindauer and completely emerged from behind his column. He was young, alert, and on guard, automatic rifle leveled.

A shot popped and Fair's chest exploded from a direct hit.

Werner Lindauer apparently could shoot.

Malone dove right, seeking cover behind another column, knowing Dark would take only a nanosecond to recover. A swift blast of automatic fire and bullets pinged off the stone a few inches from his head. He glanced across the nave at Werner, who was safe behind a column.

Dark hissed a string of obscenities, then screamed, 'I'm going to kill them both. Right now.'

'I don't give a damn,' he called out.

'Really? You sure?'

He needed to force a mistake. He motioned at Werner that he intended to advance forward, down the transept, using the columns for cover.

Now for the true test. He motioned for Werner to toss him the gun.

The man lobbed the weapon his way. He caught it and signaled to stay put.

Malone swung left and darted across the open space to the next column.

More bullets streaked his way.

He caught a glimpse of Dorothea and Christl, still tied to their column. Only two rounds remained in the gun, so he grabbed a softball-sized rock and hurled the stone toward Dark, then crossed to the next column. The projectile crashed into something and thudded away.

Five more columns remained between him and Dorothea Lindauer, who was tied on his side of the nave.

'Take a look,' Dark said.

He risked a glance.

Christl lay on the rough pavement. Ropes dangled from her wrists but they'd been cut, freeing her. Dark kept his body hidden, but Malone spotted the end of the rifle pointed down.

'You don't care?' Dark called out. 'You want to watch her die?'

A burst of bullets ricocheted off the pavement just behind where Christl lay. Fear sent her scrambling forward across the lichen-infested flooring.

'Stop,' Dark yelled at her.

She did.

'Next volley and her legs are gone.'

He paused, attuning his senses, wondering about Werner Lindauer. Where was he?

'I guess there's no way we can discuss this?' he asked.

'Toss your weapon away and get your ass out here.'

Still no mention of Werner. The gunman surely knew there was someone else here. 'Like I said. I don't give a damn. Kill her.'

He pivoted right as he spoke the challenge, his angle better now that he was closer to the altar. In the unearthly greenish light that filtered in from the fading afternoon, he saw Dark drift a couple of feet back from his column, seeking a better shot at Christl.

Malone fired but the bullet missed.

One round left.

Dark retook cover.

Malone darted to the next column. He spotted a shadow approaching Dark from the row of columns that spread to the back of the nave. Dark's attention was on Malone, so the shadow was free to scoot ahead. Its shape and size confirmed its identity. Werner Lindauer was gutsy.

'Okay, you've got a gun,' Dark said. 'I shoot her, you shoot me. But I can take the other sister without giving you a crack at me.'

Malone heard a grunt, then a thud as flesh and bones pounded something that had not given way. Malone peered around the column and saw Werner Lindauer on top of Dark, a fist raised. The two struggling men rolled out into the nave and Dark shoved Werner away, both hands still gripping the weapon.

Christl had sprung to her feet.

Dark started to stand.

Malone aimed.

The crack of a rifle reverberated across the cavernous walls.

Blood poured from Dark's neck. The gun dropped from his grip as he realized he'd been shot and reached for his throat, struggling to breathe. Malone heard another crack – a second shot – and Dark's body stiffened then fell, landing hard, spine first.

Silence engulfed the church.

Werner lay on the ground. Christl stood. Dorothea sat. Malone glared to his left.

In an upper gallery above the church's vestibule, where centuries ago a choir may have sung, Ulrich Henn lowered a scoped rifle. Beside him, grim and defiant, gazing down from her vantage point, stood Isabel Oberhauser.

57

Ramsey watched as Diane McCoy opened the car door and slipped into the passenger seat. He'd been waiting outside the administrative building for her to arrive. Her call fifteen minutes ago had signaled alarm.

'What the hell have you done?' she asked.

He wasn't about to volunteer anything.

'Daniels ordered me into the Oval Office an hour ago and reamed my ass.'

'You going to tell me why?'

'Don't play that coy crap with me. You leaned on Aatos Kane, didn't you?'

'I spoke with him.'

'And he spoke with the president.'

He sat patient and quiet. He'd known McCoy for several years. He'd studied her background. She was careful and deliberate. The nature of her job demanded patience. Yet here she was outright mad. Why?

His cell phone, resting on the dashboard, lit up, signaling an incoming message. 'Excuse me. I can't be unavailable.' He checked the display, but did not respond. 'It can wait. What's wrong, Diane? I simply asked for the senator's assistance. Are you telling me that no one else has made contact with the White House trying the same thing?'

'I'm telling you that Aatos Kane is a different animal. What did you do?'

'Not all that much. He was thrilled that I communicated with him. He said that I would make an excellent addition to the Joint Chiefs. I told him that if he felt that way, then I would appreciate any support he could show.'

'Langford, it's just you and me here, so cut the speeches. Daniels was flaming mad. He resented Kane's involvement, blamed me. Said I was in league with you.'

He screwed his face into a frown. 'In league for what?'

'You're a piece of work. You told me the other day that you could deliver Kane and you damn well did. I don't want to know how or why, but I do want to know how Daniels tied me to you. This is my ass here.'

'And a nice ass it is.'

She exhaled. 'How is that productive?'

'It's not. Just a truthful observation.'

'Are you going to offer anything to help? I've worked a long time to get this far.'

'What exactly did the president say?' He needed to know.

She slapped away his question with the back of her hand. 'Like I'm going to tell you that.'

'Why not? You're accusing me of something improper, so I'd like to know what Daniels had to say.'

'Mighty different attitude from when we last talked.' Her voice had dropped.

He shrugged. 'As I recall, you thought I'd make a fine addition to the Joint Chiefs, too. Is it not your duty, as national security adviser, to recommend good people to the president?'

'Okay, Admiral. Play the part, be a good soldier. The president of the United States is still pissed and so is Senator Kane.'

'I can't imagine why. My conversation with the senator was most pleasant, and I haven't even spoken to the president, so I can't understand why he's angry with me.'

'You going to Admiral Sylvian's funeral?'

He caught the subject shift. 'Of course. I've been asked to participate in the honor guard.'

'You've got balls.'

He threw her his most charming smile. 'I was actually touched to be asked.'

'I came because we needed to talk. I'm sitting here in a parked car, like a fool, because I got myself entangled with you—'

'Entangled in what?'

'You know damn well what. The other night you made it clear that there was going to be a vacancy in the Joint Chiefs. One that didn't exist at the time.'

'That's not what I recall. You're the one who wanted to speak to me. It was late, but you insisted. You came to my house. You were concerned about Daniels and his attitude toward the military. We spoke of the Joint Chiefs, in the abstract. Neither of us was aware that any vacancy would arise. Certainly not the next day. It's a tragedy that David Sylvian died. He was a fine man, but I fail to see how that has entangled us in any way.'

She shook her head in disbelief. 'I have to go.'

He didn't stop her.

'Have a nice day, Admiral.'

And she slammed the door.

He quickly replayed the conversation in his mind. He'd done well, delivering his thoughts in a casual manner. The night before last, when he and Diane McCoy had talked, she'd been an ally. Of that he was sure. But things had changed.

Ramsey's briefcase sat on the rear seat. Inside was a sophisticated monitor used to determine if electronic devices were either recording or broadcasting nearby. Ramsey kept one of the monitors in his house, which was how he knew no one had been listening.

Hovey had canvassed the parking lot, using a series of mounted security cameras. The call to his phone had been a text message. HER CAR PARKED IN WEST LOT. ACCESSED. RECEIVER AND RECORDER INSIDE. The monitor in the backseat had also sent a signal, so the final part of the message had been clear. SHE'S WIRED.

He exited the car and locked the doors.

Couldn't be Kane. He'd been too interested in benefits coming his way and could not risk even the possibility of exposure. The senator knew that a betrayal would mean quick and devastating consequences.

No.

This was pure Diane McCoy.

Malone watched as Werner untied Dorothea from the column and she yanked the tape from across her mouth.

'What were you thinking?' she yelled. 'Are you insane?'

'He was going to shoot you,' her husband calmly said. 'I knew Herr Malone was here, with a gun.'

Malone stood in the nave, his attention toward the upper gallery and Isabel and Ulrich Henn. 'I see you're not as ignorant of things as you wanted me to believe.'

'Those men were here to kill you,' the old woman replied.

'And how did you know they'd be here?'

'I came to make sure my daughters were safe.'

Not an answer, so he faced Christl. Her eyes gave no

indication as to her thoughts. 'I waited in the village for you to arrive, but you were way ahead of me.'

'It wasn't hard to find the connection between Einhard and Brightness of God.'

He pointed up. 'But that doesn't explain how she and your sister knew.'

'I spoke with Mother last night, after you left.'

He walked toward Werner. 'I agree with your wife. What you did was foolish.'

'You needed his attention drawn. I didn't have a gun, so I did what I thought would work.'

'He could have shot you,' Dorothea said.

'That would have ended our marriage problem.'

'I never said I wanted you dead.'

Malone understood the love–hate of marriage. His own had been the same way, even years after they separated. Luckily he'd made peace with his ex, though it had taken effort. These two, though, seemed a long way from any resolution.

'I did what I had to,' Werner said. 'And I'd do it again.'

Malone glanced back up at the choir. Henn fled his post at the balustrade and disappeared behind Isabel.

'Can we now find whatever there is to find?' Isabel asked.

Henn reappeared and he saw the man whisper something to his employer.

'Herr Malone,' Isabel said. 'There were four men sent. We thought the other two would not be a problem, but they just entered the gate.'

58

Charlie Smith studied the file on Douglas Scofield. He'd prepped this target over a year ago, but, unlike the others, this man had always been labeled optional.

Not anymore.

Apparently plans had changed, so he needed to refresh his memory.

He'd left Charlotte, heading north on US 321 to Hickory, where he'd veered onto I-40 and sped west toward the Smoky Mountains. He'd checked on the Internet, verifying that information in the file remained accurate. Dr. Scofield was scheduled to speak at a symposium he hosted every winter, this year's on the grounds of the famous Biltmore Estate. The event seemed a gathering of weirdos. Ufology, ghosts, necrology, alien abductions, cryptozoology. Lots of bizarre subjects. Scofield, though a professor of anthropology at a Tennessee university, was deeply involved with pseudo-science, authoring a host of books and articles. Since Smith had not known when, or if, he'd be ordered to move on Douglas Scofield, he hadn't given much thought to the man's demise.

He was now parked outside a McDonald's, a hundred yards from the entrance to Biltmore Estate.

He casually scanned the file.

Scofield's interests varied. He loved hunting, spending
many a winter weekend in search of deer and wild boar.
A bow was his choice of weapon, though he owned an
impressive collection of high-powered rifles. Smith still
carried the one he'd taken from Herbert Rowland's house,
lying in the trunk, loaded, just in case. Fishing and white-
water rafting were more of Scofield's passions, though this
time of year opportunities for either would be limited.

He'd downloaded the conference schedule, trying to
digest any aspects that might prove useful. He was troubled
by the previous night's escapade. Those two had not been
there by accident. Though he savored every bit of the
conceit that swirled inside him – after all, confidence was
everything – there was no sense being foolish.

He needed to be prepared.

Two aspects of the conference schedule caught his
attention, and two ideas formed.

One defensive, the other offensive.

He hated rush jobs, but wasn't about to concede to
Ramsey that he couldn't handle it.

He grabbed his cell phone and found the number in
Atlanta.

Thank goodness Georgia was nearby.

Malone, reacting to Isabel's warning, said to her, 'I only
have one round left.'

She spoke to Henn, who reached beneath his coat,
produced a handgun, and tossed it down. Malone caught
the weapon. Two spare magazines followed.

'You come prepared,' he said.

'Always,' Isabel said.

He pocketed the magazines.

'Pretty bold of you to trust me earlier,' Werner said.

'Like I had a choice.'

'Still.'

Malone glanced at Christl and Dorothea. 'You three take cover somewhere.' He motioned beyond the altar to the apse. 'Back there looks good.'

He watched as they hustled off then called up to Isabel, 'Could we take at least one of them alive?'

Henn was already gone.

She nodded. 'It depends on them.'

He heard two shots from inside the church.

'Ulrich has engaged them,' she said.

He rushed through the nave, back into the vestibule, and exited into the cloister. He spotted one of the men on the far side, scurrying between the arches. Daylight waned. The temperature had noticeably dropped.

More shots.

From outside the church.

Stephanie exited I-40 onto a busy boulevard and found the main entrance to Biltmore Estate. She'd actually visited here twice before, once, like now, during the Christmas season. The estate comprised thousands of acres, the centerpiece being a 175,000-square-foot French Renaissance château, the largest privately owned residence in America. Originally a country retreat for George Vanderbilt, built in the late 1880s, it had evolved into a swanky tourist attraction, a glowing testament to America's lost Gilded Age.

A collection of brick and pebbledash houses, many with steep gabled roofs, timbered dormers, and wide porches crowded together to her left. Brick sidewalks lined cozy, tree-lined streets. Pine boughs and Christmas ribbons draped street lamps and a zillion white lights lit the fading afternoon for the holidays.

'Biltmore Village,' she said. 'Where estate workers and servants once lived. Vanderbilt built them their own town.'

'Like something from Dickens.'

'They made it seem like an English country village. Now it's shops and cafés.'

'You know a lot about this place.'

'It's one of my favorite spots.'

She noticed a McDonald's, its architecture consistent with the picturesque surroundings. 'I need a bathroom break.' She slowed and turned into the restaurant's parking lot.

'One of their milk shakes would be good,' Davis said.

'You have a strange diet.'

He shrugged. 'Whatever fills the stomach.'

She checked her watch. 11:15 a.m. 'A quick stop, then into the estate. The hotel is a mile or so inside the gates.'

Charlie Smith ordered himself a Big Mac, no sauce, no onions, fries, and a large Diet Coke. One of his favorite meals, and since he weighed about 150 pounds sopping wet, weight had never been a concern. He was blessed with a hyper metabolism – that and an active lifestyle, exercise three times a week, and a healthy diet. Yeah, right. His idea of exercise was dialing for room service or carrying a take-out bag to the car. His job provided more than enough exertion for him.

He leased an apartment outside Washington, DC, but rarely stayed there. He needed to develop roots. Maybe it was time to buy a place of his own – like Bailey Mill. He'd been screwing with Ramsey's head the other day, but perhaps he could fix up that old Maryland farmhouse and live there, in the country. It'd be quaint. Like the buildings that now surrounded him. Even the McDonald's didn't look like any he'd ever seen. Shaped like a storybook house with a player piano in the dining room, marble tiles, and a shimmering waterfall.

He sat with his tray.

After he ate, he'd head toward the Biltmore Inn. He'd already reserved a room online for the next two nights. A classy place and pricey, too. But he liked the best. Deserved it, actually. And, besides, Ramsey paid expenses, so what did he care what it cost?

The schedule for the 14th Annual Ancient Mysteries Revealed Conference, also posted online, noted that Douglas Scofield would serve tomorrow evening as the keynote speaker at a dinner, included with the registration. A cocktail party would be held before the event in the hotel's lobby.

He'd heard of Biltmore Estate but never visited. Maybe he'd tour the mansion and see how the other half once lived. Get some decorating ideas. After all, he could afford quality. Who said killing didn't pay? He'd amassed nearly twenty million dollars from fees and investments. He'd also meant what he'd said to Ramsey the other day. He did not intend on doing this for the rest of his life, no matter how much he enjoyed the work.

He squirted a dab of mustard and a smear of ketchup on his Big Mac. He didn't like a lot of condiments, just enough to give it flavor. He munched on the burger and watched the people, many clearly here to visit Biltmore at Christmas and shop in the village.

The whole place seemed geared to tourists.

Which was great.

Lots of obscure faces among which to disappear.

★   ★   ★

Malone had two problems. First, he was pursuing an unknown gunman through a dim, frigid cloister, and second, he was relying on allies that were wholly untrustworthy.

Two things had clued him in.

First, Werner Lindauer. *I knew Herr Malone was here, with a gun.* Really? Since in their brief encounter Malone had not once mentioned who he was, how did Werner know? Nobody in the church had uttered his name.

And second, the gunman.

Never once had he seemed concerned that someone else was there, someone who'd shot his accomplice. Christl had indicated that she'd told her mother about Ossau. She could also have mentioned that he would come. But that wouldn't explain Werner Lindauer's presence or how he immediately knew Malone's identity. And if Christl had provided the information, that act showed a level of Oberhauser cooperation that he'd thought didn't exist.

All of which spelled trouble.

He stopped and listened to the wheezing of the wind. He stayed low, below the arches, knees aching. Across the garden, through the falling snow, he spotted no movement. Cold air burned his throat and lungs.

He shouldn't be indulging his curiosity, but he couldn't help it. Though he suspected what was happening, he needed to know.

Dorothea watched Werner, who confidently held the gun Malone had offered. During the past twenty-four hours she'd learned a lot about this man. Things she'd never suspected.

'I'm going out there,' Christl said.

She couldn't resist. 'I saw the way you looked at Malone. You care for him.'

'He needs help.'

'From you?'

Christl shook her head and left.

'Are you okay?' Werner asked.

'I will be when this is over. Trusting Christl, or my mother, is a big mistake. You know that.'

Cold gripped her. She wrapped her arms across her chest and sought comfort within her wool coat. They'd followed Malone's advice, retreating into the apse, playing their parts. The ruinous condition of the church cast a foreboding spell. Had her grandfather actually found answers here?

Werner grasped her arm. 'We can do this.'

'*We* have no choice,' she said, still not happy with the options her mother had offered.

'You can either make the best of it, or fight it to your detriment. Doesn't matter to anyone else, but it should matter a great deal to you.'

She caught an underlying insecurity in his words. 'The gunman was genuinely caught off guard when you tackled him.'

He shrugged. 'We told him to expect a surprise or two.'

'That we did.'

The day was sinking away. Shadows inside were lengthening, the temperature dropping.

'He obviously never believed he was going to die,' Werner said.

'His mistake.'

'What about Malone? Do you think he realizes?'

She hesitated before answering, recalling her reservations from the other day at the abbey, when she first met him.

'He'd better.'

Malone stayed beneath the arches and retreated toward one of the rooms that opened off the cloister. He stood inside, amid the snow and debris, and assessed his resources. He had a gun and bullets, so why not try the same tactic that had worked for Werner? Perhaps the gunman on the opposite side of the cloister would head toward him, making his way to the church, and he could surprise him.

'He's in there,' he heard a man shout.

He stared out the doorway.

A second gunman was now in the cloister, on the short side, passing the church entrance, rounding the corner, coming straight toward him. Apparently Ulrich Henn had not been successful in stopping him.

The man raised his gun and fired straight at Malone.

He ducked as a bullet found the wall.

Another round ricocheted past, straight through the doorway, from the other gunman, across the cloister. His refuge contained no windows and the walls and roof were unbroken. What had seemed like a sure bet had suddenly turned into a serious problem.

No way out.

He was trapped.

PART FOUR

59

Stephanie admired the Inn on Biltmore Estate, an expansive fieldstone-and-stucco building that crowned a grassy promontory, overlooking the estate's famed winery. Vehicle access was restricted to estate guests, but they'd stopped at the main gate and bought a general pass to tour the grounds, which included the hotel.

She avoided a busy valet service and parked in one of the terraced paved lots, then they climbed a landscaped incline to the main entrance, where uniformed doormen greeted them with smiles. The inside was reminiscent of what it might have been like to visit the Vanderbilts a hundred years ago. Light-paneled walls finished with a dull honey-stained gloss, marble flooring, elegant art, and rich floral patterns in the drapes and upholstery. Greenery overflowed from stone planters and warmed an airy décor that opened upward to the next floor, a coffered ceiling twenty feet overhead. The views beyond the plate-glass doors and windows, past a veranda dotted with rockers, were of the Pisgah National Forest and the Smoky Mountains.

She listened for a moment to a pianist playing near a flagstone hearth. A stairway led down to what sounded and smelled like the dining room, a steady procession of patrons coming and going. They inquired at the concierge desk and were directed through the lobby, past the pianist, to a window-lined corridor that led to meeting rooms and a conference center where they found the registration desk for Ancient Mysteries Revealed.

Davis plucked a program from a pile and studied the day's schedule. 'Scofield's not talking this afternoon.'

A perky young woman with coal-black hair heard him and said, 'The professor speaks tomorrow. Today are info sessions.'

'Do you know where Dr. Scofield is?' Stephanie asked.

'He was around here earlier, but I haven't seen him in a while.' She paused. 'You folks from the press, too?'

She caught the qualifier. 'There have been others?'

The woman nodded. 'A little while ago. Some man. He wanted to see Scofield.'

'And what did you tell him?' Davis asked.

She shrugged. 'Same thing. Haven't a clue.'

Stephanie decided to study one of the schedules and noted the next session, set to begin at one p.m. 'Pleiadian Wisdom for These Challenging Times.' She read its summary.

Suzanne Johnson is a world-acclaimed trance channeler and author of several bestselling books. Join Suzanne and the nonphysical, time-traveling, mind-boggling Pleiadians as she channels them for a stimulating two hours of mind-expanding questions and sometimes tough but always positive, life-enhancing answers. Subjects of Pleiadian interest include: the acceleration of energy, astrology, secret political and economic agendas, hidden planetary history, god games, symbols, mind control, blossoming psychic abilities, time line healing, personal self-empowerment, and much more.

The rest of the afternoon featured a host of more oddities focusing on crop circles, the world's impending end, sacred sites, and one expansive session on the rise and fall of civilization, including binary motion, change in electromagnetic waves, and the impact of catastrophic events, with an emphasis on the precession of the equinoxes.

She shook her head. Like watching paint dry. What a waste of time.

Davis thanked the woman and retreated from the table with a pamphlet still in hand. 'Nobody from the press is here to interview him.'

She wasn't so sure. 'I know what you're thinking, but our guy wouldn't be that obvious.'

'He may be in a hurry.'

'He may not be anywhere near here.'

Davis hastened back toward the main lobby.

'Where are you going?' she asked.

'It's lunchtime. Let's see if Scofield eats.'

Ramsey hurried back to his office and waited for Hovey, who arrived a few moments later and reported, 'McCoy immediately left the grounds.'

He was furious. 'I want everything we have on her.'

His aide nodded. 'That was a solo job,' Hovey said. 'You know that.'

'I agree, but she feels the need to record me. That's a problem.'

Hovey was aware of his boss's efforts to secure the Joint Chiefs position, just not the particulars. Ramsey's long-standing relationship with Charlie Smith was his alone. His aide had already been promised that he'd be going to the Pentagon with him – more than enough incentive for Hovey to actively participate. Lucky for him, every captain wanted to be an admiral.

'Get me that info on her now,' he ordered again.

Hovey left his office. He picked up the phone and dialed Charlie Smith. Four rings and the call was answered.

'Where are you?'

'Having a delicious meal.'

He didn't want any details, but he knew what was coming.

'The dining room is lovely. A large room with a fireplace, elegantly decorated. Soft lighting, relaxed appeal. And the service. Superb. My water glass has yet to get half empty and the bread basket stays full. The manager even wandered by a minute ago and made sure I was enjoying the meal.'

'Charlie, shut up.'

'Touchy today.'

'Listen to me. I assume you're doing as I asked.'

'As always.'

'I need you back here tomorrow, so make it quick.'

'They just brought a dessert sampler of crème brûlée and chocolate mousse. You really should visit here.'

He didn't want to hear another word. 'Charlie, just do it and get back by tomorrow afternoon.'

Smith clicked off his phone and turned his attention back to his dessert. Across the main dining room of the Inn on Biltmore Estate, Dr. Douglas Scofield sat at a table, with three others, eating his own lunch.

* * *

Stephanie descended the carpeted stairway and entered the inn's spacious dining room, stopping at the hostess' podium. Another flagstone hearth accommodated a crackling fire. Most of the white-clothed tables were occupied. She noticed fine china, crystal glasses, brass chandeliers, and lots of maroon, gold, green, and beige fabrics. One hundred percent southern in look and feel. Davis was still holding the conference pamphlet and she knew what he was doing. Looking for a face to match Douglas Scofield's prominent picture.

She saw him first, at a window table with three others. Then Davis caught sight. She grabbed his sleeve and shook her head. 'Not this time. We can't make a scene.'

'I'm not going to.'

'He has people with him. Let's get a table and wait until he's done, then approach him.'

'We don't have time for that.'

'And where do we have to be?'

'I don't know about you, but I'm anxious to watch the channeling with the Pleiadians at one.'

She smiled. 'You're impossible.'

'But I'm growing on you.'

She decided to surrender and released her grip.

Davis wove his way ahead and she followed.

They approached the table. Davis said, 'Dr. Scofield, I was wondering if I might have a word with you.'

Scofield appeared to be in his midsixties, with a broad nose, a bald pate, and teeth that looked too straight and too white to be real. His fleshy face betrayed a testiness that his dark eyes immediately confirmed.

'I'm having lunch at the moment.'

Davis' face stayed cordial. 'I need to speak with you. It's quite important.'

Scofield laid his fork down. 'As you can see, I am engaged with these people. I understand you're here at the conference and want some time with me, but I have to budget that carefully.'

'Why is that?'

She didn't like the sound of the question. Davis had apparently also caught the *I'm important* subtext to Scofield's explanation.

The professor sighed and pointed to the pamphlet Davis held. 'I do this every year, so that I can be available for those interested in my research. I realize you want to discuss things, and that's fine. Once I'm done here, perhaps we could talk upstairs, near the piano?'

Irritation remained in his tone. The other three diners likewise seemed annoyed. One them said, 'We've been waiting for this lunch all year.'

'And you'll have it,' Davis said. 'As soon as I'm done.'

'Who are you?' Scofield asked.

'Name's Raymond Dyals, retired navy.'

She watched as recognition clicked in Scofield.

'Okay, Mr. Dyals, and by the way you must have discovered the fountain of youth.'

'You'll be surprised what I've discovered.'

Scofield's eyes flickered. 'Then you and I definitely need to talk.'

60

Ossau

Malone decided to act. He swung the gun around and fired two rounds across the cloister garden. He had no idea of the assailant's position, but the message was clear.

He was armed.

A bullet bisected the doorway and sent him reeling back.

He determined its origin.

From the second gunman, on his side of the gallery, to his right.

He stared up. The gabled roof was held aloft by trusses formed from rough-hewn beams stretching the room's width. A jumble of broken rocks and debris littered the floor and lay piled against one of the decaying walls. He stuffed the gun into his jacket pocket and scrambled atop the largest chunks, which provided him two new feet of height. He leaped up, grabbed the cold beam, swung his legs upward, and straddled the timber like a horse. He quickly wiggled his way closer to the wall, only now he was ten feet above the doorway. He sprang to his feet, crouched, and balanced on the beam, regripping the gun, his muscles like bundles of tightly bound cord.

Shots rang out from the cloister. Several.

Perhaps Henn had joined the fray?

He heard another impact, similar to when Werner tackled Dark in the church, along with grunts, breathing, and fighting. He couldn't see anything except the stones on the floor below, cast in dimness thanks to only bleak light.

A shadow appeared.

He readied himself.

Two shots were fired and the man rushed into the room.

Malone leaped from the beam, crashing into the attacker, quickly rolling off and readying himself for a fight.

The man was hefty and broad-shouldered, the body hard, as if there were metal under the skin. He'd quickly recoiled from the assault and sprang to his feet – without the gun, which had slipped from his grasp.

Malone raked the side of his automatic across the man's face, sending him into the wall, dazed. He leveled the gun and prepared to take his prisoner, but a shot exploded behind him and the man dropped to the rubble.

He whirled.

Henn stood, gun aimed, just outside the doorway.

Christl appeared.

No need to inquire why the shot was necessary. He knew. But he wanted to know, 'The other one?'

'Dead,' Christl told him as she retrieved the weapon from the floor.

'Mind if I hold that?' he asked.

She tried to banish the surprise from her eyes. 'You're a distrustful sort.'

'It comes from people lying to me.'

She handed him the gun.

★　★　★

Stephanie sat with Davis and Scofield, upstairs, where the main lobby emptied into an alcove dotted with plush upholstered chairs, a panoramic view, and built-in bookshelves. People were studying the titles, and she noticed a small sign that said everything was available for reading.

A waiter sauntered over, but she waved him off.

'Since you're obviously not Admiral Dyals,' Scofield said, 'who are you?'

'White House,' Davis said. 'She's Justice Department. We fight crime.'

Scofield seemed to repress a shudder. 'I agreed to talk with you because I thought you were serious.'

'Like this bullshit here,' Davis said.

Scofield's face reddened. 'None of us considers this conference bullshit.'

'Really? There are what, a hundred people in a room right now trying to channel some dead civilization. You're a trained anthropologist, a man the government once used on some highly classified research.'

'That was a long time ago.'

'You'd be surprised how relevant it still is.'

'I assume you have identification?'

'We do.'

'Let me see.'

'Somebody killed Herbert Rowland last night,' Davis said. 'The night before they killed a former navy commander connected to Rowland. You may or may not remember Rowland, but he worked with you at Fort Lee, when you uncrated all that crap from Operation Highjump. We're not sure you're next to die, but it's a good possibility. That enough credentials?'

Scofield laughed. 'That was thirty-eight years ago.'

'Which doesn't seem to matter,' Stephanie said.

'I can't speak of what happened then. It's classified.'

He voiced the words as if they were some sort of shield, protecting him from harm.

'Again,' she said. 'That doesn't seem to matter, either.'

Scofield frowned. 'You two are wasting my time. I have a lot of people to speak with.'

'How about this,' she said. 'Tell us what you can.' She was hoping that once this self-important fool started talking, he'd keep talking.

Scofield checked his watch, then said, 'I wrote a book. *Maps of Ancient Explorers.* You should read it because it contains plenty of explanations. You can get a copy in the conference bookstore.' He pointed off to his left. 'That way.'

'Give us a synopsis,' Davis said.

'Why? You said we're all nuts. What does it matter what I think?'

Davis started to speak, but she waved him off. 'Convince us. We didn't drive all the way here for no reason.'

Scofield paused, seemingly searching for the right words to make his point. 'Do you know Occam's razor?'

She shook her head.

'It's a principle. Entities are not to be multiplied without necessity. Put more plainly, no elaborate solutions where simple ones will do. That applies to almost everything, including civilizations.'

She wondered if she was going to regret asking this man's opinion.

'Early Sumerian texts, including the famous *Epic of Gilgamesh,* talk repeatedly of tall, god-like people who lived among them. They called them Watchers. Ancient Jewish texts, including some versions of the Bible, refer to those

Sumerian Watchers, who are described as gods, angels, and sons of heaven. The Book of Enoch tells how these curious people sent emissaries out into the world to teach men new skills. Uriel, the angel who taught Enoch about astronomy, is described as one of these Watchers. Eight Watchers are actually named in the Book of Enoch. They were supposed experts in enchantments, root cuttings, astrology, the constellations, weather, geology, and astronomy. Even the Dead Sea Scrolls make reference to Watchers, including the episode where Noah's father becomes concerned that his child is so extraordinarily beautiful, he thinks his wife may have lain with one.'

'This is nonsense,' Davis said.

Scofield repressed a smile. 'Do you know how many times I've heard that? Here are some *historical* facts. In Mexico, Quetzalcoatl, the fair god, white-skinned, bearded, was credited with teaching the civilization that preceded the Aztecs. He came from the sea and wore long clothing embroidered with crosses. When Cortés arrived in the sixteenth century he was mistaken for Quetzalcoatl. The Mayans had a similar teacher, Kukulcán, who came from the sea where the sun rises. The Spanish burned all of the Mayan texts in the seventeenth century, but one bishop recorded a notation that survived. It talked of long-robed visitors who came repeatedly, led by someone called Votan. The Inca had a god-teacher, Viracocha, who came from the great ocean to their west. They, too, made the same mistake with Pizarro, thinking him the god returned. So, Mr. White House, whoever the hell you are, believe me, you know not of what you speak.'

She'd been right. This man liked to talk.

'In 1936 a German archaeologist found a clay vase, with a copper cylinder that held an iron rod, in a Parthian grave dated from 250 BCE. When fruit juice was poured inside a half-volt current, that lasted for two weeks, was generated. Just enough for electroplating, which we know was done during that time. In 1837 an iron plate was found in the Great Pyramid that had been smelted at over one thousand degrees Celsius. It contained nickel, which is most unusual, and was dated to two thousand years before the Iron Age. When Columbus landed in Costa Rica in 1502, he was received with great respect and taken inland to the grave of an important person, a grave decorated with the prow of a strange ship. The funeral slab depicted men who looked quite similar to Columbus and his men. To that point, no European had ever visited that land.

'China is particularly interesting,' Scofield continued. 'Its great philosopher Lao-tzu talked about Ancient Ones. As did Confucius. Lao called them wise, knowledgeable, powerful, loving, and, most important, human. He wrote of them in the seventh century BCE. His writings survive. Do you want to hear?'

'That's what we came for,' she made clear.

'*The Ancient Masters were subtle, mysterious, profound, responsive. The depth of their knowledge is unfathomable. Because it is unfathomable, all we can do is describe their appearance. Watchful, like men crossing a winter stream. Alert, like men aware of danger. Courteous, like visiting guests. Yielding, like ice about to melt. Simple, like uncarved blocks of wood.* Interesting words from a long time ago.'

Curious, she had to admit.

'Do you know what changed the world? What altered, forever, the course of human existence?' Scofield did not wait for a response. 'The wheel? Fire?' He shook his head. 'More than those. Writing. That's what did it. When we learned to record our thoughts so that others, centuries later, could know them, that changed the world. Both the Sumerians and the Egyptians left written records of a people who visited and taught them things. People who looked normal and lived and died just like them. That's not me talking. That's historical fact. Did you know that the Canadian government is, at this very moment, probing an underwater site off the Queen Charlotte Islands for traces of a civilization never known to have existed before? It's a base camp of some sort that was once on the shore of an ancient lake.'

'Where did these visitors come from?' she asked.

'The sea. They sailed with expert precision. Recently ancient marine tools were discovered off Cyprus that date back twelve thousand years, some of the oldest artifacts ever found there. Finding those means that someone was actually sailing the Mediterranean, and occupying Cyprus, two thousand years earlier than anyone ever believed. In Canada seafarers would have been drawn by rich kelp beds. It's logical these people sought out choice spots for food and trade.'

'Like I said,' Davis said. 'A bunch of science fiction.'

'Is it? Did you know that prophecy mixed with god-like benefactors from the sea forms a big part of Native American lore? Mayan records talk of Popul Vuh, a land where light and dark dwelled together. Prehistoric cave and rock drawings in Africa and Egypt show an unidentified people of the sea. The ones in France, dated to ten thousand years ago, show men and women dressed in comfortable clothes, not the furs and bones usually associated with people of that time. A copper mine found in Rhodesia has been dated to forty-seven thousand years ago. The site seemed to have been mined for a specific purpose.'

'Is this Atlantis?' Davis asked.

'There's no such thing,' Scofield said.

'I bet there's a bunch of people in this hotel who'd disagree with you.'

'And they'd be wrong. Atlantis is a fable. It's a recurring theme throughout many cultures, just as the Great Flood is part of the world's religions. It's a romantic notion, but the reality is not so fantastic. Ancient submerged megalithic constructions have been found on shallow seafloors, near coastlines, all over the world. Malta, Egypt, Greece, Lebanon, Spain, India, China, Japan – all have them. They were built before the last ice age and, when the ice melted around 10,000 BCE, sea levels rose and consumed them. These are the real Atlantis, and they prove Occam's razor. No elaborate solutions where simple ones will suffice. All explanations are rational.'

'And the rational one here is?' Davis asked.

'While cavemen were just learning to farm with stone tools and live in crude villages, there existed a people who built seaworthy vessels and charted the globe with precision. They seemed to understand their purpose and tried to teach us things. They came in peace. Never once is there any mention of aggression or hostility. But their messages became lost over time, especially as modern humankind began to consider itself the pinnacle of intellectual achievement.' Scofield cast Davis a stern look. 'Our arrogance will be our downfall.'

'Foolishness,' Davis said, 'can have the same effect.'

Scofield seemed ready for that rebuke. 'All over this planet these ancient people left messages either as artifacts, maps, or manuscripts. These messages are neither clear nor direct, granted, but they are a form of communication, one that says, *Yours is not the first civilization, nor the cultures you consider to be your roots the true beginning. Thousands of years ago we knew what you have only recently discovered. We traveled all across your young world, when ice fields blanketed the north and southern seas were still navigable. We left maps of the places we visited. We left knowledge of your world and the cosmos, of mathematics, science, and philosophy. Some of the races we visited retained that knowledge, which has helped you build your world. Remember us.'*

Davis did not seem impressed. 'What does this have to do with Operation Highjump and Raymond Dyals?'

'A great deal. But again, that's classified. Believe me, I wish it wasn't. But that I cannot change. I gave my word and I've kept it all these years. Now, since you both think I'm nuts – which, by the way, is my opinion of you – I'm leaving.'

Scofield stood. But before he walked away, he hesitated.

'One thought you might consider. A exhaustive study was done a decade ago at Cambridge University, by a team of world-renowned scholars. Their conclusion? Less than ten percent of the records from antiquity have survived till now. Ninety percent of ancient knowledge is gone. So how do we know if anything is truly nonsense?'

61

Ramsey strolled the Capitol Mall, headed for the spot where, yesterday, he'd met Senator Aatos Kane's aide. The same young man stood in the same wool overcoat, shuffling his feet from the cold. Today Ramsey had made him wait forty-five minutes.

'Okay, Admiral. I get the point. You win,' the aide said as he approached. 'Make me sweat it out.'

He knotted his brow in dismay. 'It's not a contest.'

'Right. I jammed it up your ass last time, you stuck it up my boss' ass afterward, now we're all kissin' cousins. It is a game, Admiral, and you won.'

He removed a small plastic device, the size of a television remote control, and switched it on. 'Forgive me.'

The unit quickly confirmed that no listening devices were present. Hovey was on the far side of the Mall monitoring to make sure no parabolic devices were in use. But Ramsey doubted that would be a problem. This minion worked for a pro who understood that you had to give in order to receive.

'Talk to me,' he said.

'The senator spoke to the president this morning. He told him what he wanted. The president inquired as to our interest and the senator said he admired you.'

One aspect of Diane McCoy's solo performance was now confirmed. He stood, hands in his coat pockets, and listened for more.

'The president had some reservations. He said you're not a staff favorite. His White House people had other names in mind. But the senator knew what the president wanted.'

He was curious about that. 'Tell me.'

'There's about to be a vacancy on the Supreme Court. A resignation. The justice wants to give the current administration the pick. Daniels has a name in mind and wants us to shepherd it through Senate confirmation.'

Interesting.

'We chair the Judiciary Committee. The nominee is a good one, so no problem. We can make it happen.' The aide sounded proud to be part of the home team.

'Did the president have any serious problems with me?'

The aide allowed himself a grin, then a chuckle. 'What do you want? A friggin' engraved invitation? Presidents don't like to be told what to do, nor do they like to be asked favors. They like to be the one who asks. Daniels, though, seemed receptive to the whole thing. He doesn't think the Joint Chiefs is worth a crap anyway.'

'Lucky for us he only has less than three years left in office.'

'I don't know how lucky that makes us. Daniels is a proven dealer. He knows how to give and take. We've had no problems dealing with him, and he's popular as hell.'

'The devil you know as opposed to the one you don't?'

'Something like that.'

He needed to extract what he could from this source. He had to know who else, if anyone, was aiding Diane McCoy in her surprising crusade.

'We're interested in when you'll move on the governor of South Carolina,' the aide said.

'The day after I move into my new office at the Pentagon.'

'And what if you can't deliver the governor?'

'Then I'll just destroy your boss.' He allowed an almost sexual enjoyment to sweep into his eyes. 'We'll do this my way. Clear?'

'And what is your way?'

'First off, I want to know exactly what you're doing to make my appointment happen. Every detail, and not just what you want to tell me. If my patience is tried, then I think I'll take your suggestion from last time, retire, and watch all of your careers dissolve to nothing.'

The aide held up his hands in mock surrender. 'Slow down, Admiral. I didn't come here to fight. I came to brief you.'

'Then brief me, you little piece of crap.'

The aide accepted the rebuke with a shrug. 'Daniels is on board. He says it'll be done. Kane can deliver the votes on the Judiciary Committee. Daniels knows that. Your announcement will come tomorrow.'

'Before Sylvian's funeral?'

The aide nodded. 'No need to wait.'

He agreed. But there was still Diane McCoy. 'Any objection lodged from the Office of the National Security Adviser?'

'Daniels didn't mention it. But why would he?'

'Don't you think we need to know if staffers plan to sabotage what we're doing?'

The aide threw him a wistful smile. 'That shouldn't be a problem. Once Daniels is on board, that's it. He can handle his people. What's the problem, Admiral? You got enemies over there?'

No. Merely a complication. But he was beginning to realize its limited extent. 'Tell the senator that I appreciate his efforts and to stay in touch.'

'Am I dismissed?'

His silence signaled yes.

The aide seemed glad the conversation was over and departed.

Ramsey walked over and sat on the same bench he'd warmed earlier. Hovey waited five minutes, then approached, sat beside him, and said, 'Area is clean. Nobody was listening.'

'We're fine with Kane. It's McCoy. She's doing this on her own.'

'Maybe she thinks getting you is her ticket to greater and better.'

Time to find out how bad his aide wanted *greater and better.* 'She may have to be eliminated. Just like Wilkerson.'

Hovey's silence was more explicit than words.

'Do we have much on her?' Ramsey asked the captain.

'Quite a bit, but she's relatively boring. Lives alone, no relationships, workaholic. Co-workers like her, but she's not one that everybody wants to sit next to at state dinners. She probably using this as a way to up her worth.'

Made sense.

Hovey's cell phone rang, dulled through his wool coat. The call was short and ended quickly. 'More problems.'

He waited.

'Diane McCoy just tried to access the warehouse at Fort Lee.'

Malone entered the church, Henn and Christl ahead of him. Isabel had descended from the choir and stood with Dorothea and Werner.

He decided to stop the charade and came up behind Henn, jamming the gun into the man's neck and relieving him of his weapon.

He then stepped back and aimed the barrel at Isabel. 'Tell your butler to stay cool.'

'And what would you do, Herr Malone, if I refused? Shoot me?'

He lowered the gun. 'No need. This was all a dog-and-pony show. Those four had to die. Though clearly none of them realized it. You didn't want me talking to them.'

'What makes you so sure?' Isabel asked.

'I pay attention.'

'All right. I knew they would be here, and they did think us allies.'

'Then they're bigger fools than I am.'

'Maybe not them, but certainly the man who sent them. Can we dispense with the theatrics – on both our parts – and talk?'

'I'm listening.'

'I know who's trying to kill you,' Isabel said. 'But I need your help.'

He caught the first rumors of nighttime outside the bare window frames from air turning colder by the second.

He also caught the drift of her words. 'One for the other?'

'I apologize for the deception, but it seemed the only way to attract your cooperation.'

'You should have just asked.'

'I tried that at Reichshoffen. I thought this might work better.'

'Which could have gotten me killed.'

'Come now, Herr Malone, I have much more confidence in your abilities than you seem to.'

He'd had enough. 'I'm going back to the hotel.'

He started to leave.

'I know where Dietz was headed,' Isabel said. 'Where your father was taking him in Antarctica.'

Screw her.

'Somewhere in this church is what Dietz was missing. What he went *there* to find.'

His vehemence subsided into hunger. 'I'm going to eat dinner.' He kept walking. 'I'm willing to listen while I eat, but if it isn't damn good information, I'm gone.'

'I assure you, Herr Malone, it's more than good.'

62

Asheville

'You pushed Scofield too hard,' Stephanie told Edwin Davis.

They were still sitting in the alcove. Outside, a glorious afternoon illuminated distant winter forests. To their left, toward the southeast, she caught a glimpse of the main château a mile or so away, perched high on its own promontory.

'Scofield's an ass,' Davis said. 'He thinks Ramsey cares that he's kept his mouth shut all these years.'

'We don't know what Ramsey cares about.'

'Somebody is going to kill Scofield.'

She wasn't so sure. 'And what do you propose we do about it?'

'Stick close to him.'

'We could take him into custody.'

'And lose our bait.'

'If you're right, is that fair to him?'

'He thinks we're idiots.'

She didn't like Douglas Scofield, either, but that shouldn't factor into their decisions. There was one other thing, though. 'You realize, we still have no proof of anything.'

Davis checked the clock across the lobby. 'I have to make a call.'

He left his chair and approached the windows, nestling into a floral sofa ten feet away, facing away, toward outside. She watched him. He was both troubled and complex. Interesting to know, though, like her, he struggled with emotions. And he didn't like to talk about them, either.

Davis motioned for her to come closer.

She walked over and sat beside him.

'He wants to talk to you again.'

She cradled the cell phone to her ear, knowing exactly who was on the other end.

'Stephanie,' President Daniels said, 'this is growing complex. Ramsey has maneuvered Aatos Kane. The good senator wants me to bestow the Joint Chiefs position on Ramsey. There's no way in hell that's going to happen, but I didn't let Kane know that. I once heard an old Indian proverb. *If you live in the river, then you should make friends with the crocodiles.* Apparently, Ramsey is practicing that truism.'

'Or it may be the other way around.'

'Which is what really makes this complex. Those two haven't joined forces voluntarily. Something's happened. I can kick the can down the street for a few days, but we need to make progress on your end. How's my boy?'

'Eager.'

Daniels chuckled. 'Now you see what I have to put up with from you. Tough to keep a leash on things?'

'You could say that.'

'Teddy Roosevelt said it best. *"Do what you can with what you have, where you are."* Stay with this.'

'I don't think I have much choice, do I?'

'No, but here's a tidbit. The Berlin station chief for naval intelligence, a captain named Sterling Wilkerson, was found dead in Munich.'

'Which you believe is not coincidental.'

'Crap, no. Ramsey is working something here and over there. I can't prove it, but I feel it. What about Malone?'

'Haven't heard from him.'

'Tell me straight up. Do you think this professor is in danger?'

'I don't know. But I think we ought to hang around till tomorrow, to be sure.'

'Here's something I didn't tell Edwin. I need a poker face.'

She smiled. 'Okay.'

'I have my doubts about Diane McCoy. I learned a long time ago to pay attention to my enemies 'cause they're the first to learn your mistakes. I've been watching her. Edwin knows that. What he doesn't know is that she left the building today and drove into Virginia. Right now she's at Fort Lee, inspecting a warehouse the army leases to naval intelligence. I checked. Ramsey was there himself yesterday.'

Something she already knew, thanks to her staff.

Davis motioned that he was going to get something to drink from a hospitality table near the hearth and with gestures asked if she wanted anything. She shook her head.

'He's gone,' she said into the phone. 'I assume you're telling me this for a reason.'

'It seems Diane has made friends with the crocodiles, too, but I'm worried she's going to get eaten.'

'Couldn't happen to a nicer person.'

'I do believe you have a mean streak.'

'I have a realist streak.'

'Stephanie, you sound worried.'

'As much as I may object, I have a feeling our man is here.'

'You want help?' Daniels asked.

'I do, but Edwin doesn't.'

'Since when do you listen to him?'

'This is his show. He's on a mission.'

'Love is hell, but don't let it be his downfall. I need him.'

Smith was enjoying the piano music and a crackling fire in the hearth. Lunch had been great. The salad and appetizer were both superb and the soup was delicious, but the fresh lamb with seasonal vegetables had been the best by far.

He'd come upstairs after the man and woman approached Scofield and whisked him away from his meal. He hadn't been able to hear what was said downstairs or here. He wondered, were these the same two from last night? Hard to say.

For the past few hours Scofield had been approached by one person after another. In fact, the whole conference seemed a lovefest geared toward him. The professor was listed as one of the event's original organizers. He was the keynote speaker tomorrow night. He was also conducting a candlelight tour through the main mansion this evening. Tomorrow morning was what the brochure called Scofield's Hog Wild Adventure. Three hours of boar hunting with bow and arrow, in a nearby forest, led by the professor himself. The woman at the registration desk had said the early-morning jaunt was popular, and about thirty folks went along each year. Two more people interested in Dr. Douglas Scofield was not necessarily cause for alarm. So Smith quelled his paranoia and did not allow it to get the best of him. He didn't want to admit it, but he was shaken from last night.

He watched as the man rose from the sofa and headed for a green-clothed table beside the hearth, pouring himself a glass of ice water.

Smith stood and casually walked over, refilling his teacup from a silver server. The service was a nice touch. Refreshments for guests all day. He added a little Splenda – he hated sugar – and stirred.

The man retreated toward the alcove, sipping his water, to where the woman was ending a cell phone call. The fire in the hearth had burned low, barely sputtering now. One of the attendants opened an iron grate and added a few logs. He knew he could follow those two and see where it led, but luckily he'd already decided on a more definitive tack.

Something innovative.

Guaranteed to produce results.

And fitting for the great Douglas Scofield.

Malone reentered the L'Arlequin and headed for its restaurant, where colorful rugs covered an oak-planked floor. His entourage followed him inside and peeled off their coats. Isabel spoke with the man who'd worked the registration desk earlier. The attendant left, closing the restaurant doors behind him. Malone shucked his jacket and gloves and noticed that his shirt was damp from perspiration.

'There are only eight rooms upstairs,' Isabel said, 'and I've let them all for the night. The owner is preparing a meal.'

Malone sat on one of the benches that lined two oak tables. 'Good. I'm hungry.'

Christl, Dorothea, and Werner sat opposite him. Henn stood off to the side, holding a satchel. Isabel assumed a position at the head of the table. 'Herr Malone, I'm going to be truthful with you.'

'I seriously doubt that, but go ahead.'

Her hands tightened and her fingers eagerly tapped the tabletop.

'I'm not your child,' he said, 'and I'm not in the will, so get to the point.'

'I know that Hermann visited here twice,' she said. 'Once before the war, in 1937. The other time in 1952. My mother-in-law told Dietz and I about the trips shortly before she died. But she knew nothing of what Hermann did here. Dietz himself came about a year before he disappeared.'

'You've never mentioned that,' Christl said.

Isabel shook her head. 'I never realized a connection between this place and the pursuit. I only knew that both men visited. Yesterday, when you told me about here, I immediately realized the link.'

The adrenaline rush from the church had drained, and Malone's body felt heavy with fatigue. But he needed to focus. 'So Hermann and Dietz were here. That's of little use since, apparently, only Hermann found anything. And he didn't tell anybody.'

'Einhard's will,' Christl said, 'makes clear that you *clarify this pursuit by applying the angel's perfection to the lord's sanctification*. That gets you from Aachen to here. Then *only those who appreciate the throne of Solomon and Roman frivolity shall find their way to heaven*.'

Dorothea and Werner sat silent. Malone wondered why they were even here. Maybe they'd already played their part in the church? He pointed at them and asked, 'Have you two kissed and made up?'

'Is that important to anything?' Dorothea asked.

He shrugged. 'Is to me.'

'Herr Malone,' Isabel said. 'We must solve this challenge.'

'Did you see that church? It's a ruin. There's nothing there from twelve hundred years ago. The walls are barely standing and the roof is new. The flooring is cracked and crumbled, the altar eroding away. How do you plan to solve anything?'

Isabel motioned and Henn handed her the satchel. She unbuckled its leather straps and removed a tattered map, the paper a pale rust color. She carefully unfolded and laid the sheet, maybe twenty-four by eighteen inches, flat on the table. He saw that it was not of any country or continent, but was a sectional representation of a jagged coastline.

'This is Hermann's map, used during the 1938 Nazi expedition to Antarctica. It's where he explored.'

'There's no writing,' he said.

Locations were denoted by △'s. X's seemed to note mountains. A □ pinpointed something central, and a route was shown to and from, but not a single word anywhere.

'My husband left this behind when he sailed for America in 1971. He took another drawing with him. But I know exactly where Dietz was headed.' She held up a second folded map from the satchel. Newer, blue, titled *International Travel Map of Antarctica, Scale 1:8,000,000.* 'That information is all on here.'

She reached into the satchel and brought out two final objects, both sheathed inside plastic bags. The books. One from Charlemagne's grave, which Dorothea had shown him. The other from Einhard's tomb, which Christl had possessed.

She tabled Christl's and lifted Dorothea's.

'This is the key, but we can't read it. The ability to do that is here, in that monastery. I fear that, though we know where to go in Antarctica, the trip would be unproductive unless we know what's on these pages. We must have, as Einhard wrote, a full comprehension of heaven.'

'Your husband went without one.'

'His mistake,' Isabel said.

'Can we eat?' Malone asked, tired of listening to her.

'I understand you're frustrated with us,' Isabel said. 'But I came to make a bargain with you.'

'No, you came to set me up.' He stared at the sisters. 'Again.'

'If we discover how to read this book,' Isabel said. 'If it seems worth the trip, which I believe it will be, then I assume you'll be going to Antarctica?'

'Hadn't thought that far ahead yet.'

'I want you to take my daughters with you, along with Werner and Ulrich.'

'Anything else?' he asked, almost amused.

'I'm quite serious. It's the price you'll pay to know the location. Without that location, the trip would be as futile as Dietz's.'

'Then I guess I won't know, because that's insane. We're not talking about a romp in the snow. This is Antarctica. One of the toughest places on earth.'

'I checked this morning. The temperature at Halvorsen Base, which is the closest landing strip to the location, was minus seven degrees Celsius. Not all that bad. The weather was also relatively calm.'

'Which can change in ten minutes.'

'You sound like you've been there,' Werner said.

'I have. It's not a place where you want to hang out.'

'Cotton,' Christl said. 'Mother explained this to us

earlier. They were headed for a specific location.' She pointed to the map on the table. 'Do you realize that the submarine could be lying in the water near that location?'

She'd played the one card he'd been dreading. He'd already assumed the same thing. The court of inquiry's report had noted NR-1A's last known location – *73° S, 15° W, approximately 150 miles north of Cape Norvegia*. That could now be matched with another reference point, which might be enough to allow him to find the sunken vessel. But to be able to do that, he had to play ball.

'I assume that if I agree to take along these passengers, I won't be told anything until we're in the air?'

'Actually, not until you're on the ground,' Isabel said. 'Ulrich was trained in navigation by the Stasi. He'll direct you, once there.'

'I'm positively crushed at the lack of faith you have in me.'

'About as much as you have in me.'

'You realize that I won't have the final say on who goes. I'll need help from the US military to get there. They may not allow anybody else.'

Her morose heavy face lightened by a fleeting smile. 'Come now, Herr Malone, you can do better than that. You'll have the power to make things happen. Of that I'm sure.'

He faced the others sitting across the table. 'Do you three have any idea what you're getting into?'

'It's the price *we* have to pay,' Dorothea said.

Now he understood. Their game wasn't over.

'I can handle it,' Dorothea said.

Werner nodded. 'I can, too.'

He stared at Christl.

'I want to know what happened to them,' she said, her eyes downcast.

So did he. He must be insane.

'Okay, Frau Oberhauser, if we solve the pursuit, you have a deal.'

63

Ramsey opened the hatch and exited the helicopter. He'd flown directly from Washington to Fort Lee in the chopper that naval intelligence maintained around-the-clock at administrative headquarters.

A car waited for him and he was driven to where Diane McCoy was being held. He'd ordered her detainment the moment Hovey had informed him of her visit to the base. Holding a deputy national security adviser could present a problem, but he'd assured the base commander that he'd assume full responsibility.

He doubted there'd be any fallout.

This was McCoy's jaunt, and she wasn't about to involve the White House. That conclusion was fortified by the fact that she'd made no calls from the base.

He left the car and entered the security building, where a sergeant-major escorted him to McCoy. He entered and closed the door. She'd been made comfortable in the chief of security's private office.

'About time,' she said. 'It's been nearly two hours.'

He unbuttoned his overcoat. He'd already been told she'd been searched and electronically swept. He sat in a chair beside her. 'I thought you and I had a deal.'

'No, Langford. You had a deal for you. I had nothing.'

'I told you that I would make sure you were a part of the next administration.'

'You can't guarantee that.'

'Nothing in this world is a certainty, but I can narrow the odds. Which I'm doing, by the way. But recording me? Trying to get me to admit things? Now coming here? This is not the way, Diane.'

'What's in that warehouse?'

He needed to know, 'How did you learn about it?'

'I'm a deputy national security adviser.'

He decided to be partially honest with her. 'It contains artifacts found in 1947 during Operation Highjump and again in '48 during Operation Windmill. Some unusual artifacts. They were also part of what happened to NR-1A in '71. That sub was on a mission concerning those artifacts.'

'Edwin Davis talked to the president about Highjump and Windmill. I heard him.'

'Diane, surely you can see the damage that could be done if it was revealed that the navy did not search for one of its subs after it sank. Not only didn't it search, but a cover story was fabricated. Families were lied to, reports falsified. You might have been able to get away with that then – different times – but not today. The fallout would be enormous.'

'And how do you figure into that?'

Interesting. She wasn't all that informed. 'Admiral Dyals gave the order not to search for NR-1A. Even though the crew agreed to those conditions before they left port, his reputation would be destroyed if that came out. I owe that man a lot.'

'Then why kill Sylvian?'

He wasn't going there. 'I didn't kill anybody.'

She started to speak, but he stopped her with a halting hand. 'I don't deny, though, that I want his job.'

The room grew tense, like the descending weight of a hushed poker game – which, in many ways, this encounter resembled. He bore his gaze into her. 'I'm being straight with you in the hope that you'll be straight with me.'

He knew from Aatos Kane's aide that Daniels had been receptive to the idea of his appointment, which ran contrary to McCoy's theatrics. It was vital that he maintain a set of eyes and ears within the Oval Office. Good decisions were always based on good information. Problem that she was, he needed her.

'I knew you'd come,' she said. 'Interesting that you have personal control of that warehouse.'

He shrugged. 'It's under naval intelligence. Before I headed the agency, others looked after it. That's not the only repository we maintain.'

'I imagine it's not. But there's a lot more happening here than you want to admit. What about your Berlin station chief, Wilkerson? Why did he end up dead?'

He assumed that tidbit would make it into everyone's daily briefing booklet. But there was no need to confirm any linkage. 'I'm having that investigated. The motivations may be personal, though – he was involved with a married woman. Our people are working the case right now. Too soon to say anything sinister.'

'I want to see what's in the warehouse.'

He watched her face, neither hostile nor unfriendly. 'What would that prove?'

'I want to see what this is about.'

'No, you don't.'

He watched her again. She had a pouting mouth. Her light hair hung like two inward-curving curtains on both sides of a heart-shaped face. She was attractive and he wondered if charm might work. 'Diane, listen to me. You don't need to do this. I'll honor our agreement. But to be able to do that, I have to do this my way. You coming here is jeopardizing everything.'

'I'm not prepared to trust my career to you.'

He knew a little of her history. Her father was a local Indianan politician who'd made a name for himself after getting elected lieutenant governor, then proceeded to alienate half the state. Maybe he was witnessing some of that same rebellious streak? Perhaps. But he had to make things clear. 'Then I'm afraid you're on your own.'

He sensed comprehension washing over her. 'And I'll end up dead?'

'Did I say that?'

'You didn't have to.'

No, he didn't. But there was still the problem of damage control. 'How about this. We'll say there's been a disagreement. You came here on an exploratory mission, and the White House and naval intelligence have worked out an arrangement whereby the information you want will be provided. That way, the base commander will be satisfied and no more questions, aside from what's already been raised, will be asked. We leave smiling and happy.'

He spotted defeat in her eyes.

'Don't screw with me,' she said.

'I haven't done a thing. You're the one going off half-cocked.'

'I swear to you, Langford, I'll bring you down. Don't screw with me.'

He decided diplomacy was the better tack. At least for the moment. 'As I've repeatedly said, I'll keep my end of our bargain.'

Malone enjoyed dinner, especially since he'd eaten little all day. Interesting how, when he worked in the bookshop, hunger came with a predictable regularity. But in the field, on a mission, the urge seemed to completely disappear.

He'd listened to Isabel and her daughters, along with Werner Lindauer, talk about Hermann and Dietz Oberhauser. The tension between the daughters loomed large. Ulrich Henn had eaten with them, too, and he'd watched Henn carefully. The East German had sat in silence, never acknowledging that he was even hearing, but not missing a word.

Isabel was clearly in charge, and he'd noted the waves in the others' emotions as they rode her unsteady current. Neither daughter ever rose to challenge her. They either agreed or said nothing. And Werner said little of anything useful.

He'd passed on dessert and decided to head upstairs.

In the foyerlike lobby logs burned with a warm glow, filling the room with the scent of resin. He stopped and enjoyed the fire, noticing three framed pencil drawings of the monastery on the walls. One was an exterior sketch of the towers, everything intact, and he noticed a date in one corner. 1784. The other two were interior images. One was of the cloister, its arches and columns no longer bare. Instead carved images sprang from the stones with mathematical regularity. In the center garden the fountain stood in all its glory, water overflowing from its iron basin. He imagined cowled figures flitting to and fro among the arches.

The last drawing was of the inside of the church.

An angular view from the rear vestibule facing toward the altar, from the right side, where he'd made his advance through the columns toward the gunman. No ruin was shown. Instead stone, wood, and glass assembled in a miraculous union – part gothic, part Romanesque. Artwork abounded on the columns, but with a delicate modesty, inconspicuous, a far cry from the church's current decay. He noticed that a bronze grille enclosed the sanctuary, the Carolingian curlicues and swirls reminiscent of what he'd seen in Aachen. The flooring was intact and detailed, differing shades of gray and black denoting what would have surely been color and variety. Dates on each print read 1772.

The proprietor was busy behind the front desk. He asked, 'These originals?'

The man nodded. 'They've hung here a long time. Our monastery was once glorious, but no more.'

'What happened?'

'War. Neglect. Weather. They all devoured the place.'

Before leaving the dinner table, he'd heard Isabel dispatch Henn to dispose of the bodies in the church. Her employee now donned his coat and disappeared into the night.

Malone caught a blast of cold from the front door as the owner handed him a key. He climbed wooden stairs to his room. He'd brought no clothes and the ones he wore needed cleaning, especially his shirt. Inside the room he tossed his jacket and gloves on the bed and removed his shirt. He stepped into the tiny bath and rinsed the shirt out in an enamel basin, using a little soap, then laid it across the radiator to dry.

He stood in his undershirt and studied himself in the

mirror. He'd worn an undershirt since he was six years old – a habit hammered into him. '*Nasty to be bare-chested,*' his father would say. '*You want your clothes to smell like sweat?*' He'd never questioned his father, he'd simply emulated him and always wore an undershirt – deep V neckline, since '*wearing an undershirt is one thing, seeing it is another.*' Interesting how the pull of childhood memories could so easily be triggered. They'd had so short a time together. About three years he could remember, from ages seven to ten. He still kept the flag that had been displayed at his father's memorial in a glass case beside his bed. His mother had refused the memento at the funeral, saying she'd had enough of the navy. But eight years later when he'd told her that he was joining, she hadn't objected. '*What else would Forrest Malone's boy do?*' she'd asked him.

And he'd agreed. What else?

He heard a soft rap and stepped from the bath to open the door. Christl stood outside.

'May I?' she asked.

He motioned his assent and quietly closed the door behind her.

'I want you to know that I didn't like what happened up there today. That's why I came after you. I told Mother not to deceive you.'

'Unlike yourself, of course.'

'Let's be honest, okay? If I had told you that I'd already made the connection between the will and the inscription, would you have even come to Aachen?'

Probably not. But he said nothing.

'I didn't think so,' she said, reading his face.

'You people take a lot of foolish risks.'

'There's much at stake. Mother wanted me to tell you something, not in front of Dorothea or Werner.'

He'd been wondering when Isabel would make good on her promise of *damn good information*. 'Okay, who's been trying to kill me?'

'A man named Langford Ramsey. She actually spoke with him. He sent the men who came after us in Garmisch, at Reichshoffen, and in Aachen. He also sent those today. He wants you dead. He's head of your naval intelligence. Mother deceived him into thinking she was his ally.'

'Now, there's something novel. Put my life at risk to save it.'

'She's trying to help you.'

'By telling Ramsey I'd be here today?'

She nodded. 'We staged that hostage scenario with their cooperation so they'd both be killed. We didn't anticipate the other two coming. They were supposed to stay on the outside. Ulrich thinks the shots drew them.' She hesitated. 'Cotton, I'm glad you're here. And safe. I wanted you to know that.'

He felt like a man walking to the gallows after tying the noose himself.

'Where's your shirt?' she asked.

'You live alone, you do your own laundry.'

She added a friendly smile which sweetened the otherwise tense atmosphere. 'I've lived alone all my adult life.'

'Thought you were married once?'

'We never actually lived together. One of those errors in judgment that was quickly rectified. We had a few great weekends, but that was about all. How long were you married?'

'Almost twenty years.'

'Children?'

'A son.'

'Does he carry your name?'

'His name is Gary.'

A sense of peace mingled with the silence.

She wore denim jeans, a stone-colored shirt and a navy cardigan. He could still see her tied to the column. Of course, women lying to him was nothing new. His ex-wife lied for years about Gary's parentage. Stephanie lied repeatedly, when necessary. Even his mother, a reservoir of locked emotions, a woman who rarely showed any feeling, lied to him about his father. To her, that memory was perfect. But he knew it wasn't. He desperately wanted to know the man. Not a myth, or a legend, or a memory. Just the man.

He was tired. 'It's time for bed.'

She circled to the lamp that burned beside the bed. He'd switched off the bath light when he'd answered the door so, when she pulled the chain and extinguished the bulb, the room was plunged into darkness.

'I agree,' she said.

64

Dorothea watched from her cracked-open door as her sister entered Cotton Malone's room. She'd seen her mother speak with Christl after dinner and wondered what had been said. She'd seen Ulrich leave and knew what task he'd been delegated. She wondered what her role would be. Apparently it was to make amends with her husband, as they'd been given a room together with one small bed. When she'd inquired to the proprietor about another he'd told her there were none.

'It's not that bad,' Werner said to her.

'Depends on a person's definition of *bad*.'

She actually found the situation amusing. They were both behaving like two adolescents on their first date. In one sense their predicament seemed comical, in another tragic. The tight confines made it impossible for her to escape the familiar miasma of his aftershave, his pipe tobacco, and the cloves from the gum he loved to chew. And the smells constantly reminded her that he was not one of the myriad men she'd enjoyed of late.

'This is too much, Werner. And far too fast.'

'I don't think you have a whole lot of choice.'

He stood near the window, arms clasped behind him. She was still perplexed by his actions in the church. 'Did you think that gunman would actually shoot me?'

'Things changed when I shot the other one. He was angry and he could have done anything.'

'You killed that man so easily.'

He shook his head. 'Not easily, but it had to be done. Not all that different from bringing down a stag.'

'I never realized you had that inside you.'

'Over the past few days I've realized a lot of things about myself.'

'Those men in the church were fools, thinking only about getting paid.' *Like the woman in the abbey,* she thought. 'There was absolutely no reason for them to trust us, yet they did.'

The corners of his lips turned down. 'Why are you avoiding the obvious?'

'I don't think this is the place or time to debate our personal life.'

His eyebrow raised in disbelief. 'There's no better time. We're about to make some irreversible decisions.'

Their distance these past few years had dulled her once perfect ability to know for certain when he was deceiving her. She'd for so long ignored him – simply allowed him to have his way. Now she cursed her indifference. 'What do you want, Werner?'

'The same things you want. Money, power, security. Your birthright.'

'That's mine, not yours.'

'Interesting, your birthright. Your grandfather was a Nazi. A man who adored Adolf Hitler.'

'He was no Nazi,' she declared.

'He just helped their evil along. Made it easier for them to slaughter people.'

'That's preposterous.'

'Those ridiculous theories about Aryans? Our supposed

heritage? That we were some sort of special race that came from a special place? Himmler loved that garbage. It fed right into the Nazis' murderous propaganda.'

Disturbing thoughts swirled through her mind. Things her mother had told her, things she'd heard as a child. Her grandfather's admitted right-wing philosophies. His refusal to ever speak ill of the Third Reich. Her father's insistence that Germany was no better off postwar than prewar, a divided Germany worse than anything Hitler ever did. Her mother was right. The Oberhauser family history needed to stay buried.

'You must tread lightly here,' Werner whispered.

There was something unsettling about his tone. What did he know?

'Perhaps it eases your conscience to think me a fool,' he said. 'Maybe it justifies your rejection of our marriage, and me.'

She cautioned herself that he was an expert at baiting her.

'But I'm no fool.'

She was curious. 'What do you know of Christl?'

He pointed at the door. 'I know she's in there with Malone. You understand what that means?'

'Tell me.'

'She's forging an alliance. Malone is connected to the Americans. Your mother chose her allies carefully – Malone can make things happen when we need them to happen. How else could we get to Antarctica? Christl is doing your mother's bidding.'

He was right. 'Tell me, Werner, are you enjoying the possibility of my failure?'

'If I were, I wouldn't be here. I'd simply let you fail.'

Something in his desultory tone triggered alarm. He

definitely knew more than he was saying and she hated his hedging.

She repressed a sudden shudder at the realization that this man, more stranger than husband, attracted her.

'When you killed the man at the lodge,' he asked, 'did *you* feel anything?'

'Relief.' The word slipped out from between clenched teeth.

He stood impassive, seemingly considering the admission. 'We must prevail, Dorothea. If that means cooperating with your mother, and Christl, so be it. We cannot allow your sister to dominate this quest.'

'You and Mother have been working together for some time, haven't you?'

'She misses Georg as much as we do. He was this family's future. Now its entire existence is in doubt. There are no more Oberhausers.'

She caught something in his tone and saw it in his eye. What he really wanted. 'You can't be serious?' she asked.

'You're only forty-eight. Childbirth is still possible.'

Werner came close and gently kissed her on the neck.

She slapped him across the face.

He laughed. 'Intense emotion. Violence. So you are human, after all.'

Beads of sweat formed on her forehead, though the room was not warm. She was not going to listen to him anymore.

She headed for the door.

He lunged forward, grabbed her arm, and spun her around.

'You're not going to walk away from me. Not this time.'

'Let go.' But it was a weak command. 'You are a despicable bastard. The sight of you makes me sick.'

'Your mother has made clear that if we conceive she will give it all to you.' He wrenched her close. 'Hear me, woman. Everything to you. Christl has no need for children or a husband. But maybe the same offer was made to her, as well? Where is she right now?'

He was close. In her face.

'Use your brain. Your mother has pitted the two of you against each other to learn what happened to her husband. But above all, she wants this family to continue. The Oberhausers have money, status, and assets. What they lack is heirs.'

She freed herself from his grip. He was right. Christl was with Malone. And her mother could never be trusted. Had the same offer of an heir been made to her?

'We're ahead of her,' he said. 'Our child would be legitimate.'

She hated herself. But the son of a bitch made sense.

'Shall we get started?' he asked.

65

Stephanie was a little disconcerted. Davis had decided they'd stay the night and reserved one room for them both.

'I'm not ordinarily this kind of girl,' she said to him as he opened the door. 'Going to a hotel on the first date.'

'I don't know. I heard you're easy.'

She popped him on the back of the head. 'You wish.'

He faced her. 'Here we are at a romantic four-star hotel. Last night we had a great date huddled in the freezing cold, then getting shot at. We're really bonding.'

She smiled. 'Don't remind me. And by the way, love your subtlety with Scofield. Worked great. He warmed right up to you.'

'He's an arrogant, self-absorbed know-it-all.'

'Who was there in 1971, and knows more than you and me.'

He plopped down onto a bright floral bedspread. The whole room looked like something out of a *Southern Living* magazine. Fine furnishings, elegant curtains, décor inspired by English and French manor houses. She actually would like to savor the deep tub. She hadn't bathed since yesterday morning in Atlanta. Is this what her agents routinely experienced? Wasn't she supposed to be in charge?

'Premier king room,' he said. 'It's all they had available. Its rate is way over government per diem but what the hell. You're worth it.'

She sank into one of the upholstered club chairs and propped her feet on a matching footstool. 'If you can handle all this togetherness, I can, too. I have a feeling we're not going to get much sleep anyway.'

'He's here,' Davis said. 'I know it.'

She wasn't so sure, but she could not deny a bad feeling swirling around in her stomach.

'Scofield is in the Wharton Suite on the sixth floor. He gets it every year,' Davis said.

'Desk clerk let all that slip?'

He nodded. 'She doesn't like Scofield, either.'

Davis fished the conference pamphlet from his pocket. 'He's leading a tour of the Biltmore mansion in a little while. Then, tomorrow morning, he's going boar hunting.'

'If our man's here, that's plenty of opportunities for him to make a move, not counting the time tonight in the hotel room.'

She watched Davis' face. Usually its features never gave away a thing, but the mask had faded. He was anxious. She felt a dark reluctance mingling with an intense curiosity, so she asked, 'What are you going to do when you finally find him?'

'Kill him.'

'That would be murder.'

'Maybe. But I doubt our man will go down without a fight.'

'You loved her that much?'

'Men shouldn't hit women.'

She wondered who he was talking to. Her? Millicent? Ramsey?

'I couldn't do anything before,' he said. 'I can now.' His face clouded over once again, belying all emotion. 'Now tell me what the president didn't want me to know.'

She'd been waiting for him to ask. 'It's about your co-worker.' She told him where Diane McCoy had gone. 'He trusts you, Edwin. More than you know.' She saw he caught what she hadn't said. *Don't let him down.*

'I won't disappoint him.'

'You can't kill this man, Edwin. We need him alive, to get Ramsey. Otherwise the real problem walks.'

'I know.' Defeat laced his voice.

He stood.

'We need to go.'

They'd stopped by the registration desk and signed up for the remainder of the conference before coming upstairs, obtaining two tickets for the candlelight tour.

'We have to stay close to Scofield,' he said. 'Whether he likes it or not.'

Charlie Smith entered the Biltmore mansion, following the private tour inside. When he'd registered for the Ancient Mysteries Revealed Conference under another name, he'd been presented a ticket for the event. A little quick reading in the inn's gift shop informed him that from early November until New Year's the mansion offered so-called magical evenings where visitors could enjoy the château filled with candlelight, blazing fireplaces, holiday decorations, and live musical performances. Entry times were reserved, and tonight's was extra special since it was the last tour of the day, open only for conference attendees.

They'd been ferried from the inn in two Biltmore buses – about eighty people, he estimated. He was dressed like the others, winter colors, wool coat, dark shoes. On the trip over he'd struck up a conversation about *Star Trek* with another attendee. They'd discussed which series they liked best, he arguing that *Enterprise* was by far superior, though his listener had preferred *Voyager*.

'Everyone,' Scofield was saying, as they stood in the frigid night before the main doors, 'follow me. You're in for a real treat.'

The crowd entered through an elaborate iron grille. He'd read that each room inside would be decorated for Christmas, as George Vanderbilt had done, starting in 1885 when the estate was first opened.

He was looking forward to the spectacles.

Both the house.

And his own.

Malone came awake. Christl slept beside him, her naked body against his. He glanced at his watch. 12:35 a.m. Another day – Friday, December 14 – had started.

He'd been asleep two hours.

A warm pulse of satisfaction flowed through him.

He hadn't done that in a while.

Afterward, rest had come in a no-man's-land of a twilight where detailed images roamed his restless mind.

Like the framed drawing hanging one floor below.

Of the church, from 1772.

Odd the way a solution had materialized, the answer laid out in his head like an open-faced hand of solitaire. It had happened that way two years ago. At Cassiopeia Vitt's château. He thought about Cassiopeia. Her visits of late had been few and far between, and she was God knew where. In Aachen he'd thought about calling her for help, but decided this fight was his alone. He lay still and wondered about the myriad choices life offered. The swiftness of his decision regarding Christl's advances worked his nerves.

But at least something more had come of it.

Charlemagne's pursuit.

He now knew the end.

66

Asheville

Stephanie and Davis followed the tour into Biltmore's grand entrance hall amid soaring walls and limestone arches. To her right, in a glass-roofed winter garden, a parade of white poinsettias encircled a marble-and-bronze fountain. The warm air smelled of fresh greenery and cinnamon.

A woman on the bus ride over had told them that the candlelight tour was billed as an old-fashioned festival of lights, decorations in a grand regal style, a Victorian picture postcard come to life. And true to the billing, a choir sung carols from some far-off room. With no coat check Stephanie left hers unbuttoned as they lingered at the back of the group, staying out of the way of Scofield, who seemed to relish his role as host.

'We have the house to ourselves,' the professor said. 'This is a tradition for the conference. Two hundred fifty rooms, thirty-four bedrooms, forty-three baths, sixty-five fireplaces, three kitchens, and an indoor swimming pool. Amazing I remember all that.' He laughed at his own quip. 'I'll escort you through and point out some of the interesting tidbits. We'll finish back here and then you're free to roam for another half hour or so before the buses return us to the inn.' He paused. 'Shall we?'

Scofield led the crowd into a long gallery, maybe ninety feet, lined with silk and wool tapestries that he explained were woven in Belgium around 1530.

They visited the gorgeous library with its twenty-three thousand books and Venetian ceiling, then the music room with a spectacular Dürer print. Finally, they entered an imposing banquet hall with more Flemish tapestries, a pipe organ, and a massive oak dining table that seated – she counted – sixty-four. Candlelight, firelight, and twinkling tree lights provided all of the illumination.

'The largest room in the house,' Scofield announced in the banquet hall. 'Seventy-two feet long, forty-two feet wide, crowned seventy feet up by a barrel vault.'

An enormous Douglas fir, which stretched halfway to the ceiling, was trimmed with toys, ornaments, dried flowers, gold beads, angels, velvet, and lace. Festive music from an organ filled the hall with yuletide cheer.

She noticed Davis retreating toward the dining table, so she drifted his way and whispered, 'What is it?'

He pointed to the triple fireplace, flanked with armor, as if admiring it, and said to her, 'There's a guy, short and thin, navy chinos, canvas shirt, barn coat with a corduroy collar. Behind us.'

She knew not to turn and look, so she concentrated on the fireplace and its high-relief overmantel, which looked like something from a Greek temple.

'He's been watching Scofield.'

'Everybody's been doing that.'

'He hasn't spoken to a soul, and twice he's checked out the windows. I made eye contact once, just to see what would happen, and he turned away. He's too fidgety for me.'

She pointed to more decorations that adorned the

massive bronze chandeliers overhead. Pennants hung high around the room, replicas of flags, she heard Scofield say, from the American Revolution for the original thirteen colonies.

'You have no idea, right?' she asked.

'Call it a feeling. He's checking the windows again. Don't you come for the house tour? Not what's outside.'

'You mind if I see for myself?' she asked.

'Be my guest.'

Davis continued to gawk at the hall as she casually stepped across the hardwood floor toward the Christmas tree, where the thin man in chinos stood near a group. She noticed nothing threatening, only that he seemed to pay Scofield a lot of attention, though their host was engaged in a robust conversation with some of the others.

She watched as he retreated from the aromatic tree and casually walked toward a doorway, where he tossed something into a small trash can then left, entering the next room.

She lingered a moment and followed, peering around the doorway.

Chinos wandered through a masculine billiard room that resembled a nineteenth-century gentleman's club with rich oak paneling, ornamental plaster ceiling, and deep-hued Oriental carpets. He was examining framed prints on the wall – but not all that carefully, she noted.

She quickly gazed into the trash can and spotted something on top. She bent down, retrieved it, then retreated into the banquet hall.

She noticed what she held.

Matches, from a Ruth's Chris steakhouse.

In Charlotte, North Carolina.

★   ★   ★

Malone, no longer capable of sleep, his mind racing, slipped from beneath the heavy duvet and rose from the bed. He needed to walk downstairs and study the framed print one more time.

Christl awoke. 'Where are you going?'

He retrieved his pants from the floor. 'To see if I'm right.'

'You've realized something?' She sat up and switched on the light beside the bed. 'What is it?'

She seemed utterly comfortable naked, and he was utterly comfortable staring at her. He zipped his pants and slipped on his shirt, not worrying about shoes.

'Hold up,' she said, rising and finding her clothes.

Downstairs was dimly lit by two lamps and the still-burning embers from the hearth. Nobody staffed the check-in desk, and he heard no sounds from the restaurant. He found the print on the wall and clicked on another lamp.

'That's from 1772. The church was obviously in better shape then. See anything?'

He watched as she studied the drawing.

'The windows were intact. Stained glass. Statues. The grilles around the altar seem Carolingian. Like in Aachen.'

'That's not it.'

He was enjoying this – finally being a step ahead of her. He admired her narrow waist, trim hips, and the close curls of her long blond hair. She hadn't tucked in her shirt so he caught the curve of her bare spine as she reached with one arm and traced the drawing's outline on the glass.

She turned toward him. 'The floor.'

Her pale brown eyes glowed.

'Tell me,' he said.

'There's a design. It's hard to see, but it's there.'

She was right. The print was an angled view, geared more for the towering heights of the walls and arches than the floor. But he'd noticed it earlier. Dark lines streaked through lighter slabs, a square enclosing another square, enclosing still another in a familiar pattern.

'It's a Nine Men's Morris board,' he said. 'We can't know for sure until we go look, but I think that's what that floor once depicted.'

'That's going to be hard to determine,' she said. 'I crawled across it. It's barely there anymore.'

'Part of your performance?'

'Mother's idea. Not mine.'

'And we can't tell Mother no, can we?'

A smile frayed the edges of her thin lips. 'No, we can't.'

'But only those who appreciate the throne of Solomon and Roman frivolity shall find their way to heaven,' he said.

'A Nine Men's Morris board on the throne in Aachen and one here.'

'Einhard built this church,' he said. 'He also, years later, fashioned the pursuit using the chapel in Aachen and this place as reference points. Apparently, the throne was in the Aachen chapel by then. Your grandfather made the connection, so can we.' He pointed. 'Look in the lower right corner. On the floor, near the center of the nave, around which the Nine Men's Morris board would spread. What do you see?'

She studied the drawing. 'There's something etched into the floor. Hard to tell. The lines are garbled. Look's like a tiny cross with letters. An *R* and an *L,* but the rest is meshed together.'

He saw recognition dawn within her as she visualized entirely what may have once been there.

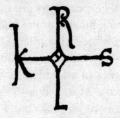

'It's part of Charlemagne's signature,' she said.

'Hard to say for sure, but there's only one way to find out.'

67

Asheville

Stephanie found Davis and showed him the matches.
'That's too damn many coincidences for me,' he said. 'He's not part of this conference. He's scoping out his target.'

Their killer was certainly cocky and confident. Being here, out in the open, with no one knowing who he was would certainly appeal to a daring personality. After all, over the past forty-eight hours he'd managed to stealthily murder at least three people.

Still.

Davis marched away.

'Edwin.'

He kept going, heading for the billiard room. The rest of the tour was scattered throughout the banquet hall, Scofield starting to herd them in Chinos' direction.

She shook her head and followed.

Davis was headed around the gaming tables toward where Chinos stood, near a pine-garland-decorated fireplace and a bearskin rug that lay across the wood floor. A few others from the tour were already in the room. The rest would be arriving shortly.

'Excuse me,' Davis said. 'You.'

Chinos turned, saw who was speaking to him, and drew back.

'I need to talk to you,' Davis said in a firm voice.

Chinos lunged forward and pushed Davis aside. His right hand slipped beneath his unbuttoned coat.

'Edwin,' she hollered.

Davis apparently saw it, too, and dove beneath one of the billiard tables.

She found her gun, leveled the weapon, and yelled, 'Stop.'

The others in the room saw her weapon.

A woman screamed.

Chinos fled out an open doorway.

Davis sprang to his feet and rushed after him.

Malone and Christl left the hotel. Silence claimed the cold, clear air. Every star glowed down with an improbable brightness, suffusing Ossau with a colorless light.

Christl had found two flashlights behind the reception desk. Though he was working in a fog of exhaustion, a blur of combative thoughts had roused his vitality. He'd just made love to a beautiful woman whom, on the one hand, he did not trust and, on the other, he could not resist.

Christl had swept her hair up from her neck and clipped the curls high on her head, a few tendrils escaping and framing her soft face. Shadows played over the rough ground. The dry air carried the scent of smoke. They trudged up the snowy inclined path with heavy footsteps, stopping at the monastery's gate. He noticed that Henn, who'd cleaned up the earlier mess, had repositioned the snipped chain so that it appeared as if the gate was locked.

He freed the chain and they entered.

A dark silence, unbroken by the night or the ages, loomed everywhere. They used the flashlights and negotiated dark passages through the cloister to the church. He felt like he was walking inside a chest freezer, the parched air chapping his lips.

He hadn't really noticed the flooring earlier, but he now searched the moss-grown pavement with his light. The masonry was rude and wide-jointed, many of the stones either cracked into pieces or missing, leaving frozen, rock-hard earth exposed. Apprehension crept into his bones. He'd brought the gun and spare magazines, just in case.

'See,' he said. 'There's a pattern. Hard to see with what little remains.' He glanced up to the choir, where Isabel and Henn had appeared. 'Come on.'

He found the stairway and they climbed. The view from up high helped. Together they saw that the floor, if all there, would have formed a Nine Men's Morris board.

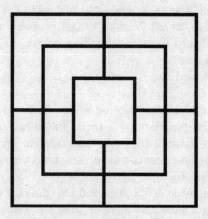

He stopped his beam at what he estimated would have been the board's center. 'Einhard was precise, I'll give him that. It's in the middle of the nave.'

'It's exciting,' she said. 'This is exactly what Grandfather did.'

'So let's get down there and see if there's anything to find.'

'All of you, listen to me,' Stephanie said, trying to regain control. Heads turned and a quick silence swept the room.

Scofield rushed in from the banquet hall. 'What's happening here?'

'Dr. Scofield, take all of these people back to the main entrance. There'll be security there. Tour's over.'

She still held the gun, which seem to add an extra aura of authority to her command. But she couldn't wait around to see if Scofield obeyed.

She darted after Davis. No telling what he was doing.

She fled the billiard room and entered a dimly lit hall. A placard announced that she was in the bachelor's wing. Two small rooms opened to her right. A stairway descended to her left. Nothing ornate, probably a servants' path. She heard footsteps thudding below.

Moving fast.

She followed.

Malone surveyed the flooring in the center of the nave. Most of the pavement was there, the joints earth-filled and lichen-encrusted. They'd descended to ground level and he shone his beam on the center stone, then crouched.

'Look,' he said.

Not much was left, but carved into the face were faint lines. A slash here and there of what was once part of a triangle and the remnants of the letters K and L.

'What else could it be but Charlemagne's mark?' she asked.

'We need a shovel.'

'There's a maintenance shed past the cloister. We found it yesterday morning when we first came.'

'Go see.'

She hustled off.

He stared at the stone embedded in the frozen earth while something nagged at him. If Hermann Oberhauser had followed the same trail, why would anything be here now? Isabel said that he first came in the late 1930s, before he traveled to Antarctica, then returned in the early 1950s. Her husband came in 1970.

Yet nobody knew a thing?

Light danced outside the church, growing in intensity. Christl returned, shovel in hand.

He grabbed the handle, surrendered his light, and wedged the metal blade into one joint. Just as he suspected, the ground was like concrete. He raised the shovel and slammed the point down hard, working the blade back and forth. After several blows he began to make progress and the ground gave way.

He again spiked the shovel into the joint and managed to wiggle it beneath, working the wooden handle like a fulcrum, loosening the stone from the earth's embrace.

He withdrew the shovel and did the same thing on the other sides.

Finally, the slab began to wobble. He pried it upward, angling the handle.

'Hold the shovel,' he told her. He dropped down and worked his gloved hands underneath, freeing the edges from the ground.

Both flashlights lay beside him. He lifted one and saw that only dirt was visible.

'Let me try,' she said.

She kneaded the hard ground with short jabs, twisting the blade, working deeper. She hit something. She withdrew the shovel and he stirred the loose dirt, scooping out cold earth until he saw the top of what at first looked like a rock, but then he realized it was flat.

He brushed away the remaining dirt.

Carved in the center of a rectangular shape, clear and distinct, was Charlemagne's signature. He cleared more earth from the sides and realized that he was looking at a stone reliquary. Maybe sixteen inches long, ten inches wide. He worked his hands down either side and discovered that it was about six inches tall.

He lifted it out.

Christl bent down. 'It's Carolingian. The style. Design. Marble. And, of course, the signature.'

'You want the honor?' he asked.

A blissful half grin claimed her mouth and she grasped the sides and lifted. The reliquary parted in the middle, the bottom portion framing the shape of something wrapped in oilcloth.

He lifted out the sheathed bundle and untied the drawstrings.

Carefully, he opened the bag as Christl shone a light inside.

68

Asheville

Stephanie descended the staircase, which turned at right angles until it found the château's basement.

Davis was waiting at the bottom. 'Took you long enough.' He wrenched the gun from her grasp. 'I need that.'

'What are you going to do?'

'Like I said, kill the piece of crap.'

'Edwin, we don't even know who he is.'

'He saw me and he ran.'

She needed to take control, as Daniels had instructed her to do. 'How did he know you? Nobody saw us last night, and we didn't see him.'

'I don't know, Stephanie, but he did.'

The man had run, which was suspicious, but she wasn't ready to order a death sentence.

Footsteps came from behind and a uniformed security guard appeared. He saw the gun in Davis' grasp and reacted, but she was ready and produced her Magellan Billet identification. 'We're federal agents and we have someone of interest down here. He fled. How many exits from this floor?'

'Another staircase on the far side. Several doors to the outside.'

'Can you cover those?'

He hesitated a moment, then apparently decided they were for real and unclipped a radio from his waist, instructing others on what to do.

'We need to get this guy, if he comes out a window. Anywhere. Understand?' she asked. 'Put men outside.'

The man nodded and gave more instructions then said, 'The tour group is out and in the buses. The house is empty, except for you.'

'And him,' Davis said, moving off.

The guard wasn't armed. Too bad. But she did notice in his shirt pocket one of the brochures she'd seen others in the tour group carrying. She pointed. 'Is there a sketch of this floor in there?'

The guard nodded. 'One of all four floors.' He handed it to her. 'This is the basement. Recreation, kitchens, servants' quarters, storage. Lots of places to hide.'

Which she didn't want to hear. 'Call the local police. Get them over here. Then cover this stairway. This guy could be dangerous.'

'You don't know for sure?'

'That's the whole problem. We don't know crap.'

Malone saw a book inside the bag and a pale blue envelope protruding near its center. He reached in and removed the book.

'Lay the bag on the floor,' he said, and he gently rested the book atop, grabbing his light.

Christl slipped the envelope free and opened it, finding two sheets of paper. She unfolded them. Both were filled by a heavy masculine script – German – in black ink.

'It's Grandfather's writing. I've read his notebooks.'

★   ★   ★

Stephanie hurried after Davis and caught up to him where the basement corridors offered a choice, one angling left, the other straight ahead. Glass-fronted doors opened off the path ahead into what looked like food pantries. She quickly checked the map. At the end of the hall she identified the main kitchen.

She heard a noise. From their left.

The schematic in the pamphlet indicated that the path ahead led to servants' bedrooms and did not connect with any other portion of the basement. A dead end.

Davis headed down the long corridor to their left, toward the noise.

They passed through an exercise room with parallel bars, barbells, medicine balls, and a rowing machine. To their right they found the indoor swimming pool, everything, including the vault overhead, white-tiled, with no windows, only harsh electric light. No water filled the deep shiny basin.

A shadow swept across the pool room's other exit.

They rounded the railed walk, Davis leading the way.

She checked the map. 'This is the only way out from the rooms beyond. Besides the main staircase, but hopefully the security guards have that covered.'

'Then we've got him. He has to come back this way.'

'Or he's got us.'

Davis stole a quick look at the map, then they passed through a doorway and down a few short steps. He gave her the gun. 'I'll wait.' He pointed left. 'That hall loops all the way around and ends back here.'

A sick feeling filled her gut. 'Edwin, this is crazy.'

'Just flush him this way.' A tremor shook his right eye. 'I have to do this. Send him my way.'

'What are you going to do?'

'I'll be ready.'

She nodded, searching for the right words, but she understood his intense desire. 'Okay.'

He retreated up the stairs they'd come from.

She advanced to the left and, at the main staircase leading up, spotted another security guard. He shook his head to indicate that no one had come his way. She nodded and pointed that she was headed left.

Two meandering, windowless corridors led her into a long rectangular room filled with historical exhibits and black-and-white photographs. The walls were painted in a collage of colorful images. The Halloween Room. She'd recalled a mention in the pamphlet about how guests at a 1920s Halloween party painted the walls.

She spotted Chinos, on the far side, weaving through the exhibits, heading for the only other exit.

'Stop,' she yelled.

He kept moving.

She aimed and fired.

Her ears stung from the gun's retort. The bullet found one of the display placards. She wasn't trying to hit the man, only scare him. But Chinos lunged through the doorway and kept running.

She followed.

She'd caught only a fleeting glance of the man, so it was impossible to know if he was armed.

She passed through a recreation room and entered a bowling alley, two lanes equipped with wood planking, balls, and pins. Had to be quite a convenience in the late nineteenth century.

She decided to try something.

'What's the point in running?' she called out. 'There's nowhere to go. The house is sealed.'

Silence.

Small dressing rooms opened to her left, one door after another. She imagined proper ladies and gentleman a hundred years ago changing into recreation clothes. The corridor ahead ended back where Davis waited near the swimming pool. She'd already made the loop.

'Just come on out,' she said. 'You're not getting to leave here.'

She sensed he was near.

Suddenly, twenty feet away, something appeared from one of the dressing rooms.

A bowling pin, propelled at her, swooshing through the air like a boomerang.

She ducked.

The pin thudded into the wall behind her and clattered away.

Chinos made his escape.

She recovered her balance and darted forward. At the corridor's end she peered around. No one in sight. She rushed to the steps and climbed the risers back into the pool room. Chinos was across, at the shallow end, where the door for the exercise room opened, rushing away. She raised her gun and aimed for his legs. But before she could fire, Davis exploded from the doorway and tackled him. They slammed into the wooden railing that surrounded the pool, which instantly gave way, and the two bodies fell three feet into the pool's empty shallow end.

Flesh and bones smacked hard tile.

69

*To my son, this may be the last sane act I ever do. My
mind is rapidly slipping into a deep fog. I have tried to
resist but with no success. Before my wits fully leave me,
I must do this. If you are reading these words then you
have successfully completed Charlemagne's pursuit. God
bless you. Know that I am proud. I also sought and
discovered the lasting heritage of our great Aryan
ancestors. I knew they existed. I told my Führer, tried to
convince him that his vision of our past was inaccurate,
but he would not listen. That greatest of kings, the man
who first foresaw a unified continent, Charlemagne,
knew well our destiny. He appreciated what the Holy
Ones taught him. He knew they were wise and he
listened to their counsel. Here, in this sacred earth,
Einhard hid the key to the language of heaven. Einhard
was taught by the High Adviser himself, and he
safeguarded what he was privileged to know. Imagine
my ecstasy, over a thousand years later, at being the first
to know what Einhard knew, what Charlemagne knew,
what we, as Germans, have to know. But not a single
soul appreciated what I'd discovered. I was, instead,
branded dangerous, deemed unstable, and forever silenced.
After the war, no one cared about our German heritage.
To speak the word Aryan was to invoke memories of
atrocities no one wanted to recall. That sickened me. If*

*they only knew. If they'd only seen. As I had. My son, if
you have come this far it is because of what I told you
of Charlemagne's pursuit. Einhard made clear that
neither he nor the Holy Ones have any patience with
ignorance. Neither do I, my son. You have proved me
right and proven yourself worthy. Now you can know
the language of heaven. Savor it. Marvel at the place
from which we came.*

'Your mother said Hermann came here the second time
in the early 1950s,' Malone said. 'Your father would have
been in his thirties then?'

Christl nodded. 'He was born in 1921. Died at fifty.'

'So Hermann Oberhauser brought back what he'd
found, replaced it, so his son could take up the pursuit.'

'Grandfather was a man of strange ideas. For the last
fifteen years of his life, he never left Reichshoffen. He knew
none of us when he died. He barely ever spoke to me.'

He recalled more of what Isabel had told him. 'Your
mother said that Dietz came here after Hermann died.
But he apparently found nothing, since the book is here.'
He realized what that meant. 'So he really did go to
Antarctica knowing nothing.'

She shook her head. 'He had Grandfather's maps.'

'You saw them. There was no writing. Like you said
in Aachen, maps are useless without notations.'

'But he had Grandfather's notebooks. There's
information there.'

He pointed to the book lying on the oilcloth. 'Your
father needed this to know what Hermann knew.'

He wondered why the navy had agreed to such a foolish
journey. What had Dietz Oberhauser promised? What had
they hoped to gain?

His ears were numb from the cold.

He stared at the cover. The same symbol from the one found in Charlemagne's grave had been stamped into the top.

He opened the ancient tome. In shape, size, and coloration it was nearly identical to the two he'd already seen. Inside was the same odd script, with additions.

'Those curlicues from the other book are letters,' he said, noting that each page contained a way to convert the alphabet into Latin. 'It's a translation of the language of heaven.'

'We can do it,' she said.

'What do you mean?'

'Mother had Charlemagne's book electronically scanned. A year ago she hired some linguists and tried to have it deciphered. They, of course, failed since it's not in any known language. I anticipated this, realizing that whatever was here had to be a way to translate the book. What else could it have been? Yesterday Mother gave me the electronic images. I have a translation program that should work. All we'd have to do is scan these pages into it.'

'Tell me you have the laptop with you.'

She nodded. 'Mother brought it from Reichshoffen. Along with a scanner.'

Finally, something had gone right.

* * *

Stephanie could do little. Davis and Chinos were rolling deeper into the empty pool, across the slick white tiles to the flat bottom of its deep end, eight feet below her.

They crashed into the lower portion of a wooden ladder, which led up to a platform that would have been submerged when the pool had been filled. Another three steps led from the platform up to her level.

Davis shoved Chinos off him, then sprang to his feet, swinging around to block any escape. Chinos seem to suffer a moment of indecision, whipping his head left and right, realizing they were encased in an unusual arena.

Davis shucked his coat.

Chinos accepted the challenge and did the same.

She wanted to stop this, but knew Davis would never forgive her. Chinos looked maybe forty to Davis' late fifties, but anger could even the odds.

She heard the sound of a fist meeting bone as Davis caught Chinos full on the jaw, sending him spiraling to the tiles. The man immediately recovered and pounced, planting a foot into Davis' gut.

She heard the wind leave him.

Chinos danced in and out, delivering quick sharp blows, ending with a jab into Davis' breastbone.

Davis, off balance, spun around. Just as he gathered his coordination and tried to swing again, Chinos lunged forward and smacked him in the Adam's apple. Davis threw a right cross that connected only with air.

A prideful smirk crept across Chinos' face.

Davis dropped to his knees, leaning forward, as if praying, head bowed, arms at his sides. Chinos stood ready. She heard Davis catch his breath. Her mouth went dry. Chinos stepped closer, seemingly intent on finishing the fight. But Davis summoned all his reserves and lurched upward, tackling his opponent, planting his head into the man's ribs.

Bone cracked.

Chinos howled in pain and fell to the tiles.

Davis pummeled the man.

Blood gushed from Chinos' nose and splattered on the tiles. His arms and legs went limp. Davis kept peppering him with hard, sharp punches from a closed fist.

'Edwin,' she called out.

He didn't seem to listen.

'Edwin,' she screamed.

He stopped. Breath wheezed from him, but he did not move.

'It's done,' she said.

Davis shot her a murderous look.

He finally crawled off his opponent and came to his feet, but his knees immediately weakened and he stumbled. He straightened one arm and caught himself, tried to remain standing, but couldn't.

He collapsed to the tiles.

70

Malone watched as Christl removed a laptop from her travel bag. They'd returned to the inn without seeing or hearing anyone. Snow had started to fall outside, a wind spinning it into fluffy eddies. She switched on the machine, then removed a handheld scanner and connected it to one of the USB ports.

'This is going to take a while,' she said. 'It's not the fastest scanner there is.'

He held the book from the church. They'd thumbed through all of the pages, which seemed a complete translation of each letter of the language of heaven into its Latin counterpart.

'You realize this is not going to be exact,' she said. 'Some of the letters could have double meanings. There could be no corresponding Latin letter or sound. That sort of thing.'

'Your grandfather did it.'

She eyed him with an odd mixture of annoyance and gratitude. 'I can also instantly convert Latin to German or English. I didn't really know what to expect. I was never quite sure if Grandfather was to be believed. A few months ago Mother allowed me access to some of his notebooks. Father's, too. But they told me little. Obviously, she withheld what she deemed important. The maps, for example. The books from Einhard's and Charlemagne's graves. So there was always a nagging doubt that Grandfather may have simply been a fool.'

He wondered about her openness. Refreshing. But also suspect.

'You saw all that Nazi memorabilia he collected. He was obsessed. The odd thing is that he was spared the disasters of the Third Reich, yet he seemed to regret not being a part of their downfall. In the end, he was just bitter. It was almost a blessing he lost his mind.'

'But he now has another chance to be proven right.'

The machine dinged, signaling it was ready.

She accepted the book from him. 'And I plan to give him every chance. What are you going to do while I work?'

He laid back on the bed. 'I intend to sleep. Wake me when you're done.'

Ramsey made sure Diane McCoy left Fort Lee and headed back to Washington. He did not revisit the warehouse so as not to draw any more attention, explaining to the base commander that he'd borne witness to a minor territorial dispute between the White House and the navy. The explanation seemed to have satisfied any questions that may have arisen from so many high-level visits over the past couple of days.

He glanced at his watch. 8:50 p.m.

He sat at a table in a small trattoria on the outskirts of Washington. Good Italian food, understated setting, excellent wine bar. None of which he cared about tonight.

He sipped his wine.

A woman entered the restaurant. Her tall, slender frame was draped by a stitched-velvet aletta coat and dark vintage jeans. A beige cashmere scarf wrapped her neck. She threaded a path around the tightly packed tables and sat with him.

The woman from the map store.

'You did good with the senator,' he told her. 'Right on the mark.'

She acknowledged his compliment with a nod.

'Where is she?' he asked. He'd ordered surveillance on Diane McCoy.

'You're not going to like it.'

A new chill sheathed his spine.

'She's with Kane. Right now.'

'Where?'

'They roamed the Lincoln Memorial, then walked the basin to the Washington Monument.'

'Cold night for a stroll.'

'Tell me about it. I have a man with her now. She's headed home.'

All disturbing. The only connection between McCoy and Kane would be him. He'd thought her placated, but he may have underestimated her resolve.

His phone vibrated in his pocket. He checked. Hovey.

'I need to take this,' he said. 'Could you wait near the door?'

She understood and left.

'What is it?' he said into the phone.

'The White House is on the line. They want to speak with you.'

Nothing unusual. 'So?'

'It's the president.'

That *was* unusual.

'Connect us.'

A few seconds later he heard the booming voice the

whole world knew. 'Admiral, I hope you're having a good night.'

'It's cold, Mr. President.'

'You got that right. And getting colder. I'm calling because Aatos Kane wants you on the Joint Chiefs. He says you're the man for the job.'

'That all depends if you agree, sir.' He kept his voice low, below the level of muffled conversations around him.

'I do. Thought about it all day, but I agree. Would you like the job?'

'I'd willingly serve wherever you like.'

'You know how I feel about the Joint Chiefs, but let's be real. Nothing's going to change, so I need you there.'

'I'm honored. When would this be made public?'

'I'll have your name leaked within the hour. You'll be the morning news story. Get ready, Admiral – it's a different ballpark than naval intelligence.'

'I'll be ready, sir.'

'Glad to have you aboard.'

And Daniels was gone.

A breathless moment passed. His defenses dropped. His fears abated. He'd done it. Whatever Diane McCoy was doing mattered not.

He was now the appointee.

Dorothea lay in the bed, trembling in that state between sleep and wakefulness where thoughts could sometimes be controlled. What had she done, making love to Werner again? That was something she'd never thought possible – a part of her life that had surely ended.

Maybe not.

Two hours ago she'd heard the door for Malone's room

open, then close. A murmur of voices seeped through the thin walls, but nothing she could decipher. What was her sister doing in the middle of the night?

Werner lay pressed beside her in the narrow bed. He was right. They were married and their heir would be legitimate. But having a baby at age forty-eight? Perhaps that was the price she would be required to pay. Werner and her mother had apparently forged some sort of alliance, strong enough that Sterling Wilkerson had to die – strong enough to transform Werner into some semblance of a man.

More voices leaked from next door.

She rose from the bed and approached the connecting wall, but could understand nothing. She padded lightly across the thinly carpeted flooring to the window. Fat snowflakes fell in silence. All of her life she'd lived in mountains and snow. She'd learned to hunt, shoot, and ski at an early age. She wasn't afraid of much – only failure, and her mother. She rested her naked body against the chilly windowsill, frustrated and mournful, and stared at her husband, curled under the comforter.

She wondered if her bitterness toward him was nothing more than grief overflowing for their dead son. For a long time afterward the days and nights had assumed a nightmarish quality, a sensation of rushing forward with no purpose or destination in view.

A chill stole the room, and her courage.

She folded her arms across her bare breasts.

It seemed with each passing year that she became more bitter, more dissatisfied. She missed Georg. But maybe Werner was right. Maybe it was time to live. To love. To be loved.

She flexed her legs in a long stretch. The room next

door had gone quiet. She turned and stared back out the window at the snow-pelted darkness.

She caressed her flat belly.

Another baby.

Why not.

71

Asheville, 11:15 p.m.

Stephanie and Edwin Davis reentered the Inn on Biltmore Estate. Davis had risen from his brawl, caught in the clutch of pain, his face bruised, but his ego intact. Chinos was in custody, albeit unconscious at a local hospital with a concussion and multiple contusions from the beating. The local police had escorted the ambulance and would remain there until the Secret Service arrived, which should be within the hour. Doctors had already told the police it would be morning before the man could be questioned. The château had been sealed and more police were combing its interior seeing what, if anything, Chinos had left behind. Tapes from security cameras located throughout the house were being carefully reviewed in search of more information.

Davis had said little since he'd climbed from the pool. A call to the White House had confirmed both their identities and credentials, so they hadn't been forced to answer questions. Which was good. She could see that Davis was not in the mood.

The estate's chief of security had accompanied them back to the inn. They approached the main registration desk and the administrator found what Davis wanted, handing him a slip of paper: 'Scofield's suite number.'

'Let's go,' Davis said to her.

They located the room on the sixth floor and Davis banged on the door.

Scofield answered, wearing one of the inn's signature robes. 'It's late and I have an early morning tomorrow. What could you two possibly want? Didn't you cause enough havoc earlier?'

Davis brushed the professor aside and marched into the suite, which contained a generous living area with a sofa and chairs, a wet bar, and windows that surely provided spectacular mountain views.

'I put up with your asshole attitude this afternoon,' Davis said, 'because I had to. You thought we were nuts. But we just saved your ass, so we'd like some answers in gratitude.'

'Someone was here to kill me?'

Davis pointed at his bruises. 'Look at my face. He's in the hospital. It's time you tell us some things, Professor. Classified things.'

Scofield seemed to swallow some of his insolence. 'You're right. I was an ass to you today, but I didn't realize—'

'A man came to kill you,' Stephanie made clear. 'Though we need to question him to be sure, it certainly looks like we have the right person.'

Scofield nodded and offered them a seat.

'I can't imagine why I'm a threat after all these years. I've kept my oath. I never spoke of anything, even though I should have. I could have made quite a name for myself.'

She waited for him to explain.

'I've spent all my time since 1972 trying to prove, in other ways, what I know to be true.'

She'd read a brief synopsis of Scofield's book, which

her staff had provided by e-mail yesterday. He supposedly had established that an advanced worldwide civilization existed thousands of years before ancient Egypt. His evidence was a reappraisal of maps, long known to scholars, like the famous Piri Reis drawing, which had all been drawn, Scofield concluded, using more ancient maps, now lost. Scofield believed that those ancient mapmakers were much more advanced scientifically than the civilizations of Greece, Egypt, Babylonia, or even the later Europeans, mapping all of the continents, outlining North America thousands of years before Columbus, and charting Antarctica when its coasts were ice-free. No serious scientific study corroborated any of Scofield's assertions but, as the e-mail had noted, none had refuted his theory, either.

'Professor,' she said. 'In order for us to learn why they want you dead, we need to know what's involved. You have to tell us about your work with the navy.'

Scofield bowed his head. 'Those three lieutenants brought me crates full of rocks. They'd been collected during Highjump and Windmill back in the 1940s – just sitting in a warehouse somewhere. No one had paid them any mind. Can you imagine? Evidence like that and nobody cared.

'I was the only one allowed to examine the crates, though Ramsey could come and go as he pleased. The rocks were engraved with writing. Unique curlicue-like letters. No known language corresponded to them. Making it even more spectacular was that they came from Antarctica, a place that has been under ice for thousands of years. Yet we found them. Or, more accurately, the Germans found them. They went to Antarctica in 1938 and located the initial sites. We went back in 1947 and '48 and collected them.'

'And again in '71,' Davis said.

Disbelief spread over Scofield's face. 'We did?'

She could see he truly didn't know, so she decided to offer a bone. 'A submarine went, but was lost. That's what started all this now. There's something about that mission somebody doesn't want anyone to know.'

'I was never told about that. But that's not surprising – I didn't need to know. I was retained to analyze the writing, to see if it could be deciphered.'

'Could it?' Davis asked.

Scofield shook his head. 'I wasn't allowed to finish. Admiral Dyals ended the project abruptly. I was sworn to secrecy and dismissed. It was the saddest day of my life.' His manner matched his words. 'There it was. Proof that a first civilization existed. We even had their language. If we could somehow learn to understand it, we'd know all about them – know for certain if they were the ancient sea kings. Something told me that they were, but I never was allowed to find out.'

He sounded both thrilled and brokenhearted.

'How would you have learned to read the language?' Davis asked. 'It would be like writing down random words and trying to know what they say.'

'That's where you're wrong. You see, on those rocks were also letters and words I recognized. Both Latin and Greek. Even some hieroglyphs. Don't you see? That civilization had interacted with us. There was contact. Those stones were messages, announcements, pronouncements. Who knows? But they were capable of being read.'

Her annoyance with her own stupidity changed to a strange uncertainty, and she thought about Malone and what was happening to him. 'Did you ever hear the name *Oberhauser*?'

Scofield nodded. 'Hermann Oberhauser. He went to Antarctica in 1938 with the Nazis. He's partially the reason we went back with Highjump and Windmill. Admiral Byrd became fascinated with Oberhauser's views on Aryans and lost civilizations. Of course, at that time, post-World War II, you couldn't speak of those things too loudly, so Byrd conducted private research while there with Highjump and found the stones. Since he may have confirmed what Oberhauser had theorized, the government slammed a lid on the whole thing. Eventually, his findings were simply forgotten.'

'Why would anyone want to kill over this?' Davis muttered out loud. 'It's ludicrous.'

'There's a bit more,' Scofield said.

Malone awoke with a start and heard Christl say, 'Come on, get up.'

He shook sleep from his eyes and checked his watch. He'd been out two hours. When his eyes adjusted to the room's lamps he saw Christl staring at him with a look of triumph.

'I did it.'

Stephanie waited for Scofield to finish.

'When you view the world through a different lens, things change focus. We measure locations with latitude and longitude, but those are relatively modern concepts. The prime meridian runs through Greenwich, England, because that was the point arbitrarily chosen in the late nineteenth century. My study of ancient maps revealed something quite to the contrary and quite extraordinary.'

Scofield stood and found one of the hotel's notepads and a pen. Stephanie watched as he sketched a crude world map, adding latitude and longitude markings around its perimeter. He then drew a line down the center from the thirty-degree east longitude position.

'This is not to scale, but it'll do for you to see what I'm talking about. Believe me, applied to a scaled map everything I'm about to show you is proven clear. This center line, which would be thirty-one degrees, eight minutes east, passes directly through the Great Pyramid at Giza. If this now becomes the zero-degree longitude line, here's what happens.'

He pointed to a spot where Bolivia would be in South America. 'Tiahuanaco. Built around 15,000 BCE. The capital of an unknown pre-Inca civilization near Lake Titicaca. Some say it may be the oldest city on earth. One hundred degrees west of the Giza line.'

He pointed to Mexico. 'Teotihuacán. Equally as old. Its name translates as "birthplace of the gods." No one knows who built it. A sacred Mexican city, one hundred twenty degrees west of the Giza line.'

The pen's point rested in the Pacific Ocean. 'Easter Island. Loaded with monuments that we can't explain. One hundred forty degrees west of the Giza line.' He moved farther out into the South Pacific. 'The ancient Polynesian center of Raiatea, sacred beyond measure. One hundred eighty degrees west of the Giza line.'

'Does it work the other way?' she asked.

'Of course.' He found the Middle East. 'Iraq. The biblical city of Ur of the Chaldees, the birthplace of Abraham. Fifteen degrees east of the Giza line.' He shifted the pen point. 'Here, Lhasa, the holy Tibetian city, old beyond measure. Sixty degrees east.

'There are many more sites that fall at defined intervals from the Giza line. All sacred. Most constructed by unknown peoples, involving pyramids or some form of raised structure. It cannot be a coincidence that these are located at precise points on the globe.'

'And you think whoever carved the writing in the stones was responsible for all that?' Davis asked.

'Remember, all explanations are rational. And when you consider the megalithic yard, the conclusion becomes inescapable.'

She'd never heard the term.

'From the 1950s until the mid-1980s, Alexander Thom, a Scottish engineer, undertook an analysis of forty-six neolithic and Bronze Age stone circles. He eventually surveyed more than three hundred sites and discovered that there was a common unit of measure used in every one of them. He called it the megalithic yard.'

'How is that possible,' she asked, 'considering the varied cultures?'

'The fundamental idea is quite sound.

'Monuments like Stonehenge, which exist all over the planet, were nothing more than ancient observatories. Their builders deciphered that if they stood in the center of a circle and faced the sunrise, marking the location of the event each day, after one year 366 markers would lie on the ground. The distance between those markers was a constant 16.32 inches.

'Of course those ancient people did not measure in inches,' Scofield said, 'but that was the modern equivalent from reproducing the technique.'

Those same ancient peoples then learned that it took 3.93 minutes for a star to move from one marker to the next.

'Again, they didn't utilize minutes, but they nonetheless observed and noted a constant unit of time.' Scofield paused. 'Here's the interesting part.

'For a pendulum to swing 366 times over 3.93 minutes, it has to be exactly 16.32 inches long.

'Amazing, wouldn't you say? And no way coincidental. That's why 16.32 inches was chosen by the ancient builders for the megalithic yard.'

Scofield seemed to catch their disbelief.

'It's not all that unique,' he said. 'A similar method was once proposed as an alternative for determining the length of a standard meter. The French ultimately decided that it would be better to use a division of the meridian quadrant, as they didn't trust their timepieces.'

'How could ancient peoples know this?' Davis asked. 'It would take a sophisticated understanding of mathematics and orbital mechanics.'

'There's that modern arrogance again. These people were not ignorant cavemen. They possessed an intuitive intelligence. They were conscious of their world. We narrow our senses and study little things. They widened their perceptions and learned the cosmos.'

'Is there any scientific evidence to prove this?' she asked.

'I just gave you physics and mathematics – which, by the way, that seafaring society would have understood. Alexander Thom posited that wooden measuring rods of a megalithic yard length could have been used for surveying purposes, and that they must have been produced from a central place in order to maintain the consistency he observed at the building sites. These people taught their lessons well to willing students.'

She could see that he believed everything he was saying.

'There are a number of numerical coincidences with other measuring systems used throughout history that provide some support to the megalithic yard. When studying the Minoan civilization, the archaeologist J. Walter Graham proposed that the people of Crete used a standard measure, which he termed the Minoan foot. There's a correlation. Three hundred sixty-six megalithic yards equal exactly one thousand Minoan feet. Another amazing coincidence, wouldn't you say?

'There's also a connection between the ancient Egyptian measurement of the royal cubit and the megalithic yard. A circle with a diameter of one-half a royal cubit will have a circumference equal to one megalithic yard. How could such a direct correlation be possible without a common denominator? It's as if the Minoans and the Egyptians were taught the megalithic yard, then they adapted the unit to their own situations.'

'Why have I never read or heard of any of this?' Davis asked.

'Mainstream scientists can neither confirm nor deny the megalithic yard. They argue that there's no evidence that pendulums were in common use, or even that the principle of the pendulum was known before Galileo. But there's that arrogance again. Somehow we are always the first to realize everything. They also say that neolithic peoples had no system of written communication able to record information about orbits and planetary motions. But—'

'The rocks,' she said. 'They contained writing.'

Scofield smiled. 'Precisely. Ancient writing in an unknown language. Yet until such time as they can be deciphered, or a neolithic measuring rod is actually found, this theory will remain unproven.'

Scofield went silent. She was waiting for that *more*.

'I was only allowed to work with the stones,' he said. 'Everything was brought to a warehouse at Fort Lee. But there was a refrigerated section of that warehouse. Locked off. Only the admiral went inside. Its contents were already there when I arrived. Dyals told me that if I solved the language problem, then I'd get a look inside.'

'No clue what was in there?' Davis asked.

Scofield shook his head. 'The admiral was crazy about secrecy. He always kept those lieutenants up my ass. I was never alone inside the building. But I sensed that the important items were stored in that freezer.'

'Did you get to know Ramsey?' Davis asked.

'Oh, yes. He was Dyals' favorite. Clearly in charge.'

'Ramsey is behind this,' Davis declared.

Scofield's gloom and annoyance seemed to mount. 'Does he have any idea what I could have written about those stones? They should have been shown to the world. They would confirm all that I've researched. A previously unknown culture, seafaring, that existed long before our civilization ever rose, capable of language. It's revolutionary.'

'Ramsey could not care less,' Davis said. 'His only interest is himself.'

She was curious. 'How did you know this culture was seafaring?'

'Reliefs on the stones. Long boats, sophisticated sailing crafts, whales, icebergs, seals, penguins, and not the small ones. Tall ones, the size of a man. We now know a species like that once existed in the Antarctic, but they've been extinct for tens of thousands of years. Yet I saw carvings of them.'

'So what happened to that lost culture?' she asked.

He shrugged. 'Probably the same thing that happens to all of man's societies. We wipe ourselves out either intentionally or recklessly. Either way, we're gone.'

Davis faced her. 'We need to go to Fort Lee and see if that stuff is still there.'

'It's all classified,' Scofield said. 'You'll never get near it.'

He was right. But she saw that Davis would not be deterred. 'Don't be so sure.'

'Can I go to sleep now?' Scofield said. 'I have to be up in a few hours for our annual hunt. Wild boar and bows and arrows. I take a group from the conference every year out into the woods.'

Davis stood. 'Sure. We'll be out of here in the morning, too.'

She stood.

'Look,' Scofield said, resignation in his voice. 'I am sorry about the attitude. I appreciate what you did.'

'You ought to consider not going hunting,' she said.

He shook his head. 'I can't disappoint the participants. They look forward to it each year.'

'It's your call,' Davis said. 'But I think you're okay. Ramsey would be a fool to come after you again, and he's anything but that.'

72

Bacchus tells me that they have communicated with many peoples and they respect all forms of language, finding each beautiful in its own way. The language of this gray land is a flowing tongue in an alphabet long ago perfected. On writing they are conflicted. It is necessary, but they warn that writing encourages forgetfulness and discourages memory and they are correct. I wander freely among the people with no fear. Crime is rare and punished by isolation. One day, I was asked to help lay the cornerstone of a wall. Bacchus was pleased with my involvement and urged me to irritate the vessels of the earth, for they distill a strange wine that grows under my hand and covers the whole of heaven. Bacchus says that we should worship this marvel for it provides life. Here the world is broken by mighty winds and voices that cry aloud in a tongue mortal men cannot speak. To the sounds of this primal joy I enter the house of Hathor and offer five jewels upon an altar. The wind sings loudly, so much that all who are there seem entranced and I truly think we are in heaven. Before a statue we kneel and give praise. The sound of a flute haunts the air. Snows are eternal and a strange perfume smokes upward. One night Bacchus broke forth into a monstrous speech that I could not appreciate. I asked to be taught the means of understanding and Bacchus agreed and I willingly embraced the language of heaven. I am glad my king allowed me to come to this wild country of the waning sun. These people rave and howl, they froth out folly. For a time I was afraid of being alone. I dreamed of warm sunsets, bright flowers, and thick vines. But no longer. Here the soul is drunken. Life is full. It slays, and suffices, but never disappoints.

. . .

I have noticed a strange constant. Everything that turns, naturally turns to the left. Lost people move to the left. Snow swirls to the left. The tracks of the animals in the snow bear to the left. The sea creatures swim in left-banked circles. Flocks of birds approach from a leftward direction. The sun in summer moves all day around the horizon, always from right to left. Youth are encouraged to know their natural surroundings. They are taught how to anticipate a storm or the approach of danger, they grow to be aware, at peace with themselves, prepared for life. I joined a trek one day. Hiking is favored but a dangerous pursuit. A good sense of direction and agile feet are needed. I noticed that even when our guide consciously turned right, the sum of his several turns was always left so that, without landmarks, which this land totally lacks, it is almost impossible to avoid returning to your starting point from anywhere but left. Man, bird, and sea creature are integrated. This left-turning mechanism seems entirely subconscious to them all. None of those who inhabit this gray land have any realization of the habit and, when I point out the observation, they simply shrug and smile.

. . .

Today Bacchus and I visited Adonai, who had been told of my interest in mathematics and architecture. He is a teacher of skills and showed me measuring rods used to both design and construct. To be consistent is to be accurate, I am told. I tell him how the design of the king's chapel at Aachen had been greatly influenced by his students and he was pleased. Instead of being fearful, distrusting, or ignorant of the world, Adonai insists we should learn from what nature created. The contours of the land, the location of underground heat, the angle of the sun, and the sea are all factors considered when locating both a city and a building. Adonai's wisdom is sound and I thank him for the lesson. I am also shown a garden. Many plants are preserved, but many more have perished. Plants are grown indoors in a soil rich with ash, pumice, sand, and minerals. Plants are also grown in water, both from the sea and fresh. Flesh is rarely eaten. I am told it depletes the energy within the body and makes one more susceptible to illness. After eating a diet mainly of plants, with an occasional dish of fish, I have never felt better.

What pleasure to see the sun again. The long winter darkness has ended. The crystal walls come alive with a glitter of colored light. A choir sings a low, sweet, rhythmic chant. The level increases as the sun climbs into a new sky. Trumpets sound the final note and all bow their heads in appreciation of the power of

life and strength. The city welcomes the summer
season. People play games, attend lectures, visit with
one another, and enjoy the Festival of the Year. Each
time the central pendulum in the plaza comes to rest,
all face the temple and watch as a crystal splashes
color across the city. After the long winter, the
spectacle is much appreciated. The time of unions
arrives and many appear to pledge their love and
allegiance. Each accepts a promise bracelet and tells
of their pledge to the other. This time brings great
joy. To live harmoniously is the goal I am told. But
on this occasion three unions required dissolution.
Two birthed children and the parents agreed to share
responsibility, even though no longer together. The
third union refused. Neither wanted the children. So
others who had long desired to parent were given
the offspring and there was again great joy.

. . .

I stay in a house where four rooms encircle a
courtyard. No windows in any of the walls but the
rooms are splendidly lit from above by a crystal
ceiling and always remain full of warmth and light.
Pipes reach across the city and into every house,
like roots trailing on the ground, and bring a never-
yielding heat. There are but two rules that govern
the house. No eating and no sanitation. The rooms
cannot be desecrated by eating, I am told. Meals are
taken with everyone in the dining halls. Washing,
bathing, and all other sanitation is performed in
other halls. I inquire about such rules and I am told
that all impure matter is instantly sent from the

dining and sanitation halls to the fire that never ends, where it is consumed. That is what keeps Tartarus clean and healthy. The two rules are the sacrifices each person makes for the purity of the city.

. . .

This gray land is divided into nine Lots, each with a city that radiates from a central plaza, which seems a gathering spot. An Adviser administers each Lot, selected from the people of the Lot through a vote, in which both men and women participate. Laws are enacted by the nine Advisers and inscribed upon the Righteous Columns in the central plaza of each city so that all will know. Solemn agreements are made consistent with the law. Advisers meet once, during the Festival of the Year, in the central plaza of Tartarus, and choose one of their number to be High Adviser. A single rule governs their law: Treat the land and one another as you would want to be treated. Advisers deliberate for the good of all beneath the symbol of righteousness. Atop is the sun, half ablaze in its glory. Then the earth, a simple circle, and the planets represented by a dot within the circle. The cross reminds them of the land, while the sea waves below. Forgive my crude sketch but this is how it appears.

73

Asheville

Stephanie was jarred from her sleep by the bedside phone. She glanced at the digital clock. 5:10 a.m. Davis lay on the other queen bed, also fully clothed, sleeping. Neither of them had even bothered to unmake their bed before lying down.

She snatched up the receiver, listened for a moment, then sat up. 'Say that again.'

'The man in custody is named Chuck Walters. We've verified that through fingerprints. He has a record, mostly petty stuff, nothing that relates here. He lives and works in Atlanta. We checked his alibi. Witnesses place him in Georgia two nights ago. No question. We interviewed them all and it checks out.'

She cleared her head. 'Why'd he run?'

'He said a man came charging after him. He's been sleeping with a married woman the past few months and thought it was her husband. We checked with the woman and she confirmed the affair. When Davis approached him, he freaked and ran. When you shot at him he really freaked and tossed the bowling pin. He didn't know what was happening. Then Davis beat the crap out of him. He says he's going to sue.'

'Any chance he's lying?'

'Not that we can see. This guy is no professional assassin.'

'What was he doing in Asheville?'

'His wife threw him out two days ago, so he decided to come up here. That's all. Nothing sinister.'

'And, I assume, the wife confirmed all that.'

'That's what we get paid for.'

She shook her head. Dammit.

'What do you want me to do with him?'

'Let him go. What else?'

She hung up the phone and said, 'It's not him.'

Davis was sitting on the side of his bed. The realization dawned within them both at the same time.

Scofield.

And they rushed for the door.

Charlie Smith had been perched in the tree for nearly an hour. Winter engulfed the limbs with aromatic resin, the thick needles ideal cover among a cluster of tall pines. The early-morning air was bitingly cold, an abundance of moisture only magnifying his discomfort. Thankfully, he'd dressed warmly and chosen his spot with care.

The show last night inside Biltmore house had been classic. He'd organized the charade with great style and watched as the woman not only took the bait, but swallowed the line, rod, reel, and the whole damn boat. He'd needed to know if he was walking into a trap, so he'd called Atlanta and found the operative, whom he'd employed before on other jobs. His instructions had been clear. *Watch for a signal and then draw attention to himself.* Smith had noticed the man and woman from the lobby earlier when they'd stepped onto the bus that transported the tour group from the inn to the château. He'd suspected they might be his problem but, once inside the house, he'd come to know for sure. So he'd given the signal and his man had given an Oscar-worthy performance. He'd stood on the far side of the enormous Christmas tree, in the banquet hall, and watched as all hell broke loose.

His orders to the operative had been clear. No weapons. Do nothing except run. Let them catch you, then plead ignorance. He'd made sure that his man possessed a clean alibi for his whereabouts two nights ago, since he knew everything would be double-checked. The fact that his helper was indeed experiencing marital problems and sleeping with a married woman only aided in the alibi and provided the perfect reasons for fleeing.

All in all, the spectacle had played itself out with perfection.

Now *he'd* come to finish the job.

Stephanie banged on the door for the conference coordinator, and her summons was finally answered. The front desk had provided them the room number.

'Who the hell are—'

Stephanie flashed her identification. 'Federal agents. We need to know where that hunt is located this morning.'

The woman hesitated a second, then said, 'It's on the estate, about twenty minutes from here.'

'A map,' Davis said. 'Draw it, please.'

Smith watched the hunting party through a pair of binoculars he'd purchased yesterday afternoon at a nearby Target. He was glad he'd kept the rifle from Herbert

Rowland's house. It contained four rounds, more than enough. Actually, he'd only need one.

Hunting wild hogs certainly was not for everyone. He knew a little about the sport. Hogs were mean, nasty, and tended to inhabit only densely vegetated areas, off the beaten path. The file on Scofield indicated that he loved hog hunting. When Smith learned yesterday about this jaunt, his mind had quickly formulated the perfect way to eliminate his target.

He looked around. The environment was ideal. Plenty of trees. No houses. Dense woods for miles. Wreaths of mist encircled the forested peaks. Fortunately, Scofield did not bring any dogs – they would have posed a problem. He'd learned from the conference staff that the participants always met at a staging area about three miles from the inn, near the river, and followed a well-marked route. No guns. Only bows and arrows. And they didn't necessarily come back with a hog. More private time with the professor, talking shop, enjoying a winter's morning in the woods. So he'd arrived two hours ago, well before dawn, and made his way down the trail, finally deciding on the highest and best location, near the start of the trek, hoping he'd get an opportunity.

If not, he'd improvise.

Stephanie drove and Davis navigated. They'd sped away from the inn, west into the 8,000 acres that made up the Biltmore Estate. The road was a narrow, unlined asphalt lane that eventually crossed the French Broad River and entered thick forest. The conference coordinator had said the hunt's staging area was not far past the river, and the trail into the woods would be easy to follow.

She caught sight of cars ahead.

Once she'd parked in a clearing they sprang from the car. A pale hint of dawn touched the sky. Her face was chilled by the damp air.

She spotted the trail and ran.

Smith caught sight of orange among the winter foliage, maybe a quarter mile away. He was ensconced on a limb, braced against a pine trunk. A blowing wind swept past under what was slowly developing into an azure December sky, crisp and chilling.

Through field glasses, he watched as Scofield and his party trudged north. He'd gambled as to their ultimate route, hoping they would stay on the trail. Now, with Scofield in sight, that chance had paid off.

He looped the binoculars' strap across a protruding branch and cradled the rifle, focusing through a long-range scope. He would have preferred to work more unnoticed, using a high-pressure sound suppressor, but he hadn't brought one of his own and they were illegal to purchase. He gripped the wooden stock and patiently waited for his quarry to draw close.

Just a few more minutes.

Stephanie raced ahead, panic firing through her in sharp bursts. She kept her eyes trained ahead, searching the woods for movement. Her breath tore at her lungs.

Wouldn't they all be wearing bright vests?

Was the killer out here?

Smith glimpsed movement behind the hunting party. He grabbed the binoculars and focused on the two from last night, rushing ahead, maybe fifty yards behind on a winding trail.

Apparently, his ruse had only partially worked.

He envisioned what would happen after Scofield died. A hunting accident would be immediately assumed, though the two intrepid souls closing the gap would scream murder. There'd be an inquiry by the local sheriff's department and the state department of natural resources. Investigators would measure, photograph, and search, angles and trajectories would be noted. Once it was realized the bullet came from above, the trees would come under scrutiny. But hell, there were tens of thousands of those around.

Which ones would they search?

Scofield stood five hundred yards away, his two saviors closing. In a few moments, they'd make a turn on the trail and spot their target.

He refocused through the rifle scope.

Accidents happen all the time. Hunters mistake one another for game.

Four hundred yards away.

Even when they wear fluorescent orange vests.

The rifle's crosshairs filled with his objective.

The shot needed to be in the chest. But the head would eliminate the necessity of a second round.

Three hundred yards.

Those two being here were a problem, but Ramsey expected Dr. Douglas Scofield to die today.

He squeezed the trigger.

The rifle barked across the valley and Scofield's head erupted.

So the chance would have to be taken.

PART FIVE

74

Malone had read enough of Christl's translation to know that he must go to Antarctica. If he had to take along four passengers, then so be it. Einhard had obviously experienced something extraordinary, something that had also enthralled Hermann Oberhauser. Unfortunately, the old German had sensed his impending doom and returned the book to where it had sat for twelve hundred years in the hope that his son might make the return journey. Yet Dietz had failed and had taken the crew of NR-1A down with him. If there was a chance in hell of finding that sunken sub, he had to take it.

They'd spoken to Isabel and told her what they'd found.

Christl was completing the translation, polishing her effort, making sure they possessed accurate information.

So he stepped from the inn into a frigid afternoon, and walked toward Ossau's central square, each step like a crisp Styrofoam squeak on the fresh snow. He'd brought his phone and, while he walked, dialed Stephanie's number. She answered on the fourth ring and said, 'I've been waiting to hear from you.'

'That doesn't sound good.'

'Being played for a fool never is.' He listened as she told him about the past twelve hours and what had happened at Biltmore Estate. 'I watched the man's skull be blown off.'

'You tried to tell him not to go, but he wouldn't listen. No trace of the shooter?'

'A lot of woods between us and him. No way to find him. He chose his spot well.'

He understood her frustration but noted, 'You still have a trail to Ramsey.'

'It's more like he has us.'

'But you know the connection. He has to make a mistake at some point. And you said Daniels told you that Diane McCoy went to Fort Lee, and Ramsey visited there yesterday. Think, Stephanie. The president didn't tell you that for nothing.'

'I thought the same thing.'

'I think you know your next move.'

'This sucks, Cotton. Scofield is dead because I wasn't thinking.'

'Nobody said it's fair. The rules are tough and the consequences tougher. Like you'd tell me. Do your job and don't sweat it, but don't screw up again.'

'The student teaching the teacher?'

'Something like that. Now I need a favor. A big one.'

Stephanie phoned the White House. She'd listened to Malone's request and told him to stand by. She agreed. It had to be done. She also agreed that Danny Daniels was plotting.

She'd dialed a private line directly to the chief of staff. When he answered, she explained her need. A few moments later the president came on the line and asked, 'Scofield's dead?'

'And it's our fault.'

'How's Edwin?'

'Mad as hell. What are you and Diane McCoy doing?'

'Not bad. I thought I hid that one good.'

'No, Cotton Malone is the bright one. I was just smart enough to listen to him.'

'It's complicated, Stephanie. But let's just say I wasn't as confident in Edwin's approach as I'd like to be and, it seems, I was right.'

She couldn't argue. 'Cotton needs a favor, and it relates to this.'

'Go ahead.'

'He's connected Ramsey, NR-1A, Antarctica, and that warehouse at Fort Lee. Those rocks with the writing on them – he found a way to read them.'

'I've been hoping that would happen,' Daniels said.

'He's e-mailing a translation program. I suspect that's the reason NR-1A went in 1971 – to learn more about those rocks. Now Malone needs to go to Antarctica. Halvorsen Base. Immediately. With four passengers.'

'Civilians?'

'Afraid so. But they're part of the deal. They have the site location. No them, no location. He'll need air and ground transportation and equipment. He thinks he may be able to solve the NR-1A mystery.'

'We owe him this one. Done.'

'Back to my question, what are you and Diane McCoy doing?'

'Sorry. Presidential privilege. But I need to know, are you going to Fort Lee?'

'Can we use that private jet that brought the Secret Service here?'

Daniels chuckled. 'Yours for the day.'

'Then yes, we'll go.'

Malone sat on a frozen bench and watched knots of people pass by, everyone laughing, full of festivity. What was waiting in Antarctica? Impossible to say. But for some reason he feared it.

He sat alone, his emotions as brittle and cold as the air around him. He barely remembered his father, but there'd never been a day since he was ten years old that he hadn't thought of the man. When he'd joined the navy, he'd met many of his father's contemporaries and quickly learned that Forrest Malone had been a highly respected officer. He'd never felt any pressure to measure up – perhaps because he'd never known the standard – but he'd been told that he was a lot like him. Forthright, determined, loyal. He'd always considered that a compliment, but damn if he didn't want to know the man for himself.

Unfortunately, death intervened.

And he was still angry at the navy for lying.

Stephanie and the court of inquiry report had explained some of the reasons for that deception. The secrecy of NR-1A, the Cold War, the mission's uniqueness, the fact that the crew agreed to no rescue. But none of that was satisfactory. His father died on a foolhardy venture searching for nonsense. Yet the US Navy had sanctioned that folly and a bold cover-up.

Why?

His phone vibrated in his hand.

'The president has okayed everything,' Stephanie said when he answered. 'There's usually lots of prep and procedures that have to be followed before anyone goes to Antarctica – training, vaccinations, medical exams – but he's ordered them suspended. A helicopter is on its way to you now. He wishes you well.'

'I'll send the translation program by e-mail.'

'Cotton, what do you hope to find?'

A deep breath calmed his jangled nerves. 'I'm not sure. But there's a few of us here who have to make the journey.'

'Sometimes ghosts are better left alone.'

'I don't recall you believing that a couple of years ago, when the ghosts were yours.'

'What you're about to do. It's dangerous, in more ways than one.'

His face was cast down at the snow, phone to his ear. 'I know.'

'Careful with this one, Cotton.'

'You, too.'

75

Fort Lee, Virginia, 2:40 p.m.

Stephanie drove a rental car obtained at the Richmond airport, where the Secret Service jet had landed after its quick flight from Asheville. Davis sat beside her, his face and ego still bruised. He'd been played twice for an idiot. Once years ago by Ramsey with Millicent, and yesterday by the man who'd skillfully murdered Douglas Scofield. The local police were treating the death as a homicide, solely on information Stephanie and Edwin had provided, though not a trace of an assailant had been found. Both of them realized that the killer was long gone, their task now to determine where. But first they needed to see what all the ruckus was about.

'How do you plan to get into that warehouse?' she asked Davis. 'Diane McCoy didn't manage.'

'I don't think that's going to be a problem.'

She knew what or, more accurately, who that meant.

She approached the base's main gate and stopped at the security point. To the uniformed sentry, she presented their identifications and said, 'We have business with the base commander. Classified.'

The corporal retreated into his gate station and quickly returned, holding an envelope. 'This is for you, ma'am.'

She accepted the packet and he waved them through.

She handed the envelope to Davis and drove forward as he opened it.

'It's a note,' he said. 'Says to follow these directions.'

Davis navigated and she drove through the base until they entered a compound filled with metal warehouses, lying beside one another like half loaves of bread.

'The one marked 12E,' Davis said.

She saw a man waiting for them outside. Dark-skinned, hair jet black, cut short, his features more Arab than European. She parked and they both clambered out.

'Welcome to Fort Lee,' the man said. 'I'm Colonel William Gross.'

He was dressed in jeans, boots, and a lumberjack shirt.

'A bit out of uniform,' Davis said.

'I was hunting today. Was called in and told to come as I am and be discreet. I understand you want a look inside.'

'And who told you that?' she asked.

'Actually, the president of the United States. Can't say I've ever been called by one before, but I was today.'

Ramsey stared across the conference table at the *Washington Post* reporter. This was the ninth interview he'd granted today and the first in person. The others had all been by telephone, which had become standard operating procedure for a press with tight deadlines. Daniels, true to his word, had announced the appointment four hours ago.

'You have to be thrilled,' the woman said. She'd covered the military for several years and had interviewed him before. Not all that bright, but she clearly thought herself so.

'It's a good post in which to end my career with the navy.' He laughed. 'Let's face it, that's always been the last billet for anyone chosen. Not many places to go higher.'

'The White House.'

He wondered if she was knowledgeable or simply baiting him. Surely the latter. So he decided to have some fun with it. 'True, I could retire out and make a run for the presidency. Seems like a plan.'

She smiled. 'Twelve military men made it that far.'

He held up a hand in surrender. 'I assure you, I have no plans for that. None at all.'

'Several people I spoke with today mentioned that you'd be an excellent political candidate. Your career has been exemplary. Not a hint of scandal. Your political philosophies are unknown, which means they could be molded however you choose. No party affiliation, which gives you choices. And the American people always love a man in uniform.'

Exactly his reasoning. He firmly believed that an opinion poll would reveal an overall approval of him, both as a person and a leader. Though his name was not that well known, his career spoke for itself. He'd dedicated his life to military service, been stationed around the globe, serving in every conceivable trouble spot. He'd received twenty-three commendations. His political friends were numerous. Some he'd cultivated himself, like Winterhawk Dyals and Senator Kane, but others gravitated toward him simply because he represented a high-ranking officer in a sensitive position who could be of help whenever they might need it.

'Tell you what, I'll leave that honor to some other military person. I'm simply looking forward to serving on the Joint Chiefs. Going to be a terrific challenge.'

'I've heard Aatos Kane is your champion. Any truth to that?'

This woman was far more informed than he'd assumed. 'If the senator spoke for me, then I'm grateful. With confirmation looming, it's always nice to have friends on the Senate floor.'

'You think confirmation will be a problem?'

He shrugged. 'I don't presume anything. I simply hope the senators think me worthy. If not, I'll be pleased to finish my career right where I am.'

'You sound like it doesn't matter whether you get the job or not.'

One piece of advice many a nominee had failed to heed was simple and clear. Don't ever appear anxious or entitled.

'That's not what I said, and you know it. What's the problem here? No story beyond the appointment itself, so you're trying to make one?'

She seemed not to enjoy his reprimand, however tacit. 'Let's face it, Admiral. Yours was not the name most people would have associated with this appointment. Rose at the Pentagon, Blackwood at NATO – those two would have been naturals. But Ramsey? You came out of nowhere. That fascinates me.'

'Perhaps the two you mentioned weren't interested?'

'They were, I checked. But the White House came straight to you, and my sources say it was thanks to Aatos Kane.'

'You need to ask Kane that question.'

'I did. His office said they'd get back to me with a comment. That was three hours ago.'

Time to placate her. 'I'm afraid there's nothing sinister here. At least not on my part. Just an old navy man grateful for a few more years to serve.'

*   *   *

Stephanie followed Colonel Gross into the warehouse. He'd gained entrance through a numeric code and digital thumb scanner.

'I personally supervise maintenance of all these warehouses,' Gross said. 'My coming here will raise no suspicions.'

Which, Stephanie thought, was precisely why Daniels had enlisted his aid.

'You understand the secrecy of this visit?' Davis asked.

'My CO explained, as did the president.'

They stepped into a small anteroom. The rest of the dimly lit storage facility loomed ahead through a plate-glass window that revealed row after row of metal shelving.

'I'm supposed to give you the history,' Gross said. 'This building has been on lease to the navy since October 1971.'

'That's before NR-1A sailed,' Davis said.

'I don't know anything about that,' Gross made clear. 'But I do know that the navy has maintained this building ever since. It's equipped with a separate refrigerated chamber—' He pointed through the window. '—beyond the last row of shelves, which is still operational.'

'What's in it?' she asked.

He hesitated. 'I think you need to see that for yourself.'

'Is that why we're here?'

He shrugged. 'No idea. But Fort Lee has made sure this warehouse stayed in tip-top shape for the past thirty-eight years. I've been on the job for six of those. No one other than Admiral Ramsey himself enters this building, without me by their side. I stay with any cleaning or repair crew at all times. My predecessors did the same. The scanners and electronic locks were installed five years ago. A computer record is maintained of all who enter and is provided daily to the Office of Naval Intelligence, which has direct managerial oversight of the lease. Whatever anyone sees in here is classified, and all personnel understand what that means.'

'How many times has Ramsey visited?' Davis asked.

'Only once in the past five years – that the computer record shows. Two days ago. He also entered the refrigerated compartment. It has a separate recorded lock.'

She was anxious. 'Take us.'

Ramsey showed the *Post* reporter from his office. Hovey had already told him about three more interviews. Two for television, one for radio, and they would happen downstairs, in a briefing room, where crews were setting up. He was beginning to like this. Much different from living in the shadows. He was going to make a great Joint Chief of Staff and, if all went according to plan, an even better vice president.

He'd never understood why the number two constitutional office couldn't be more active. Dick Cheney had demonstrated the possibilities, becoming a quiet molder of policy without the attention the presidency continually attracted. As vice president, he could involve himself in what he wanted, when he wanted. And just as quickly un-involve himself, since – as John Nance Garner, FDR's first vice president, had so wisely noted – most believed the office wasn't worth a 'warm bucket of spit,' though legend says reporters changed the spelling of the last word for print.

He smiled.

Vice President Langford Ramsey.

He liked that.

His cell phone alerted him with a barely audible chime.

He lifted the unit from his desk and noted the caller. Diane McCoy.

'I need to speak with you,' she said.

'I don't think so.'

'No tricks, Langford. You name the place.'

'I haven't the time.'

'Make it, or there won't be any appointment.'

'Why do you persist in threatening me?'

'I'll come to your office. Surely you feel safe there.'

He did, but wondered, 'What's this about?'

'A man named Charles C. Smith Jr. It's an alias, but that's what you call him.'

He'd never heard anyone speak that name before. Hovey handled all payments, but they were issued to another name in a foreign bank, protected behind the National Security Act.

Yet Diane McCoy knew.

He checked the clock on his desk. 4:05 p.m.

'Okay, come on over.'

76

M alone settled in to the LC-130. They'd just completed a ten-hour flight from France to Cape Town, South Africa. A French military chopper had ferried them from Ossau to Cazau, Teste-de-Buch, the nearest French military base, about 150 miles away. There a C-21A, the military version of a Learjet, had flown them just under Mach 1 across the Mediterranean and lengthwise down the African continent, with only two quick stops for refueling.

In Cape Town a fully fueled LC-130 Hercules, with two crews from the 109th Air Wing of the New York Air National Guard, sat waiting, engines revved. Malone realized that the ride in the Learjet was going to seem luxurious next to what he and his cohorts were about to experience on the twenty-seven hundred miles south to Antarctica, across storm-tossed ocean for all but the last seven hundred miles, which would be over solid ice.

Truly, a no-man's-land.

Their gear had been waiting on board. He knew the key word. *Layers.* And he knew the objective. Eliminate body moisture without it freezing. Under Armour shirts and pants, made of a fast-wicking material, went on first to keep the skin dry. Over that came a wool long john union suit, breathable, also with water-wicking properties, then a nylon jacket-and-pant set with a fleece backing. Finally, a Gore-Tex fleece-lined parka and cold-weather wind pants. Everything was in a camouflage digital pattern, courtesy of the US Army. Gore-Tex gloves and boots, along with two pairs of socks each, protected the extremities. He'd provided their sizes hours ago and noticed that the boots were the requisite size and a half too big to accommodate the thick socks. A black wool balaclava protected the face and neck with openings only for the eyes, which would be shielded by tinted goggles. Like going for a space walk, he mused, which wasn't far off the mark. He'd heard stories of how the Antarctic cold caused fillings in teeth to contract and fall out.

Each of them had brought a rucksack with a few personal items. He noticed that a cold-weather version, thicker and better insulated, had been provided.

The Hercules lumbered toward the runway.

He turned to the others, who sat on canvas seats with web backings across from him. None of them had yet donned the wool balaclava, so their faces remained exposed. 'Everybody okay?'

Christl, who sat beside him, nodded.

He noticed they all seemed uncomfortable in their thick clothing. 'I assure you, this flight is not going to be warm and these clothes are about to become your best friends.'

'This may be too much,' Werner said.

'This is the easy part,' he made clear. 'But if you can't take it, you can always stay at the base. The Antarctic camps are plenty comfortable.'

'I've never done this before,' Dorothea said. 'Quite an adventure for me.'

More like the adventure of a lifetime, since supposedly no human had touched the Antarctic shore until 1820, and only a precious few made it there now. He knew there was a treaty, signed by twenty-five nations, that labeled the entire continent as a place of peace, with a free exchange of scientific information, no new territorial claims, no military activities, and no mining unless all signers of the treaty agreed. Five point four million square miles, about the size of the United States and Mexico combined, 80 percent of which was swathed in a mile-thick shroud of ice – 70 percent of the world's fresh water – making the resulting ice plateau one of the highest on earth, with an average elevation of over eight thousand feet.

Life existed only at the edges, as the continent received less than two inches of rain a year. Dry as a desert. Its white surface lacked the ability to absorb light or heat, reflecting back all radiation, keeping the average temperature around seventy degrees below zero.

He also knew the politics from his two previous visits while with the Magellan Billet. Currently seven nations – Argentina, Britain, Norway, Chile, Australia, France, and New Zealand – laid claim to eight territories, defined by degrees of longitude that intersected at the South Pole. They were flying to the portion claimed by Norway, known as Dronning Maud Land, which extended from 44° 38'E to 20°W. A sizable chunk of its western portion – from 20°E to 10°W – had been claimed by Germany in 1938 as Neuschwabenland. And though the war ended that claim, the region remained one of the least known of the continent. Their destination was Halvorsen Base, operated by Australia in the Norwegian section, situated on the northern coast facing the southern tip of Africa.

They'd been given foam earplugs – which he noticed everyone had inserted – but the noise was still there. The pungent smell of engine fuel swirled around his head, but he knew, from past flights, that the odor would soon go unnoticed. They sat forward, near the flight deck, accessible via a five-step ladder. For the long flight, two crews had been provided. He'd once sat on the flight deck while landing on Antarctic snow. Quite an experience. Now here he was again.

Ulrich Henn had said nothing on the flight from France and sat impassive in his seat beside Werner Lindauer. Malone knew this man was trouble, but couldn't determine whether he or some of the others were the object of Henn's interest. No matter, Henn carried the information they needed once on the ground, and a deal was a deal.

Christl tapped him on the arm and mouthed *Thank you*.

He nodded in gratitude.

The Hercules turboprops revved to full throttle, and they accelerated down the runway. First slow, then faster, then airborne, climbing out over open ocean.

It was nearly midnight.

And they were on their way to who knew what.

77

Fort Lee, Virginia

Stephanie watched as Colonel Gross released the electronic lock and opened the refrigerated compartment's steel door. Cold air rushed out in a chilling fog. Gross waited a few seconds until the air cleared, then motioned inside.

'After you.'

She entered first. Davis followed. The compartment was about eight feet square, two of the walls bare metal, the third lined from floor to ceiling with a rack of shelving upon which stood books. Five rows. One after another. She estimated maybe two hundred.

'They've been here since 1971,' Gross said. 'Before that, I have no idea where they were kept. But it had to be cold since, as you can see, they're in great shape.'

'Where'd they come from?' Davis asked.

Gross shrugged. 'I don't know. But the rocks outside are all from Operation Highjump in 1947 and Windmill in '48. So, it's reasonable to assume that these came from then, too.'

She approached the shelves and studied the volumes. They were small, maybe six by eight inches, wood-bound, held together by tight cords, the pages coarse and thick.

'Can I see one?' she asked Gross.

'I was told to let you do whatever you want.'

Carefully, she removed a frozen sample. Gross was right. It was perfectly preserved. A thermometer near the door indicated a temperature of ten degrees Fahrenheit. She'd read an account once of Amundsen and Scott's dual expeditions to the South Pole – how decades later, when their food stores had been found, the cheese and vegetables were still edible. The biscuits retained their crispiness. Salt, mustard, and spices remained in perfect condition. Even the pages of magazines appeared as the day they were printed. Antarctica was a natural freezer. No rot, rust, fermentation, mold, or disease. No moisture, dust, or insects. Nothing to break down any organic debris.

Like books with wooden covers.

'I read a proposal once,' Davis said. 'Somebody suggested that Antarctica would be the perfect repository for a world library. The climate wouldn't affect a single page. I thought the idea ludicrous.'

'Maybe not.'

She laid the book on the shelf. Embossed into the pale beige cover was an unrecognizable symbol.

Carefully, she examined the stiff pages, each covered with writing from top to bottom. Curlicues, swirls, circles. A strange cursive script – tight and compact. Drawings, too. Plants, people, devices. Every succeeding folio was the same – all in crisp clear brown ink, not a smudge anywhere.

Before Gross had opened the refrigerated compartment he'd shown them the warehouse shelves, which contained a multitude of stone fragments with similar writing etched into them.

'A library of some sort?' Davis asked her.

She shrugged.

'Ma'am,' Gross said.

She turned. The colonel reached up to the top shelf and retrieved a leather-bound journal wrapped with a cloth strap. 'The president said to give this to you. It's Admiral Byrd's private diary.'

She instantly recalled what Herbert Rowland had said about seeing it.

'It's been classified since 1948,' Gross said. 'Here since '71.'

She noticed several strips of paper marking spots.

'The relevant parts are flagged.'

'By who?' Davis asked.

Gross smiled. 'The president said you'd ask that.'

'So what's the answer?'

'I took this to the White House earlier and waited while the president read it. He said to tell you that, contrary to what you and other staffers may think, he learned to read a long time ago.'

Returned to dry valley, Spot 1345. Set up camp. Weather clear. Sky cloudless. Little wind. Located previous German settlement. Magazines, food stores, equipment all indicate 1938 exploration. Wooden shed erected then still standing. Sparsely furnished with table, chairs, stove, radio. Nothing significant at site. Moved fourteen miles east, Spot 1356, another dry valley. Located carved stones at mountain base. Most too large to transport, so we gathered smaller ones. Helicopters called. I examined the stones and made a tracing.

Oberhauser in '38 reported similar finds. These represent confirmation of war archives. Germans clearly here. Physical evidence beyond dispute.

. . .

Investigated a crevice in mountain at Spot 1578 that opened into a small room carved from rock. Writing and drawings similar to Spot 1356 found on walls. People, boats, animals, carts, the sun, representations of sky, planets, moon. Photographs taken. A personal observation: Oberhauser came in '38 in search of lost Aryans. Clearly, some sort of civilization once existed here. Physical images of the people are of a tall, thick-haired, muscular race with Caucasian features. Woman are full-breasted with long hair. I was disturbed looking at them. Who were they? Before today I thought Oberhauser's theories on Aryans ridiculous. Now I do not know.

. . .

Arrived Spot 1590. Shown another chamber. Small. More writing on walls. Few images. 212 wood-bound volumes found inside, stacked on stone table. Photographs taken. Same unknown writing from the stones inside the books. Time short. Operation ends in eighteen days. Summer season fading. Ships must depart before ice packs return. Ordered books crated and ferried to ship.

Stephanie glanced up from Byrd's diary. 'This is amazing. Look what they found – yet they did nothing with it.'

'A sign of their times,' Davis quietly said. 'They were too busy worrying about Stalin and dealing with a destroyed Europe. Lost civilizations mattered little, especially one that might have a German connection. Byrd was clearly concerned about that.' Davis looked at Gross. 'Photographs are mentioned. Can we get those?'

'The president tried. They're gone. In fact, everything is gone except for that diary.'

'And these books and rocks,' she added.

Davis thumbed through the diary, reading other passages out loud. 'Byrd visited a lot of sites. A shame we don't have a map. They're only identified by numbers, no coordinates.'

She wished the same thing, especially for Malone's sake. But there was one salvation. The translation program Malone mentioned. What Hermann Oberhauser found in France. She stepped from the freezer, found her cell phone, and dialed Atlanta. When her assistant told her an e-mail had been sent by Malone she smiled and clicked off.

'I need one of these books,' she said to Gross.

'They have to be kept frozen. It's how they're preserved.'

'Then I want to be allowed back in here. I have a laptop, but I'll need Internet access.'

'The president said whatever you want.'

'You have something?' Davis asked.

'I think I do.'

78

6:30 p.m.

Ramsey reentered his office, finished with the last interview of the day. Diane McCoy sat inside, where he'd told Hovey to have her wait. He closed the door. 'Okay, what's so important?'

She'd been electronically swept and was clean of listening devices. He knew his office was secure, so he sat with confidence.

'I want more,' she told him.

She wore a gun-check wool tweed suit in calming shades of brown and camel, with a black turtleneck underneath. A tad casual and expensive looking for a White House staffer, but stylish. Her coat lay across another of the chairs.

'More of what?' he asked.

'There's a man who goes by the name Charles C. Smith Jr. He works for you, and has for a long time. You pay him well, albeit through a variety of false names and numbered accounts. He's your killer, the one who took care of Admiral Sylvian and a whole group of others.'

He was amazed, but stayed composed. 'Any proof?'

She laughed. 'Like I'm going to tell you. Just suffice it to say I know, and that's what matters.' She grinned. 'You may well be the first person in US military history to have actually murdered his way to the top. Damn, Langford, you truly are an ambitious SOB.'

He needed to know. 'What do you want?'

'You have your appointment. That's what *you* wanted. I'm sure that's not all, but that's all for the moment. So far the reaction has been good to your selection, so you seem on your way.'

He agreed. Any serious problems would quickly surface once the public knew he was the president's choice. That's when anonymous phone calls to the press would start and the politics of destruction would take over. After eight hours, nothing had yet surfaced, but she was right. He had murdered his way to the top so, thanks to Charlie Smith, anyone who could possibly be a problem was already dead.

Which reminded him. Where was Smith?

He'd been so busy with interviews, he'd forgotten all about him. He'd told the idiot to take care of the professor and return by nightfall, and the sun was now setting.

'You've been a busy girl,' he said.

'I've been a smart girl. I have access to information networks you could only dream about.'

He didn't doubt that. 'And you plan to hurt me?'

'I plan to wreck the living hell out of you.'

'Unless what?'

A ripple of amused laughter drifted across her face. This bitch was definitely enjoying herself.

'This is all about you, Langford.'

He shrugged. 'You want to be a part of what happens after Daniels? I'll make that happen.'

'Do I look like I just fell off the turnip truck?'

He grinned. 'Now you sound like Daniels.'

'That's because he says that to me at least twice a week.

Usually I deserve it, since I am playing him. He's smart, I'll give him that. But I'm no fool. I want a damn lot more.'

He had to hear her out, but a strange uneasiness accompanied his forced patience.

'I want money.'

'How much?'

'Twenty million dollars.'

'How did you arrive at that figure?'

'I can live comfortably off the interest for the rest of my life. I did the math.'

An almost sexual enjoyment danced in her eyes.

'I assume you would want this offshore, in a blind account, accessible only to you?'

'Just like Charles C. Smith Jr. With a few more stipulations, but those can come later.'

He tried to remain calm. 'What brought this on?'

'You're going to screw me. I know it, you know it. I tried to get you on tape, but you were too smart. So I thought, *Lay it on the table. Tell him what I know. Make a deal. Get something, up front.* Call it a down payment. An investment. That way you'll be more hesitant to shaft me later. I'll be bought and paid for, ready to use.'

'And if I refuse?'

'Then you'll end up in prison or, better yet, maybe I'll find Charles C. Smith Jr. and see what he has to say.'

He said nothing.

'Or maybe I'll just dangle you out in the press.'

'And what will you tell the reporters?'

'I'll start with Millicent Senn.'

'And what would you know of her?'

'Young naval officer, assigned to your staff in Brussels. You had a relationship with her. And then, lo and behold, she becomes pregnant and a few weeks later is dead. Failed heart. The Belgians ruled it natural. Case closed.'

This woman was well informed. He worried that his silence might be more explicit than any response, so he said, 'No one would believe that.'

'Maybe not now, but it makes for a great story. The kind of thing the press loves. Especially *Extra* and *Inside Edition*. Did you know that Millicent's father still believes, to this day, she was murdered? He'd gladly go on camera. Her brother – who's a lawyer, by the way – also has doubts. Of course, they don't know anything about you or your relationship with her. They also don't know that you liked to beat the crap out of her. What do you think they, the Belgian authorities, or the press would do with all that?'

She had him, and knew it.

'This is no setup, Langford. It's not about getting you to admit anything. I don't need your admissions. It's about looking after me. I. Want. Money.'

'And, for the sake of argument, if I agreed, what would stop you from shaking me down again?'

'Not one thing,' she said through clenched teeth.

He allowed himself a grin, then a chuckle. 'You are a devil.'

She returned the compliment. 'Seems we're perfect for each other.'

He liked the amicable note in her voice. Never had he suspected that so much larceny coursed through her veins. Aatos Kane would like nothing more than to rid himself of his obligation, and even the hint of scandal would offer the senator a perfect opportunity. *I'm willing to hold up my end,* Kane would say, *you're the one with problems.*

And there'd be nothing he could do.

It would take reporters less than an hour to verify that

his tour of duty in Brussels coincided with Millicent's. Edwin Davis had also been there and that romantic fool had had a thing for Millicent. He'd known that at the time, but could not have cared less. Davis had been weak and unimportant. Not anymore. God knew where he was. He'd heard nothing about Davis in several days. But the woman sitting across from him was a different matter. She had a loaded gun, aimed straight at him, and knew where to shoot.

'Okay. I'll pay.'

She reached into her jacket pocket and removed a sheet of paper. 'Here's the bank and routing number. Make the payment, in full, within the next hour.'

She tossed it on the desk.

He did not move.

She smiled. 'Don't look so glum.'

He said nothing.

'Tell you what,' she said, 'To show you my good faith, and my willingness to work with you on a permanent basis, once the payment is confirmed I'm going to give you something else you really want.'

She stood from the chair.

'What's that?' he asked.

'Me. I'm yours tomorrow night. So long as I get paid in the next hour.'

79

Saturday, December 15, 12:50 a.m.

Dorothea was not happy. The plane bumped its way through rough air like a truck on a pitted dirt road, which brought back memories of her childhood and trips to the lodge with her father. They'd loved the outdoors. While Christl shunned guns and hunting, she'd loved both. It had been something she and her father had shared. Unfortunately, they'd only enjoyed a few seasons. She was ten when he died. Or, better put, when he never came back home again. And that sad thought scooped out another crater in the pit of her stomach, deepening an emptiness that seemed to never abate.

It was after her father's disappearance that she and Christl had drifted farther apart. Different friends, interests, tastes. Lives. How did two people who sprang from the same egg grow so distant?

Only one explanation made sense.

Their mother.

For decades she'd forced them to compete. And those battles had bred resentment. Dislike came next. An easy jump from there to hatred.

She sat strapped into her seat, bundled in her gear. Malone had been right about the clothing. This misery wouldn't end for at least another five hours. The crew had distributed box lunches when they'd boarded. Cheese roll, cookies, chocolate bar, a drumstick, and an apple. No way she could eat a bite. Just the thought of food made her sick. She pressed her parka tight into the seat's web backings and tried to be comfortable. An hour ago Malone had disappeared up into the flight deck. Henn and Werner were asleep, but Christl seemed wide awake.

Perhaps she was anxious, too.

This flight was the worst of her life, and not just from the discomfort. They were flying to their destiny. Was something there? If so, was it good or bad?

After suiting up, they'd each packed their insulated rucksacks. She'd brought only a change of clothes, a toothbrush, some toiletries, and an automatic pistol. Her mother had sneaked it to her in Ossau. Since this was not a commercial flight, there'd been no security inspections. Though she resented allowing her mother to make yet another decision for her, she felt better with the gun nearby.

Christl's head turned.

Their eyes met in the half-light.

What a bitter piece of irony that they were here, on this plane, thrust together. Would speaking to her do any good?

She decided to try.

She unbuckled her harness and rose from the seat. She crossed the narrow aisle and sat beside her sister. 'We have to stop this,' she said over the noise.

'I plan to. Once we find what I know is there.' Christl's expression was as cold as the plane's interior.

She tried again. 'None of that matters.'

'Not to you. It never did. All you cared about was passing the wealth to your precious Georg.'

The words pierced her, and she wanted to know, 'Why did you resent him?'

'He was all that I could never have, dear sister.'

She caught the bitterness as conflicting emotions collided inside her. Dorothea had wept by Georg's coffin for two days, trying, with everything she possessed, to release his memory. Christl had come to the funeral, but left quickly. Not once had her sister offered any condolences.

Nothing.

Georg's death had signaled a turning point in Dorothea's life. Everything changed. Her marriage, her family. And, most important, herself. She did not like what she'd become, but had readily accepted anger and resentment as substitutes for a child she'd adored.

'You're barren?' she asked.

'You care?'

'Does Mother know you can't have children?' she asked.

'What does it matter? This isn't about children anymore. It's about the Oberhauser legacy. What this family believed.'

She could see that this effort was futile. The gulf between them was far too wide to either fill or bridge.

She started to rise.

Christl cracked her hand down on her wrist. 'So I didn't say I was sorry when he died. At least you know what it is like to have a child.'

The pettiness of the comment stunned her. 'God help any child you would have had. You could have never cared for one. You're incapable of that kind of love.'

'Seems you didn't do such a great job. Yours is dead.'

Damn her.

Her right hand formed a fist and her arm powered upward, smashing into Christl's face.

★　　★　　★

Ramsey sat at his desk and prepared himself for what lay ahead. Surely more interviews and press attention. Admiral Sylvian's funeral was tomorrow, at Arlington National Cemetery, and he reminded himself to make mention of that sad event to every interviewer. *Focus on the fallen comrade. Be humble that you've been chosen to follow in his footsteps. Regret the loss of a fellow flag officer.* The funeral would be a full-dress affair with honors. The military certainly knew how to bury its own. They'd done it often enough.

His cell phone rang. An international number. Germany. About time.

'Good evening, Admiral,' a gravelly woman's voice said.

'Frau Oberhauser. I've been expecting your call.'

'And how did you know I would call?'

'Because you're an anxious old bitch who likes to be in control.'

She chuckled. 'That I am. Your men did a good job. Malone is dead.'

'I prefer to wait till they report that fact to me.'

'I'm afraid that's going to be impossible. They're dead, as well.'

'Then you're the one with a problem. I have to have confirmation.'

'Have you heard anything about Malone in the last twelve hours? Any reports of what he might be doing?'

No, he hadn't.

'I saw him die.'

'Then we have nothing more to say.'

'Except you owe me an answer to my question. Why did my husband never come back?'

What the hell? Tell her. 'The submarine malfunctioned.'

'And the crew? My husband?'

'They didn't survive.'

Silence.

Finally, she said, 'You saw the submarine and the crew?'

'I did.'

'Tell me what you saw.'

'You don't want to know.'

Another long pause, then, 'Why was it necessary to cover this up?'

'The submarine was top secret. Its mission was secret. There was no choice at the time. We couldn't risk the Soviets finding it. Only eleven men aboard, so it was easy to conceal the facts.'

'And you left them there?'

'Your husband agreed to those conditions. He knew the risks.'

'And you Americans say Germans are heartless.'

'We're practical, Frau Oberhauser. We protect the world, you folks tried to conquer it. Your husband signed on for a dangerous mission. His idea, actually. He's not the first to make that choice.'

He was hoping this would be the last he heard from her. He didn't need her aggravation.

'Good-bye, Admiral. I hope you rot in hell.'

He heard the emotion in her voice, but could not care less. 'I wish only the same for you.'

And he clicked off.

He made a mental note to change his cell phone number. That way he'd never have to talk to that crazy German again.

Charlie Smith loved a challenge. Ramsey had delegated him a fifth target, but made clear that the job had to be done today. Absolutely nothing could arouse suspicions.

A clean kill, no aftertaste. Usually that would not be a problem. But he was working with no file, only a few scant facts from Ramsey, and a twelve-hour window. If successful, Ramsey had promised an impressive bonus. Enough to pay for Bailey Mill, with plenty left over for remodeling and furnishing.

He was back from Asheville, at his apartment, the first time home in a couple of months. He'd managed a few hours' sleep and was ready for what lay ahead. He heard a soft chime from the kitchen table and checked his cell phone ID. Not a number he recognized, though it was a Washington-area exchange. Perhaps it was Ramsey calling from an anonymous phone. He'd do that sometimes. The man was eaten up by paranoia.

He answered.

'I'm calling for Charlie Smith,' a woman's voice said.

The use of that name brought his senses alert. He used that label only with Ramsey. 'You got the wrong number.'

'No, I don't.'

'Afraid so.'

'I wouldn't hang up,' she said. 'What I have to say could make or break your life.'

'Like I said, lady, wrong number.'

'You killed Douglas Scofield.'

A cold chill swept through him as realization dawned. 'You were there, with the guy?'

'Not me, but they work for me. I know all about you, Charlie.'

He said nothing, but her having the phone number and knowing his alias were major problems. Actually, catastrophic. 'What do you want?'

'Your ass.'

He chuckled.

'But I'm willing to trade yours for someone else's.'

'Let me guess. Ramsey?'

'You are a bright guy.'

'I don't suppose you plan to tell me who you are?'

'Sure. Unlike you, I don't live a false life.'

'Then who the hell are you?'

'Diane McCoy. Deputy national security adviser to the president of the United States.'

80

Malone heard someone scream. He was on the flight deck talking with the crew and rushed to the aft doorway, staring down into the tunnel-like interior of the LC-130. Dorothea was across the aisle, beside Christl, who was struggling to free herself from the harness and shrieking. Blood gushed from Christl's nose and stained her parka. Werner and Henn had come awake and were unbuckling themselves.

With open palms, Malone slid down the ladder's railings and rushed toward the mêlée. Henn had managed to yank Dorothea away.

'You crazy bitch,' Christl screamed. 'What are you doing?'

Werner took hold of Dorothea. Malone dropped back and watched.

'She slugged me,' Christl said, dabbing her sleeve onto her nose.

Malone found a towel on one of the steel racks and tossed it to her.

'I should kill you,' Dorothea spit out. 'You don't deserve to live.'

'You see,' Christl yelled. 'This is what I mean. She's nuts. Totally nuts. Crazy as hell.'

'What *are* you doing?' Werner asked his wife. 'What brought this on?'

'She hated Georg,' Dorothea said, struggling in Werner's grasp.

Christl stood, facing her sister.

Werner released his hold on Dorothea and allowed the two lionesses to appraise each other, both seemingly trying to calculate a hidden purpose in the other. Malone watched the women, dressed in identical thick gear, their faces identical, but their minds so different.

'You weren't even there when we finally buried him,' Dorothea said. 'All the rest of us stayed, but not you.'

'I hate funerals.'

'I hate you.'

Christl turned toward Malone, the towel pressed to her nose. He grabbed her gaze and quickly saw the threat in her eyes. Before he could react, she dropped the towel, whirled, and smacked Dorothea in the face, sending her sister careering back into Werner.

Christl cocked her fist, readying another blow.

Malone caught her wrist. 'You owed her one. That's all.'

Her whole countenance had darkened and a fiery gaze told him that this was none of his business.

She wrenched her arm free and snatched the towel from the floor.

Werner helped Dorothea down. Henn just watched, like always, never saying a word.

'Okay, enough prizefighting,' Malone said. 'I suggest all of you get some sleep. We have less than five hours to go and I plan to hit the ground running when we land. Anybody who bitches or can't keep up stays at the base.'

Smith sat in his kitchen and stared at the phone lying on the table. He'd doubted the caller's identity so she'd given him a contact number, then hung up. He grabbed the unit and punched in the number. Three rings and a pleasant voice informed him that he'd dialed the White House and wanted to know how to direct his call.

'Office of the National Security Adviser,' he said in a weak voice.

She connected him.

'Took you long enough, Charlie,' a woman said. The same voice. 'Satisfied?'

'What do you want?'

'To tell you something.'

'I'm listening.'

'Ramsey intends to terminate his relationship with you. He has big plans, major plans, and they don't include you being around to possibly interfere with them.'

'You're barking up the wrong tree.'

'That's what I'd say, too, Charlie. But I'll make it easy for you. You listen and I'll talk. That way if you think you're being recorded it won't matter. Sound like a plan?'

'If you got the time, go ahead.'

'You're Ramsey's personal problem solver. He's used you for years. Pays you well. In the last few days you've been a busy guy. Jacksonville. Charlotte. Asheville. Am I getting warm, Charlie? Do you want me to name names?'

'You can say whatever you want.'

'Now Ramsey has given you a new assignment.' She paused. 'Me. And let me guess. Has to be done today. That makes sense since I shook him down yesterday. He tell you about that, Charlie?'

He did not reply.

'No, I didn't think so. See, he's making plans and they don't include you. But I don't plan to end up like the others. That's why we're talking. Oh, and by the way, if I was your enemy the Secret Service would be at your door right now and we'd have this talk in a private place, just you and me and somebody big and strong.'

'That thought had already occurred to me.'

'I knew you'd be reasonable. And just so you understand that I really do know what I'm talking about, let me tell you about three offshore accounts you have, the ones Ramsey makes his deposits into.' She rattled off the banks and account numbers, even passwords, two of which he'd changed only a week ago. 'None of those accounts is really private, Charlie. You just have to know where and how to look. Unfortunately for you, I can seize those accounts in an instant. But to show you my good faith, I haven't touched them.'

Okay. She was the real deal. 'What do you want?'

'Like I said, Ramsey has decided that you have to go. He's made a deal with a senator, one that doesn't include you. Since you're practically dead anyway, what with no identity, few roots, no family, how hard would it be for you to permanently disappear? Nobody would ever miss you. That's sad, Charlie.'

But true.

'So I have a better idea,' she said.

Ramsey was so close to his goal. Everything had gone as planned. Only one obstacle remained. Diane McCoy.

He still sat at his desk, a swig of chilled whiskey resting nearby. He thought about what he'd told Isabel Oberhauser. About the submarine. What he'd retrieved from NR-1A and kept ever since.

Commander Forrest Malone's log.

Through the years he'd occasionally glanced at the handwritten pages, more out of morbid curiosity than genuine interest. But the log represented a memento from a journey that had profoundly changed his life. He wasn't sentimental, but there were times that deserved remembering. For him, one of those moments came under the Antarctic ice.

When he followed the seal.

Upward.

He broke the surface and swung his light out of the water. He was in a cavern formed of rock and ice. Maybe a football field long and half that wide, faintly illuminated in a gray-and-purple silence. To his right he heard the bark of a seal and saw the animal leap back into the water. He pushed his face mask to his forehead, spit the regulator from his mouth, and tasted the air. Then he saw it. A bright orange conning tower, stunted, smaller than normal, distinctive in shape.

NR-1A.

Holy Mother of God.

He treaded water toward the surfaced boat.

He'd served aboard NR-1, one of the reasons why he'd been chosen for this mission, so he was familiar with the sub's revolutionary design. Long and thin, the sail forward, near the front of a cigar-shaped hull. A flat fiberglass superstructure mounted atop the hull allowed the crew to walk the length of the boat. Few openings existed in the hull, so that it could dive deep with minimal risk.

He floated close and caressed the black metal. Not a sound. No movement. Nothing. Only water slapping the hull.

He was near the bow, so he drifted down the port side. A rope ladder rested against the hull – used, he knew, for ingress and egress to inflatable rafts. He wondered about its deployment.

He grabbed hold and tugged.

Firm.

He slipped off his fins and slid the straps across his left wrist. He clipped the light to his belt, gripped the ladder, and hauled himself from the water. On top, he collapsed to the decking and rested, then slipped off his weight belt and air tank. He swiped cold water from his face, braced himself, regripped his light, then used the sail fins like a ladder and hoisted himself to the top of the conning tower.

The main hatch hung open.

He shuddered. From the cold? Or from the thought of what waited below?

He climbed down.

At the ladder's bottom he saw that the flooring plates had been removed. He shone his light across where he knew the boat's batteries were stored. Everything appeared charred – which might explain what had happened. A fire would have been catastrophic. He wondered about the boat's reactor but, with everything pitch dark, apparently it had been shut down.

He moved through the forward compartment to the conn. The chairs were empty, the instruments dark. He tested a few circuits. No power. He inspected the engine room. Nothing. The reactor compartment loomed silent. He found the captain's corner – not a cabin, NR-1A was too small for such luxuries, just a bunk and a desk attached to the bulkhead. He spotted the captain's journal, which he opened, thumbing through, finding the last entry.

Ramsey remembered that entry exactly. *Ice on his fingers, ice in his head, ice in his glassy stare.* Oh, how right Forrest Malone had been.

Ramsey had handled that search with perfection. Anyone who could now be a problem was dead. Admiral Dyals' legacy was secure, as was his own. The navy was likewise safe. The ghosts of NR-1A would stay where they belonged.

In Antarctica.

His cell phone came alive with light, but no sound. He'd silenced it hours ago. He looked. Finally.

'Yes, Charlie, what is it?'

'I need to see you.'

'Not possible.'

'Make it possible. In two hours.'

'Why?'

'A problem.'

He realized they were on an open phone line and words needed to be chosen with care.

'Bad?'

'Enough I need to see you.'

He checked his watch. 'Where?'

'You know. Be there.'

81

Fort Lee, Virginia, 9:30 p.m.

Computers were not Stephanie's strong point, but Malone had explained in his e-mail the translation procedure. Colonel Gross had provided her with a high-speed portable scanner and an Internet connection. She'd downloaded the translation program and experimented with one page, scanning the image into the computer.

Once she applied the translation program, the result had been extraordinary. The odd assortment of twists, turns, and curlicues first became Latin, then English. Rough in places. Parts missing here and there. But enough for her to know that the refrigerated compartment contained a treasure trove of ancient information.

Inside a glass jar suspend two piths by a thin thread. Rub a shiny metal rod briskly on clothing. There will be no sensation, no tingle, no pain. Bring the rod close to the jar and the two spheres will fly apart and stay apart even after the rod is withdrawn. The force from the rod flows outward, unseen and unfelt but there nonetheless, driving the piths apart. After a time the piths will sink, driven so by the same force that keeps everything that is tossed into the air from remaining there.

. . .

Construct a wheel, with a handle at its rear, and attach small metal plates to its edge. Two metal rods should be fixed so that a spray of wires from each lightly touches the metal plates. From the rods a wire leads to two metal spheres. Position them one-half commons apart. Twirl the wheel by the handle. Where the metal plates contact the wires, flashing will occur. Spin the wheel faster and blue lightning will leap and hiss from the metal spheres. A strange smell will occur, one that has been noticed after a fierce storm in lands where rain falls in abundance. Savor it and the lightning, for that force and the force that drives the piths apart is the same, only generated in differing ways. Touching the metal spheres is as harmless as touching the metal rods rubbed to the clothing.

. . .

Moonstone, crownchaka, five milks from the banyan, fig, magnet, mercury, mica pearl, saarasvata oil, and nakha taken in equal parts, purified, should be ground and allowed to rest until congealed. Only then mix bilva oil and boil until a perfect gum forms. Spread the varnish evenly on a surface and allow it to dry before exposing it to light. For dulling, to the mixture add pallatory root, maatang, cawries, earthen salt, black lead, and granite sand. Apply in abundance onto any surface for strength.

. . .

The peetha is to be three commons wide and one-half high, square or round. A pivot is fixed to the center. In front is placed a vessel of acid dellium. To the west is the mirror for enhancing darkness and in the east is fixed the solar ray attraction tube. In the center is the wire operating wheel and to the south is the main operating switch. On turning the wheel toward the southeast the two-faced mirror fixed to the tube will collect solar rays. By operating the wheel in the northwest the acid will activate. By turning the wheel west, the darkness-intensifying mirror will function. By turning the central wheel, the rays attracted by the mirror will reach the crystal and envelop it. Then the main wheel should be revolved with great speed to produce an enveloping heat.

. . .

Sand, crystal, and suvarchala salt, in equal parts, filled in a crucible, placed in a furnace then cast will yield a pure, light, strong, cool ceramic. Pipes fashioned of this material will transport and radiate heat and can be bound strongly together with salt mortar. Color pigments made from iron, clay, quartz, and calcite are both rich and lasting and adhere well after casting.

Stephanie stared at Edwin Davis. 'On the one hand they were playing around with electricity in infant stages while, on the other hand, they were creating compounds and mechanisms we've never heard of. We have to find out where these books came from.'

'Going to be difficult since, apparently, every record from Highjump that could tell us is gone.' Davis shook his head. 'What damn fools. Everything top secret. A few narrow minds made monumental decisions that affected us all. Here is a repository of knowledge that could well change the world. It could also be garbage, of course. But we'll never know. You realize in the decades since these books were found, foot after foot of new snow has accumulated down there. The landscape is totally different from what it was then.'

She knew Antarctica was a mapmaker's nightmare. Its coastline constantly changed as ice shelves appeared and disappeared, shifting at will. Davis was right. Finding Byrd's locations could prove impossible.

'We've only looked at a handful of pages in a few scattered volumes,' she said. 'There's no telling what's in all these.'

Another page caught her eye, filled with text and a sketch of two plants, roots and all.

She scanned that folio into the computer and translated.

Gyra grows in dim damp recesses and should be freed from the ground prior to the summer sun leaving. Its leaves, crushed and burned, abate fever. But take care that the Gyra stays free of moisture. Wet leaves are ineffective and can cause illness. Yellowed leaves the same. Bright red or orange is preferable. They also bring sleep and can be used to quell dreams. Too much can cause harm, so administer with care.

She imagined what an explorer must have felt when standing on a virgin shore, staring at a new land.

'This warehouse is going to be sealed,' Davis declared.

'That's not a good idea. It'll alert Ramsey.'

Davis seemed to see the wisdom of her observation. 'We'll work it through Gross. If anybody moves on this cache, he'll let us know and we can stop it.'

That was a better idea.

She thought about Malone. He should be nearing Antarctica. Was he on the right trail?

But there was still unfinished business here.

Finding the killer.

She heard a door across the cavernous interior open, then close. Colonel Gross had maintained a vigil in the anteroom to afford them privacy, so she assumed it must be him. But then she heard two sets of footsteps echoing through the dark. They sat at a table just outside the refrigerated compartment with only two lamps burning. She glanced up and saw Gross materialize from the dimness followed by another man – tall, bushy-haired, wearing a navy-blue windbreaker and casual pants, the emblem of the president of the United States over his left breast.

Danny Daniels.

82

Maryland, 10:20 p.m.

Ramsey left the dark highway and drove into the woods, toward the Maryland farmhouse where he'd met Charlie Smith a few days ago.

Bailey Mill, Smith had called it.

He hadn't liked Smith's tone. Smart-ass, cocky, irritating – that was Charlie Smith. Angry, demanding, belligerent? No way.

Something was wrong.

Ramsey seemed to have acquired a new ally in Diane McCoy, one that had cost him twenty million dollars. Luckily, he'd stashed much more than that in various accounts across the globe. Money that had fallen his way from operations that either ended prematurely or were aborted. Thankfully, once a CLASSIFIED stamp was placed on a file, little in the way of a public accounting ever occurred. Policy required that whatever resources had been invested be returned, but that wasn't always the case. He needed funds to pay Smith – capital to finance covert investigations – but his need was becoming more finite. Yet as that need tightened, so did the risks.

Like here.

His headlights revealed the farmhouse, a barn, and another car. Not a light on anywhere. He parked and reached into the center console, removed his Walther automatic, then stepped out into the cold.

'Charlie,' he called out. 'I don't have time for your crap. Get your ass out here.'

His eyes, attuned to the darkness, registered movement to his left. He aimed and ticked off two shots. The bullets thudded into the old wood. More movement, but he saw that it wasn't Smith.

Dogs.

Fleeing the porch and the house, racing off toward the woods. Like last time.

He exhaled.

Smith loved to play games, so he decided to accommodate him. 'Tell you what, Charlie. I'm going to flatten all four of your tires and you can freeze your ass off here tonight. Call me tomorrow when you're ready to talk.'

'You're not a bit of fun, Admiral,' a voice said. 'Not a bit at all.'

Smith emerged from the shadows.

'You're lucky I don't kill you,' he said.

Smith stepped from the porch. 'Why would you do that? I've been a good boy. Did everything you wanted. All four dead, nice and clean. Then I hear on the radio that you're going to be promoted to the Joint Chiefs. Just movin' on up, to the east side. To that deluxe apartment in the sky. You and George Jefferson.'

'That's unimportant,' he made clear. 'Not your concern.'

'I know. I'm just hired help. What's important is that I get paid.'

'You did. Two hours ago. In full.'

'That's good. I was thinking of a little vacation. Someplace warm.'

'Not until you deal with your new task.'

'You aim high, Admiral. Your latest goes straight into the White House.'

'Aiming high is the only way to achieve anything.'

'I need double the usual price for this one, half down, balance on completion.'

Didn't matter to him how much it cost. 'Done.'

'And there's one more thing,' Smith said.

Something poked into his ribs, through his coat, from behind.

'Nice and easy, Langford,' a woman's voice said. 'Or I'll shoot you before you move.'

Diane McCoy.

Malone checked the plane's chronometer – 7:40 a.m. – and gazed out the flight deck at the panorama below. Antarctica reminded him of an upturned bowl with a chipped rim. A vast ice plateau almost two miles thick was bordered for at least two-thirds of its circumference by black jagged mountains lined with crevasse-ridden glaciers that flowed toward the sea – the northeast coast below no exception.

The pilot announced that they were making a final approach to Halvorsen Base. Time to prepare for landing.

'This is rare,' the pilot said to Malone. 'Superb weather. You're lucky. Winds are good, too.' He adjusted the controls and gripped the yoke. 'You want to take us down?'

Malone waved him off. 'No thanks. Way beyond me.' Though he'd landed fighter jets on tossing carriers, dropping a one-hundred-thousand-pound aircraft onto perilous ice was a thrill he could do without.

The brawl between Dorothea and Christl still concerned him. They'd behaved themselves the past few hours, but their bitter conflict could prove vexing.

The plane began a steep decline.

Though the attack had raised warning flags, something else he'd witnessed caused him even more concern.

Ulrich Henn had been caught off guard.

Malone had spotted the momentary confusion that swept Henn's face before the mask rehardened. He clearly hadn't expected what Dorothea had done.

The plane leveled and the engine's turbines slackened.

The Hercules was equipped with landing skis and he heard the copilot confirm that they were locked. They continued to drop, the white ground growing in size and detail.

A bump. Then another.

And he heard the scrape of skis on crusty ice as they glided. No way to brake. Only friction would slow them. Luckily there was plenty of room to slide.

Finally the Hercules stopped.

'Welcome to the bottom of the world,' the pilot told everyone.

Stephanie stood from her chair. Force of habit.

Davis did, too.

Daniels motioned for them to stay put. 'It's late and we're all tired. Sit.' He grabbed a chair. 'Thank you, Colonel. Would you make sure we're not disturbed?'

Gross disappeared toward the front of the warehouse.

'You two look like hell,' Daniels said.

'Comes from watching a man's head get blown off,' Davis said.

Daniels sighed. 'I've seen that myself, once or twice. Two tours in Vietnam. Never leaves you.'

'A man died because of us,' Davis said.

Daniels' lips tightened. 'But Herbert Rowland is alive because of you.'

Little consolation, Stephanie thought, then asked, 'How are you here?'

'Slipped out of the White House and rode *Marine One* straight south. Bush started that. He'd fly all the way to Iraq before anyone knew. We have *procedures* in place to accommodate that now. I'll be back in bed before anyone knows I'm gone.' Daniels' gaze drifted toward the refrigerator door. 'I wanted to see what was in there. Colonel Gross told me, but I wanted to see.'

'It could change how we view civilization,' she said.

'It's amazing.' And she could see that Daniels was genuinely impressed. 'Was Malone right? Can we read the books?'

She nodded. 'Enough to make sense.'

The president's usual boisterous bearing seemed in check. She'd heard he was a notorious night owl, sleeping little. Staffers constantly complained.

'We lost the killer,' Davis said.

She caught the defeat in his tone. So different from the first time they'd worked together, when he'd tossed out an infectious optimism that had driven her into central Asia.

'Edwin,' the president said, 'you've given this your best shot. I thought you were nuts, but you were right.'

Davis' eyes were those of someone who'd given up expecting good news. 'Scofield's still dead. Millicent is still dead.'

'The question is, do you want their killer?'

'Like I said, we lost him.'

'See, that's the thing,' Daniels said. 'I found him.'

83

Maryland

Ramsey sat in a rickety wooden chair, his hands, chest, and feet bound with duct tape. He'd contemplated attacking McCoy outside but realized that Smith was surely armed – and he could not elude them both. So he'd done nothing. Bided his time. And hoped for a fumble.

Which may not have been smart.

They'd herded him into the house. Smith had lit a small camping stove that now provided weak illumination and welcome heat. Interesting how one section of the bedroom wall was swung open, the rectangle beyond pitch-black. He needed to know what these two wanted, how they'd joined forces, and how to appease them.

'This woman tells me that I've been added to the expendable list,' Smith said.

'You shouldn't listen to people you don't know.'

McCoy stood, propped against an open windowsill, holding a gun. 'Who says we don't know each other?'

'This isn't hard to decipher,' he said to her. 'You're playing both ends against the middle. Did she tell you, Charlie, that she shook me down for twenty million?'

'She did mention something about that.'

Another problem.

He faced McCoy. 'I'm impressed you identified Charlie and made contact.'

'Wasn't all that hard. You think no one pays attention? You know cell phones can be monitored, bank transfers traced, confidential agreements between governments used to access accounts and records that no one else could get to.'

'I never realized I interested you so.'

'You wanted my help. I'm helping.'

He yanked on his restraints. 'Not what I had in mind.'

'I offered Charlie half the twenty million.'

'Payable in advance,' Smith added.

Ramsey shook his head. 'You're an ungrateful fool.'

Smith lunged forward and raked the back of his hand across Ramsey's face. 'I've wanted to do that for a long time.'

'Charlie, I swear to you, this you're going to regret.'

'Fifteen years I've done what you asked,' Smith said. 'You wanted people dead. I made them dead. I know you've been planning something. I could always tell. Now you're moving to the Pentagon. Joint Chiefs of Staff. What's next? No way you'll be satisfied and retire out. That's not you. So I've become a problem.'

'Who said that?'

Smith pointed at McCoy.

'And you believe her?'

'She makes sense. And she did have twenty million dollars, because I now have half of it.'

'And we both have you,' McCoy said.

'Neither one of you has the guts to murder an admiral, the head of naval intelligence, nominee for the Joint Chiefs. Going to be tough to cover that one up.'

'Really?' Smith said. 'How many people have I killed

for you? Fifty? A hundred? Two hundred? I can't even remember. Not a one of which has ever been tagged murder. I'd say cover-up is my specialty.'

Unfortunately the cocky little weasel was right, so he decided to try diplomacy. 'What can I do to assure you, Charlie? We've been together a long time. I'm going to need you in the years ahead.'

Smith did not answer.

'How many women did he kill?' McCoy asked him.

Ramsey wondered about that question. 'Does it matter?'

'Does to me.'

Then he realized. Edwin Davis. Her co-worker. 'This about Millicent?'

'Did Mr. Smith here kill her?'

He decided to be honest and nodded.

'She was pregnant?'

'That's what I was told. But who knows? Women lie.'

'So you just killed her?'

'Seemed the simplest way to end the problem. Charlie here was working for us in Europe. That's when we first met. He handled the job well, and he's been mine ever since.'

'I'm not yours,' Smith said, contempt in his voice. 'I work for you. You pay me.'

'And there's lots more money to be made,' the admiral made clear.

Smith stepped toward the open panel in the wall. 'Leads down to a concealed cellar. Probably came in handy during the Civil War. Good place to hide things.'

He caught the message. *Like a body.*

'Charlie, killing me would be a really bad idea.'

Smith turned and aimed his gun. 'Maybe so. But it sure as hell will make me feel better.'

★   ★   ★

Malone left the bright sunshine and entered Halvorsen Base, followed by the others. Their host, waiting for them on the ice when they'd deplaned into a blast of frigid air, was a swarthy, bearded Australian – stocky, robust, and seemingly competent – named Taperell.

The base comprised an assembly of high-tech buildings buried beneath thick snow, powered by a sophisticated solar and wind array. State-of-the-art, Taperell said, then added, 'You're fortunate today. Only minus thirteen degrees Celsius. Bloody warm for this part of the world.'

The Aussie led them into a spacious wood-paneled room, filled with tables and chairs, that smelled of cooking food. A digital thermometer on the far wall read nineteen degrees Celsius.

'Hamburgers, chips, and drinks will be here in a tick,' Taperell said. 'I thought you'd need some tucker.'

'I assume that means food,' Malone said.

Taperell smiled. 'What else, mate?'

'Can we get going as soon as we eat?'

Their host nodded. 'No worries, that's what I was told. I have a chopper ready. Where you headin'?'

Malone faced Henn. 'Your turn.'

Christl stepped forward. 'Actually, I have what you need.'

Stephanie watched as Davis stood from his chair and asked the president, 'What do you mean, you found him?'

'I offered the vacancy on the Joint Chiefs to Ramsey today. I called him and he said yes.'

'I assume there's a good reason you did that,' Davis said.

'You know, Edwin, we seem to stay twisted around. It's

like you're the president and I'm the deputy national security adviser – and I say that with a special emphasis on the word *deputy*.'

'I know who's the boss. You know who's the boss. Just tell us why you're here in the middle of the night.'

She saw that Daniels didn't mind the brash insolence.

'When I went to Britain a few years ago,' the president said, 'I was asked to join a foxhunt. Brits love that crap. Get all dressed up, early in the morning, mount a smelly horse, then take off following a bunch of howlin' dogs. They told me how great it was. Except, of course, if you're the fox. Then, it's a bitch. Being the compassionate soul that I am, I kept thinking about the fox, so I passed.'

'Are we going hunting?' she asked.

She saw a twinkle in the president's eye. 'Oh, yes. But the great thing about this trek is, the foxes don't know we're coming.'

Malone watched as Christl unfolded a map and spread it out on one of the tables. 'Mother explained it to me.'

'And what made you so special?' Dorothea asked.

'I assumed she thought I'd keep a level head, though apparently she believes me to be a vengeful dreamer out to ruin our family.'

'Are you?' Dorothea asked.

Christl's gaze bore into Dorothea. 'I'm an Oberhauser. The last of a long line, and I plan to honor my ancestors.'

'How about we focus on the problem at hand,' Malone said. 'The weather is great out there. We need to take advantage of that while we can.'

Christl had brought the newer map of Antarctica that Isabel had tempted him with in Ossau, the one she'd failed to unfold. Now he saw that all of the various continental bases were denoted, most along the coast, including Halvorsen.

'Grandfather visited here and here,' Christl said, pointing to spots marked 1 and 2. His notes say that most of the stones he brought back come from Site 1, though he spent a great deal of time at Site 2. The expedition brought a cabin, disassembled, to erect somewhere to firmly stake Germany's claim. They chose to build the cabin on Site 2, here, near the coast.'

Malone had asked Taperell to stay. He now faced the Aussie and said, 'Where is that?'

'I know it. About fifty miles west of here.'

'It's still there?' Werner asked.

'Deadset,' Taperell said. 'She'll be right – wood doesn't rot here. That thing would be like the day they erected it. And especially there – the entire region is designated a protected area. A site of "special scientific interest" under the Antarctic Conservation Act. You can only visit with an okay from Norway.'

'Why is that?' Dorothea asked.

'The coast belongs to seals. It's a breeding area. No people allowed. The cabin sits in one of the inland dry valleys.'

'Mother says that Father told her he was taking the Americans to Site 2,' Christl said. 'Grandfather always wanted to return and explore more, but was never allowed.'

'How do we *know* that's the spot?' Malone asked.

He caught mischief in Christl's eye. She reached back into her pack and retrieved a thin, colorful book titled in German. He silently translated. *A Visit to Neuschwabenland, Fifty Years Later.*

'This is a picture volume published in 1988. A German magazine sent a film crew and a photographer. Mother came across it about five years ago.' She thumbed through, searching for a particular page. 'This is the cabin.' She showed them a striking, two-page color image of a gray wooden structure set within a black rock valley, streaked with bright snow, dwarfed by bare gray mountains. She turned the page. 'This is a shot of the inside.'

Malone studied the picture. Not much there. A table with magazines scattered on top, a few chairs, two bunks, packing crates adapted into shelving, a stove, and a radio.

Her amused eyes met his. 'See anything?'

She was doing to him what he'd done to her in Ossau. So he accepted her challenge and carefully scanned the picture, as did the others.

Then he saw it. On the flooring. Carved into one of the planks.

He pointed. 'The same symbol from the book cover found in Charlemagne's tomb.'

She smiled. 'This has to be the place. And there's this.' She slid a folded sheet of paper from the book. A page from an old magazine, yellowed and brittle with a grainy black-and-white image from inside the cabin.

'That came from the Ahnenerbe records I obtained,' Dorothea said. 'I remember. I looked at it in Munich.'

'Mother retrieved them,' Christl said, 'and noticed this photograph. Look on the floor – the symbol is clearly visible. This was published in the spring of 1939, an article

Grandfather wrote about the previous year's expedition.'

'I told her those records were worthwhile,' Dorothea said.

Malone faced Taperell. 'Seems that's where we're going.'

Taperell pointed to the map. 'This area here, on the coast, is all ice shelf with seawater beneath. It extends inland about five miles in what would be a respectable bay, if not frozen. The cabin is on the other side of a ridge, maybe a mile inland on what would be the bay's west shore. We can drop you there and pick you back up when you're ready. Like I said, reckon you're in luck with the weather, it's a scorcher out there today.'

Minus thirteen degrees Celsius wasn't his idea of tropical, but he got the point. 'We'll need emergency gear, just in case.'

'Already have two sleds prepared. We were expecting you.'

'You don't ask a lot of questions, do you?' Malone quizzed.

Taperell shook his head. 'No, mate. I'm just here to do my job.'

'Then let's eat that tucker and get going.'

84

Fort Lee

'Mr. President,' Davis said. 'Would it be possible for you to simply explain yourself. No stories, no riddles. It's awfully late, and I don't have the energy to be patient and respectful.'

'Edwin, I like you. Most of the assholes I deal with tell me either what they think I want to hear or what I don't need to know. You're different. You tell me what I have to hear. No sugarcoating, just straight up. That's why when you told me about Ramsey, I listened. Anybody else, I would have let it go in one ear and out the other. But not you. Yes, I was skeptical, but you were right.'

'What have you done?' Davis asked.

She'd sensed something, too, in the president's tone.

'I simply gave him what he wanted. The appointment. Nothing rocks a man to sleep better than success. I should know – it's been used on me many times.' Daniels' gaze drifted to the refrigerated compartment. 'It's what's in there that fascinates me. A record of a people we've never known. They lived a long time ago. Did things. Thought things. Yet we had no idea they existed.'

Daniels reached into his pocket and removed a piece of paper. 'Look at this.'

'It's a petroglyph from the Hathor Temple at Dendera. I saw it a few years ago. The thing's huge, with towering columns. It's fairly recent, as far as Egypt goes, first century before Christ. Those attendants are holding what looks like some kind of lamp, supported on pillars, so they must be heavy, connected to a box on the ground by a cable. Look at the top of the columns, beneath the two bulbs. Looks like a condenser, doesn't it?'

'I had no idea you were so interested in things like this,' she said.

'I know. Us poor, dumb country boys can't appreciate anything.'

'I didn't mean it that way. It's just that—'

'Don't sweat it, Stephanie. I keep this to myself. But I love it. All those tombs found in Egypt, and inside the pyramids – not a single chamber has smoke damage. How in the crap did they get light down into those places to work? Fire was all they had, and lamps burned smoky oil.' He pointed at the drawing. 'Maybe they had something else. There's an inscription found at the Hathor Temple that says it all. I wrote it down.' He turned the drawing over. '*The temple was built according to a plan written in ancient writing upon a goatskin scroll from the time of the Companions of Horus.* Can you imagine? They're saying right there that they had help from a long time ago.'

'You can't really believe Egyptians had electric lights,' Davis said.

'I don't know what to believe. And who said they were electric? They could have been chemical. The military has tritium gas-phosphor lamps that shine for years without electricity. I don't know what to believe. All I know is that petroglyph is real.'

Yes, it was.

'Look at it this way,' the president said. 'There was a time when the so-called experts thought all of the continents were fixed. No question, the land has always been where it is now, end of story. Then people started noticing how Africa and South America seem to fit together. North America, Greenland. Europe, too. Coincidence, that's what the experts said. Nothing more. Then they found fossils in England and North America that were identical. Same kind of rocks, too. Coincidence became stretched. Then plates were located beneath the oceans that move, and the so-called experts realized that the land could shift on those plates. Finally, in the 1960s, the experts were proven wrong. The continents were all once joined together and eventually drifted apart. What was once fantasy is now science.'

She recalled last April and their conversation at The Hague. 'I thought you told me that you didn't know beans about science.'

'I don't. But that doesn't mean I don't read and pay attention.'

She smiled. 'You're quite a contradiction.'

'I'll take that as a compliment.' Daniels pointed at the table. 'Does the translation program work?'

'Seems to. And you're right. This is a record of a lost civilization. One that's been around a long time and apparently interacted with people all over the globe, including, according to Malone, Europeans in the ninth century.'

Daniels stood from his chair. 'We think ourselves so smart. So sophisticated. We're the first at everything. Bullshit. There's a crapload out there we don't know.'

'From what we've translated so far,' she said, 'there's apparently some technical knowledge here. Strange things. It's going to take time to understand. And some fieldwork.'

'Malone may regret that he went down there,' Daniels muttered.

She needed to know, 'Why?'

The president's dark eyes studied her. 'NR-1A used uranium for fuel, but there were several thousand gallons of oil on board for lubrication. Not a drop was ever found.' Daniels went silent. 'Subs leak when they sink. Then there's the logbook, like you learned from Rowland. Dry. Not a smudge. That means the sub was intact when Ramsey found it. And from what Rowland said, they were on the continent when Ramsey went into the water. Near the coast. Malone's following Dietz Oberhauser's trail, just like NR-1A did. What if the paths intersect?'

'That sub can't still exist,' she said.

'Why not? It's the Antarctic.' Daniels paused. 'I was told half an hour ago that Malone and his entourage are now at Halvorsen Base.'

She saw that Daniels genuinely cared about what was happening, both here and to the south.

'Okay, here it is,' Daniels said. 'From what I've learned,

Ramsey employed a hired killer who goes by the name Charles C. Smith Jr.'

Davis sat still in his chair.

'I had CIA check Ramsey thoroughly and they identified this Smith character. Don't ask me how, but they did it. He apparently uses a lot of names and Ramsey has doled out a ton of money to him. He's probably the one who killed Sylvian, Alexander, and Scofield, and he thinks he killed Herbert Rowland—'

'And Millicent,' Davis said.

Daniels nodded.

'You found Smith?' she asked, recalling what Daniels had originally said.

'In a manner of speaking.' The president hesitated. 'I came to see all this. I truly wanted to know. But I also came to tell you exactly how I think we can end this circus.'

Malone stared out the helicopter's window, the churn of the rotors pulsating in his ears. They were flying west. Brilliant sunshine streamed in through the tinted goggles that shielded his eyes. They girdled the shore, seals lounging on the ice like giant slugs, killer whales breaking the water, patrolling the ice edges for unwary prey. Rising from the coast, mountains poked upward like tombstones over an endless white cemetery, their darkness in stark contrast with the bright snow.

The aircraft veered south.

'We're entering the restricted area,' Taperell said through the flight helmets.

The Aussie sat in the chopper's forward right seat while a Norwegian piloted. Everyone else was huddled in an unheated rear compartment. They'd been delayed three hours by mechanical problems with the Huey. No one had stayed behind. They all seemed eager to know what was out there. Even Dorothea and Christl had calmed, though they sat as far away from each other as possible. Christl now wore a different-colored parka, her bloodied one from the plane replaced at the base.

They found the frozen horseshoe-shaped bay from the map, a fence of icebergs guarding its entrance. Blinding light reflected off the bergs' blue ice.

The chopper crossed a mountain ridge with peaks too sheer for snow to cling to. Visibility was excellent and winds were weak, only a few wispy cirrus clouds loafing around in a bright blue sky.

Ahead he spotted something different.

Little surface snow. Instead, the ground and rock walls were colored with irregular lashings of black dolerite, gray granite, brown shale, and white limestone. Granite boulders littered the landscape in all shapes and sizes.

'A dry valley,' Taperell said. 'No rain for two million years. Back then mountains rose faster than glaciers could cut their way through, so the ice was trapped on the other side. Winds sweep down off the plateau from the south and keep the ground nearly ice- and snow-free. Lots of these in the southern portion of the continent. Not as many up this way.'

'Has this one been explored?' Malone asked.

'We have fossil hunters who visit. The place is a treasure trove of them. Meteorites, too. But the visits are limited by the treaty.'

The cabin appeared, a strange apparition lying at the base of a forbidding, trackless peak.

The chopper swept over the pristine rocky terrain, then wheeled back over a landing site and descended onto gravelly sand.

Everyone clambered out, Malone last, the sleds with equipment handed to him. Taperell gave him a wink as he passed Malone his pack, signaling that he'd done as requested. Noisy rotors and blasts of freezing air assaulted him.

Two radios were included in the bundles. Malone had already arranged for a check-in six hours from now. Taperell had told them that the cabin would offer shelter, if need be. But the weather looked good for the next ten to twelve hours. Daylight wasn't a problem since the sun wouldn't set again until March.

Malone gave a thumbs-up and the chopper lifted away. The rhythmic thwack of rotor blades receded as it disappeared over the ridgeline.

Silence engulfed them.

Each of his breaths cracked and pinged, the air as dry as a Sahara wind. But no sense of peace mixed with the tranquility.

The cabin stood fifty yards away.

'What do we do now?' Dorothea asked.

He started off. 'I say we begin with the obvious.'

85

Malone approached the cabin. Taperell had been right. Seventy years old, yet its white-brown walls looked as if they'd just been delivered from the sawmill. Not a speck of rust on a single nailhead. A coil of rope hanging near the door looked new. Shutters shielded two windows. He estimated the building was maybe twenty feet square with overhanging eaves and a pitched tin roof pierced by a pipe stack chimney. A gutted seal lay against one wall, gray-black, its glassy eyes and whiskers still there, lying as if merely sleeping rather than frozen.

The door possessed no latch so he pushed it inward and raised his tinted goggles. Sides of the seal meat and sledges hung from iron-braced ceiling rafters. The same shelves from the pictures, fashioned from crates, stacked against one brown-stained wall with the same bottled and canned food, the labels still legible. Two bunks with fur sleeping bags, table, chairs, iron stove, and radio were all there. Even the magazines from the photo remained. It seemed as if the occupants had left yesterday and could return at any moment.

'This is disturbing,' Christl said.

He agreed.

Since no dust mites or insects existed to break down any organic debris, he realized the Germans' sweat still lay frozen on the floor, along with flakes of their skin and bodily excrescences – and that Nazi presence hung heavy in the hut's silent air.

'Grandfather was here,' Dorothea said, approaching the table and the magazines. 'These are Ahnenerbe publications.'

He shook away the uncomfortable feeling, stepped to where the symbol should be carved in the floor, and saw it. The same one from the book cover, along with another crude etching.

'It's our family crest,' Christl said.

'Seems Grandfather staked his personal claim,' Malone noted.

'What do you mean?' Werner asked.

Henn, who stood near the door, seemed to understand and grasped an iron bar by the stove. Not a speck of rust infected its surface.

'I see you know the answer, too,' Malone said.

Henn said nothing. He just forced the flat iron tip beneath the floorboards and pried them upward, revealing a black yawn in the ground and the top of a wooden ladder.

'How did you know?' Christl asked him.

'This cabin sits in an odd spot. Makes no sense, unless it's protecting something. When I saw the photo in the book, I realized what the answer had to be.'

'We'll need flashlights,' Werner said.

'Two are on the sled, outside. I had Taperell pack them, along with extra batteries.'

Smith awoke. He was back in his apartment. 8:20 a.m. He'd managed only three hours' sleep, but what an excellent day already. He was ten million dollars richer, thanks to Diane McCoy, and he'd made a point to Langford Ramsey that he wasn't someone to be taken lightly.

He switched on the television and found a *Charmed* rerun. He loved that show. Something about three sexy witches appealed to him. Naughty *and* nice. Which also seemed best how to describe Diane McCoy. She'd coolly stood by during his confrontation with Ramsey, clearly a dissatisfied woman who wanted more – and apparently knew how to get it.

He watched as Paige orbed from her house. What a trick. To dematerialize from one place, then rematerialize at another. He was somewhat like that. Slipping in, doing his job, then just as deftly slipping away.

His cell phone dinged. He recognized the number.

'And what may I do for you?' he asked Diane McCoy as he answered.

'A little more cleanup.'

'Seems the day for that.'

'The two from Asheville who almost got to Scofield. They work for me and know far too much. I wish we had time for finesse, but we don't. They have to be eliminated.'

'And you have a way?'

'I know exactly how we're going to do it.'

* * *

Dorothea watched as Cotton Malone descended into the opening beneath the cabin. What had her grandfather found? She'd been apprehensive about coming, both for the risks and unwanted personal involvements, but she was glad now that she'd made the trip. Her pack rested a few feet away, the gun inside bringing her renewed comfort. She'd overreacted on the plane. Her sister knew how to play her, keep her off balance, rub the rawest nerve in her body, and she told herself to quit taking the bait.

Werner stood with Henn, near the hut's door. Christl sat at the radio desk.

Malone's light played across the darkness below.

'It's a tunnel,' he called out. 'Stretches toward the mountain.'

'How far?' Christl asked.

'A long-ass way.'

Malone climbed back to the top. 'I need to see something.'

He emerged and walked outside. They followed.

'I wondered about the strips of snow and ice streaking the valley. Bare ground and rock everywhere, then a few rough paths crisscrossing here and there.' He pointed toward the mountain and a seven- to eight-yard-wide path of snow that led from the hut to its base. 'That's the tunnel's path. The air beneath is much cooler than the ground so the snow stays.'

'How do you know that?' Werner asked.

'You'll see.'

Henn was the final one to climb down the ladder. Malone watched as they all stood in amazement. The tunnel stretched ahead in a straight path, maybe twenty feet wide, its sides black volcanic rock, its ceiling a luminous blue, casting the subterranean path in a twilight-like glow.

'This is incredible,' Christl said.

'The ice cap formed a long time ago. But it had help.' He pointed with his flashlight at what appeared to be boulders littering the floor, but they reflected back in a twinkly glow. 'Some kind of quartz. They're everywhere. Look at their shapes. My guess is they once formed the ceiling, eventually fell away, and the ice remained in a natural arch.'

Dorothea bent down and examined one of the chunks. Henn held the other flashlight and offered illumination. She joined a couple of them together: They fit like pieces in a puzzle. 'You're right. They connect.'

'Where does this lead?' Christl said.

'That's what we're about to find out.'

The underground air was colder than outside. He checked his wrist thermometer. Minus twenty degrees Celsius. He converted the measurement. Four below Fahrenheit. Cold, but bearable.

He was right about length – the tunnel was a couple of hundred feet long and littered with the quartz rubble. Before descending they'd lugged their gear into the hut, including the two radios. They'd brought down their backpacks and he toted spare batteries for the flashlights, but the phosphorescent glow filtering down from the ceiling easily showed the way.

The glowing ceiling ended ahead where, he estimated, they'd found the mountain and a towering archway – black and red pillars framing its sides and supporting a tympanum filled with writing similar to the books. He shone his light and noted how the square columns tapered inward toward their base, the polished surfaces shimmering with an ethereal beauty.

'Seems we're at the right place,' Christl said.

Two doors, perhaps twelve feet tall, were barred shut. He stepped close and caressed their exterior. 'Bronze.'

Bands of running spirals decorated the smooth surface. A metal bar spanned their width, held in place by thick clamps. Six heavy hinges opened toward them.

He grasped the bar and lifted it away.

Henn reached for the handle of one of the doors and swung it outward. Malone gripped the other, feeling like Dorothy entering Oz. The door's opposite side was adorned with the same decorative spirals and bronze clamps. The portal was wide enough for all of them to enter simultaneously.

What had appeared topside as a single mountain, draped in snow, was actually three peaks crowded together, the wide cleaves between them mortared with translucent blue ice – old, cold, hard, and free of snow. The inside had once been bricked with more of the quartz blocks, like a towering stained-glass window, the joints thick and jagged. A good portion of the inner wall had fallen, but enough remained for him to see that the construction feat had been impressive. More iridescent showers of blue-tinted rays rained down through three rising joints, like massive light sticks, illuminating the cavernous space in an unearthly way.

Before them lay a city.

Stephanie had spent the night at Edwin Davis' apartment, a modest two-bedroom, two-bath affair in the Watergate towers. Canted walls, intersecting grids, varying ceiling heights, and plenty of curves and circles gave the rooms a cubist composition. The minimalist décor and walls the color of ripe pears created an unusual but not unpleasant feel. Davis told her the place had come furnished and he'd grown accustomed to its simplicity.

They'd returned with Daniels to Washington aboard *Marine One* and managed a few hours' sleep. She'd showered, and Davis had arranged for her to buy a change of clothes in one of the ground-floor boutiques. Pricey, but she'd had no choice. Her clothes had seen a lot of wear. She'd left Atlanta for Charlotte thinking the trip would take one day, at best. Now she was into day three, with no end in sight. Davis, too, had cleaned up, shaved, and dressed in navy corduroy trousers and a pale yellow oxford-cloth shirt. His face was still bruised from the fight but looked better.

'We can get something to eat downstairs,' he said. 'I can't boil water, so I eat there a lot.'

'The president is your friend,' she felt compelled to say, knowing last night was on his mind. 'He's taking a big chance for you.'

He cracked a brittle smile. 'I know. And now it's our turn.'

She'd come to admire this man. He was nothing like she imagined. A bit too bold for his own good, but committed.

The house phone rang and Davis answered.

They'd been waiting.

In the apartment's hushed quiet she could hear the caller's every word.

'Edwin,' Daniels said. 'I have the location.'

'Tell me,' Davis said.

'You sure? Last chance. You might not come back from this one.'

'Just tell me the location.'

She cringed at his impatience, but Daniels was right. They might not come back.

Davis shut his eyes. 'Just let us do this.' He paused. 'Sir.'

'Write this down.'

Davis grabbed a pen and pad from the counter and wrote quickly as Daniels provided the information.

'Careful, Edwin,' Daniels said. 'Lots of unknowns here.'

'And women can't be trusted?'

The president chuckled. 'I'm glad you said it and not me.'

Davis hung up and stared at her, his eyes a kaleidoscope of emotions. 'You need to stay here.'

'Like hell.'

'You don't have to do this.'

His cool assumption made her laugh. 'Since when? You're the one who involved me.'

'I was wrong.'

She stepped close and gently caressed his bruised face. 'You would have killed the wrong man in Asheville if I hadn't been there.'

He grasped her wrist in a light embrace, his hand jittery. 'Daniels is right. This is wholly unpredictable.'

'Hell, Edwin, that's my whole life.'

86

Malone had seen some impressive things. The Templar treasure. The Library of Alexandria. The tomb of Alexander the Great. But none of those compared to what he now saw.

A processional way of irregularly shaped and polished slabs, lined on both sides with close-packed buildings of varying shapes and sizes, stretched ahead. Streets crisscrossed and intersected. The cocoon of rock that encased the settlement reached hundreds of feet into the air, the farthest wall maybe two football fields away. Even more impressive were the vertical rock faces rising like monoliths, polished smooth from ground to ceiling, etched with symbols, letters, and drawings. His flashlight revealed in the wall nearest him a melding of whitish yellow sandstone, greenish red shale, and black dolerite wedges. The effect was like that of marble – of standing inside a building rather than a mountain.

Pillars lined the street at defined intervals, and supported more of the quartz that gently glowed, like night-lights, investing everything with a dim mystery.

'Grandfather was right,' Dorothea said. 'It truly does exist.'

'Yes, he was,' Christl proclaimed, her voice rising. 'Right about everything.'

Malone heard the pride, felt her flush of excitement.

'All of you thought him a dreamer,' Christl continued. 'Mother berated him and Father. But they were visionaries. They were right about it all.'

'This *will* change everything,' Dorothea said.

'Of which you have no right to share,' Christl said. 'I always believed in their theories. It's why I pursued that line of study. You laughed at them. No one will laugh at Hermann Oberhauser anymore.'

'How about we hold off on the accolades,' Malone said, 'and have a look.'

He led the group forward, peering down the side streets as deep as their flashlight beams would allow. A strong foreboding rocked through him, but curiosity nudged him forward. He almost expected people to drift out from the buildings and greet them, but only their footsteps could be heard.

The buildings were a mixture of squares and rectangles with walls of cut stone, laid tight, polished smooth, held together with no mortar. The two flashlights revealed façades ablaze with color. Rust, brown, blue, yellow, white, gold. Low-pitched roofs produced pediments filled with elaborate spiral designs and more writing. Everything seemed tidy, practical, and well organized. The Antarctic freezer had preserved it all, though there was evidence of geological forces at work. Many of the quartz blocks in the towering light crevices had fallen. A few walls had collapsed, and the street contained buckles.

The thoroughfare drained into a circular plaza with more buildings lining its circumference, one a colonnaded temple-like structure with beautifully decorated square columns. In the center of the plaza stood the same unique symbol from the book cover, an enormous shiny red monument surrounded by tiers of stone benches. His eidetic memory instantly recalled what Einhard had written.

> The Advisers stamped their approval to enactments with the symbol of righteousness. Its shape, carved into red stone, centers the city and watches over their annual deliberations. Atop is the sun, half ablaze in glory. Then the earth, as a simple circle, and the planets represented by a dot within the circle. The cross beneath them reminds of the land, while the sea waves below.

Square pillars dotted the plaza, maybe ten feet tall. Each crimson and topped with swirls and ornamentation. He counted eighteen. More writing had been etched onto their façades in tight rows.

Laws are enacted by the Advisers and inscribed upon the Righteous Columns in the center of the city so that all will know the provisions.

'Einhard was here,' Christl said. She'd apparently realized the same thing. 'It's as he described.'

'Since you didn't share what he wrote with us,' Dorothea said. 'It's hard to know.'

He watched as Christl ignored her sister and studied one of the columns.

They were walking on a collage of mosaics. Henn examined the pavement with his light. Animals, people, scenes of daily life – each alive with bright color. A few yards away stood a circular stone ledge, perhaps thirty feet in diameter and four feet tall. He walked toward it and gazed over. A black stone-lined hole opened in the earth.

The others approached.

He found a rock the size of a small melon and tossed it over the side. Ten seconds passed. Twenty. Thirty. Forty. A minute. Still no sound of the bottom.

'That's a deep hole,' he said.

Similar to the predicament he'd dug for himself.

Dorothea drifted away from the pit. Werner followed and whispered, 'You okay?'

She nodded, again uncomfortable with his husbandly concern. 'We need to finish this,' she whispered. 'Move it along.'

He nodded.

Malone was studying one of the square red pillars.

Each breath she took parched her mouth.

Werner said to Malone, 'Would it be faster if we divide into two groups and explore, then meet back here?'

Malone turned. 'Not a bad idea. We have another five hours before we check in, and it's a long way back down that tunnel. We need to make that trek only once.'

No one argued.

'So there's no fight among anyone,' Malone said, 'I'll take Dorothea. You and Christl go with Henn.'

Dorothea glanced at Ulrich. His eyes told her that would be fine.

So she said nothing.

Malone decided that if anything was going to happen, now was the time, so he'd quickly agreed with Werner's suggestion. He was waiting to see who'd make the first move. Keeping the sisters and the married people apart seemed smart, and he noticed that no one objected.

That meant he'd now have to play the hand he'd dealt himself.

87

Malone and Dorothea left the central plaza and ventured deeper into the cluster, the buildings packed tight like dominoes in a box. Some of the structures were shops with one or two rooms, opening directly to the street with no other obvious function. Others were set back, accessed by walkways leading between the shops to front doors. He noticed no cornices, eaves, or guttering. The architecture seemed eager to use right angles, diagonals, and pyramidal forms – curves appeared in restraint. Ceramic pipes, married with thick gray joints, ran house to house, and up and down the exterior walls – each beautifully painted – part of the décor, but also, he surmised, practical.

He and Dorothea investigated one of the dwellings, entering through a sculpted bronze door. A mosaic-paved central courtyard was surrounded by four square rooms, each carved from stone with clear depth and precision. Onyx and topaz columns seemed more for decoration than support. Stairs led to an upper story. No windows. Instead, the ceiling consisted of more quartz, the pieces arched together with mortar. The weak light from outside refracted through and was magnified, making the rooms more resplendent.

'They're all empty,' Dorothea said. 'As if they took everything and left.'

'Which may be exactly what happened.'

Images sheathed the walls. Groups of well-dressed woman seated on either side of a table, surrounded by more people. Beyond, a killer whale – a male, he knew from the tall dorsal fin – swam in a blue sea. Jagged icebergs floated nearby, dotted with colonies of penguins. A boat cruised the surface – long, thin, with two masts and the symbol from the plaza, emblazoned in red, on square sails. Realism seemed a concern. Everything was well proportioned. The wall reflected the flashlight beam, which drew him closer to caress the surface.

More of the ceramic pipes ran floor to ceiling in every room, their exterior painted to blend with the images.

He examined them with unconcealed wonder.

'Has to be some sort of heating system. They had to have a way to keep warm.'

'The source?' she asked.

'Geothermal. These people were smart, but not mechanically sophisticated. My guess is that pit in the central plaza was a geothermal vent that would have heated the whole place. They channeled more heat into these pipes and sent it all over the city.' He rubbed the shiny exterior. 'But once the heat source faded, they would have been in trouble. Life here would have been a daily battle.'

A fissure marred one of the interior walls and he traced it with his light. 'This place has taken some earthquake hits over the centuries. Amazing it's still standing.'

No reply had been offered to either of his observations, so he turned.

Dorothea Lindauer stood across the room, a gun pointed at him.

*   *   *

Stephanie studied the house that Danny Daniels' directions had led them to find. Old, dilapidated, isolated in the Maryland countryside, surrounded by dense woods and meadows. A barn stood to its rear. No other cars were in sight. They'd both come armed, so they stepped from the vehicle, weapons in hand. Neither of them said a word.

They approached the front door, which hung open. Most of the windows were shattered clear. The house was, she estimated, two to three thousand square feet, its glory having faded long ago.

They entered cautiously.

The day was clear and cold and bright sunshine flooded in through the exposed windows. They stood in a foyer, parlors opening to their left and right, another corridor ahead. The house was single-story and rambling, connected by wide hallways. Furniture filled the rooms, draped in filthy cloths, the wall coverings peeling, the wood floors buckling.

She caught a sound, like scraping. Then a soft *tap, tap, tap*. Something moving? Walking?

She heard a snarl and growl.

Her eyes focused down one of the halls. Davis brushed past and led the way. They came to a doorway into one of the bedrooms. Davis dropped behind her but kept his gun aimed. She knew what he wanted her to do, so she eased close to the jamb, peeked inside, and saw two dogs. One tawny and white, the other a pale gray, both busy eating something. They were each a good size and sinewy. One of them sensed her presence and raised its head. Its mouth and nose were bloodstained.

The animal growled.

His partner sensed danger and came alert, too.

Davis moved up behind her.

'Do you see it?' he asked.

She did.

Beneath the dogs, lying on the floor, was their meal.

A human hand, severed at the wrist, three fingers missing.

Malone stared at Dorothea's gun. 'You plan to shoot me?'

'You're in league with her. I saw her go into your room.'

'I don't think a one-night stand qualifies as being in league with someone.'

'She's evil.'

'You're both nuts.'

He stepped toward her. She jutted the weapon forward. He stopped, near a doorway that led out into the adjacent room. She stood ten feet away, before another wall of shiny mosaics.

'You two are going to destroy each other, unless you stop,' he made clear.

'She's not going to win this.'

'Win what?'

'I'm my father's heir.'

'No. You're not. You both are. Trouble is, neither one of you can see that.'

'You heard her. She's vindicated. She was right. She'll be impossible to deal with.'

True, but he'd had enough and now was not the time. 'Do what you have to do, but I'm walking out of here.'

'I'll shoot you.'

'Then do it.'

He turned and started out the doorway.

'I mean it, Malone.'

'You're wasting my time.'

She pulled the trigger.

Click.

He kept walking. She pulled the trigger again. More clicks.

He stopped and faced her. 'I had your bag searched while we ate at the base. I found the gun.' He caught the abashed look on her face. 'I thought it a prudent move, after your tantrum on the plane. I had the bullets taken from the magazine.'

'I was shooting at the floor,' she said. 'I wouldn't have harmed you.'

He extended a hand for the gun.

She walked over and surrendered it. 'I hate Christl with all my being.'

'We've established that, but at the moment it's counterproductive. We found what your family has been searching for – what your father and grandfather worked their whole lives to find. Can't you be excited about that?'

'It's not what I've been searching for.'

He sensed a quandary, but decided not to pry.

'And what about what you've been searching for?' she asked him.

She was right. No sign of NR-1A. 'The jury's still out on that one.'

'This could have been where our fathers were coming.'

Before he could answer her speculation, two pops broke the silence outside, far off.

Then another.

'That's gunfire,' he said.

And they raced from the room.

Stephanie noticed something else. 'Look farther right.'

Part of the interior wall swung open, the rectangle beyond deep with shadows. She studied paw prints in the dirt and dust that led to and from the open panel. 'Apparently they know what's behind that wall.'

The dogs' bodies tensed. Both started barking.

Her attention returned to the animals. 'They need to go.'

Their guns remained aimed, the dogs holding their ground, guarding their meal, so Davis shifted to the other side of the doorway.

One of the dogs lunged forward, then abruptly stopped. 'I'm going to fire,' he said.

He leveled his gun and sent a bullet into the floor between the animals. Both shrieked, then rushed around in confusion. He fired again and they bolted through the doorway into the hall. They stopped a few feet away, realizing that they'd forgotten their food. She fired into the floorboards and they turned and ran, disappearing out the front door.

She let out a breath.

Davis entered the room and knelt beside the severed hand. 'We need to see what's down there.'

She didn't necessarily agree – what was the point? – but knew Davis needed to see. She stepped to the doorway. Narrow wooden steps led below, then dog-legged right into pitch darkness. 'Probably an old cellar.'

She started the descent. He followed. At the landing she hesitated. Slivers of darkness evaporated as her pupils adjusted and the ambient light revealed a room about ten feet square, its curtain wall hacked from the ground rock, the floor a powdery dirt. Thick wooden beams spanned the ceiling. The frigid air was unmolested by ventilation.

'At least no more dogs,' Davis said.

Then she saw it.

A body, wearing an overcoat, lying prone, one arm a

stump. She instantly recognized the face, though a bullet had obliterated the nose and one eye.

Langford Ramsey.

'The debt is paid,' she said.

Davis bypassed her and approached the corpse. 'I only wish I could have done it.'

'It's better this way.'

There was a sound overhead. Footsteps. Her gaze shot to the wood floor above.

'That's not a dog,' Davis whispered.

88

Malone and Dorothea fled the house and found the empty street. Another pop sounded. He determined its direction.

'That way,' he said.

He resisted breaking into a run, but quickened his pace toward the central plaza, their bulky clothing and backpacks slowing progress. They rounded the circular walled pit and trotted down another wide causeway. Here, deeper into the city, more evidence of geological disturbances could be seen. Several of the buildings had collapsed. Walls were cracked. Rocks littered the street. He was careful. Their legs couldn't be trusted over such unsure footing.

Something caught his eye. Lying near one of the faintly glowing elevated crystals. He stopped. Dorothea did, too.

A cap? Here? In this place of ancient and abandoned possession, it seemed a strange intrusion.

He stepped close.

Blue cloth. Recognizable.

He bent down. Above its bill was stitched:

UNITED STATES NAVY
NR-1A

Mother of God.

Dorothea read it, too. 'It can't be.'

He glanced at the inside. Written in black ink was the name VAUGHT. He recalled the court of inquiry report. *M M 2 Doug Vaught.* One of the crew of NR-1A.

'Malone.'

His name had been called out across the vast interior.

'Malone.'

It was Christl. His mind jolted back to reality.

'Where are you?' he yelled.

'Over here.'

Stephanie realized they needed to flee the dungeon. It was the last place they'd want to confront anybody.

A single set of footsteps thumped above, moving to the other side of the house, away from the room at the top of the stairs. So she lightly climbed the wooden risers, stopping at the top. Carefully, she peered around the open panel, saw no one, and exited. She motioned and Davis flanked one side of the hallway door, she the other.

She risked a glance.

Nothing.

Davis went first, not waiting for her. She followed him back to the foyer. Still no one. Then movement from beyond the parlor into which she was staring – what would be the kitchen and dining room.

A woman appeared.

Diane McCoy.

Just as Daniels had said.

She walked straight toward her. Davis abandoned his position across the foyer.

'The Lone Ranger and Tonto,' McCoy said. 'Come to save the day?'

McCoy wore a long wool coat, open in front, slacks, shirt, and boots beneath. Her hands were empty and the rhythmic *thump, thump* of her leather heels matched what they'd heard below.

'Do you have any idea,' McCoy asked, 'how much trouble you two have caused? Prancing around. Interfering in things that totally don't concern you.'

Davis aimed his gun at McCoy. 'Like I care. You're a traitor.'

Stephanie did not move.

'Now, that isn't nice,' a new voice said. Male.

Stephanie turned.

A short, wiry man with a round face appeared in the opposite parlor with an HK53 pointed at them. She knew the assault rifle well. Forty rounds, rapid fire, messy. She also realized who held it.

Charlie Smith.

Malone stuffed the cap into his coat pocket and ran. A series of extended step-downs, twenty or so feet long, steadily lowered the street to a semicircular plaza that faced a tall colonnaded building. Statues and sculptures ringed its perimeter, displayed atop more square pillars.

Christl stood among the columns on the building's portico, a gun lowered at her side. He'd had her pack searched, but not her person. To do that would have alerted everyone that he wasn't as dumb as they apparently thought him to be, and he had not wanted to lose the advantage of being underestimated.

'What's happening?' he asked, winded.

'It's Werner. Henn killed him.'

He heard Dorothea gasp. 'Why?'

'Think, dear sister. Who gives Ulrich commands?'

'Mother?' Dorothea asked in answer.

No time for a family debate. 'Where's Henn?'

'We split up. I came back just as he shot Werner. I found my gun and fired, but Henn fled.'

'What are you doing with a gun?' he asked.

'I'd say it's a good thing I brought it.'

'Where's Werner?' Dorothea asked.

Christl motioned. 'In there.'

Dorothea bounded up the steps. He followed. They entered the building through a door wrapped in what appeared to be ornamented tin. Inside was a long hall with a high ceiling, the floor and walls tiled in blue and gold. Basins, their bottoms paved with well-worn pebbles, dotted the floor, one after the other, a stone balustrade on either side. Unglazed window openings were cased in bronze lattice and mosaics sheathed the walls. Landscapes, animals, young men wearing what appeared to be kilts and women in flounced skirts, some carrying jars, others bowls, filling the basins. Outside he'd noticed what appeared to be copper topping the pediment and silver adorning the columns. Now he spotted bronze cauldrons and silver fittings. Metallurgy had clearly been an art form to this society. The ceiling was quartz, a wide arch supported by a center beam that ran the length of the rectangle. Drains in the sides and bottoms of the basins confirmed that they had once held water. This was a bathhouse, he concluded.

Werner lay sprawled in one of the basins.

Dorothea ran to him.

'Touching scene, isn't it?' Christl said. 'The good, faithful wife lamenting the loss of her precious husband.'

'Give me your gun,' he demanded.

She threw him a cutting glare but handed over the weapon. He noticed it was the same make and model as

Dorothea's. Isabel had apparently made sure the daughters' odds were even. He removed the magazine and pocketed both.

He approached Dorothea and saw that Werner had been shot with a single round to the head.

'I fired twice at Henn,' Christl said. She pointed to the end of the hall, past a low-stepped platform, at another doorway. 'He escaped there.'

Malone slipped the rucksack off his shoulders, unzipped the center compartment, and found a 9mm automatic. When Taperell had searched the others' belongings and found Dorothea's gun, he'd wisely asked the Aussie to stash a weapon in his own pack.

'Different rules for you?' Christl asked.

He ignored her.

Dorothea stood. 'I want Ulrich.'

He heard the hate. 'Why would he kill Werner?'

'It's Mother. Why else?' Dorothea screamed, her words echoing through the bathhouse. 'She killed Sterling Wilkerson just to keep him from me. Now she's killed Werner.'

Christl seemed to sense his ignorance. 'Wilkerson was an American agent that the Ramsey man sent to spy on us. Dorothea's latest lover. Ulrich shot him in Germany.'

He agreed, they needed to locate Henn.

'I can help,' Christl said. 'Two would be better than one. And I know Ulrich. How he thinks.'

He was certain of that observation, so he reinserted a magazine from his pocket and handed the gun back to her.

'I want mine, too,' Dorothea said.

'She came armed?' Christl asked him.

He nodded his head. 'You two are just alike.'

★   ★   ★

Dorothea felt vulnerable. Christl was armed and Malone flatly refused her request for a gun.

'Why give her an advantage?' she asked. 'Are you an idiot?'

'Your husband is dead,' Malone reminded her.

She glanced down at Werner. 'He hasn't been my husband in a long time.' Her words were remorseful. Sad. Just as she felt. 'But that doesn't mean I wanted him dead.' She glared at Christl. 'Not like this.'

'This quest is proving costly.' Malone paused. 'For you both.'

'Grandfather was right,' Christl said. 'History books will be rewritten, all thanks to the Oberhausers. It's our job to see that happens. For the family.'

She imagined that her father and grandfather may have thought and said the exact same thing. But she wanted to know, 'What about Henn?'

'There's no telling what Mother ordered him to do,' Christl said. 'My guess is he's going to kill me and Malone.' She motioned at Dorothea with the gun. 'You were to be the sole survivor.'

'You're a liar,' Dorothea hissed.

'Am I? Then where's Ulrich? Why did he flee when I confronted him? Why kill Werner?'

Dorothea could provide no answers.

'Arguing is pointless,' Malone said. 'Let's go get him and be done with this.'

Malone passed through a doorway and exited the bath hall. A series of rooms opened off a long corridor, spaces that appeared to be either storage facilities or workrooms, since they were less elaborate in color and design and devoid of murals. The ceiling remained quartz, its refracted light still illuminating the way. Christl advanced with him, Dorothea trailing behind them.

They came to a series of tiny rooms that may have been a dressing area, then more storage and work spaces. The same ceramic pipes ran along the floor, against the wall, doubling as a baseboard.

They found an intersection.

'I'll go that way,' Christl said.

He agreed. 'We'll take the other route.'

Christl moved right, then disappeared around a corner into the cold gray dimness.

'You know she's a lying bitch,' Dorothea whispered.

He kept his attention on where Christl had gone and said, 'You think?'

89

Charlie Smith had the situation under control. Diane McCoy had briefed him well, telling him to wait in the barn until both of their visitors were inside, then quietly assume a position here, in the front parlor. McCoy would then enter the house and announce her presence, then they would deal with the problem.

'Drop the guns,' he ordered.

Metal clattered across the wood floor.

Smith wanted to know, 'You were the two in Charlotte?'

The woman nodded. Stephanie Nelle. Magellan Billet. Justice Department. McCoy had told him their names and positions.

'How'd you know I'd be at Rowland's place?' He was genuinely curious.

'You're predictable, Charlie,' Nelle said.

He doubted that. Still, they had been there. Twice.

'I've known about you for a long time,' Edwin Davis said to him. 'Not your name, or what you look like, or where you live. But I knew you were out there, working for Ramsey.'

'You like my little show at Biltmore?'

'You're quite the pro,' Nelle said. 'That round went to you.'

'I take pride in my work. Unfortunately, I'm between jobs, and employers, at the moment.'

He stepped forward a few feet, into the foyer.

'You realize,' Nelle said, 'that people know we're here.'

He chuckled. 'That's not what she told me.' He motioned toward McCoy. 'She knows the president is suspicious of her. He's the one who sent you here – to trap her. Did Daniels mention me by any chance?'

Nelle gave a surprised look.

'I didn't think so. Just supposed to be you three. Come to talk it out?'

'That's what you told him?' Nelle asked McCoy.

'It's the truth. Daniels sent you to get me. The president can't afford for word of this to get out in public. Too many questions. That's why you're the whole damn army.'

McCoy paused.

'Like I said, the Lone Ranger and Tonto.'

Malone had no idea where the maze of corridors led. He had no intention of doing what he'd told Christl, so he said to Dorothea, 'Come with me.'

They retraced their steps and reentered the bath hall.

Three other doorways opened from the outer walls. He handed her the flashlight. 'See what's in those rooms.'

She gave him a puzzled look, then he saw realization dawn inside her. She was quick, he'd give her that. The first one revealed nothing, but at the second doorway she motioned for him to come.

He approached and saw Ulrich Henn, dead on the floor.

'The fourth shot,' he said. 'Though it was surely the first one Christl fired, since he represented the greatest threat. Especially after the note your mother sent. She figured you three were in league to get her.'

'The bitch,' Dorothea muttered. 'She killed them both.'

'And she means to kill you, too.'

'And you?'

He shrugged. 'I can't imagine why I'd be allowed to leave.'

He'd let his guard down last night, caught up in the moment. Danger and adrenaline had that effect. Sex had always been a way to ease his fears – which had gotten him into trouble years ago, when he first started with the Magellan Billet.

But not this time. He stared back out into the bath hall, deciding what to do next. Lots happening fast. He needed –

Something smashed into the side of his head.

Pain jolted through him. The hall winked in and out.

Another blow. Harder.

His arms trembled. His fists clenched.

Then his mind lost all awareness.

Stephanie assessed their situation. Daniels had sent them here with precious little information. But the intelligence business was all about improvising. Time to practice what she preached.

'Ramsey was lucky to have you,' she said. 'Admiral Sylvian's death was a work of art.'

'I thought so,' Smith said.

'Bottomed out his blood pressure. Ingenious—'

'That how you killed Millicent Senn?' Davis interrupted. 'Black woman. Navy lieutenant in Brussels. Fifteen years ago.'

Smith seemed to be searching for the memory. 'Yeah.

Same way. But that was a different time, different continent.'

'Same me,' Davis said.

'You were there?'

Davis nodded.

'What was she to you?'

'More important, what was she to Ramsey?'

'Got me. I never asked. Just did what he paid me to do.'

'Did Ramsey pay you to kill him?' Stephanie asked.

Smith chuckled. 'If I hadn't, I would have been dead soon. Whatever he was planning, he didn't want me around, so I shot him.' Smith motioned with the rifle. 'He's back there in the bedroom, a nice clean hole through his no-good brain.'

'Got a little surprise for you, Charlie,' Stephanie said.

He threw her a quizzical look.

'That body ain't there.'

Dorothea slammed the heavy steel flashlight into the side of Malone's skull a final time.

He shrank to the floor.

She grabbed his weapon.

This was going to end between her and Christl.

Right now.

Stephanie saw that Smith was puzzled.

'What did it do? Walk away?'

'Go see.'

He jammed the assault rifle into her face. 'You lead the way.'

She sucked a deep breath and steeled her nerves.

'One of you pick up those guns and toss them out the window,' Smith said, keeping his eyes locked on her.

Davis did as instructed.

Smith lowered the rifle. 'Okay, let's all have a look. You three first.'

They crept down the corridor and entered the bedroom.

Nothing there but a bare window frame, the open wall panel, and a bloody hand.

'You're being played,' Stephanie said. 'By her.'

McCoy reeled back from the accusation. 'I paid you ten million dollars.'

Smith didn't seem to care. 'Where's the friggin' body?'

Dorothea pressed ahead. She knew Christl was waiting for her. Their entire lives had been spent in competition. One trying to outdo the other. Georg had been the one thing she'd managed that Christl had never matched.

And she'd always wondered why.

Now she knew.

She shook all troubling thoughts from her mind and concentrated on the murky scene before her. She'd hunted at night, stalking prey through the Bavarian woods under a silvery moon, waiting for the right moment to kill. At best, her sister was a double murderess. Everything she'd ever believed about her had now been confirmed. Nobody would blame her for shooting the bitch.

The hallway ended ten feet ahead.

Two doorways – one left, one right.

She fought a spasm of panic.

Which one?

90

Malone opened his eyes and knew what had happened. He rubbed a throbbing knot on the side of his head. Damn. Dorothea had no idea what she was doing.

He heaved himself up and caught a wave of nausea.

Crap – she may have cracked his skull.

He hesitated and allowed the frigid air to clear his brain.

Think. Focus. He'd set this whole thing up. But it wasn't playing out as expected, so he shook himself free of unwanted speculation and found Dorothea's gun in his pocket.

He'd confiscated Christl's, identical in make and model. When he'd returned it to her, though, he'd taken advantage of the situation to load the blank magazine that had originally come from Dorothea's. Now he popped the fully loaded magazine into the remaining Heckler & Koch USP, forcing his foggy mind to concentrate, his fingers to move.

Then he staggered for the doorway.

Stephanie was improvising, using whatever she could think of to keep Charlie Smith off balance. Diane McCoy had played her part to perfection. Daniels had briefed them on how he'd sent McCoy to Ramsey, first to become a co-conspirator, then as an adversary, all to keep Ramsey in constant motion. '*A bee can't sting you if it's flying,*' the president had observed. Daniels had also explained that when told about Millicent Senn and what had happened in Brussels years ago, McCoy had immediately volunteered. For the deception to have any chance at success, it required someone at her level, since Ramsey would never have dealt with, nor believed, subordinates. Once the president learned about Charlie Smith, McCoy had easily manipulated him, too. Smith was a vain, greedy soul, too accustomed to success. Daniels had informed them that Ramsey was dead – shot by Smith – and that Smith would appear, but unfortunately that was all the intel offered. McCoy confronting them had also been part of the script. What would happen after that was anybody's guess.

'Back to the front,' Smith ordered, gesturing with the gun.

They walked to the foyer between the two front parlors.

'You have quite a problem,' Stephanie said.

'I'd say you're the one with a problem.'

'Really? You going to kill two deputy national security advisers and a high-level Justice Department agent? I don't think you want the kind of heat that'll bring. Shooting Ramsey? Who cares? We certainly don't. Good riddance. Nobody's going to bother you on that one. We're a different story.'

She saw that her reasoning had struck home.

'You've always been so careful,' Stephanie said. 'That's your trademark. No traces. No evidence. Shooting us would be totally out of character. And besides, we may want to hire you. After all, you do good work.'

Smith chuckled. 'Right. I doubt you'd use my services.

Let's get this straight. I came to help her' – he gestured to McCoy – 'tend to a problem. She did pay me ten million, and let me kill Ramsey, so that buys her a favor. She wanted you two gone. But I can see that was a bad idea. I think the wise thing is for me to leave.'

'Tell me about Millicent,' Davis said.

Stephanie had wondered why he'd been so quiet.

'Why is she so important?' Smith asked.

'She just is. I'd like to know about her before you go.'

Dorothea eased forward toward the two doorways. She pressed herself close to the corridor's right-side wall and watched for any change in the shadows ahead.

Nothing.

She came to the doorway's edge and quickly stole a glance inside the room to her right. Maybe ten meters square, lit from above. Nothing inside except a figure lying propped against the far wall.

A man wrapped in a blanket, wearing a blue nylon one-piece jumper. Dimly illuminated, like an old black-and-white photo, he sat cross-legged, his head inclined left, and stared at her with eyes that did not blink.

She was drawn toward him.

He was young, maybe late twenties, with dusty brown hair and a thin angular face. He'd died where he sat, perfectly preserved. She almost expected him to speak. He wore no coat, but his blue cap was the same from the one outside. US Navy. NR-1A.

Her father, during times when they'd hunted, had always cautioned her about frostbite. The body, he'd said, would sacrifice fingers, toes, hands, noses, ears, chins, and cheeks to keep blood flowing to vital organs. But if the cold persisted, and no relief was found, the lungs eventually hemorrhaged and the heart stopped. Death was slow, gradual, and painless. But the long conscious fight against it was the real agony. Especially when nothing could be done to stop it.

Who was this soul?

She caught a noise, behind her.

She whirled.

Someone appeared in the room across the hall. Twenty meters away. A black form, framed by another doorway.

'What are you waiting for, sister?' Christl called out. 'Come and get me.'

Malone reentered the back corridors of the bath hall and heard Christl call out to Dorothea. He turned left, which seemed the direction from which the words had come, and made his way down another long corridor that eventually spilled into a room forty feet ahead. He advanced, watchful of open doorways to his left and right. He gave a quick glance inside each as he kept moving. More storage and work spaces. Nothing of interest in any of the gloomy alcoves.

In the next to last one he halted.

Someone lay on the floor.

A man.

He entered the room.

The face was of a middle-aged Caucasian, with short rust-brown hair. He lay prone, arms at his side, feet stretched straight, like some human form of petrified rock, a blanket flat beneath him. He wore a blue navy regulation jumpsuit with the name JOHNSON stitched to his left pocket. His mind made the connection. *EM2 Jeff Johnson, Ship's Electrician.* NR-1A.

His heart gave a sudden leap.

The seaman seemed to have simply lain down and allowed the cold to steal over him. Malone had been taught in the navy that no one froze to death. Instead, as cold air enveloped bare skin, vessels near the surface constricted, reducing heat loss, forcing blood to vital organs. *Cold hands, warm heart,* was more than a cliché. He recalled the warning signs. First a tingling, a stinging, a dull ache, then numbness and finally a sudden whitening. Death came once the body's core temperature fell and vital organs shut down.

Then you froze.

Here, in a world with no moisture, the body should have been perfectly preserved, but Johnson had not been so lucky. Black scraps of dead skin hung from his cheeks and chin. Mottled yellow scabs caked his face, some hardened into a grotesque mask. His eyelids had frozen shut, ice clinging to the lashes, and his last breaths were condensed into two icicles that hung from his nose to his mouth, like the tusks of a walrus.

Anger at the US Navy swelled inside him. The sorry no-good SOBs let these men die.

Alone.

Helpless.

Forgotten.

He heard footsteps and retreated back to the hall, glancing right just as Dorothea appeared in the last room, then disappeared through another doorway.

He let her go ahead.

Then followed.

91

*S*mith stared down at the woman. She lay still in the bed.
He'd waited for her to pass out, the effects of the alcohol
working as the perfect sedative. She'd drunk a lot, more than
usual, celebrating what she thought would be a marriage to
a rising captain in the US Navy. But she'd chosen the wrong
beau. Captain Langford Ramsey had no desire to marry her.
Instead he wanted her dead, and he'd paid handsomely for
that to happen.

She was lovely. Long, silky hair. Smooth, dark skin.
Beautiful features. He folded back the blanket and studied her
naked frame. She was thin and shapely, offering no sign of
the pregnancy he'd been told existed. Ramsey had provided
him with her naval medical records, which indicated an
irregular heartbeat that had required two treatments over the
past six years. Hereditary, most likely. Low blood pressure was
also a concern.

Ramsey had promised him more work if this job went
smoothly. He liked the fact they were in Belgium, as he'd found
Europeans far less suspicious than Americans. But it shouldn't
matter. The cause of the woman's death would be untraceable.

He found the syringe and decided the armpit would be the
best injection point. A tiny hole would remain, but hopefully
it would go unnoticed – absent an autopsy. Even if an autopsy
occurred, there'd be nothing in the blood or tissue to find.

Just a tiny hole under the arm.

He gently grasped her elbow and inserted the needle.

Smith recalled exactly what happened that night in Brussels, but wisely decided not to share any details with the man standing six feet away.

'I'm waiting,' Davis said.

'She died.'

'You killed her.'

He was curious. 'Is all this about her?'

'It's about you.'

He didn't like the bitter edge in Davis' voice, so he declared again, 'I'm leaving.'

Stephanie watched as Davis challenged their captor. Smith might not *want* to kill them, but he certainly would if need be.

'She was a good person,' Davis said. 'She didn't have to die.'

'You should have had this conversation with Ramsey. He's the one who wanted her dead.'

'He's the one who beat the crap out of her all the time.'

'Maybe she liked it?'

Davis advanced forward, but Smith halted him with the rifle. Stephanie knew that with a single pull of the trigger not much of Davis would be left.

'You're an edgy one,' Smith said.

Davis' eyes were suffused with hate. He seemed to hear and see only Charlie Smith.

But she caught movement behind Smith, outside the bare window frame, past the covered front porch, where bright sunshine was soothed by the winter cold.

A shadow.

Moving closer.

Then a face peered inside.

Colonel William Gross.

She saw that McCoy had spotted him, too, and wondered why Gross didn't just shoot Smith. Surely he was armed and, apparently, McCoy had known the colonel was out there – two guns flying out the window had certainly conveyed the message that they needed help.

Then it occurred to her.

The president wanted this one alive.

He didn't necessarily want a lot of attention drawn to this situation – hence there wasn't a cadre of FBI and Secret Service here – but he wanted Charlie Smith in one piece.

McCoy gave a slight nod.

Smith caught the gesture.

His head whirled.

Dorothea left the building and descended a set of narrow stairs back to the street. She was next to the bathhouse, beyond the plaza that stretched out in front, near the cavern's end and one of the polished rock walls that rose hundreds of meters.

She turned right.

Christl was thirty meters away, running through a gallery of alternating light and dark that caused her to appear and disappear.

She pursued.

Like chasing a deer in the forest. Give it room. Allow it to think itself safe. Then strike when least expected.

She passed through the light gallery and entered another plaza, similar to the one before the bathhouse in size and shape. Empty, except for a stone bench upon which a figure sat. He wore a white cold-weather suit similar to her own, except his was unzipped in front, arms exposed, the top half rolled down to the waist, exposing a chest clothed only in a wool sweater. His eyes were dark hollows in a shallow face, the lids closed. His frozen neck had craned to one side, his dark hair brushing the tops of ashen white ears. An iron-gray beard was streaked with congealed moisture and a blissful grin danced across closed lips. His hands were folded peacefully before him.

Her father.

Her nerves racked into numbness. Her heart pounded. She wanted to look away, but couldn't. Corpses were meant to be entombed, not sitting on benches.

'Yes, it's him,' Christl said.

Her attention swung back to the danger around her, but she did not see her sister, only heard her.

'I found him earlier. He's been waiting for us.'

'Show yourself,' she said.

A laugh permeated the silence. 'Look at him, Dorothea. He unzipped his coat and allowed himself to die. Can you imagine?'

No, she couldn't.

'That took courage,' the disembodied voice said. 'To hear Mother speak, he had no courage. To hear you speak, he was a fool. Could you have done that, Dorothea?'

She spotted another of the tall gates, framed by square columns, sealed with bronze doors, these swung open, no metal bar holding them shut. Beyond, steps led down and she felt a breeze of cold air.

She stared back at the dead man.

'Our father.'

She whirled. Christl stood perhaps seven meters away, with a gun pointed.

She stiffened her arm and started to raise her weapon.

'No, Dorothea,' Christl said. 'Keep it down.'

She did not move.

'We found him,' Christl said. 'We solved Mother's quest.'

'This resolves nothing between us.'

'I totally agree.'

'I was right,' Christl said, 'About every single thing. And you were wrong.'

'Why did you kill Henn and Werner?'

'Mother sent Henn to stop me. Loyal Ulrich. And Werner? Seems you'd be glad he's gone.'

'You plan to kill Malone, too?'

'I have to be the only one who walks from here. The lone survivor.'

'You're insane.'

'Look at him, Dorothea. Our precious father. The last time we saw him we were ten years old.'

She didn't want to look. She'd seen enough. And she wanted to remember him as she'd known him.

'You doubted him,' Christl said.

'So did you.'

'Never.'

'You're a murderess.'

Christl laughed. 'Like I care what you think of me.'

There was no way she could raise her gun and shoot before Christl pulled her trigger. Since she was dead anyway, she decided to act first.

Her arm started up. Christl pulled the gun's trigger. Dorothea braced herself to be shot. But nothing happened. Only a click.

Christl seemed shocked. She worked the trigger more, but to no avail.

'No bullets,' Malone said, as he entered the plaza. 'I'm not a complete idiot.'

Enough.

Dorothea pointed and fired.

The first shot caught Christl square in the chest, piercing her thick arctic wear. The second bullet, also in the chest, challenged her sister's balance. The third shot, to the skull, caused her forehead to burst red, but the frigid cold instantly coagulated the blood.

Two more shots and Christl Falk sank to the pavement. Not moving.

Malone came closer.

'It had to be done,' she muttered. 'She was no good.'

Her head turned toward her father. She felt as if she were awakening from an anesthetic, some thoughts clearing, others remaining cloudy and distant. 'They actually made it here. I'm glad he found what he'd been searching for.'

She faced Malone and saw that a frightening salvation had seeped into his thoughts, too. The exit portal drew both of their attention. She didn't have to say it. She'd found her father. He hadn't.

Not yet.

92

Stephanie questioned the wisdom of McCoy's warning. Smith, unsettled, had stepped back and swung around, trying to focus on them while sneaking a peek at the window.

More shadows fluttered outside.

Smith fired a short burst that obliterated the brittle walls, shattering the wood with jagged wounds.

McCoy lunged toward him.

Stephanie feared he might shoot her, but instead he whirled the rifle around and jammed the butt hard into her stomach. She buckled forward, gasping for breath, and he thrust a knee upward into her chin, flipping her to the floor.

Instantly, before either Stephanie or Davis could react, Smith releveled the gun and alternated his focus between them and the window, probably trying to decide where the greater threat lay.

Nothing moved outside.

'Like I said, I wasn't interested in killing you three,' Smith said. 'But I think that's changed.'

McCoy lay on the floor, moaning in the fetal position, cradling her stomach.

'Can I see about her?' Stephanie asked.

'She's a big girl.'

'I'm going to see about her.'

And without waiting for further permission, she knelt beside McCoy.

'You're not leaving here,' Davis said to Smith.

'Brave words.'

But Charlie Smith seemed unsure, as if he were trapped inside a cage, staring out for the first time.

Something thudded against the outer wall, near the window. Smith reacted, swinging the HK53 around. Stephanie tried to stand, but he popped her square in the neck with the rifle's metal stock.

She gasped and found the floor.

Her hand went to her Adam's apple – the pain of a kind she'd never felt before. She struggled to breathe, fighting an urge to choke. She rolled and watched as Edwin Davis catapulted himself into Charlie Smith.

She struggled to stand, fighting both to breathe and to overcome the throbbing in her throat. Smith still clung to his assault rifle, but it was useless as he and Davis rolled through the battered furniture, ending against the far wall. Smith used his legs and tried to wiggle free, keeping a grip on his gun.

Where was Gross?

Smith lost the rifle, but his right arm wrapped around Davis and a new gun appeared – a small automatic – jammed into Davis' neck.

'Enough,' Smith yelled.

Davis stopped struggling.

They came to their feet and Smith released his grip, shoving Davis to the floor near McCoy.

'You're all crazy,' Smith said. 'Friggin' nuts.'

Stephanie slowly came to her feet, shaking a fog from her brain, as Smith regripped the assault rifle. This had gyrated out of control. The one thing she and Davis had agreed on during the drive over was not to agitate Smith.

Yet Edwin had done just that.

Smith retreated to the window and quickly peered out. 'Who is he?'

'Mind if I look?' she managed to say.

He nodded his assent.

She slowly approached and spotted Gross, lying on the porch, his right leg bleeding from a bullet wound. He seemed conscious, but in extreme pain.

He works for McCoy, she mouthed.

Smith's gaze searched beyond the porch, to the brown grassy meadow and thick woods. 'Who's a lying bitch.'

She gathered her strength. 'But she did pay you ten million.'

Smith clearly did not appreciate her levity.

'Tough choices, Charlie? Always you made the call when to kill. Your choice. Not this time.'

'Don't be so sure. Get back over there.'

She did as told but couldn't resist, 'And who moved Ramsey?'

'You need to shut the hell up,' Smith said, continuing to snatch glimpses out the window.

'I'm not letting him go,' Davis muttered.

McCoy rolled onto her back and Stephanie saw the pained look on her colleague's face.

Coat . . . pocket, McCoy's lips said, without a sound.

Malone descended steps on the other side of the portal feeling as if he were walking to his execution. Tingles of fright – unusual for him – danced down his spine.

Below stretched a huge cavern, most of its walls and ceiling ice, casting the same bluish light across the orange sail of a submarine. The hull was short, rounded, with a flat superstructure atop, and totally encased by ice. More of the tile pavement looped from the staircase around to the cavern's far side four to five feet above the ice.

Some sort of wharf, he concluded.

Perhaps this harbor had once opened to the sea?

Ice caves existed all across Antarctica, and this one loomed long enough to accommodate multiple submarines.

Moved by a common impulse, they both walked. Dorothea held her gun and so did he, though the only threat to either of them now was the other.

The rock portion of the cavern's wall was polished smooth and adorned similarly to the inside of the mountain, with symbols and writing. Stone benches lined the wall base. On one sat a shadow. Malone closed his eyes and hoped it was only an apparition. But when he opened them, the ghostly figure remained.

He sat upright, like the others, back straight. He wore a khaki naval shirt and pants, the trousers tucked into laced boots, a blue cap lying on the bench beside him.

Malone inched his way closer.

His senses reeled. His sight went dim.

The face was the same as the picture back in Copenhagen, next to the glass case with the flag the navy had handed his mother at the memorial ceremony, the one she'd refused to accept. Long, equine nose. Protruding jaw. Freckles. Gray-blond crew cut. Eyes open, staring, as if in deep communion.

Shock paralyzed his body. His mouth parched.

'Your father?' Dorothea asked.

He nodded, and self-pity pierced him – a sharp arrow that drove down his throat, into his gut, as if he'd been skewered.

His nerves stretched taut.

'They just died,' she said. 'No coats. No protection. As if they sat down and welcomed it.'

Which, he knew, was exactly, what they'd done. No sense prolonging the agony.

He noticed papers lying in his father's lap, the pencil writing as fresh and clear as it must have been thirty-eight years ago. The right hand rested atop them, as if making sure they would not be lost. He slowly reached out and slid them free, feeling as if he was violating a sacred site.

He recognized the heavy script as his father's.

His chest ballooned. The world seemed both dream and reality. He fought against a reservoir of unlocked grief. Never had he cried. Not when he married, or when Gary was born, or when his family disintegrated, or when he learned that Gary was not his biological son. To suppress a growing urge, he reminded himself that tears would freeze before they left his eyes.

He forced his mind to focus on the pages he held.

'Could you read them out loud?' Dorothea asked. 'They could affect my father, too.'

Smith needed to kill all three of them and get out of here. He was working with no information after trusting a woman he knew he shouldn't have trusted. And who had moved Ramsey's body? He'd left it in the bedroom, intent on burying the corpse somewhere on the property.

Yet somebody had taken it below.

He gazed out the window and wondered if there was anybody else out there. Something told him that they were not alone.

Just a feeling.

Which he had no choice but to follow.

He gripped the rifle and readied himself to turn and fire. He'd take out the three inside with a short burst, then finish off the one outside.

Leave the damn bodies.

Who cared? He'd bought the property under an assumed name with false identification, paying cash, so there was nobody to find.

Let the government worry about the cleanup.

Stephanie watched as Davis' right hand eased into McCoy's coat pocket. Charlie Smith was still positioned at the window, holding the HK53. She had no doubt he planned to kill them, and she was equally concerned that there was nobody here to help them. Their backup was bleeding on the front porch.

Davis stopped.

Smith's head whipped their way, satisfied all was well, then he stared back out the window.

Davis withdrew his hand, holding a 9mm automatic.

She hoped to heaven he knew how to use it.

The hand with the gun dropped to McCoy's side and Davis used her body to block Smith's view. She could see that Edwin realized that their choices were limited. He'd have to shoot Charlie Smith. But thinking about that act and doing it were two entirely different things. A few months ago she'd killed for the first time. Luckily there hadn't been a nanosecond to consider the act – she'd simply been forced to fire in an instant. Davis was not to be afforded such a luxury. He was thinking, surely wanting to do it, but at the same time not wanting to. Killing was serious business. No matter the reason or the circumstances.

But a cold excitement seemed to steady Davis' nerves.

His eyes were watching Charlie Smith, his face loose and expressionless. What was about to provide him the courage to kill a man? Survival? Possibly. Millicent? Surely.

Smith started to turn, his arms swinging the rifle barrel their way.

Davis raised his arm and fired.

The bullet tore into Smith's thin chest, staggering him back toward the wall. One hand left the rifle as he tried to steady himself with an outstretched arm. Davis kept the gun pointed, stood, and fired four more times, the bullets tearing a path through Charlie Smith. Davis kept shooting – each round like an explosion in her ears – until the magazine emptied.

Smith's body contorted, his spine arching and twisting involuntarily. Finally, his legs buckled and he toppled forward, smacking the flooring, his lifeless body rolling onto his spine, his eyes wide open.

93

The underwater electrical fire destroyed our batteries.
The reactor had already failed. Luckily the fire
burned slow and radar was able to locate a break in
the ice and we managed to surface just before the air
became toxic. All hands quickly abandoned the boat
and we were amazed to find a cavern with polished
walls and writing, similar to the writing we'd
observed on stone blocks lying on the seafloor.
Oberhauser located a stairway and bronze doors,
barred from our side, which, when opened, led into an
amazing city. He explored for several hours, trying to
locate an exit, while we determined the extent of
damage. We tried repeatedly to restart the reactor,
violating every safety protocol, but nothing worked. We
carried only three sets of cold-weather gear and there
were eleven of us. The cold was numbing, relentless,
unbearable. We burned what little paper and refuse we
had on board, but it wasn't much and provided only
a few hours of relief. Nothing inside the city was
flammable. Everything was stone and metal, the
houses and buildings empty. The inhabitants seemed
to have taken all of their belongings with them. Three
other exits were located but they were barred from the
outside. We possessed no equipment to force the bronze
doors open. After only twelve hours we realized that

*the situation was desperate. There was no way out of
the cocoon. We activated the emergency transponder
but doubted its signal could reach far considering the
rock and ice and the thousands of miles from the
nearest ship. Oberhauser seemed the most frustrated.
He found what we came in search of, yet would not
live to know its extent. We all realized that we were
going to die. No one would come search for us since
we agreed to that condition prior to leaving. The sub
is dead and so are we. Each man decided to die in
his own way. Some went off alone, others together. I
sat here and kept watch over my boat. I write these
words so all will know my crew died bravely. Each
man, including Oberhauser, accepted his fate with
courage. I wish I could have learned more about the
people who built this place. Oberhauser told us they
are our forefathers, that our culture came from them.
Yesterday I would have said he was insane.
Interesting how life deals us cards. I was given
command of the navy's most sophisticated undersea
sub. My career was set. Captain's bars would have
eventually come my way. Now I'll die alone in the
cold. There's no pain, only a lack of strength. I am
barely able to write. I served my country to the best
of my ability. My crew did the same. I felt pride as
they each shook my hand and walked off. Now, as the
world starts to fade, I find myself thinking of my son.
My one regret is that he will never know how I truly
felt about him. Telling him what was in my heart
always came hard. Though I was gone for long
periods of time, not a moment in a day went by that
he wasn't at the top of my thoughts. He was
everything to me. He's only ten and surely knows*

*nothing of what life holds for him. I regret that I
won't be a part of shaping who he becomes. His
mother is the finest woman I've ever known and she'll
make sure he becomes a man. Please, whoever finds
these words, give them to my family. I want them to
know I died thinking of them. To my wife, know that
I love you. It was never difficult for me to say those
words to you. But to my son, let me say now what
was so hard for me. I love you, Cotton.*

Forrest Malone, USN
November 17, 1971

Malone's voice trembled as he read his father's final
four words. Yes, they had been difficult for his father to
say. In fact, he could never recall them ever being voiced.

But he'd known.

He stared at the corpse, the face frozen in time. Thirty-
eight years had passed. During which Malone had grown
into a man, joined the navy, become an officer, then an
agent for the US government. And while all that occurred,
Commander Forrest Malone had sat here, on a stone
bench.

Waiting.

Dorothea seemed to sense his pain and gently grabbed
his arm. He watched her face and could read her thoughts.

'Seems we all found what we came for,' she said.

He saw it in her eyes. Resolution. Peace.

'There's nothing left for me,' she said. 'My grandfather
was a Nazi. My father a dreamer who lived in another
time and place. He came here seeking truth and faced his
death with courage. My mother has spent the past four
decades trying to take his place, but all she could do was
pit Christl and me against each other. Even now. Here.

She tried to keep us at odds, and was so successful that Christl was killed because of her.' She went silent, but her eyes conveyed submission. 'When Georg died, a large part of me died, too. I thought by securing wealth I could find happiness, but that's impossible.'

'You're the last Oberhauser.'

'We are a sorry lot.'

'You could change things.'

She shook her head. 'To do that, I would have to place a bullet in Mother's head.'

She turned and walked toward the steps. He watched her go with an odd mix of respect and contempt, knowing where she was headed.

'There will be repercussions from all this,' he said. 'Christl was right. History will change.'

She kept walking. 'It doesn't concern me. All things must end.'

Her comment was colored by anguish, her voice trembling. But she was right. There came a time when everything ended. His military career. Government service. Marriage. Life in Georgia. His father's life.

Now Dorothea Lindauer was making a final choice of her own.

'Good luck to you,' he called out.

She stopped, turned, and threw him a weak smile. '*Bitte,* Herr Malone.' She let out a long breath and seemed to steel herself. 'I need to do this alone.' Her eyes implored him.

He nodded. 'I'll stay here.'

He watched as she climbed the stairs and passed through the portal, into the city.

He stared at his father, whose dead eyes caught no glint of light. He had so much to say. He wanted to tell him that he'd been a good son, a good naval officer, a good agent, and, he believed, a good man. Six times he'd been awarded commendations. He'd been a failure as a husband, but was working on being a better father. He wanted to be a part of Gary's life, always. All his adult life he'd wondered what had happened to his own father, imagining the worst. Sadly, reality was more terrible than anything he'd ever concocted. His mother had been similarly tormented. She'd never remarried. Instead she'd endured decades, clutching her grief, always referring to herself as Mrs. Forrest Malone.

How was it that the past never seemed to end?

A shot sounded, like a balloon popping beneath a blanket.

He envisioned the scene above.

Dorothea Lindauer had ended her life. Normally suicide would be deemed the result of a sick mind or an abandoned heart. Here, it was the only means to stop a madness. He wondered if Isabel Oberhauser would even comprehend what she'd wrought. Her husband, grandson, and daughters were gone.

A loneliness crept into his bones as he absorbed the deep silence of the tomb. Proverbs came to mind.

A simple truth from long ago.

He that troubleth his own house shall inherit the wind.

94

Washington, DC, Saturday, December 22, 4:15 p.m.

Stephanie entered the Oval Office. Danny Daniels stood and greeted her. Edwin Davis and Diane McCoy were already seated.

'Merry Christmas,' the president said.

She returned the greeting. He'd summoned her from Atlanta yesterday afternoon, providing the same Secret Service jet that she and Davis had used, over a week ago, to travel from Asheville to Fort Lee.

Davis looked fine. His face had healed, the bruising gone. He wore a suit and tie and sat stiffly in an upholstered chair, his granite façade back in place. She'd managed a fleeting glance into his heart and wondered if that privilege would doom her from ever knowing him any further. He did not seem a man who liked to bare his soul.

Daniels offered her a seat, next to McCoy. 'I thought it best we all have a talk,' the president said, sitting in his own chair. 'The past couple of weeks have been tough.'

'How's Colonel Gross?' she asked.

'Doing good. His leg is healing fine, but that round did some damage. He's a bit irritated with Diane for giving him away, but grateful that Edwin can shoot straight.'

'I should go see him,' McCoy said. 'I never meant for him to get hurt.'

'I'd give it a week or so. I meant what I said about the irritation.'

Daniels' melancholy eyes were the embodiment of woe.

'Edwin, I know you hate my stories, but listen up anyway. Two lights in a fog. On one, an admiral stands on the ship's bridge and radios the other light saying he's commanding a battleship and the light should veer right. The other light radios back and tells the admiral *he* should veer right. The admiral, being a testy sort, like me, comes back and reorders the other ship to go right. Finally, the other light says, "Admiral, I'm the seaman manning the lighthouse and you better damn well go right." I went out on a limb for you, Edwin. Way out. But you were the guy in the lighthouse, the smart one, and I listened. Diane, there, the moment she heard about Millicent, signed on and took a hell of a chance, too. Stephanie you drafted, but she went the distance. And Gross? He took a bullet.'

'And I appreciate everything that was done,' Davis said. 'Immensely.'

Stephanie wondered if Davis harbored any remorse for killing Charlie Smith. Probably not, but that didn't mean he'd ever forget. She looked at McCoy. 'Did you know when the president first called my office, looking for Edwin?'

McCoy shook her head. 'After he hung up, he told me. He was concerned that things might get out of hand. He thought a backup plan might be needed. So he had me contact Ramsey.' McCoy paused. 'And he was right. Though you two did a great job flushing Smith our way.'

'We still have some fallout to deal with, though,' Daniels said.

Stephanie knew what he meant. Ramsey's death had been explained as a murder by a covert operative. Smith's death was simply ignored since no one knew he even existed. Gross' injuries were attributed to a hunting accident. Ramsey's chief aide, a Captain Hovey, was questioned and, on threat of court-martial, revealed everything. In a matter of days the Pentagon cleaned house, assigning a new management team to naval intelligence, ending the reign of Langford Ramsey and anyone associated with him.

'Aatos Kane came to see me,' Daniels said. 'He wanted me to know that Ramsey had tried to intimidate him. Of course, he was long on complaints and short on explanations.'

She caught a twinkle in the president's eye.

'I showed him a file we found in Ramsey's house, inside a safe. Fascinating stuff. No need to go into the details – let's just say that the good senator will not be running for president and will retire, effective December thirty-first, from Congress to spend more time with his family.' A look of unmistakable command swept over Daniels. 'The country will be spared his leadership.' Daniels shook his head. 'You three did a great job. So did Malone.'

They'd buried Forrest Malone two days ago in a shady south Georgia cemetery, near where his widow lived. The son, on behalf of the father, refused interment in Arlington National Cemetery.

And she'd understood Malone's reluctance.

The other nine crewmen had likewise been brought home, their bodies delivered to families, the true story of NR-1A finally being told by the press. Dietz Oberhauser had been sent to Germany, where his wife claimed his and her daughters' remains.

'How is Cotton?' the president asked.

'Angry.'

'If it matters,' Daniels said, 'Admiral Dyals is taking a lot of heat from the navy and the press. The story of NR-1A has struck a nerve with the public.'

'I'm sure Cotton would like to ring Dyals' neck,' she said.

'And that translation program is yielding a wealth of information about that city and the people who lived there. There are references to contacts with cultures all over the globe. They did interact and share, but thank heaven they weren't Aryans. No super race. Not even war-like. The researchers stumbled onto a text yesterday that may explain what happened to them. They lived in Antarctica tens of thousands of years ago, when it wasn't iced over. But as the temperatures fell, they gradually retreated into the mountains. Eventually, their geothermal vents cooled. So they left. Hard to say when. They apparently used a different time measurement and calendar. Just like with us, not everyone had access to all of their knowledge, so they couldn't reproduce their culture elsewhere. Only bits and pieces – here and there – as they worked their way into our civilization. The best informed left last and wrote the texts, leaving them as a record. Over time, those immigrants were absorbed into other cultures, their history lost, nothing of them but legend remained.'

'Seems sad,' she said.

'I agree. But the ramifications from this could be enormous. The National Science Foundation is sending a team to Antarctica to work the site. Norway has agreed to give us control of the area. Malone's father, and the rest of NR-1A's crew, did not die for no good reason. We may learn a great deal about ourselves, thanks to them.'

'I'm not sure that would make Cotton, or those families, feel better.'

'*Study the past, if you would divine the future,*' Davis said. 'Confucius. Good advice.' He paused. 'For us, and for Cotton.'

'Yes, it is,' Daniels said. 'I hope this is over.'

Davis nodded. 'For me, it is.'

McCoy agreed. 'Nothing would be served by hashing this out in public. Ramsey's gone. Smith's gone. Kane's gone. It's over.'

Daniels stood, stepped to his desk, and grabbed a journal. 'This came from Ramsey's house, too. It's the logbook from NR-1A. The one Herbert Rowland told you about. The asshole kept it all these years.' The president handed it to Stephanie. 'I thought Cotton might like it.'

'I'll get it to him,' she said, 'once he calms down.'

'Check out the last entry.'

She opened to the final page and read what Forrest Malone had written. *Ice on his finger, ice in his head, ice in his glassy stare.*

'From *The Ballad of Blasphemous Bill,*' the president explained. 'Robert Service. Early twentieth century. He wrote about the Yukon. Cotton's daddy was obviously a fan.'

Malone had told her how he'd found the frozen body, *ice in his glassy stare.*

'Malone's a pro,' Daniels said. 'He knows the rules and his father knew them, too. It's tough for us to judge folks from forty years ago by today's standards. He needs to get over it.'

'Easier said than done,' she made clear.

'Millicent's family needs to be told,' Davis said. 'They deserve the truth.'

'I agree,' Daniels said. 'I assume you want to do that?'

Davis nodded.

Daniels smiled. 'And there was one bright spot through all this.' The president pointed at Stephanie. 'You didn't get fired.'

She grinned. 'For which I'm eternally grateful.'

'I owe you an apology,' Davis said to McCoy. 'I misread you. I haven't been a good co-worker. I thought you were an idiot.'

'You always so honest?' McCoy asked.

'You didn't have to do what you did. You put your ass on the line for something that didn't really involve you.'

'I wouldn't say that. Ramsey was a threat to national security. That's in our job description. And he killed Millicent Senn.'

'Thank you.'

McCoy gave Davis a nod of gratitude.

'Now that's what I like to see,' Daniels said. 'Everybody getting along. See, a lot of good can come from wrestling rattlesnakes.'

The tension in the room abated.

Daniels shifted in his chair. 'With that out of the way, unfortunately we have a new problem – one that also involves Cotton Malone, whether he likes it or not.'

Malone switched off the ground-floor lights and climbed to his fourth-floor apartment. The shop had been busy today. Three days before Christmas and books seemed to be on Copenhagen's gift list. He employed three people who kept the store open while he was gone, for which he was grateful. So much that he'd made sure each of them received a generous holiday bonus.

He was still conflicted about his father.

They'd buried him where his mother's family lay. Stephanie had come. Pam, his ex-wife, was there. Gary had been emotional, seeing his grandfather for the first time lying in the casket. Thanks to the deep freeze and a skillful mortician, Forrest Malone lay as if he'd died only a few days before.

He'd told the navy to go to hell when they suggested a military ceremony with honors. Too late for that. Didn't matter that no one there had participated in the inexplicable decision not to search for NR-1A. He'd had enough of orders and duty and responsibility. What had happened to decency, righteousness, and honor? Those words seemed always forgotten when they really counted. Like when eleven men disappeared in the Antarctic and no one gave a damn.

He made it to the top floor and switched on a few lamps. He was tired. The past couple of weeks had taken a toll, capped off by watching his mother burst into tears as the coffin was lowered into the ground. They'd all lingered after and watched as workers replaced the dirt and erected a tombstone.

'*You did a wonderful thing,*' his mother had said to him. '*You brought him home. He would have been so proud of you, Cotton. So very proud.*'

And those words had made him cry.

Finally.

He'd almost stayed in Georgia for Christmas but decided to come home. Strange, how he now considered Denmark home.

Yet he did. And that no longer gave him pause.

He walked into the bedroom and lay down on the bed. Nearly eleven p.m. and he was exhausted. He had to stop this intrigue. He was supposed to be retired. But he was glad he'd called in his favor with Stephanie.

Tomorrow he'd rest. Sunday was always a light day.

Stores were closed. Maybe he'd drive north and visit with Henrik Thorvaldsen. He hadn't seen his friend in three weeks. But maybe not. Thorvaldsen would want to know where he'd been, and what had happened, and he wasn't ready to relive it.

For now, he'd sleep.

Malone awoke and cleared the dream from his mind. The bedside clock read 2:34 a.m. Lights were still on throughout the apartment. He'd been sleeping for three hours.

But something had roused him. A sound. Part of the dream he'd been having, yet not.

He heard it again.

Three squeaks in quick succession.

His building was seventeenth century, completely remodeled a few months ago after being firebombed. Afterward, the new wooden risers from the second to the third floor always announced themselves in a precise order, like keys on a piano.

Which meant someone was there.

He reached beneath the bed and found the rucksack he always kept ready – a habit from his Magellan Billet days. Inside, his right hand gripped the Beretta automatic, a round already chambered.

He crept from the bedroom.

WRITER'S NOTE

This book was a personal journey for both Malone and myself. While he found his father, I got married. Not necessarily something new for me, but definitely an adventure. As far as traveling, this story led me to Germany (Aachen and Bavaria), the French Pyrénées, and Asheville, North Carolina (the Biltmore Estate). Lots of cold, snowy places.

Now it's time to separate speculation from reality.

The super-secret NR-1 submarine (prologue) is real, as are its history and its exploits. NR-1 continues to this day, after almost forty years, to serve our nation. NR-1A is my concoction. There are precious few written accounts of NR-1, but the one I drew upon is *Dark Waters*, by Lee Vyborny and Don Davis, which is a rare firsthand observation of what it was like to be aboard. The court of inquiry report on the sinking of NR-1A (chapter 5) is modeled on actual investigative reports regarding the sinking of *Thresher* and *Scorpion*.

The Zugspitze and Garmisch are faithfully described (chapter 1), as is the Posthotel. Holiday time in Bavaria is wonderful, and the Christmas markets detailed in chapters 13, 33, and 37 are, without question, part of the attraction. Ettal Abbey (chapter 7) is accurately described, save for the rooms beneath.

Charlemagne is, of course, pivotal to the story. His

historical context, as presented, is accurate (chapter 36), as is his signature (chapter 10). He remains one of the world's most enigmatic figures and still carries the title *Father of Europe*. The authenticity of the story of Otto III entering Charlemagne's grave in 1000 CE is a matter of debate. The tale featured in chapter 10 has been repeated many times – though, of course, the strange book Otto finds is my addition. There are equally strong stories that say Charlemagne was buried lying down, inside a marble sarcophagus (chapter 34). No one knows for sure.

Einhard's *Life of Charlemagne* continues to be regarded as one of the great works from that period. Einhard himself was a learned man, and his involvement with Charlemagne, as described, is accurate. Only their connection to the Holy Ones is my invention. Einhard's accounts quoted in chapters 21 and 22 are loosely based on portions of the Book of Enoch – an ancient, enigmatic text.

Operations Highjump and Windmill happened as described (chapter 11). Both were extensive military operations. Much about them remained classified for decades and is still shrouded in mystery. Admiral Richard Byrd was co-leader of Highjump. My descriptions of the technological resources Byrd brought south with him (chapter 53) are accurate, as is the tale of his extensive exploration of the continent. His secret diary (chapter 77) is fictitious, as are his supposed findings of carved stones and ancient tomes. The German Antarctic expedition of 1938 (chapter 19) happened and is accurately detailed – including the dropping of little swastikas all over the icy surface. Only Hermann Oberhauser's exploits are my creations.

The strange writing and manuscript pages (chapters 12 and 81) are reproduced from the Voynich manuscript.

That book rests in the Beinecke Rare Book and Manuscript Library at Yale University, and is generally regarded as the most mysterious writing on the planet. No one has ever been able to decipher its text. A good primer on this oddity is *The Voynich Manuscript,* by Gerry Kennedy and Rob Churchill. The symbol first seen in chapter 10 – a monad – came from their book, an archetypal representation originally found in a sixteenth-century treatise. The strange Oberhauser family crest (chapter 25) also is from Kennedy and Churchill's book and is actually the Voynich family coat of arms, created by Voynich himself.

The true explanation of the term *Aryan* (chapter 12) demonstrates how something so innocuous can become so lethal. The Ahnenerbe, of course, existed. Only in the past few years have historians begun to reveal both its pseudo-scientific chaos and its horrible atrocities (chapter 26). One of the best resources on the topic is *The Master Plan,* by Heather Pringle. The Ahnenerbe's many international expeditions, detailed in chapter 31, happened and were used extensively to fashion its scientific fiction. Hermann Oberhauser's involvement with the organization is my invention, but his efforts and discrediting are based on the experiences of actual participants.

The concept of a first civilization (chapter 22) is not mine. The idea has been the basis for many books, but Christopher Knight and Alan Butler's *Civilization One* is excellent. All of the arguments Christl Falk and Douglas Scofield advance for the existence of this first civilization belong to Knight and Butler. Their theory is not all that far-fetched, but the reaction to it is similar to how mainstream science once viewed continental drift (chapter 84). Of course, the most obvious question remains. If such a culture existed, why are there no remnants?

But maybe there are.

The stories detailed by Scofield in chapter 60 about 'god-like' people interacting with cultures around the world are true, as are the inexplicable artifacts found and the story of what Columbus was shown. Even more amazing are the image and inscription from Hathor Temple in Egypt (chapter 84), which clearly show something extraordinary. Sadly, though, Scofield's observation that 90 percent of the ancient world's knowledge will never be known is potentially true. Which means we may never have a definitive answer to this fascinating inquiry.

Locating the first civilization in Antarctica (chapters 72, 85, and 86) was my idea, as are the civilization's knowledge and limited technology (chapters 72 and 81). I didn't visit Antarctica (it's definitely at the top of my Must-See list), but its beauty and danger are faithfully reported using firsthand accounts. Halvorsen Base (chapter 62) is fictitious, but the cold-weather gear Malone and company don is real (chapter 76). The politics of the Antarctic continent (chapter 76), with its various international treaties and unique cooperative rules, remains complex. The area where Malone explores (chapter 84) is indeed controlled by Norway, and some texts note that it is designated as off limits for supposed environmental reasons. The underwater sequences with Ramsey are taken from those who have dove those pristine waters. The dry valleys (chapter 84) exist, though they're generally confined to the southern portion of the continent. The preserving and destructive effects of absolute cold on human bodies are accurately portrayed (chapters 90 and 91). *Ice*, by Mariana Gosnell, is an excellent account of these phenomena.

Aachen Cathedral (chapters 34, 36, 38, and 42) is well

worth a visit. The Book of Revelation played a key role in its design, and the building remains one of the last from Charlemagne's time still standing. Of course, my interjection of the Holy Ones into its history is simply part of this story.

The Latin inscription inside the chapel (chapter 38) is from Charlemagne's time and is reproduced exactly. While counting every twelfth word I discovered that only three words would be revealed, the last count stopping at number eleven. Then, amazingly, the three words formed a recognizable phrase – *Brightness of God*.

Charlemagne's throne does indeed have a Nine Men's Morris board etched into its side (chapter 38). How and why it's there, nobody knows. The game was played in Roman and Carolingian times, and is still played today.

The Charlemagne pursuit, with all of its various clues, including Einhard's will, are my invention. Ossau, France (chapter 51), and the abbey (chapter 54) are concocted, but Bertrand is based on a real abbot who lived in that area.

Fort Lee (chapter 45) is real, though the warehouse and refrigerated compartment are not. I've recently acquired an iPhone, so Malone had to have one, too. All of the peculiar investigations conducted by the US government during the Cold War into paranormal and extraterrestrial phenomena (chapter 26) happened. I simply added one more.

Biltmore Estate (chapters 58, 59, and 66) is one of my favorite places, especially at Christmastime. The inn, mansion, village, hotel, and grounds are accurately portrayed. Of course, the Ancient Mysteries Revealed Conference does not exist, but it is based on a variety of real gatherings.

The Piri Reis map and other portolans (chapter 41) are real, and each one raises a host of perplexing questions. *Maps of the Ancient Sea Kings,* by Charles Hapgood, is regarded as the definitive work on this subject. The prime meridian debate happened as described (chapter 41), and Greenwich was arbitrarily chosen. Using the Giza pyramid as zero longitude (chapter 71), though, does produce some fascinating connections with sacred sites around the globe. The megalithic yard (chapter 71) is another interesting concept that rationally explains similarities engineers have long noticed at ancient construction sites. But proof of its existence has not, as yet, been established.

This story poses some interesting possibilities. Not of a mythical Atlantis with surreal engineering and fantastic technology, but instead the simple idea that we may not have been the first to achieve intellectual consciousness. Perhaps there were others whose existence is simply unknown, their history and fate extinguished, lost among the 90 percent of ancient knowledge we may never recover.

Far-fetched? Impossible?

How many times have the so-called experts been proven wrong?

Lao-tzu, the great Chinese philosopher who lived 2,700 years ago and is still regarded as one of humankind's most brilliant thinkers, may have known best when he wrote:

> *The Ancient Masters were subtle, mysterious,*
> *profound, responsive.*
> *The depth of their knowledge is unfathomable.*
> *Because it is unfathomable, all we can do is describe*
> *their appearance.*

Watchful, like men crossing a winter stream. Alert,
like men aware of danger.
Courteous, like visiting guests. Yielding, like ice
about to melt.
Simple, like uncarved blocks of wood.